KT-144-480

31513500118695

Owen S... ... ...ny,
South W... ...05
Welsh B... ...ty
of Literature Ondaatje Prize. He is also the acclaimed author of
two po... ...*Book* and *Skirrid Hill*, for which
he re... ...

Furth... ...'ate

'An... ...The heart of... ...ook is the relationship
between the valley's women and the soldiers, and particularly that
between Sarah and the cerebral German captain, Albrecht. From
this clash of worlds, Sheers conjures a moving meditation on what
war does to people . . . The result is impossible to resist.' Adrian
Turpin, *Financial Times*

'[It] dances brilliantly with the possibilities of an alternative out-
come to the Second World War . . . In a polyphonous novel filled to
bursting with evocative images, the most graphic is itself a piece of
writing. One of the women writes letters to her missing husband in
the back of their farm accounts. She gradually fills in the book from
both ends until there is no more space, and she has to find another
way forward.' Ingrid Wassenaar, *The Daily Telegraph*

'[Sheers] creates around his imagined history a credible and moving
story of loyalty and quiet courage . . . *Resistance* is an impressive
debut and confirms Sheers as a writer whose talent encompasses a
variety of literary forms.' Stephanie Merritt, *Observer*

'There are many beauties in the novel's delineations of the land's
harsh demands and intimate rewards, and of those human spirits
who have derived sustenance from it.' Paul Binding, *Independent*

'*Resistance* is a genuinely rewarding poet's novel, unlike many
comparable examples of the genre. Sheers, who has always avoided
writing narrative poems, demonstrates that he has an ability to
tackle the demands of the longer form. We must hope that this is
the first of his many excursions into fiction.' Andrew Biswell,
Scotland on Sunday

WITHDRAWN

by the same author

Non-fiction

THE DUST DIARIES

Poetry

THE BLUE BOOK

SKIRRID HILL

OWEN SHEERS

Resistance

faber and faber

First published in 2007
by Faber and Faber Limited
3 Queen Square London WC1N 3AU
This paperback edition first published in 2008

Printed AND BOUND BY CPI GROUP (UK) LTD, CROYDON, CR0 4YY

All rights reserved
© Owen Sheers, 2007

The right of Owen Sheers to be identified as author of this work has been
asserted in accordance with Section 77 of the Copyright, Designs and
Patents Act 1988

*This book is sold subject to the condition that it shall not, by way of trade
or otherwise, be lent, resold, hired out or otherwise circulated without the
publisher's prior consent in any form of binding or cover other than that
in which it is published and without a similar condition including this
condition being imposed on the subsequent purchaser*

A CIP record for this book
is available from the British Library

ISBN 978-0571-22964-2

6 8 10 9 7

500118695
Don 12/17

For those who would have
and those who did

SEPTEMBER–NOVEMBER 1944

Everything
Would have been different. For it would have been
Another world

Edward Thomas, 'As the team's head-brass'

In the months afterwards all of the women, at some point, said they'd known the men were leaving the valley. Just as William Jones used to forecast the weather by studying the sky or the formations of migrating birds, so the women said they'd been able to forecast the men's sudden departure. After all, they were their men, their husbands. No one could read them like they could. So no surprise if they should see what was coming. That's what the women said in the long silence afterwards.

But in truth none of them saw any change in the men's behaviour. None of them knew the men were leaving and in many ways this was the hardest part of what happened. Their husbands left in the night. Just days after news of the invasion came crackling through on Maggie's wireless, propped on a Bible on her kitchen table, the men, lit by a hunter's moon, met at William's milking shed and slipped out of the valley. Moving in single file they walked through the higher fields and up over the Hatterall ridge; an ellipsis of seven dark shapes decreasing over the hill's shoulder, shortening to a last full stop and then nothing, just the blank page of the empty slope. The women, meanwhile, slept soundly in their beds. It was only in the morning when a weak September sun shone into the valley that they realised what had happened.

*

For Sarah Lewis it began in her sleep. The drag, rattle and bark of the dogs straining on their chains was so persistent it entered her dreams. A ship in storm, the sailors shouting for help from the deck, their pink faces and open mouths obscured by the spray blown up the sides of the hull. Then the noise became Marley's ghost, dragging his shackles over a flagstone floor. Clink, *slump*, clink, *slump*. Eventually, as the light brightened about the edges of the blackout curtain and Sarah surfaced through the layers of her sleep, the sound became what it was. Two dogs, urgent and distressed, pulling again and again on their rusty chains and barking, short and sharp through the constraint of their collars.

Without opening her eyes Sarah slid her hand across the sheet behind her, feeling for the warm impression of her husband's body. The old horsehair mattress they slept on could hold the shape of a man all day and although Tom was usually up before her, she found comfort in touching the warm indentation of where he'd lain beside her. She stroked her palm over the thin cotton sheet. A few hairs poking through the mattress caught against her skin, hard and stubborn as the bristles on a sow's back.

And there he was. A long valley where his weight had pressed the ball of his shoulder and his upper arm into the bed; a rise where his neck had lain beneath the pillow. She explored further down. A deeper bowl again, sunk by a protruding hip and then the shallower depression of his legs tapering towards the foot of the bed. As usual, Tom's shape, the landscape of him, was there. But it was cold. Normally Sarah could still feel the last traces of his body's heat, held in the fabric of the sheet just as the mattress held his form. But this morning that residue was missing.

With fragments of her dreams still fading under her lids she slid her hand around the curves and indentations again,

4

and then beyond them, outside the borders of his body. But the sheet was cold there too. The dogs below her window barked and barked, their sound making pictures in her mind's eye: their sharp noses tugging up with each short yap, exposing the white triangles of their necks, flashing on and off like a warning. She lay there listening to them, their chains rising and falling on the cobbles of the yard.

Tom must have been up early. Very early. Not in the morning at all but in the night. She turned on her side and shifted herself across the bed. The blankets blinked with her movement and she felt a stab of cold air at her shoulder. Pulling them tight about her neck she lay there within the impression of her husband, trying not to disturb the contours of his map. Everything about her felt heavy, as if her veins were laced with lead. She was trying to think where Tom could be but the barks of the dogs were distracting her. Her mind was blurred, as buckled as a summer's view through a heat haze. Why hadn't he taken the dogs? He always took the dogs. Did he say something last night? She couldn't remember. She couldn't remember anything past their dinner. She opened her eyes.

In front of her the bedroom window was bright about the ill-fitting blackout cloth, a thin square outline of light burning into the darkened room. She blinked at it, confused. The window looked into the western flank of the valley, and yet there was light. Too much light. The sun must already be over the Black Hill on the other side of the house. She must have slept late. She never slept this late.

She rose quickly, hoping movement would dispel her mild unease. Tugging roughly on the heavy blankets she made the bed, tucking their edges under the mattress. Then she plumped the pillows, shaking them as if to wake them. Brushing a few of Tom's hairs from the one beside hers she paused for a second and stilled herself, as if the hairs might summon Tom himself. She listened, one hand still resting on the pillow. But there was nothing. Just the usual ticks and groans of the old building waking and warming, and outside, the dogs, barking and barking.

She pulled back the blackout cloth and opened the thin curtains behind it with both hands, unveiling the room to light. It was a bright, clear day. She closed her eyes against the glare. When she opened them again white spots shimmered over her vision. Drawing the sleeve of her nightdress over her wrist she wiped away the veneer of condensation from one of the small panes and looked down into the yard below. The dogs, both border collies, both bitches, sensed the movement above them and barked and strained harder in response, pulling their chains taut behind them. Sarah looked above the outhouse where they were tied. Over the top of its jigsaw slate roof she could see the lower paddock rising up to meet the sweep and close of the valley's end wall. Except for a few grazing sheep it was empty, and so were the steep-sided hills on either side, their edges bald against the blue sky.

Turning away from the window she pulled her nightdress over her head. Again she felt the cold air on her skin. The dress's neckline held her hair for a moment, then let it go all at once so it fell heavily about her shoulders. She sat on the edge of the bed, put on her knickers, a vest, and began balling a pair of woollen stockings over her hand, her forehead puckered in a frown. Catching herself in the dressing-table mirror she paused and ran a finger up the bridge of her nose between her eyebrows. A slight crease was forming there. She'd only noticed it recently; a short line that remained even when her brow was relaxed. Still sitting on the edge of the bed she gathered up her hair and, turning her profile to the mirror, held it behind her head with one hand, exposing her neck. That crease was the only mark on her face. Other than that her skin was still smooth. She turned the other way with both hands behind her head now. She should like a wedding to go to. Or a dance, a proper dance where she could wear a dress and her hair up like this. That dress Tom bought for her on their first anniversary. She couldn't have worn it more than twice since. Tom. Where was he? She dropped her hair and pulled on her stockings. Reaching into the dressing table drawer she put on a blouse and began doing up the buttons, the crease on her forehead deepening again.

Bad news had been filtering into the valley every day for the last few weeks. First the failed landings in Normandy. Then the German counter-attack. The pages of the newspapers were dark with the print of the casualty lists. London was swollen with people fleeing north from the coast. They had no phone lines this far up and apart from Maggie's farm, which sat higher in the valley, the whole area was dead for radio reception. But news of the war still found its way to them. The papers, often a couple of days old, the farrier when he came, Reverend Davies on his fortnightly visits to The Court, all of them brought a trickle of stories from the changing world beyond the valley. Everyone was unnerved but Sarah knew these stories had unsettled Tom more than most. He rarely spoke of it, but for him they threw a shadow in the shape of his brother, David. David was three years younger than Tom. He'd had no farm of his own so he'd been conscripted to fight. Two months ago he was declared missing in action and, while Tom maintained an iron resolve that his brother would appear again, the sudden shift in events had shaken his optimism.

For Sarah news of the war still seemed to have an unreal

quality, even when a few days ago the names of the battle-grounds changed from French villages to English ones. There were marks of the conflict all about her: the patch-work of ploughed fields down by the river once kept for grazing; the boys from her schooldays and the farmhands, many of them gone for years now. But unlike Tom she didn't have a relative in the fighting. Her own older brothers had been absent from her life ever since they'd argued with her father and broken from the family home when she was still a girl. They'd bought a farm together outside Brecon, large enough to have saved them both from the army. So Sarah didn't possess that vital thread connecting her to the war that brought the news stories so vividly to life for so many others. There were women here, in the valley, who had lost sons and in the early years she'd seen other mourning moth-ers and wives in Longtown and Llanvoy. But even these women, with their swollen eyes and dark dresses, seemed to have passed into a different place, a parallel world of grief. The sight of them evoked sympathy in Sarah, sometimes a flush of silent gratitude that Tom was in a reserved occupa-tion, but never empathy.

Only once in the last five years had the war really impacted upon her. When the bomber crashed up on the bluff. Then, suddenly, it had become physical. She'd been woken by the whine of its dive followed by the terrible land-locked thun-der of its explosion. Tom held her afterwards, speaking softly into her hair, 'Shh, bach, shh now.' In the morning they'd all gone up to look. Tom and she took the ponies. When they got there the Home Guard and the police from Hereford had already put a cordon around the wreckage so they just stood at a distance and watched, the thin rope singing and whip-ping in the hilltop wind. Beyond the crashed plane she'd glimpsed a tarpaulin sheet laid over a shallow hump. 'One of

8

the crew,' Tom had said with a jerk of his chin. She'd agreed with him. 'Yes, must be,' although she'd thought the hump looked too small, too short, to be the body of a man. The ponies shifted uneasily under them, pawing the ground, tossing their heads. They were disturbed by this sculpture of twisted metal that had appeared on their hill, by this charred and complicated limb half embedded in the soil as if it had erupted from the earth, not fallen from the sky. And so was Sarah. She'd heard about the Blitz, and about Liverpool and Coventry, its cathedral burning through the night. She'd even seen their own bombers out on training runs. But she'd never seen an enemy plane before. Usually they were just a distant drone to her, a long revolving hum above the clouds as they returned from a raid on Swansea or banked for home after emptying their payloads over Birmingham. But now, here was one of them, on the hill above her farm. Massive and perfunctory. So ordinary in its blunt engineering. And under that tarpaulin was a real German. A man from over there who had flown over here to kill them.

She dressed quickly in a long skirt and cardigan and went downstairs to pull on her boots in the porch by the kitchen door. As she bent to lace them she noticed Tom's weren't there. Not just his work boots but his summer ones too; both pairs were missing. She stared for a moment at the space where they'd been, four vague outlines in a scattering of dust blown in under the door. Leaning forward on her knee she touched one of these empty footprints as if it could tell her where he'd gone. But there was nothing, just the cold stone against her fingertips. She shook her head. What was she doing? She stood up, took her coat from the hook on the back of the door, pushed her arms through its sleeves and drew its belt tight about her waist. Lifting the door's latch she stepped out into the brightness of the cobbled yard where the day fell in on her with a cool wash of air. She breathed in deeply, feeling the first metallic tang of autumn at the back of her throat. Shards of sunlight reflected off the stones. The dogs barked faster and louder to greet her. She moved towards them and they settled back on their haunches, stepping the ground with their forepaws, quivering with anticipation as if a voltage ran under their skins.

The dogs, let loose of their chains, wove and slipped about her as she walked up the slope across the lower paddock and through the coppiced wood behind the farm. The extra hours of restraint had charged them with a frantic energy and they raced ahead of her, ears flat, before doubling back, their sorrowful eyes looking up at hers, their heads low and their coats slickly black in the dappled sunlight. Sarah, in contrast, felt her legs heavy and awkward beneath her. She took the slope with more pace, pressing the heels of her palms into her thighs with each step. Twice she found herself stopping to rest against the trunk of a tree. She was twenty-six years old, worked every day and was usually through this wood before she knew it, but this morning it was as if one of the dogs' chains had snagged around her feet and was dragging her back down the hill with every step she took.

Ten minutes of this stop–start walking brought her out of the wood and across their upper land until she stood on the edge of the top field where the cultivated valley gave to the hill, the mapped countries of bracken tapering to meet the sheep-cropped grass. She sat down with this bracken at her back. Picking at a few fronds, already rusting at their tips, she looked out over the valley.

When Sarah was a girl her mother had once described this range of long hills as a giant outstretched hand. It wasn't an original description – Sarah had often heard people refer to the 'Black Mountains Hand' – but then her mother was a cautious woman who'd rarely said anything that hadn't been tested in the voice of someone else first. She'd had a deep fondness, a belief almost, in such figurative language. As she got older these phrases became her hand holds, a semiotic map by which she navigated her way through the days, weeks and seasons. Her mother had died two years ago but Sarah had inherited this map and she still found herself repeating her sayings nearly every day. This weather for example. Despite the high mackerel clouds and the brightness of the day a soft rain had begun to fall, folds of moisture turning the air milky. 'The devil's beating his wife today,' that's how her mother would have translated such weather; one hand on her hip, nodding at the view out the kitchen window, 'Yes, my girl,' she'd say, turning to Sarah at her side, 'the devil's beating his wife for sure.' Sarah had never understood what connection there could be between these autumn showers and the devil beating his wife, but she knew what her mother meant. There was something odd about this kind of rain, as if the calibration of the seasons had slipped, become unbalanced. Something unnatural about it, something wrong.

She looked out over the valley, hoping to see Tom somewhere in the view. But there was nothing. The whole valley was still, much stiller than it should have been at this time of day. William Jones usually had his tractor out by now. It was the first and only one in the valley and he was always finding an excuse to use it, petrol rationing or not. But she couldn't see it anywhere in his fields. Or hear it. Viewed through the gauze of the sunlit rain the valley looked like a painted landscape.

Sarah called the dogs. 'Fly! Seren! Cumby!'

Fly came and sat nervously at her side. Sarah stroked her,

drawing a hand across her head over her ears and down her damp neck. She could feel the dog's muscles bunched tightly over the bone.

'Shh, cwtch ci,' she said, trying to relax her.

Maybe Tom had gone into town. But what for? They'd been told not to hoard or stock up on supplies, and they had everything they needed on the farm anyway. She still couldn't remember anything of last night; why was that? She tried to picture herself in the house. She remembered cooking their meal. She'd burnt her calf on the oven door. She could still feel the tightness of the burn-mark under her woollen stocking. They'd taken tea by the fire in the front room. Tom hadn't spoken much, but then he often didn't.

Fly slipped away from under her hand and trotted over the field to find Seren. Sarah watched her go then looked out at the valley once more, as if by looking hard enough she could conjure Tom from its fields and trees. Drawing a deep breath, she called his name into the morning air.

'Tom!'

Her voice echoed off the facing valley wall and immediately she felt stupid, childish, calling for him like that. The dogs pricked their ears and began running back up the slope towards her, their tongues hanging out the side of their mouths. She listened, but there was just the fading of her own voice and then the sticky breaths of Seren and Fly panting either side of her. She stood to rise above the sound of them and called for Tom again, straining to hear a reply beyond her own echo. But again there was nothing. Just the intermittent bleat of a ewe, a blackbird mining its notes in a nearby tree and underscoring everything the distant rustle of the river running its course through the valley below.

*

Tom didn't hear Sarah call for him but Maggie Jones did. She was standing in a field beside the river, one hand resting on the angular rump of a cow, when she heard Sarah shout from higher up the valley. Like Sarah she too was out looking for her husband. She'd checked the barn and the outhouses, the tool shed, but found no trace of him. The tractor was still in the yard, fresh soil stuck to the cleats of its wheels, but William was nowhere to be seen. She wasn't worried. There was always work to be done somewhere on the farm. But then she came to the field by the river and found the cows. The three of them and their calves were crowded around the gate that opened onto the lane, licking at their nostrils, their breath steaming in the cold morning air. Their unmilked udders swung heavily between their legs.

In thirty years of marriage Maggie had never known William to leave the cows unmilked. His father had been a dairy farmer and William had inherited his habit, if not his herd. Through sickness, holidays, bad weather, even on the morning of their wedding day, he'd been up with the dawn to usher them through the lane to the milking shed, then back again two hours later. A jostling, shitting, pissing ebb and flow you could set your watch by, as regular as any tidal chart.

Lifting the gate off its latch she shouldered the two heifers at the front back a few steps, their hooves sucking in the mud as she pushed through to look over the rest of the field. It was empty. She sighed. She'd have to do the cows herself. She'd planned to go into Llanvoy this morning, and take some butter up to Edith. There were potatoes to be dug. But now she'd have to do the milking. William knew her back was playing up. Where the hell was he? She tried another sigh, heavier this time, but it was no use, her irritation lacked conviction. A more worrying thought was welling

13

beneath it, draining her exasperation of its usual energy. She looked out at the open field again, retracing the last few days as she did; things William had said, things he hadn't. The thought welled larger in her mind. She tried dismissing the possibility as ridiculous. William simply wouldn't do that and she would surely have known about it if he did. But then Maggie heard Sarah call for Tom, her voice carried down the valley on the still air. It was all the confirmation she needed and standing there among the cows with their swollen udders the thought broke within her. She knew with a terrible and sudden certainty that her husband wasn't just up on the hill checking the sheep or out in the fields patching a hedge. She should have known as soon as she'd seen the cows, she realised that now. Known that wherever William had gone he wasn't coming back.

'You stupid bugger,' she said under her breath, hitting the flank of the cow beside her with the heel of her fist. 'You daft, stupid bugger William Jones.' The cow shifted its weight and she felt its hip joint move under her hand. She rested her forearm along its back and her head upon her arm. 'At your age. You bloody stupid bugger.' The trees beside the river blurred and multiplied in her vision. She blinked and brought them back into focus. Sarah's voice filtered down to her a second time, calling for Tom again. She looked up the hill in her direction. It was a beautiful day, a blue sky despite the light rain, the berries clustered red and thick in the hawthorn. Just a few high clouds. Up on the hill Sarah called a third time. The cows would have to wait. Everything would have to wait. Maggie pushed her way back through the small herd, opened the gate and, closing it behind her, started walking up the lane towards Upper Blaen. She's still young, she told herself as she went, still a girl really. She'd have to break this to her gently. But she wouldn't lie to her either, she promised herself that. To lie to Sarah would be the worst thing she could do, to tell her it was going to be all right. Because it wasn't, Maggie knew that now. She'd heard the news on the wireless these past days. It wasn't going to be all right. But that didn't mean they couldn't be; they could still be prepared, they could still carry on, however long the men were away.

Fourteen days.

'Fourteen days of activity. You can expect around fourteen days from the invasion date. Still up for it?'

That's what Tommy Atkins had said. He'd made it clear what he meant too; what would happen after the 'activity' ended. Fourteen days before you're caught, tortured and shot, that's what he was saying. George Bowen shifted in his narrow bed. He came out in a cold sweat every time he thought of it. According to the papers the first landing craft beached at Dover eight days ago. Just six days then, was that it? He counted them off on his hand under the bedclothes, opening a finger from his fist for each day of the week. Wednesday, Thursday, Friday, Saturday, Sunday, Monday. Next Monday then. Or maybe Tuesday if he was lucky. His turn to 'perish in the common ruin'. That's how Churchill had put it on the wireless last week: 'perish in the common ruin rather than fail or falter in your duty'. But what if he did fail or falter? What if he didn't do his duty? What would happen then?

He turned over again. He was still wearing his clothes and his boots lay beside the bed where he'd kicked them off just hours before. He'd taken to sleeping like this ever since it started again, so he could be up quickly when his father shouted for him from the bottom of the stairs. He was often too tired to get undressed anyway.

Fourteen days. Two weeks. But Atkins had said that four years ago. He was planning for a different invasion altogether then. So perhaps it wouldn't be the same this time. Things were different now, weren't they? Perhaps it would be sooner. Or maybe later. After all he hadn't seen a thing yet, other than some of their own troop movements and the activities of the Home Guard. But there had been lots of messages. For the last four nights in a row he'd been to all three drop points. The loose stone at the church; the plank in the barn door; the split tennis ball in the yew bole. Every night he'd been all over his patch and he knew others had too. The wireless operators had been at their stations day in, day out. So it was close, no doubt about it.

According to one message he'd taken last night the operational patrols had already left. He tried to imagine them slipping from under the covers, their wives' sleep-breathing, warm and slow in the dark bedrooms. The men creeping down the stairs, pulling on their regulation dungarees and picking up their rucksacks from the hiding places. Then turning their backs on their homes and walking up into the hills, ink black against the stars. So yes, it was close now. They'd be here soon. At last, after four years, it was happening.

For George this had all begun eight months after his seventeenth birthday. Like every boy in the area he'd received a call-up for a services medical in Newport. It was July, the long hot summer of 1940. The beaches were packed with sunbathers. The contrails of dog-fighting planes etched smoke patterns against the blue skies of the southern coast. George's mother had made him wear a suit to the medical and when he'd arrived at the building opposite County Hall he was sweating heavily after the walk from the station. He registered at the entrance and then a sergeant led him and seventy other boys into a large room with desks where he told them to take a seat. In front of them, an officer informed them, was a short educational test. 'You have twenty minutes, gentlemen. Begin.'

The sun was glaring through the windows high in the wall and at first George found it hard to concentrate in the flat heat of the room. Once he'd removed his jacket and rolled up his sleeves, however, he'd started to enjoy the test, unlike most of the boys around him who crouched over their papers, frowning into their desks. He finished the test before the twenty minutes were up. After checking over his answers he sat back and looked over the bent heads of his companions, patches of pink sunburnt skin showing through the close-cropped hair on the back of their necks. Seeing them like that, sitting in regimented lines, he couldn't help wondering what lay ahead for all of them. He thought of the casualty lists he'd seen, the reports from Dunkirk and other news from France. Some of these boys would join the army, some the RAF, others the navy. Some would be sent down the mines, others into the factories. One thing was for sure, by this time next year, if things carried on as they were, some of them would be dead. All of them perhaps, including himself.

After the test had come the medical, a surly army doctor who'd told him to undress and examined him as his father might a ram or a horse he was buying at market. Then along with a few other boys he'd been sent to wait outside a room in a windowless corridor deeper in the building. A fan thrummed on the ceiling and the sound of faraway doors opening and closing echoed along the exposed pipes running the length of the walls. It was much cooler here than in the testing room and as he waited George leant his head against the painted stone to feel the relief of its touch against his neck. Eventually a clerk called his name and directed him into a small office. An older man with grey hair and heavy eyelids stood from behind a desk, shook George's hand and introduced himself as Colonel Hughes. The colonel told him he'd done well in the educational test, very well. He asked him a few basic questions, about his schooling, where he lived. Then, licking his thumb, he looked back down at his papers for a moment, holding the corner of one page off the table, before telling him that was all. Someone would visit him in a few days' time, but that was all for now. 'Thank you, Mr Bowen,' he said without looking up. It was the first time anyone had ever called him Mr Bowen and when George boarded the train for Abergavenny an hour later he felt significantly older than when he'd stepped off it that morning.

He'd seen the fishing flies first, flashing in the sun. There were so many of them George thought the man was wearing some kind of polished steel helmet. But as he got closer he saw they were fishing flies pinned tightly together on a flat tweed cap, their bright yellow and red feathers trembling in the breeze.

'Mr Bowen?' the man called out as he walked across the field.

'Yes, sir.'

'Ah, good.' He held out his hand as he approached. 'Tommy Atkins,' he smiled, raising his eyebrows as if to acknowledge the sobriquet. George leant his scythe against the hedge and, wiping his fingers against his trousers, shook the man's hand. He was taller than George, in his early forties with a taut angular face. The kind of man who'd look comfortable with a shotgun broken over one arm and a brace of pheasants over the other.

'Hot work,' Atkins said, nodding towards the scythe.

19

'Yes, sir. All this bracken has to be cleared. And in the next field. We'll be ploughing it up soon. Ministry orders.'

'Yes, of course, of course. Need every scrap we can get, don't we?'

He spoke casually but George was unnerved by the way he looked him straight in the eye, as if his voice and his vision were unconnected.

A skylark ascended from the field behind them, drilling its song through the heavy summer air. Atkins broke his stare to watch it rise, shielding his eyes with his hand. George followed his gaze, trying to locate the tiny bird against the sky, but it was already too high.

'You were expecting me, Mr Bowen, weren't you?' Atkins said, taking off his jacket and sitting on a tree stump beside the hedge. 'Colonel Hughes said someone would come and visit you?'

'Yes sir, he did.'

'Well, that's me.' He paused and folded his jacket across his knee. 'I'll get straight to the point, Mr Bowen. I'm a British Intelligence officer. I've come to see you because you scored very highly in your test the other day. You're a clever lad. We think you could be of great service to your country.'

George opened his mouth to speak but Atkins held up his hand to stop him.

'What I'm going to propose to you may sound unusual but I assure you I'm serious. Before I go any further, however, I'll need a promise of your complete discretion. As I'm sure you understand, everything I tell you is strictly confidential.'

He reached into the pocket of his jacket and drew out a small black Bible.

'We can't have any signing of papers with this business, I'm afraid, so I'm going to have to ask you to swear on this instead.' He held out the Bible. George looked at it, both his hands dug deep in his pockets.

'If you have no objection, Mr Bowen?'

George looked down at him, this man who called himself Tommy Atkins. He thought of the Ministry of Information posters he'd seen at the railway station. 'Vigilance at all times.' 'Loose talk costs lives.'

'I'm sorry, sir,' he said, 'but how do I know who you are? That you are who you say you are? Shouldn't you show me some identification?'

Atkins looked down at his feet for a moment then back up at George, nodding his head. 'I suppose I should, Mr Bowen, I suppose I should. But really, what's the use of me showing you some papers? Easiest thing in the world to forge, you know that. Never trust someone's identification Mr Bowen, never. Please, sit down.' He gestured to the ground in front of him as if showing George to a chair in his office. George remained standing by his scythe. Atkins's smile tightened. He looked out over the patchwork of summer fields and sighed. In the distance a horse and cart was making halting progress between a pattern of haystacks in the field opposite them. A team of men followed, pitching the loose hay up into the cart, their voices caught in snatches on the light breeze. A darker expression passed over his face, the brief shadow of a thought. He took a deep breath, inhaling the sweet smell of the freshly cut bracken at his feet.

'You have a scar on your left shin approximately two inches long,' he said, still looking out over the fields. 'You fell out of a tree when you were six years old and broke your arm. You have some scarring on your right lung, the result of a bout of pleurisy when you were twelve. You're slightly deaf in your left ear, possibly also as a result of the fall from the tree.' He turned to look at George. 'Incidentally, this is what they'll cite if you accept my proposal. Unfit for duty due to deafness.' A smile twitched at the corner of his mouth again, 'You see, George, I know more about you than you do about yourself.'

He held out the Bible. 'Are you sure you don't want to hear what I've got to say? I'll be honest, I think you're making a mistake if you don't.'

George looked back at Atkins, meeting his stare. He bit his lower lip. Atkins kept the Bible held out towards him but said nothing further. George took his right hand out of his pocket and laid it on the leather cover.

'Good lad,' Atkins said, 'now repeat after me . . .'

And that was how it began. In a field four years ago, Atkins reciting by rote, in a tone that reminded George of when they said the Lord's Prayer at school, the Oath of Allegiance, the Defence Act and the Official Secrets Act. At the end of each sentence he paused for George to repeat his words. When they'd finished Atkins put the Bible back in his jacket pocket, asked George to sit down and told him everything. He told him about Operation Sea Lion, Hitler's directive for the invasion of Britain. About the government's plan for a resistance movement to be activated in the event of such an invasion. He explained to George how this organisation, the Auxiliary Units, would live or die not just on its weapons and its training but also on its information, on its eyes and ears. How, if George was willing, he could be part of that listening and watching machine, running messages, observing enemy troop movements. Atkins talked like this for over half an hour, explaining everything in the fullest detail. He wanted George to understand completely, to leave no part of this possible future he was describing unexamined. He returned again and again to the need for absolute secrecy.

'No one must know we've had this conversation, George; no one. Not your mother or father, your sister, your friends. It's the same for everyone. Even the men in the operational patrols will only know the other men in their patrol. You won't know who they are and they certainly won't know about you. Understand?'

The resistance wouldn't try to halt the German advance, Atkins explained. That was the job of the army and the Home Guard (George thought of his uncle and his grandfather doing drill in the school yard last week, their uniforms sagging at the knees, broom handles over their shoulders). No, the resistance would retreat to underground bunkers that were, as they spoke, already being constructed by the army. Once the Germans had passed they'd attack them from behind, sabotaging supply lines, planting roadside bombs, ambushing isolated military posts. The units would not give up, he assured George. 'They'll be well supplied and they'll be well trained. They'll give Jerry a bloody hard time, believe me they will.' The reprisals would be severe. Hostages executed. Whole villages wiped out in revenge. The resistance, Atkins told him, would not survive. And neither would he. If the invasion was successful, in the end they would all die. 'Fourteen days, that's what you can expect. Around fourteen days of activity from the date of the invasion.' He looked at George from under his tweed cap, the multi-coloured feathers of the fishing flies quivering in the breeze. 'Still up for it?'

George averted his eyes from Atkins's gaze and looked down at his feet for a moment before looking back up at him. 'Yes, sir', he said, frowning.

Atkins leant forward. 'You don't have to call me sir, you know? Mr Atkins is fine.' Then, giving George a tap on the shoulder like a judge striking his gavel to signal court out of session, he stood up and put on his jacket. Reaching into an inside pocket he drew out a sheaf of papers.

'These are for you. This is rice paper. It's edible. Only ever write your observations on this. If you think you're going to get caught, eat them.' He tore off a corner and handed it to George. 'Try a bit, not as bad as all that. Bit like the gum the Yanks chew.'

George bit off a bit of the paper and chewed on it as Atkins unfolded another sheet. It was illustrated with hand-drawn symbols: rectangles and triangles patterned with shaded crosses and chevrons. 'These,' he said, 'are the insignia of every German unit from the Hook of Holland to Cap Gris Nez. I want you to learn them all by heart. I'll test you on them when we meet next week, so make sure you do learn them, George. You might need them even sooner than that.' He handed the sheet to him. 'That's all for now,' he said, then turned away and began walking back across the field towards the lane. 'I'll see you next week,' he called over his shoulder.

'Sir?'

Atkins turned back, one eyebrow cocked.

'Sorry. Mr Atkins.'

'Yes, George?'

'How will I know where to meet you?'

Atkins gave another of his sudden smiles, 'Better start checking those drop points, hadn't you, George?' Then he turned away again and kept walking towards the gate, the smile shedding from his face immediately. He hated this. Too much like fattening lambs for slaughter. This boy, he looked so young. With his dusting of a moustache, his sunburnt ears, his fair hair cut under a bowl by his mother. What chance did he stand? But then what chance did any of them stand once the beachheads were breached? Just 167 anti-

24

tank guns in the whole of the country, museums being ransacked for 300-year-old canons. He glanced back at George as he climbed over the gate into the lane. He was already back at work, the bracken bowing before the swing of his scythe like Japanese courtiers before their emperor. Atkins knew he had to do this. What else could they do? But that didn't mean he had to like it. He mounted his bicycle and cycled on down the lane, the rhythmical swish of George's scythe rising and falling as he passed him on the other side of the hedge. It was he, Atkins thought, him, 'Tommy Atkins', with his secrets and promises, not George, who should be holding that scythe.

The meeting with Atkins had happened too quickly for George to think on the consequences yet. His head was light, open, and he swung his scythe with a renewed energy. He felt exposed, as if a layer of skin had been shaved from him, bringing him into closer contact with the world. The blade's edge against the young stalks of bracken, the calligraphy of the swallows above him. Everything seemed clearer, brought into a sharper focus. Just over an hour ago the war was a different country, the contours of which he'd traced through the newspapers, in radio reports. But now he was involved, connected. He had the strange sensation of his life simultaneously diminishing and expanding under the impression of Atkins's words and for the second time that week he felt older than his seventeen years.

'George! George, you lazy bastard! Get up!'

His father. His father who had slept, snoring all night while he was out running messages. His father who now thought his 21-year-old son was a lazy good for nothing as well as a coward, always yawning, tripping over his boots and knocking things over.

He got out of bed, nausea swelling through his belly. His eyelids felt lined with sandpaper.

'I'm coming! Be down now in a minute!'

Dropping to his knees he reached under the bed. He pulled out some bags of old clothes, a train set he'd had as a boy. Then he put his arm deep under again, his head resting on the mattress, like a farmer feeling for the hooves of a lamb in the womb. His fingers groped about the knots and cracks of the wooden floorboards before touching the smoother polish of the case. He drew it out. It was long and narrow, like the cue cases of the snooker players he'd seen waiting at the bus stop to go into the club in town. Flicking the latches with his thumbs he opened the lid slowly, as if it was a music box, pulled away the oily rag inside and lifted out the rifle. He tested its mechanism, the slide of the bolt, the trigger weight, then took a narrow brush from inside the case and pulled it through the barrel. Resting it across his knee he fitted the telescopic sight and silencer, then lifted the stock to his shoulder. With one elbow resting on the bed he bent his head to the eyepiece of the scope. The cross hairs wavered for a moment, the view through the telescopic sight swinging from half, to crescent, to full moon before coming to rest on the pencil mark he'd drawn on the far wall of his bedroom. He held them there, counting in his head. One thousand, two thousand, three thousand, four thousand. Relaxing his thumb he squeezed his finger until he felt the click of the trigger. The cross hairs trembled slightly as if shaken in a breeze, but kept their bearing on the pencil mark on the wall. He breathed out slowly, just as he'd been instructed. Not by Atkins, who didn't like guns, he knew that now, but as the other man from British Intelligence had taught him. The other man who'd also come to visit George one day that long hot summer four years ago.

Guide on How Troops are to Behave in England

1. A firm and cautious attitude toward the civilian population is to be adopted; correct soldierly behaviour is a self-evident duty.

2. Strict reticence will be observed when conversing with the local population. *Enemy intelligence* will be particularly active in occupied territory, endeavouring to obtain information on installations and measures of military importance. Any thoughtlessness, boasting, or misplaced confidences may, therefore, have the direst consequences.

3. Acts of violence against orderly members of the population and looting will incur the severest penalties under military law; the death sentence may be imposed.

4. Works of art and historic monuments are to be preserved and protected. Any disparagement of the religious practices of the country will be punished.

5. The soldier will be provided with all essentials by his unit. Unnecessary purchases are to be avoided. Any private purchases by individual soldiers are to be paid for in cash. Any wastefulness is harmful to the unit.

6. Unnecessary interference with the economic life of the country is to be avoided. Factories, workshops, and offices are not to be disturbed; except where operationally necessary, such places may only be entered
by soldi
use of stocks of petrol, oil, machiner
operational area exceptions ma
unit commanders from batt

7. Goods of all kind

The print ended in a ragged sepia burn mark, like an aerial photograph of a coastline. Captain Albrecht Wolfram of the 14th Panzergrenadier Division let the Wehrmacht pamphlet fall from his hand. Its owner wouldn't have any use for it now, not if the state of the book was anything to go by. He watched it land in the mud at his feet, then, rubbing the bridge of his nose under his glasses, he lifted his head to look about him. There'd been heavy fighting here as there had been all along the southern coast. The smells of cordite, burnt flesh, wood smoke and petrol still hung heavy in the air, while the sky over the Channel was dark with the thick plumes of the oil slicks the British had lit to slow the progress of their landings. The charred invasion pamphlet was just one of thousands of pieces of debris that scattered the ground; boots, a burnt-out armoured car, empty cans of food, a child's bicycle, its rear tyre melted by the heat of a recently extinguished fire. Inside the house behind him one of his men had found a letter and wedding ring pinned to the wall with a knife. The writer lay beneath them, his pistol still in his hand, a band of white skin around one of his dirty fingers.

Albrecht leant back against the picket fence and drew a packet of cigarettes from the breast pocket of his tunic. A couple of Stukas passed low overhead, their engines screaming. He glanced up at their crooked wings, acknowledging them with the slightest of twitches about his right eye.

Albrecht was patting his other pockets for some matches, the cigarette balanced on his lower lip, when he saw the dust trail of the dispatch rider rise along the road ahead. As the motorbike got closer he recognised the uniform of the Waffen SS. He took the unlit cigarette out of his mouth and pushed himself away from the fence.

'Captain Wolfram?' the dispatch rider asked him, removing his goggles, leaving his face a clown's mask of grime, pale circles about his eyes.

'Yes.'

'Telegram from regional headquarters.' He handed Albrecht an envelope bearing the SS stamp, saluted and turned on his heel. Albrecht returned his salute and watched him kick the bike into life before racing back up the road, the growl of its exhaust another seam in the montage of engine noises all around him.

Albrecht felt his stomach turn as he opened the envelope and pulled out the thin sheet of telegram paper. He'd been expecting something like this, hoping he might be called back to Intelligence, but from his own commanding officers perhaps, or the staff at Southern Headquarters, the Gestapo even, not from the SS. Why would they be contacting him? They had their own translators just as they had their own everything. When he'd registered as a fluent English speaker before the invasion he'd hoped for an easy position with the liaison units or, even better, safely behind a desk at HQ. But he couldn't expect something like that from the SS. Nothing was ever easy with them. He unfolded the telegram slowly, as if it contained something that might bite him.

He read the order twice. The typewriter ribbon needed replacing. The letters were chipped and bitten, every 'r' faded, ghosts among crowds of the living. Like every order he'd ever read it was dry and direct. Report to Southern Headquarters immediately. He'd expected that. It was always immediately, even here on the fringes of the front line. Even here where the smell of burnt flesh still thickened the air.

'REPORT TO SOUTHERN HEADQUARTERS
IMMEDIATELY STOP SELECT FIVE MAN PATROL

STOP SUPPLY NAMES RANKS SERVICE RECORDS
STOP'

He glanced at the necessary permission from his own regiment's HQ stapled to the back of the order, then looked
back at the telegram. A patrol. He hadn't expected that.
Whatever it was they wanted him for, it wasn't translating
documents in a back room at HQ or explaining orders of
civil obedience to cowed town mayors. No, a patrol meant
he'd be moving. But where?

The thump and crumple of artillery rose again in the near
distance and a thick rumble signalled the arrival of a Panzer
division from around the corner of the hamlet they'd taken
that morning. All around him the machinery of battle
ground on regardless, of him, of anything.

Albrecht watched as the tracks of one of the tanks clipped
the fence of the house next to the one he stood beside, pluck-
ing the wooden stakes from the ground as if they were can-
dles from the icing of a cake. An infantry company followed
the tanks; boys' faces numb under steel helmets. One of
them glanced at Albrecht as they passed but there was nothing in his eyes. He was going forward, Albrecht was staying
here. That's all they said. You will live today, I may not.
Except, of course, Albrecht was going forward now. He too
was going on, not back. Isn't that what a patrol meant? That
they were sending him forward. Again. Just when he'd
thought they would get a chance to rest.

He turned and looked at his own men sitting against the
walls of the cottage behind him. Some of them were lying on
its lawn, already asleep despite the massive groaning of the
tanks and the muffled punches of the field guns. Lying like
that they looked disturbingly like the corpses they'd passed
on the roads as they came up this morning and Albrecht

found himself staring at their chests, watching for movement to assure himself they hadn't just given up and died.

A five-man patrol. For what purpose he didn't know, but wherever it meant going at least it wasn't here. It could be somewhere worse, of course, but right now Albrecht couldn't imagine that. Where could be worse than here? Not in hell yet, but waiting to enter it, on the brink. Ahead of them, beyond the towns and villages of Kent, lay London, a battered city filling every hour with what was left of the Allied armies and, to Albrecht's mind even more dangerously, a fleeing population with their backs to the wall.

If they'd done this four years ago when he was first conscripted in '40, after Dunkirk, then perhaps it wouldn't have been so bad. For several months back then an invasion of England had seemed imminent. As a fluent English speaker Albrecht had been posted to Wehrmacht Intelligence in Belgium where he'd observed the massing of troops, the arrival of Italian flyers and the conversion of hundreds of Dutch barges into makeshift landing craft. On one evening, while strolling by the docks in Antwerp, he'd been shown an entire warehouse of English signposts. There were thousands of them, leaning together along each wall, their destinations all pointing in the same direction: *Tonbridge, Sevenoaks, Ludlow.* The next day he'd even watched the 'Invasion of England' being filmed in advance for the newsreels at home, entire battalions emptying onto St Anne's bathing beach as the cameras whirred from the decks of boats and along the beach itself. So unquestionable was the impending event this film was meant to represent that officers buying jewellery in town would often replace the ring or the necklace they'd been examining and walk out the door, telling the owner they'd find something better in London next week instead. But then, despite the Führer's assurances, the invasion date slipped from 15 August to 15 September, before eventually disappearing from the plans of High Command altogether. Albrecht was posted to Holland and then, after a clash of characters with a superior officer, to a fighting unit at the vanguard of the Russian offensive. It was, Albrecht knew, intended as an execution posting, but he'd survived, as much to his own surprise as that of his superiors. And not just survived either. He had, over the course of that terrible campaign, discovered something of a talent for leading men in combat, for killing, for garnering the respect and even love of those under his command. It was these men, the men of his company, whom he thought about now as he looked over the devastated scene before him, recognising how much better it would have been for all of them if the dummy invasion he'd seen filmed in Antwerp had been followed closely by the real one. England had lain exposed then, belly up. There were no Americans. But now this wounded island was only exposed in the way an injured lion or bear is exposed. Vulnerable but rageful and thrashing too. Open to its enemy and to the very extremities of aggression as well. Albrecht knew London. He'd walked its narrow streets, felt its buckled, broken history seaming under his feet. He knew what attacking that city would be like. It would be boiling at every turn, with resentment, with anger, with desperation. It would fall, of course; it seemed they all did in the end. Even Moscow and Stalingrad had fallen. But how many of them would it swallow first? How many of them would have to tip themselves into London's jaws before the city finally choked on their blood running in the veins and arteries of her streets?

Albrecht put the cigarette back in his mouth, found his matches and lit it. Drawing the smoke deep into his lungs he cast his eye over the exhausted soldiers heaped about the cottage. Its two gutted windows were streaked with soot around their sills, ravaged and dark against the white walls. They reminded him briefly of Ebbe's cried-out eyes at a party years ago, the mascara smeared over her pale cheekbones as he held her, the scent of lavender hanging heavy and sweet above them.

So which five? Who would make up the patrol? Albrecht found these decisions harder every time. Not so much because of the new faces he didn't know, the characters that were still uncharted territory to him, but more because of the older ones he did. The men he'd fought with, the men to whom he was joined by the shared loss of other men. He had made too many of these decisions over the last three years and now he was incapable of considering them without seeing their consequences spiralling into the future before him. The sentry he'd posted in the evening only to find him dead in the morning. The six men he'd ordered to advance into a street in Stalingrad, four of them returning minutes later carrying a fifth between them. He no longer thought as a soldier because he had been a soldier. He had seen too much. And now he had to choose again. Which of these men would he take? To which of them would he grant an alternative future? What that future was, he couldn't say. A few more weeks alive perhaps? The lucky wound that would send them home? The bullet or shrapnel splinter that ends it all tomorrow. Whatever it was, at least it wasn't London. They'd be sending no patrols there for weeks, maybe months, he was sure of that.

It was ridiculous, as Albrecht knew full well. There were a thousand other vagaries beyond his own decisions that held more sway over the spun threads of these men's lives. Blocks of wood pushed across a table in Berlin. Arrows drawn on a map pinned to the wall at the new Southern UK

Headquarters. The Führer's toothache. A general's capricious fit of arrogance. The trembling cross hairs of a sniper's sights settling over an Adam's apple. All of these held more potency than anything Albrecht could do or command. But as he cast his eye over the vestiges of his company he still felt the edge of fate biting into his shoulders, the thousands of possible alternatives offered up to these men in this moment's thought.

The telegram threw up another choice too. If he was assigned to this patrol, then who would lead the company? That question, he knew, held the balance of more than just five men's lives in its answer. But it was also not for him. He could leave that choice to old Hertz the battalion commander. Major Hertz who made this kind of decision in his sleep, who never saw anything other than the broadest of consequences emanating from them. Old Hertz, probably the most successful battalion commander in the regiment. Albrecht need only focus on the five then. The five names this telegram had demanded, like an ancient god requesting five sacrificials for its altar. So, the same question. Which five? Who would he take with him?

He pulled on the cigarette again, felt the heat of its slow ember creep nearer his knuckle. The column of infantry was still passing. They would always be passing, Albrecht thought. Always a column of boys marching on tired feet, staring at the hairline of the man in front of them with tired eyes and even more exhausted minds. He turned his back on them to face his own men.

He would need a wireless operator. That was a relief. That was one choice made for him. There was only one operator in the company. They'd have to find another from somewhere, but that wasn't his problem. If it was a patrol Albrecht needed him, no question. He looked over the men

34

and found the solitary operator. Crouched at the corner of the cottage, sitting back on his haunches unwrapping a ration of biscuits, his steel helmet tipped back to release a tuft of short blond hair. A new boy, a replacement. Steiner . . . He couldn't remember his first name. Young. The defence of Normandy had been his first action. He'd held up well. Or so Albrecht had been told. He hadn't seen it himself, but the reports were good. Steiner then. That was one.

They'd need a medic too. A good one if Albrecht could help it. Again he felt a sense of relief at another easy decision. The company had two medics at the moment. Sebald and Weiss. He'd take Sebald. He'd been with the company much longer. Always in the thick of it, weaving his stumbling, ducking run through the battlefield to answer the cry they'd come to know too well, 'Medic! Medic!' He deserved the break. And he was calmer. Weiss swore too much as he worked. Albrecht was sure he didn't know he was doing it, but he did. It unnerved the men. Just yesterday in a back street in Eastbourne he'd watched Weiss fumble inside a man's groin for the end of a severed artery. As he groped deeper inside the wound his swearing got louder and faster. The man's cries kept pace, getting more and more frantic, which in turn wound Weiss up another notch until the two of them were caught in a tangled race of damns and shits and fucks. Suddenly, with Weiss's hand still up to his wrist inside the wound, the blood gulping around it like a thick red tongue, the man won the race and fell silent. His eyes flicked wide and he stopped, mouth open, like a wind-up toy reaching the end of its coil. So Weiss would stay. He hoped they'd find a good replacement for Sebald. They'd need one. But there was no way Albrecht was taking Weiss on a patrol, however short it might be.

He made a mental note of their names. Steiner, Sebald . . .

35

Steiner, Sebald . . , repeating them as if they were the start of a forgotten childhood chant and he was searching for the next name in the list. As if the choice had already been made for him and all he had to do was remember the sequence, the roll-call, rather than create it himself.

Steiner, Sebald . . .

He didn't have to move. From where he stood he could see the whole company, or what was left of it. Just sixty-seven men. More than fifty short of full strength.

Steiner, Sebald . . .

It was like making a recipe, finding the right combination of characters, experience. He had a young soldier and an older medic. He needed another older soldier now. A keystone man around which the patrol could gather and form. A foundation stone.

Alex. Sergeant Alex Klepper. He wasn't much older than Steiner but he may as well have been. One of the few, along with Albrecht, who'd been with the company since the Russian campaign. Albrecht looked for him now and saw him lying flat out, his head resting beside a flower bed at the side of the cottage. Stretched out like that he covered the ground from the cottage wall to the picket fence so the other men had to step over him to pass round to the back of the house. Alex was a steady soldier. Big enough to carry the 42mm for days on end if he had to. So, Steiner, Sebald, Klepper . . . He was making progress. Almost there.

Who was he fooling? He knew he'd yet to make a real decision, a real choice. The first two had chosen themselves and if he was honest with himself Albrecht always knew he was going to take Alex. Alex from Bavaria who had so often saved his skin, who had so often laid himself on the line for the sake of Albrecht and the company. Albrecht didn't want Alex going into London. He'd do it again. Put himself in the line of fire. He wouldn't survive that city, Albrecht was sure of it. And they were so close now. Let someone else take that bullet. Someone who hadn't come all the way just to fall at the final fence.

Time was running out. Any minute now they'd be on the move again, packing up and pulling back off the line. He must choose the five men now, let them know they wouldn't be retiring with the rest of the company. Otherwise it would come as an even greater blow, once their bags were packed, once they'd set their minds on the idea of rest, even if only for a few days.

Steiner, Sebald, Klepper . . .

He looked over the faces of the men again. Filthy most of them. Bloodied. Eyes closed. There was hardly a wrinkle between them. He searched out the few older heads but there was no point. These men would be needed in the company. And what counted as older now anyway? A man who had been with them a couple of months? A few weeks even? On this accelerated scale of maturity Albrecht, at thirty-three, knew he was practically a geriatric. Lucky enough to have survived this far but not enough of a Party man to have risen any further, away from the fighting units. No, Alex and Sebald would be his two experienced soldiers on the patrol. That would be enough.

Then Albrecht saw Otto. Unlike most of the company he was still standing, rifle slung over his shoulder, holding his helmet against his stomach, his hands resting over it like a pregnant woman waiting at the bus stop. The dirt on his face stopped short of his hairline, just above his eyebrows where his helmet had previously sat; a sharply defined tide mark of battle, a festival mask of grime. His eyes showed in it like those of a blacked-up minstrel singer. Wide, unblinking. He was looking away from the marching infantry behind them, out towards the skyline where the rising columns of smoke met the descending clouds of an English autumn.

As far as Albrecht knew Otto had not spoken for the past fortnight. Not a word since the defence of Normandy. They'd shared the same bunker on the beachhead. Otto had manned the machine gun. Albrecht seemed to remember this was a mistake. He'd only been covering for another man when the attack began. Otto was not usually the machine gunner. But once it started there was no chance for him to leave his post. The waves of men seemed endless. Most of the Allied tanks sank or were knocked out by their own camouflaged Panzer divisions, but the men kept coming. A desperate, ancient pulse of men. It was as if an entire generation was being emptied onto the beaches before them. And so Otto had fired that machine gun all day and into the night. Until both his hands were burnt on the metal handles. Until its barrel glowed orange like the end of Albrecht's cigarette when he took another pull. Fired it constantly, sweeping it left and right, right and left. How many men had Otto killed that day? Five, six hundred? More, probably. After all, he'd carried on firing through their retreat too, left and right, right and left, cutting up the surf, planting reefs of bullets on which the Allied soldiers foundered and drowned.

He was a slight boy, Otto. Pale with deep black hair. Thin wrists. But strong enough to swing that machine gun, left and right, right and left. His physique made Albrecht aware again of the perverted nature of this war. That a boy as slim, as small, as bird-like as Otto could kill so many men. Half way through that morning Albrecht had caught his face, motionless under his helmet, lit by the narrow slit in the bunker and dirty like today except for the white tributaries of tear marks mapping down his cheeks. By the evening these were covered with dirt too and he'd looked as he did now. Open eyes, unblinking. Impassive. Something inside him had broken, stretched and snapped. One bullet in the thousands had been a bullet too far. Albrecht had seen it before, but never so cleanly. Never such a clean fracture of the soul. And never such a silent break either. Silent ever since. Sebald had looked him over and passed him fit but no one had yet pushed him to speak. There was no need. They'd all seen what he'd done that day and they were all grateful for it; grateful he'd done it and grateful it was him who had, not them.

Albrecht took a last drag on the cigarette, studying Otto's profile as he did so. He would take Otto. A strange choice perhaps, but for all his silence he'd proved himself an efficient soldier in the fighting since. And in the more intimate company of a patrol it was just possible he might be nurtured back to voice. He'd passed his watershed, his own tidemark. He'd stepped through the looking glass and was therefore probably, despite his temporary muteness, more stable than many of the other privates who, as yet, appeared to be functioning normally.

So, Steiner, Sebald, Klepper and Schütze Mann. Private Mann. Albrecht couldn't help acknowledging to himself the appropriateness of the English translation. He flicked the cigarette stub from his fingers and ground it into the soil with the toe of his boot, like a dancer powdering the points of his shoes. Placing his hands on the fence before him he took a deep breath and then regretted it. The burnt rubber from the burning bicycle still hung in the air. The tail of the marching infantry was passing behind him. The slow ones. The blistered ones. The broken souls with broken soles.

Albrecht was looking for his final note. The note to set against Otto that would complete the melody of his patrol. The answer to Otto's silence. That was how he would, once again, lift the pressure of his choice. How he would decide which man's life he would alter. How he would choose who he would save or sacrifice, depending on what this patrol held in store for them. A young private gave him his answer, provided the counterpoint as he hoped one of them would. He was sitting in a circle with others, resting against an upturned British ammo box, and as Albrecht's eye passed over him, he laughed. And there, in that laugh, he made his own fate, decided his future. That laugh, as he took an offered cigarette from another soldier, was the note that met and answered the silence of Otto Mann.

The private's name was Ehrhardt, Private Gernot Ehrhardt. Another replacement like Steiner. Just this morning Albrecht had seen him bayonet a British soldier as they took a gun position south of this village. The British soldier was old. Not old like Albrecht, but old like Albrecht's father had been old. Grey hair, a rheumy eye. Ehrhardt had bayoneted him with force, with anger, in textbook style. And now here he was laughing. Was that any more cause for concern than Otto's silent stare? Albrecht didn't care. He'd seen Ehrhardt laugh before, many times since he'd joined the company, and he wanted him with them for that laugh. For that ability to prevent one side of his actions, his character, washing up against the rest of him.

Steiner, Sebald, Klepper, Mann, Ehrhardt.

Albrecht took out his notebook and pencil and wrote the names down in his clearest handwriting. Calling to one of the runners he ordered him back to battalion headquarters to find these men's records and to confirm battalion clearance for this request. In the meantime he'd get Alex to inform the men they'd been selected for a patrol. Once he had their records he'd find a motorbike to take him over to Southern Headquarters, where he hoped he'd discover exactly what choice he'd just made for them. Where they were going, for how long and why. He also hoped he'd find out why he'd been chosen. Why an SS order to a Wehrmacht officer? Why a patrol when they were still only on the fringes of this country? He was a fluent English speaker. He'd studied here before the war, in Oxford and London. But whatever the reason for the patrol, it couldn't be London, that's what he told himself again. Not London, and therefore whatever their mission, it had to be good news for him and the men. Better news at least. Anywhere was better than London.

As if to confirm this thought another Panzer division came rumbling round the corner past the cottage accompanied again by more infantry. All of them were heading north, towards the capital. Albrecht turned and watched the sullen progression of the tanks once more. A dog, a scruffy Jack Russell, had appeared from somewhere. It leant back on its haunches and barked and snarled at the feet of the passing soldiers. One of them swung a lazy kick at its head and missed. Another, a few rows later, threw it the bitten end of a piece of salami. The dog snatched it from the air and lay down to chew on it, keeping one wary eye on the passing soldiers. French salami, bought just a few days ago, thrown to an English dog. Once again the speed of all this overtook Albrecht. The speed and momentum of this spiralling, unnatural world he had somehow found himself caught up in, like a man woken from a coma into a life no longer his.

'Of course they'll be back. Don't talk nonsense.'

Maggie spoke over her shoulder, still fussing with the kettle steaming from its spout on the front hob of her Rayburn. This was their third pot of tea. The other women murmured in agreement, nodding their heads at Mary, who sat at the end of the table, an anxious frown slanting over her eyes. Mary, who had finally said what they'd all been thinking. Maggie went back to the kettle, wrapping a cloth round its handle and lifting it in a smooth movement from the hob onto the sideboard. Just as William had got the first tractor in the valley so Maggie had got the first Rayburn and she moved about it with the authority of a captain at the bridge of a ship. Sarah sipped at her tepid tea. One bird ticked away irregularly outside Maggie's kitchen window like a one-finger typist taking the minutes of the day. It was left to Menna Probert, the other younger woman in the room, to break the silence.

'I don't understand it. Jack's got a whole field of mangels t'do this morning. He wouldn't just leave that.'

Maggie glanced at Sarah. No, Menna didn't understand, and Maggie was beginning to lose her patience. Bringing the pot of new tea to the table she sat down beside the younger woman, put her hand on her arm and tried once more. And again all of them listened as Maggie attempted to explain the impossible to Menna, as she tried to paint a picture of an altered world sitting there in her kitchen that looked so familiar, so unchanged and unchangeable that it challenged every word she spoke.

When Sarah had got back from looking for Tom on the hill she'd found Maggie waiting for her in the cobblestoned yard. The dogs had got to her first and were sniffing round her legs. Maggie ruffled their heads, shielding her eyes with one hand as she looked up at Sarah.

'Hello, Maggie,' Sarah had said, trying to sound as natural as possible but still unable to prevent her relief at seeing Maggie tinge her greeting.

'William's gone too.'

She hadn't even said hello.

'What d'you mean?'

'He's not at the farm. Or in the fields. He's gone. Like Tom.'

Sarah laughed. 'Tom hasn't gone anywhere.'

Maggie laid a hand on Sarah's arm, just as she had again now with Menna. 'Hasn't he, bach?'

Standing there in the bright, rain-polished yard, the two women had suddenly felt their ages upon them. Sarah felt like a girl again, that one word sending her back to her mother and her childhood. Back to when her brothers had left, when she never seemed to know the whole story and there was always something left to explain. Maggie, meanwhile, saw her own age reflected in Sarah's younger face, in the deep furrow of confusion between her eyebrows, in all the unworry and unspent hope that was so evidently still welling within her. Why had Maggie felt none of that? Just the knowing, the dull, certain knowing of experience. She envied Sarah then, standing in that yard. But she pitied her

43

too. She'd had hardly any distance to fall herself, but this young girl, she had the whole height of her hope. Maggie could still remember what that felt like. Just last year when her eldest was declared missing. When the telegram finally came confirming he was dead she'd cursed herself for not coming down off that pillar of hope sooner. Of not waking up earlier.

'Why don't we have a sit inside?'

Sarah was still looking at her with an uncertain smile on her face. 'Are you all right, Maggie?'

'I'm fine, Sarah. It's just I heard you calling. Just now. For Tom.'

'Yes. I can't find him. I don't know where he's got to.'

'I know. That's why I've come up. Let's go inside is it?'

At first, when Maggie told Sarah what she thought might have happened to their husbands, Sarah refused to credit the idea at all. But then she thought of the bed, Tom's outline, cold like it never was except maybe right in the depth of lambing when he'd been out all night. And she thought of his boots, both pairs missing. Of his silences this past week, deeper than usual. But there was still so much Maggie hadn't explained. All she'd said was she thought this was to do with the invasion. That there would have been plans. Plans maybe they wouldn't have known about. That Tom, William and the others were some of the only men left. If something had to be set up, if something had to be organised, they'd be the ones to help with it. After all, who else knew this area as well as they did?

'But why didn't they tell us then?' Sarah had asked, feeling like that girl once more, tugging at the sleeve of her father, asking him to explain.

Maggie didn't know. In fact she didn't know anything, she admitted. Nothing certain. She just knew. They'd all heard the wireless reports, hadn't they? All of them had listened to the announcements from the BBC. Britain was being invaded. A massive counter-attack is what the newsreader called it, speaking as calmly as if he were reporting that day's business news. Britain was being invaded and the Germans were coming. Reinforcements flooding in from the victories on the collapsed Eastern Front. The Allies' attempted invasion had been a disaster and now the Germans were staging their own. Chasing the ravaged Allied armies back across the Channel.

They should have nothing to worry about here though, that's what Reverend Davies had told them. And the Home Guard officer who'd come round handing out the leaflets a week ago. 'Disable all vehicles so only you can use them. Hide food stores and essential supplies. Offer no resistance but offer no help either.' He'd said these sentences in a flat tone, their intonations worn thin through repetition. But then he'd given Maggie a quick smile and briefly found his own voice again. 'I wouldn't worry too much though, Mrs Jones. Really. There's no way Churchill'll let them past the beaches. And even if he did, well, to be honest, I doubt you'd see a Jerry up a valley like this.'

And now Tom and William were gone. And some of the others too, she'd bet. 'So it has to be something to do with what's happened, doesn't it?' Maggie said, looking hard into Sarah's eyes. She was looking for the start of that fall, the connection of possibility and reality, the gear change from doubt to concern. They'd known each other ever since Sarah came into the valley four years ago. Maggie was Sarah's nearest neighbour. They'd soon become friends, although always along the axis of their ages. Always Maggie leading, playing the role of the mother, the aunt.

Sarah looked down at the old wooden table, traced the swirls and eddies of the knots in the wood. 'Like fingerprints,' her mother would have said. 'Fingerprints in the wood from those gone before.'

She shook her head slowly. 'No, Maggie, Tom wouldn't go anywhere without telling me first. He just wouldn't.'

Maggie sighed. She wouldn't fall. God bless her, she wouldn't fall.

'Let's go an' call on Mary,' she said, ignoring Sarah's refusal to address the idea. 'And then we'll see if Jack's down at The Firs.'

Sarah looked up at Maggie as if she were speaking another language and for a moment it made Maggie feel foolish. Was she jumping ahead? Was the girl right?

'It's best we check,' she said at last, 'and then we'll know, won't we?'

They'd found Mary Griffiths feeding her chickens at the back of the farmhouse. She'd sent her daughter Bethan out on the pony to look for her husband, Hywel. She wasn't back yet. Mary had noticed Hywel's winter coats weren't hanging in the spare bedroom where they usually were. Both Bethan and her mother had overslept that morning and hadn't been awake for long.

Mary had two sons in the war, one of them in Intelligence, as she often told people. She was proud, but their absence these past four years had eroded her previously pretty face, leaving it worn with missing and marked with a perpetual frown. Sarah recognised Maggie's deference to Mary's fragility. She said nothing of the fears she'd expressed to Sarah. Just that William and Tom had gone off somewhere and they'd wondered if Hywel had seen them. No doubt he'd be back soon. If he had, could she send Bethan over and let them know?

So they'd left Mary throwing handfuls of seed to her chickens, their urgent beaks drilling around her feet, the cockerel standing tall to stretch his wings and shake his blood-red wattle and comb.

They'd walked down the slope from Mary's farm, through a lower field and across the river, fording it where Jack Probert had thrown in a number of large rocks to create a pattern of makeshift stepping stones. Then they'd climbed back up the slope, through the trees where a few early mushrooms were showing brilliant white and stubby in the grass and up onto the track that cut into the side of the valley. As they walked along it towards The Firs they spoke of other things than what had brought them out on this morning walk. The Home Service's morning announcement, the withdrawal from Eastbourne, the wandering tomcat that had left Maggie with a litter of kittens to deal with. Anything other than where their husbands might be at that moment.

At The Firs Menna Probert was busy with her two young children, three-year-old Tudor, whom she held balanced on one hip as she answered the door, and one-year-old Emma, who lay crying somewhere in the darkened farmhouse behind her. Maggie and Sarah didn't go in. They didn't have to. Menna answered the door talking, her voice rising up the hallway towards them,

'Aboutime too. Where've you been? Your tea's cold now and I've put the cake back in . . .' – she opened the door – 'Oh. Sorry. I thought you were Jack,' she said, shifting Tudor another notch higher on her hip. 'Has his hands full sometimes. Can't get to the handle.'

Back in the house Emma filled her lungs behind her mother and launched into another rising scale of cries. Menna winced and frowned over her shoulder into the hallway. Again Maggie said nothing more than ask if she'd seen

William or Tom about. No? Well, not to worry, she said, stroking and pinching at Tudor the same way she might pet a dog or one of her horses. If she saw Jack she'd tell him his tea was cold. And she'd bring some of those old toys of her boys round for Tudor. She'd been meaning to for ages. No, of course she would, no trouble. She didn't really want them around the house anyway.

They'd left The Firs, Emma's cries dulling behind them as her mother closed the door of the farmhouse, and walked back down onto the track. If they turned right it would lead them all the way back to Upper Blaen. Turn left and it led out towards the mouth of the valley, gradually becoming a lane as it emerged from under the shadow of the slope and only evolving into a proper tarred road eight or nine miles further on, once it was free of the valley altogether.

Maggie was quiet as they walked away from The Firs. She picked leaves from the hedge and kept her head down as if looking for something in the soft rutted mud beneath her feet. The blackberries were beginning to ripen, swelling from tight red clusters into claret-dark bunches. Sarah wanted to stop and pull at the ripest ones but Maggie's pace had quick-ened and she was walking ahead. Sarah jogged a couple of strides to draw level with her.

'So, what d'you think?'

Maggie stopped in the lane. The light rain had passed and the sun through the leaves dappled across her face, making her squint when the breeze shifted the shadows from her eyes.

'I think I was right, Sarah, that's what I think. They're up t'something. All of them. They've gone somewhere. The bloody fools,' she added with a shake of her head.

'But where'd they go? The leaflets all say stay put. And the radio. And they can't leave the farms for long, can they?'

'I don't know, bach. You're right, they can't leave the farms for long.' Maggie paused, looking back down at her feet. 'But they've left us, haven't they?'

Sarah shook her head again, the notch between her eyebrows deepening, 'They haven't "left" us. They've just gone somewhere. They'll be back soon enough. I know Tom, he won't be gone for long.'

'An' I know William,' Maggie said, looking back up at Sarah. 'He's never left the cows unmilked. Never. He's been milking cows every morning since he was a lad. An' he's never done anything I didn't know about first.'

Maggie made this last assertion with some pride and Sarah wondered if this wasn't all just about her unease at being usurped by William, who, it was true, rarely moved from the house without Maggie's blessing or knowledge.

'We should get together,' Maggie said. 'Mary will start worrying. As soon as Bethan's back and she hasn't got Hywel in tow.'

'But she might. Have found him I mean.'

Maggie looked hard at Sarah. Don't be so stupid girl. Grow up. That's what she wanted to say to her. Snap out of your dreams, your pretty life. What do you know? You've never lost anyone. This is war. Things happen. Don't you realise, everything's different now. Don't you know what happened in France? In Holland? Belgium? Even Russia? Things happen. Even here, things happen. But she didn't say this to Sarah. She just nodded her head instead, said, 'Hmm, yes, she might,' and started walking on again, still talking, but more to herself than to Sarah, 'but I still think we should get together an' talk. Just in case isn't it?'

Sarah didn't object again. She knew better than to question Maggie more than once.

'So,' Maggie continued, quickening her pace again and

49

throwing her handful of leaves away, 'why don't you go back and tell Mary t'come up to ours. An' tell Bethan to go Over t'The Firs. She can take care of Tudor an' Emma so Menna can come over too. Actually, you'd better go to Menna first, let her know. Gently mind.'

'And what are you going t'do?' Sarah asked.

'I'm going down The Court. See if Reg and the boys are there,' Maggie answered. 'An' then I'm going to milk those bloody cows,' she added, striding on, leaving Sarah standing in the middle of the track.

A magpie, disturbed by Maggie, flew from a tree leaning over the track ahead of her. 'One for sorrow' Sarah thought, hearing her mother's voice again. She looked around for the second bird that would make that curse a blessing. But it wasn't there. And once Maggie had rounded the bend in the track, neither was anything else.

That had been over an hour ago. And now here they were, the four of them, sitting around Maggie's kitchen table listening to her as she explained to Menna once more that their husbands might be gone for a while. For more than just a day. They'd tried the wireless but it hadn't told them anything. The fighting in the south continued. The Allied forces were resisting the German counter-attack. The population along the south coast had been evacuated north. America had pledged more reinforcements but the U-boats in the Atlantic were sinking two ships out of every three. Japan was making advances in the Pacific. And then the signal had gone, fuzzed and whined out into static as it so often did, blunted by the hills that surrounded them.

'So what d'we do?' Mary asked when Maggie had finished. Menna's eyes had begun to fill and Mary's voice had a different, harder tone to it. One Sarah hadn't heard before.

'Well, carry on, I suppose,' Maggie said. 'Tha's all we can do, isn't it? Carry on, keep everything going.'

'It doesn't make sense,' Menna said, her voice thick with suppressed tears and muffled under the handkerchief she held over her mouth. 'It doesn't make any sense.'

Maggie put a hand on her shoulder but carried on talking to Mary. 'I don't know about The Court though.'

When Maggie had gone to call on Reg and his boys at Olchon Court she'd found the morning's pattern complete. Reg had no wife to leave behind so Maggie had simply found the old house empty. The Court sat a mile or so further down the valley's western wall than Maggie's farm. It was a square, solid building, a fourteenth-century fortified farmhouse with walls several feet thick and initials carved into its pitted beams by boys over 700 years dead. Reg Powell had inherited it from a long line of fathers and sons. When his wife died he carried on living at The Court with his own two boys, Malcolm and John. Malcolm had been born with a club foot so, given The Court's large acreage, John had been allowed to stay to help his father run the farm. But this morning Maggie had found the place deserted, the sun flashing off the diamond-shaped panes in the higher windows and the chickens roaming the lawn, picking at the flower beds. It was The Court that made her sure. Every man in the valley had gone. Last night there were seven of them here. With their pipes and their cigarettes, with their caps, their boots, their rare laughter, their wind-weathered faces and their earth-hardened hands. But this morning there were none. It was as if the valley had experienced its very own Passover and they, the women, had somehow been left untouched by whatever dark angel had visited in the night and taken their men.

'We can't cope with everything on our own. There's no

way.' Mary was hardening against Maggie's assumed authority.

'Yes we can,' Maggie said. 'Of course we can. The dipping's done, isn't it?'

'And it won't be for long,' Sarah said.

The two older women looked down the table at her but said nothing.

'And what if the Germans get this far?'

Mary's question hung in the air. Maggie shot her a look as if to say, not now, not yet. Menna whispered 'Oh God,' into her handkerchief.

'Well, I've got to think of Bethan,' Mary continued, and for the first time her eyes weakened and filled, like groundwater rising through waterlogged moss.

Maggie rose from her chair and went over to the dresser where she picked out a leaflet from between two framed photos of her boys. It was dull green with 'Stand Fast' printed across the cover. All of them had seen it before, propped on shelves and on sideboards in their own houses. It was the leaflet the Home Guard officer handed out the previous week. Returning to the table Maggie took her reading glasses out of her apron pocket and sitting down beside Menna again, read from the leaflet:

German troops moving across the country would not stop to attack a single house . . . The public must stay indoors as long as there is fighting around them . . . A slit trench in the garden may be dug for added protection. Diagrams to assist with the construction and buttressing of such trenches can be obtained from your local Women's Institute . . .

(a snort of derision from Mary)

52

The civilian must not attempt independent acts of armed resistance, but must also do nothing which would be of the slightest help to the enemy . . . On the contrary, the enemy should be hindered and frustrated whenever possible . . . If a civilian's help is asked for by friendly military, as it may well be, it is his duty to answer wholeheartedly any call, however exacting, that may be made upon him . . . Hide your maps. Hide your food. See that the enemy gets no petrol.

The leaflet ended with a simple statement in capital letters:

THINK BEFORE YOU ACT. BUT ALWAYS THINK OF YOUR COUNTRY BEFORE YOU THINK OF YOURSELF.

The four women sat in silence when Maggie finished. The single bird ticking outside the window was replaced by the rise and fall of a song thrush, repeating its melody again and again. The twigs of an overgrown bush brushed against the glass. And it was then Sarah fell. She was looking at a framed piece of needlework hung beside Maggie's dresser. It had been made by Maggie's mother when she was a girl. A simple house and garden in bright primary colours; animals around the house, a woman feeding the animals and Maggie's mother's name neatly picked out in red thread above the picture, 'Catrin Roderick – 1862'. Everything Maggie had just read to them seemed to threaten that needlework picture. It was like the bomber again. The war had finally come to them. Even here in the valley, where events just over the hill could go unknown, unnoticed for months. And Tom had left. They'd all left. Now, just when the German guns were firing on English soil, when the German army was marching towards them.

Sarah had never known Tom keep anything from her before, and as she sat there she began to work through all he must have done to keep this secret. That was why Mary was angry, she understood that now. The men had abandoned them, now of all times. And they'd planned it, behind their backs. Together and without them.

'Why have they gone? Why now, Maggie? And where? You said it's t'do with the invasion. How?'

All three of the other women looked up at Sarah in surprise. Maggie let out a heavy sigh. She recognised the falling.

'Well?' Sarah asked again, looking at the other women, her voice urgent, 'Where d'you think they've gone? Hereford? Brecon?'

Menna began crying again and Mary's face was drawn with worry. Sarah stood up and paced to the window. Looking out onto Maggie's yard she half expected to see a German troop carrier coming up the lane.

'What do you know, Maggie?' she asked, her back to the room.

'Nothing, bach', Maggie replied. 'Only . . . I suppose. Well, that it must be to protect us.'

Sarah turned from the window. 'Protect us? What d'you mean? They've gone. Tom, William, Jack, Hywel, The Court boys. They've all bloody gone.'

Mary raised her eyebrows at Sarah's cursing.

'Well, maybe that's it, isn't it?' Maggie said fixing Sarah with her eye. 'Maybe we're safer with them gone. For now.'

Menna lifted her head from her hands and turned to look at Maggie. But she said nothing more, just looked up at the dark beams, her own eyes pricking with tears, as if she'd said too much already.

'What d'you mean?' Mary said, her voice hard-edged again.

'Well,' Maggie said, speaking slowly. 'It's usually the men they want, isn't it? In the other places they've been. The men they're worried will cause them trouble. With the men gone, there's nothing here to worry them, is there? Just us.' She broke off, removing her glasses. She looked at the faces of the three women looking back at her, all of them frowning. A thin smile lifted and fell across her lips. 'But we're not going to see any Germans here anyway, are we? I mean, what would they want here? The tractor? Some eggs? We've hardly got anything ourselves and for once that's a good thing, because it means we haven't got anything for them either. They're not going to bother coming all the way up here. Not in winter they won't. No,' she continued, looking round at all of them, warming to her theme, 'the only thing we should worry about is carrying on 'til they get back. And we can do that. We'll need to help each other, of course. Like we always do, just a bit more, that's all. Bethan can help with your two, Menna. Can't she, Mary?'

Mary looked uncertain but gave a curt nod. 'Yes, I suppose she can.'

'What about Edith?' Sarah said from the window.

'Well,' Maggie said. 'Nothin's changed for her has it? We'll just carry on as usual with Edith, just like we always have.'

Edith Evans lived up at The Gaer, the highest house in the valley. A low-lying stone cottage with a broken-backed roof that took its name from the Iron Age hill fort that once occupied the ridge above it. Like most of the houses in the valley The Gaer had been whitewashed and when Sarah first moved to Upper Blaen she remembered seeing it on bright mornings, shining above the Black Hill's shadow line thrown across the steep wall of the ridge. Its position meant that over the years she'd come to use it as a crude barometer.

If she came out into the yard and The Gaer was obscured by low cloud, she knew the day was set in rain. If she could see its whitewash, bright against the hill's tawny canvas, she knew the sun would be strong all morning.

The hill fort itself was now no more than a series of faint concentric rings buried beneath centuries of soil and grass. It was as subtle a feature on the ridge as the banks and dips of Tom's body had been in the horsehair mattress of Sarah's bed. Like Tom's outline the missing physical presence of the fort, its ramparts and defences, could be traced only by someone who knew the place intimately, who could still see what was no longer there in the earth echoes underfoot. A careful eye, sensitive to the landscape, could make out where a gate once stood or the foundations of huts where men had once slept and fought and loved and cooked. To the casual observer, however, there was nothing there, just a toothless gap in a long grassy jawbone of earth and a few faint humps beneath a tangled mass of bracken and gorse.

Edith had lived at The Gaer alone with her son ever since her husband was killed in an accident in Longtown. A motorbike skidding on black ice, him unsteady on market-day legs, his arms full with a box of shopping, still talking to the shopkeeper over his shoulder. This was before Sarah moved into the valley but Maggie had told her how at one time there'd been a hope that after an appropriate period Edith might marry Reg at The Court. There'd even been an awkward attempt at courting, Reg stooping through the low doorway of The Gaer, a bunch of wild flowers in one hand, a leg of lamb in the other, the residue of carbolic soap cracking in the creases around his neck. But neither was made for romance. Both had only ever known their dead spouses and their capacity for companionship had been formed and died with them. Reg might have lived at The Court but he was of the same stock as the other men in the valley; spare of speech, tender as a wet nurse with a new-born lamb, clumsy as a schoolboy with a woman. And Edith wasn't interested anyway. She was too busy for love or anything like it. As well as keeping The Gaer going she had her son Roderick to raise. Edith had high hopes for Roderick. Tending sheep about a wind-whipped cottage on the prow of a ridge wasn't for him. No, she wanted university for her boy, an education. Every Monday morning she'd see him off on the ten-mile walk down to Pandy where he'd catch the train into the grammar school in Hereford. He'd won a scholarship as a weekly boarder, one of only two in the district. During the week he lodged in the town with a spinster and her brother, whose house Edith had checked over thoroughly first, running her damp finger over every lintel and door jamb. Her son would be a doctor, an engineer, a lawyer even. His health must be protected. Roderick became the focus of Edith's life, as if her husband's death, having amputated one channel of her love, left the one still flowing to her son doubled in force to the point of breaking its banks. Which is exactly what happened when Roderick went to war and was killed in a training accident before he'd ever fired a shot in anger.

The blackout regulations had stopped them all white-washing the outside walls of their homes but in the years following Roderick's death Edith stopped cleaning hers too. The Gaer's brightness dulled with mildew and mould. The little garden of rhododendrons and azaleas, fenced in from the sparse hillside, grew wild. The slates slipped and skewed in the gales, leaving the roof a crossword puzzle of dark square gaps. Edith's defences, once as strong and deeply rooted as those of the fort above her, collapsed under the weight of Roderick's death, just as those of the fort had dis-integrated under the weight of time.

One day William was bringing his flock off the mountain when he found Edith wandering through the bilberry bushes, barefoot, her hair wild and her hands black with the peaty soil. She'd been following Roderick's voice, she told him. He was out on the mountain and she had to find him. She had to bring him home. Ever since then they'd made sure someone visited Edith every day. She was still fiercely independent and wouldn't hear of moving down into the valley. With her boys gone Maggie would have had room for her. And Mary too. But Edith wouldn't leave The Gaer. They were retreating into the hillside together, her and the cottage, sinking back into the soil. She still managed to feed herself, tended her small flock, kept a sow she offered to William's boar every autumn. But she'd become wild in other ways. One night a couple of days after William found her ranging the hillside Sarah took her turn to stay over at The Gaer. In the middle of the night she'd been woken by Edith's voice drifting up the stairs. When she'd gone down to investigate, feeling her way through the dark cottage with her hands along its walls, she'd found Edith in her nightdress in the living room, a single candle throwing a weak, flickering light over the lettered board on the table in front of her. When Sarah had spoken her name, 'Edith?', she'd knocked the upturned glass to the floor and started like a frightened pony, white-eyed and ready for flight. To this day none of them could work out how she'd got that board. Maggie said it must have always been there, in the cottage, that there was a lot of that stuff around after the Great War. She told Sarah that after the Somme she remembered sermons being preached down at Longtown discouraging a rash of desperate forays into the occult. It was the devil's work, the minister had told them, knuckles white over the edge of the pulpit, this twisting of grief. But still, Maggie said, she'd known of young women all over, up all night using boards, cards, even psychics, trying to speak to the ghosts of their dead husbands, sons and fathers.

'What's to say they won't be back tonight? They've only been gone a few hours, haven't they?'

And now here they were, holding their own kind of séance for their own lost men; trying to conjure a reason for their leaving from the spaces they'd so suddenly left in their lives.

'Well, Maggie?' Mary continued. 'What makes you so sure? Did William say anything?'

'No,' Maggie replied, shaking her head and sighing again. 'No, he didn't say anything.'

There was something in Maggie's tone, the slightest of inflexions over the way she'd said 'say' that made the other women expectant. Mary stopped her questioning and all of them looked at Maggie, silently asking her to carry on. Maggie looked back at each of them in turn as if making a calculation, weighing their responses. Eventually, under the weight of their shared gaze, she stood and went over to the dresser once more. This time she pulled a pamphlet from the middle drawer.

'But I did find this. Just now when I came back to milk the cows.'

She dropped the pamphlet on the table in front of Mary. Sarah came over from the window and looked over Menna's shoulder, her hands on the back of the chair. The pamphlet had a dull brown cover with the same typeface as the 'Stand Fast' leaflet. The title, which they could just make out under smears of mud and a hole torn at its centre, curved around some illustrations of tools; a hoe, a plough and a spade: 'The Countryman's Diary – 1944'.

'It was in the milking shed,' Maggie said. 'On the floor. I only saw it because one of the heifers was standing on it.'

Mary opened the cover and turned the first few pages. Maggie sat back down. She looked beaten, deflated. Whatever had been holding her firm from within had buckled and sagged.

'Stupid bugger must have dropped it. What chance has he got if he can't even keep hold of that?' she said, looking out the window.

As Mary turned the pages Sarah caught glimpses of headings, diagrams and snatches of text:

SILENT KILLING . . . insert the knife an inch below the ear and twist . . , DELAY MECHANISMS I. The Time Pencil . . . The Time Pencil looks rather like a propelling pencil. One end is copper, the other brass . . . TARGETS I. Shell and Bomb Dumps . . . IV Semi-Tracked Vehicles . . . Fix a charge of 2lb Gelignite at any of the following points . . . I. The Pull Switch . . . The pull switch is designed so that when a wire fitted to the eye at the end is pulled, a cap is fired . . . OB Maintenance . . . ensure to keep all vents clear of debris . . . Escape Routes . . . In the event of hostile intrusion . . .

All three of them were silent as Mary carried on turning the pages. It was not a thick pamphlet and she soon came to the last one, closing it to reveal the innocuous cover once more: 'The Countryman's Diary – 1944'.

Maggie spoke first. 'That's why I think they might not be back today. Or tomorrow.'

'How . . .?' was all Menna could manage.

Sarah sat down at the table again. 'It isn't possible. Tom never had the time . . .'

'I know, bach,' Maggie said. 'I know. But there it is.' She looked at the other three women. Each of them looked as if they'd been slapped. The blood was shallow beneath their cheeks and they looked numb, lost in their thoughts, retracing days, nights, any scrap of time their husbands hadn't been home or on the farm.

'I thought he had a woman,' Mary said at last, looking straight ahead, her eyes unfocused. 'Over in Llanthony or down in Longtown. That barmaid at The New Inn. I thought it might be her.'

Maggie gave Sarah a beseeching look. Come on, girl, help me now. Now you know. Help me with this. But Sarah's eyes were also distant, staring out the window.

'I'll get some cake,' Maggie said, standing from her chair and wiping her eyes. 'Why don't you put the kettle on Sarah? Mash us some more tea, bach?'

It was well into the afternoon when the women left Maggie's kitchen, each of them walking back to their farmhouses, loosened by the resonance of that pamphlet dropped onto the table like a pebble thrown into the still waters of their lives. Their husbands had not been who they thought they were. At least, not this last year. Or had it been for longer than that? They didn't know. All they did know was the men had left; that they had been left. That if 'The Countryman's Diary' was anything to go by, the men had left the valley because of the invasion edging north from the southern coast. They had left to perform their duties, their secret duties. To sabotage, to kill (Sarah remembered the first time she'd seen Tom stick a pig, the resolute way he'd worked the knife into its throat . . . *insert an inch below the ear . . .*) and then to disappear. It was unthinkable. None of them were fighting men. William was in his late fifties and Hywel and Reg couldn't have been far behind him. Malcolm walked with a limp, dragging his club foot like a ball and chain. Jack, Tom and John were younger, it was true, but they'd been farmers all their lives. They'd hardly ever left the valley except for the market or the occasional farm sale. Sarah could count on one hand the nights Tom had spent away from the farm. They were not soldiers.

And yet this is what the handbook would have them believe. This is what Maggie would have them believe, and that's why they'd agreed to tell no one about this. No one. If their husbands had kept this secret from them, their wives, then they must keep that secret too. Until the men returned they'd say nothing of their going. They'd stay in the valley and keep the farms running. There was no need to leave. Between them there was plenty of food. Maggie's cows produced enough milk for butter and cheese for all of them. The potatoes were newly dug and the Ministry hadn't yet collected their share. They had enough salted pork and bacon hanging in their larders to see them through the winter. Some lamb too. It would still be hard work though. Impossible, maybe, to keep all the farms going as they should, to manage the flocks. Maggie, ever the organiser, was already working out a routine, a weekly diary of mutual help. But that was nothing new. The valley had always run on a basis of co-operation. Everyone gathered each other's hay, picked each other's potatoes. William lent his tractor whenever it was needed. Tools, implements, horses, ploughs, all of them were shared. The only difference now was that it was just the women who were left to handle them. But still, everything would be shared. The work and the results of the work, everything. At least, everything that could be. This, this returning to empty homes, was something each of the women had to experience alone. The sitting in quiet rooms that were somehow quieter than yesterday when they knew their husbands were out in the fields. Turning your head to catch the shadow of a movement and finding nothing, again. The intimate silences of their loss, each unique and individual, shaped by the man who had gone, these each woman suffered alone. But it was best to go to their homes, that is what they'd decided. In case the men came back. In case they left a message. It was best to be there, where the men could find them.

For Sarah that first day ended as it began. All the way back up the track to Upper Blaen she heard the dogs and their chains. Scenting her approach they'd come out of their shelter and were straining on them again, pulling and barking, taut with unspent energy. As she came back into the yard they let the chains slacken and sat back on their haunches, nudging the air with their noses.

'Hello, girls,' Sarah said.

When she let them off they spun and turned about her, slick and supple as two freshly landed fish.

Unsure what else to do, Sarah bridled Bess the pony in the back paddock and rode out bare-back to check on the flock. She also wanted to look on the hill again. She was sure there'd be some kind of a sign up there, that Tom couldn't have left without making some kind of mark indicating where he'd gone. She took Fly and Seren with her, weaving ahead of the pony, trotting back now and then, their heads low. She wanted them for the company but she also thought there was the chance they'd pick up Tom's scent and somehow lead her to him.

Half-way up the slope Sarah eased Bess to a halt and turned to look back down the long V of the valley. If she were to follow her mother's description of the Black Mountains Hand, then where she rode now was in the hollow between the thumb and forefinger. The Hatterall ridge, on her right, was the forefinger, a long slice of land pointing south-east towards Pandy with Offa's Dyke running the length of its knuckles.

63

The Black Hill, meanwhile, or Crib Y Gath, the Cat's Back, as her mother would have called it, was the thumb; shorter, thicker, the last bulk of earth before Herefordshire's patchwork of farmland. Between the thumb and the forefinger ran the river Olchon, after which the valley was named.

Just like a thumb, the Black Hill opened at a wider angle than the other hills, making the valley broader at its mouth. From where Sarah was sitting this gave it the illusion of accessibility, a stadium view right down to the distant hill-islands of Skirrid Fawr and Mynydd Merddin, rising from the lowland fields. Viewed from this lowland, however, Sarah knew the Olchon actually appeared more secluded, more secretive than the other valleys. There was something about the severity of its slopes, as if a cleaver had been driven into the soil and wrenched out with no movement from side to side. And the roads. The roads didn't turn here naturally, warded off by the depth of the valley's shadow. The one lane that did pass around its long bowl petered out into a track and doubled back on itself just below their farm as if retreating at the last moment from the hill in its path. No one ever came into the valley by accident. You only ever came here if you needed to, and apart from those who lived here few people ever did.

Sarah moved into the valley herself four years ago when Tom brought her to live with him at Upper Blaen, his late uncle's farm.

'The last valley in Wales,' her mother had said the evening before their wedding. 'You'll be living in the last valley in Wales, bach.' She'd shaken her head, her eyes glazed with tears, enjoying the small drama of the moment.

'More like the first in England,' her father had retorted from behind his paper. 'May as well live in Hereford itself as in the Olchon.'

Her parents had spoken as if she were to travel across the country and yet the next evening Tom only had to drive the pony and trap from Llanthony around the tip of the Hatterall ridge's forefinger to bring his new bride home.

It was Sarah's first move. She'd been born in the Llanthony valley and lived there all her life. She'd gone to school in the valley, had her first kiss there, known her first death there. It was even where she'd courted Tom, taking long walks with him along its upper slopes. Llanthony was where her life was shaped and where she'd come to terms with its boundaries and borders. Her mother had been born in the valley further west again between the middle finger of Tal Y Cefn and Gadir Fawr, while her grandmother was born outside the hand altogether at a farm beside Llangorse Lake, beyond Allt Mawr. Generation by generation the women of the family had moved eastward. Like pieces of driftwood floated loose from a shipwreck they'd been drawn towards the shallower waters of the English plain. It was a journey Sarah could trace on the inside cover of her family Bible. Along with their birth, marriage and death dates, all of her mother's family were there, a copperplate roll call with spots of ink dotting the facing page where the book had been closed too soon after writing. It was these names that told the story of her family's eastward movement. From the Welsh names of her ancestors, drawn from the myths of the Mabinogion: Branwen, Olwen and Rhiannon, to her grandmother's Megan, her mother's Ruth and finally her own Sarah. With each new wave-hill that rolled them nearer England, with each man that took them east, their names were smoothed in the wash of the tide. The Mabinogion was replaced by the Bible and the ornate Welsh was rounded and buffed to the simpler shapes of English.

Every name in the Bible above Sarah's and those of her

two older brothers was matched with a complete set of dates. Some of them were pitifully similar, with only one or maybe two different numbers to set their years apart. Others, like those next to the sister she'd never known, were echoed by the same year altogether:

Mary Lewis, 13th April 1916 – 10th May 1916

Sarah's was the last birth date on the page.

Sarah Lewis, 15th March 1918 –

She'd often looked at that dash leading nowhere and wondered who would write the pairing date. Whose hand at some moment in the future would pick up the pen and seal her life with four carefully written numbers.

Gathering up the reins Sarah gave Bess a tap with her heels and began riding on up the slope towards the rest of the flock, scattered about the rocky crevice of the river and over the higher ground. Three hundred hefted ewes, yearlings to wethers, their inherited borders instinctively wired within them, passed on over the generations from mother to lamb.

As the pony picked its way along the narrow sheep tracks through the bracken Sarah scanned the ground on either side of her, checking for sick ewes. A healthy sheep will graze with the flock but a sick one would often break away to lie on its own. The bracken was still thick at this time of year despite the hints of rust on the stems and edges of the leaves. You could pass a ewe by a couple of feet and still not know it was there. Even Tom often found them too late, when it was just the squawking of crows fighting with a buzzard that eventually led him to the carcass, already thick with maggots.

She wondered what else she should be looking for. This was Tom's job. This is what he did when not seeing to the lower fields. Tend and guide the flock through its annual cycle

66

of tupping, lambing, weaning, shearing, dipping. At least they'd be staying on the upland for a few more weeks. But then the lambing ewes would need to be brought down to the meadows for flushing. It seemed impossible to Sarah that Tom wouldn't be back by then, but what would she do if he wasn't? She'd often watched him work the dogs, but she'd never worked them herself. With him they'd lie either side of him, ears cocked, ready to move on his slightest instruction. Sometimes he didn't even have to speak; the timbre of an intake of breath was enough for them to know the command he was about to give. A nod, the slightest of sounds in the back of his throat. Then, as they fanned out either side of him, still bodies over their quick legs, he'd switch to a palette of whistles, playing the dogs at a distance as if they were tethered to his fingers by invisible lengths of string. And they were good dogs too. Even William had to admit that. Never drove the flock too fast. Could bring them all the way off the mountain just by standing, poised, in the exact positions where Tom placed them. How could she ever hope to replicate that? With her the dogs associated the hill with rides like this, or when she went picking bilberries, when they could loop out and back to her in a loose pattern of coming and going. With Tom the hill was their place of work, a tight map of pressure and release, of give and take as the flock flowed before them like a shoal, three hundred animals moving as one.

The pony worked hard against the slope beneath her and as she leant forward on its withers she felt its shoulder muscles slipping over the bone. They came out of the bracken and the land levelled off into the mosaic of moorland and heathland of the hill top. The last high clouds had dissolved, leaving the sky a deep evening blue. To her left the Black Mountains ranged out into the distance, buckled and shadowed, the coarse wire-grass, still bleached from the summer, catching the unhindered low sun. As she rode on the view on the other side of the Black Hill revealed itself from under the ridge. A wide expanse of undulating fields, crossed and divided by hedges, punctuated by houses and hamlets, stretching out far below her, as if viewed from a low-flying aeroplane. She'd lived here for four years and yet it still managed to catch her unawares, somewhere under the ribs, every time. This contrast, from the claustrophobic view of the valley, its steep walls framing the sky, bringing your head back all the time, to this: an entire country laid out before her, tangible, open and yet so out of reach.

But Tom wasn't down there, she was sure of it. He was a hill man. They all were. She remembered one of the diagrams she'd glimpsed in 'The Countryman's Diary'. A cross section of a deep underground burrow stocked with supplies, rudimentary bunk beds, a thin tunnel leading horizontally from one end, another leading up vertically from the other. A disguised entrance covered with grass and leaves. She looked back over the moorland behind her again. It was bare and massive, shot with spring flushes and pitted with dark pools filling the peaty hollows. Maybe they were here, right now, under that sparse, empty ground. Maybe they could hear Bess's hooves above them. Maybe they could even see her. An electric thrill ran through her at the thought of Tom emerging from that tuft of deergrass there, or from under those bushes of heather. Still half turned on the back of the pony she shouted his name to the hill again.

'Tom!'

She listened but again there was nothing. Just the wind, hushing and rushing in her ears, rising and falling like her own blood, like distant waves, endlessly folding against a stubbornly silent shore.

That night Sarah tried to sleep with the dogs in the bedroom but it was no good. Tom rarely let them into the house, let alone upstairs. They turned and whined at the side of her bed, their claws scraping on the wooden floor until Sarah took them back outside and chained them in the yard. She returned to the bedroom alone, a single candle lighting her way up the narrow staircase. Getting under the heavy layers of blankets she stretched her hand across the sheet to feel for the impression of Tom once more. He was still there, just, but growing fainter all the time. The mattress was expanding back into his shape, like water seeping into those hollows on the hill, steadily rising up the banks until there was no hollow, just an undisturbed surface reflecting the blankness of a cloud-covered sky.

It was around midnight, suspended somewhere between sleep and wakefulness, that the thought came to her. If Tom was going to be away then she wanted him to know she'd managed the farm without him; that everything was ready for him to carry on as usual when he came back. What she'd done each day, how many animals were ill when, how many eggs, how many lambs even, if he was away that long. She'd write it all in the back of the accounts book they kept in the dresser downstairs. She would write it every day so that when he returned he could read it. And once he had, he'd know how she'd spent these weeks without him. He'd know everything, just as if they'd never been apart at all.

October 12th

The first frost this morning. We didn't expect that.

Fed the pullets warm mash and gave some to the pig too. Three of the pullets laid today. Only one hen still laying.

Helped Menna Probert pull Hywel's field of mangels. Menna and me pulled and docked. Bethan did the cart and Mary loaded. Maggie looked after Menna's two.

Gone five when we finished.

Took Bess around the flock. The cut above her fore off hock is healing good.

Drove a batch of ewes off the heavy grazing on the top marsh.

Maggie came and we made supper here. Still no news from her wireless today.

Maggie said she'll take eggs and cheese into market tomorrow.

The leaves are turning fast. The birch is all yellow and the sycamore is browning. I saw a thrush this morning, hammering a snail shell on the wall. That tawny owl is back, calling all through the night.

The pen felt awkward in Sarah's hand. Her fingers were stiff from picking and docking the mangels and it slipped in her grip. It felt too thin, too fragile. She'd been writing this diary every night for two weeks now but she still wasn't used to it. She hadn't written like this since school. She'd always kept the accounts but that was different. That was numbers, dates, lists of words. The money they got from an auction of lambs, the coins she spent in the village, the stuffed sacks of freshly sheared wool, they all translated onto the pages of the accounts book. The numbers and dates she wrote represented what happened. But this diary, written at the other end of the book, the other way up, was different. She still couldn't make her days translate onto these pages. She looked at the words she'd just written. *Helped Menna pull Hywel's field of mangels*. That didn't describe how they'd spent the day at all. How they'd gathered in Menna's kitchen for a breakfast of oatmeal and tea before tramping down to Hywel's lower meadow. How the valley was still dark in shadow as the cart trundled and bucked over the frost-hardened ruts behind them. How they'd started at the top of the field where the sun first touched and followed that line, that border of shadow, as it steadily moved up the slope. How they'd followed it all day, a couple of feet behind, giving it time to warm the mangels and soften the earth so the waterlogged roots wouldn't bruise when they eased them from the soil. How Bethan didn't speak to any of them yet whispered and coaxed the old cart horse all day, scratching at its withers, geeing it on with sharp clicks of her tongue against her teeth. How that early sun caught the frost on the ploughed ridges, transforming the crop into a field of diamonds. How when Menna cut her finger with the curved blade of the docking knife she'd cursed then laughed at herself right after, hand over her mouth, shocked at her own profanity. How the blood curled around her finger like a molten wedding ring. How this evening her own fingers are sore and cramped, how her back aches after hours of bending to pull at the mangels, shaking them free of the earth. How she never thought it would be for this long. How she wants Tom back. How she wants all of them back. How she wants it to be like before.

The men have been gone for two weeks now and all the women agree the best dreams are the nightmares. The worst are the good ones, the ones that give them what they want, the ones that make them forget. They have all been surprised how cruel the mind can be in this way. How willing the imagination is to put them through the mill again and again. For Sarah it's when she dreams of sleeping beside Tom, knowing that his warm weight is just inches away from her. When she dreams of waking and going downstairs to light the fire to heat the water for his wash; of hearing his tread on the floorboards above her, him coming down and appearing at the bottom of the stairs pulling on his waistcoat, doing up the buttons with his thick thumbs. Him telling her what his plans for the day are, or asking her how much butter they have left, or maybe just sitting at the table and taking his tea from her with a creased smile. When she dreams of all this and then wakes, to the creaking house, to the dull static of the river, to the empty bed beside her, it is like losing him all over again as her stomach swings away from her and she has to let all she remembers to be true come flooding back.

So far this truth has been a silent one. None of them has heard anything from or about their husbands. Mary and Bethan rode over into Llanthony a few days afterwards and found nothing changed. The farmers were still there, working their land. Everyone was worried, of course, and the Ministry hadn't been to collect the potatoes, but otherwise nothing had changed. The valley, they said, had felt as busy as ever, its through road to Hay-on-Wye lending it a subtle flow of life unlike their own dead-end which invited no travellers, no passers-through. They'd said nothing of the missing men to anyone. Menna suggested they should tell the police or even the Home Guard, but Maggie had quashed that idea. Sarah was surprised when Mary had agreed with her, as if this was something the two older women both knew was right, simply because of their age. And so they'd all waited instead. For a word, a message or for the men just to come back, as suddenly as they'd left.

Maggie's wireless was of little help. Every now and then it picked up transmissions, giving them a piecemeal idea of what was happening elsewhere in the country. The fighting continued. There had been calls for peace, for surrender from politicians the Home Service called 'traitors'. Civilian men along the south coast had been deported. No one knew to where. There was one report of a massacre at a village in Cornwall. 'A reprisal', the announcer had called it. A whole village shot. The women and children. Maggie had flicked the switch and cut off the report mid-speech. Since then every time they'd tried to tune in to the news they'd got nothing but the whine and snow of white noise, the crackle of disconnection.

Through it all, they worked. In some ways with the men gone there were fewer jobs to do each day. Fewer meals to be cooked, clothes to wash, plates to clean. But there were new jobs to take the place of these. Harder, heavier, unfamiliar tasks. They decided to break the flock at The Court and divide it between their farms. The new sheep weren't hefted to their grazing areas and often drifted back towards The Court's land. Over the past fortnight Sarah had been out three times driving her portion of the broken flock back to Upper Blaen. As well as keeping the flock and the chickens and the pig, Sarah also set about the other jobs Tom usually

left for this time of year, the round of mendings and prepa-
rations that filled the last weeks of October as the days
steadily grew colder towards winter. So she began trimming
the hedges around the lower fields, anxious to finish them
before the first frost while there was still sap in the wood.
She checked and fixed the hurdles, cleaned out the pens,
patched the thatch on the hay ricks, laid down poison for the
rats and fixed the broken slates on the little barn beside the
house, musty with piles of potatoes and sheaves of straw
glowing in the dark. There was also work to be done on the
farms of the others. All-day jobs like the pulling of Hywel's
mangels or the winter ploughing of William's meadows
down by the river. In line with Ministry guidelines William
had decided to give over his best alluvial land to oats.
Maggie was determined this should still be done, that they
should carry on as usual, so at the end of that first week
Mary and Sarah found themselves sitting in her kitchen once
more, booted and scarved, ready for work.

None of them had ever driven the tractor and Maggie
thought the fuel should be saved anyway so they resorted to
the horse-drawn plough, the two big-hoofed cart horses
from The Court, their heads nodding like pistons, lifting
their knees high out of the cloying soil, drawing Jack's single
plough. The first furrows of the day were a mess. Maggie
insisted on driving the plough, leaving Mary to follow with
the presser drawn by her own elderly horse. 'Don't you
think I've watched them do it all my life?' Maggie said when
Mary questioned why she should drive the plough. 'Every
year we're down at Pandy for the match. Four times
William's won that he has. An' him a valley farmer too. Four
times mind,' she added, as if William's skill with the
ploughshare would somehow reflect upon her.

Sarah helped Mary with the presser and from that position, following the plough, soon saw that, however accomplished a ploughman William might have been, his wife had learnt little in all her years of observation. Maggie couldn't hold the blade deep enough and it often skidded over the field's stubble or only nicked at its surface. When she did manage to engage the share the earth turned away clumsily, breaking into clumps rather than folding over like a wave from the prow of a ship as Sarah had seen it do the few times Tom ploughed or when she'd also gone down to the ploughing match herself.

After five uneven, crooked furrows and four awkward, mud-churning turns Maggie finally gave over to Mary. She joined Sarah on the presser, breathing heavily, a dew of sweat on her forehead despite the bitter day. Together they drove the machine behind Mary's steady, straight furrows, the clods bowing away neatly, glinting in the weak morning sun.

Mary was a slight woman compared to Maggie and yet she was able to handle the balance of the heavy plough, to ride its bucking and swinging, bringing the blade in deep and true on each turn. They were not the furrows of a regular ploughman, but they were sufficient.

'Only child,' she called over her shoulder at them. 'My father had me ploughing soon as I was big enough to reach both handles.' Sarah couldn't see Mary's face, but she could hear the smile in her voice.

That had been last week. Now, at the end of the second since the men's departure, Sarah and the others were exhausted. There were less bad good dreams, simply because they often fell into bed and slept too deeply for even their own unconsciousness to reach them. And it wasn't even winter yet, although the season could be sensed every morning, in the steelier taste of the air, in the first falling of the leaves and in their clouded breaths as they walked out into the fields. The lambing ewes and yearlings would have to be brought down soon. The yearlings for protection and the ewes for flushing, for two weeks of good grazing on the richer meadow grass. So Sarah had her own challenges to consider ahead of her. The ones she hadn't yet thought about, fearing to jinx Tom's return. But now, increasingly, the work to be done tomorrow, next week, next month even, occupied her mind. At least it distracted her from where the men were, although that was a thought that never left her completely. It ran on beneath all the farm work like a stream going underground, under all her other thoughts every day. For Sarah it took the form of a growing sense of disbelief. She simply couldn't give herself to the scenario Maggie had painted. Who's to say 'The Countryman's Diary' was connected to why the men had gone? Who's to say it wasn't just William who'd owned a copy, or if he hadn't just picked it up from a friend in town?

The night before the mangle picking Sarah had spent the evening with Maggie. Over dinner she'd asked to see 'The Countryman's Diary' again. When she did Maggie had looked down into her steaming bowl of soup. 'Afraid you can't, Sarah,' she said simply.

'Why not? We all saw it. I just want a proper read of it, that's all.'

'I know, bach,' Maggie said looking up at her. 'But I burnt it. After you all left. I put it on the fire.'

Sarah looked back at her, her soup spoon held half way to her mouth. She placed it in the bowl, feeling a flush of anger pulse through her chest. That pamphlet had been the only thing left; the only sign, the only marker. It was their only connection to their husbands and now Maggie had destroyed it. She felt her anger melt towards tears, tears of frustration, not sadness. The kind of tooth-grinding frustration she'd felt as a child when accused of doing something wrong. A frustration against the flow of events that seemed to always be running counter to her own direction.

'I couldn't have it around here,' Maggie continued. 'What if someone else found it?'

Sarah knew who Maggie was talking about. 'I thought you said they wouldn't come this far. That there was nothing for them here.'

'Well now there isn't, is there?' Maggie replied, an edge to her voice. 'And honestly, Sarah,' she continued more softly, 'you wouldn't have wanted to see it. There was some horrid stuff in there, really.' She returned to her soup, shaking her head. 'Awful,' she muttered between spoonfuls, 'awful.'

Sarah walked home through the dark lanes that night still nursing her disbelief, her reluctance to accept the story that appeared to have unfolded before them all. She knew she would still ride out on the hill when she could though, looking. Just in case. And it didn't stop her thinking all the time of where Tom and the other men would go, where, if Maggie's story was true, they would build their underground shelter. In the meantime, however, the farm demanded her as a suckling baby demands its mother; without malice, without agenda, just simply because it was the way of things. Her farm and the farms of the other women. The whole valley was there, with its cycle of birth, sowing, harvesting and slaughter, and they, the women, had to keep it turning or it would leave them behind altogether. And that's why, despite her aching limbs and the gritty tiredness in her eyes, Sarah had woken the next morning and gone to pull mangels with Menna and the others.

When she came back to Upper Blaen that evening she saw to her own animals then cooked herself some bacon and potatoes before tying up the dogs for the night. Then, with a slow rain tapping faster at the window, she sat by the fire to write her diary, picking up the thin pen through which she found it so hard to speak faithfully to Tom about how she'd spent her days without him.

November 1st

4.30 p.m. Wehrmacht Unit, <u>Poss.</u> 4th Infantry Div. (Wehrheis IV) temp. attached to 14th Panzergren. Div.? Travelling N.W. out of Pandy. Dest. Longtown/ Michaelchurch?

1 x Mercedes Benz staff car. One driver (1 x sergeant?) three passengers. 1 x officer. Light arms. 2 x MP38 sub machine guns.

1 x BMW R35 motorbike and sidecar. Two men. 1 x MG 42 heavy machine gun (7.92mm) on side car mount. Light arms.

Shrapnel damage to left wheel arch of staff car.

The tip of the pencil broke through the rice paper as George marked the full stop. He pulled it free, leaving a grey-edged puncture like a tiny bullet hole at the end of the sentence. His hand was shaking. He was too excited. Stay calm, he told himself. Too excited and too tired.

George had been observing troop movements for the past week but this was the first sign of the enemy probing deeper into the hills, away from the focus points of the railway and the main road. It had all begun as Atkins had predicted, just much slower. The fourteen days had passed and George was still here. Still going about his farm work by day and running messages at night. But eventually it unfolded exactly as he'd told George it would, as if Atkins himself had planned the invasion.

First there had been their own troops along with scatterings of Americans and Canadians. Mixed regiments, even some Home Guard units, retreating up the railway towards Hereford. There was talk of the smaller towns being handed over to the advancing Germans without putting up a fight, to save the civilians. The newspapers stopped coming and there was less news, more light music, on the radio. Through it all they kept broadcasting light music. George suspected the songs chosen and the order in which they were played were a code, but he couldn't be sure.

Then, two weeks ago as they'd sat to breakfast, George's family heard the guns for the first time. Over the course of the next day they got closer until George could make out the exact metronomic rhythm of the thud, whine, crash of their firing. From what they could make out, several small units of Allied artillery had stayed behind to slow the German advance. It was among these units the German shells were now landing. George tried to imagine the damage inflicted each time he heard that final crash, but he couldn't. He hadn't even seen bombs dropped, let alone artillery fire, and he found it difficult to associate these soft crumples with what he knew must have been terrible explosions.

More messages started appearing at the drop points. It looked as if one of the German invasion armies was moving north and west before curling east again towards London, like a giant wave on the point of breaking. Another was securing the southern approach to the capital and another again was pushing north-east towards the mouth of the Thames. They were closing a pincer around the city, cutting off all escape routes other than those to the north. Bristol fell. The German navy docked warships at Newport.

After the day of the guns George saw a flurry of civilians moving north, most of them on the main road. Cars crammed with people, luggage, boxes, mattresses tied to their roofs. Horses straining against their yokes, the carts behind them piled high with children, old women and possessions. The army closed the railway line to civilians. There were protests and a man was shot trying to break through the cordons to the station. Leaflets appeared urging people to stay in their homes, not to try and travel anywhere. George heard of a German parachute agent, caught landing outside Hereford. Apparently they were dropping all over the country just in front of the advancing armies, spreading rumours, panic. This one was killed by the crowd before the police could get to him. His accent had been perfect but then it transpired this was because he wasn't German at all but English. A Nazi sympathiser who'd moved to Germany before the war.

And then there was silence. No more guns, just the odd drone of bombers flying north. The occasional crackle of anti-aircraft fire. All at a distance. Eventually a telephone call came through to the local police station. The news spread throughout the area within hours. A column of German troops was marching into Hereford. Another had already established a Western Headquarters in Abergavenny. After that there were always messages at all the drop points. The wireless operator, whom George guessed was most probably Reverend Sheldon at the church, must have been active non-stop for forty-eight hours.

For the first three days after that telephone call George saw nothing. But then he found an excuse to go down to the railway station during the day. Constable Evans, looking pale and strained, had visited his father and confirmed the area was now under German occupation. He also said that, for now, essential movement of livestock was still being allowed. George's father was expecting a batch of chicks on the Hereford train and it was there, at the two-track station in Pandy he'd known all his life, that George saw his first German soldiers.

He'd waited in line behind the other farmers at the freight desk the Germans had set up and eyed the guards on the station forecourt. They looked younger than him, thin. He hated them, he was sure of that. Atkins had been clear about what these men did in the name of fighting for their country. And the other man too, the man who'd visited George after Atkins, the man who'd never told him his name, he'd been at his most articulate when telling George what the occupying soldiers would do to him and his loved ones. Men castrated like male lambs. The young women 'spread' among the elite officers. Yes, he hated them. And yet here, in the flesh, these young guards looked so normal, so human. They looked like the young Allied soldiers he'd seen retreating through this same station just the week before. Only the colour and cut of their uniforms were different. The dirt, dust and the shabbiness of the material were all the same. Under those odd mushroom-shaped helmets George saw how these guards were boys like him. He even noticed two of them share a joke, the language angular on his ear. They'd laughed. And then he'd hated them again. These boys playing at soldiers, laughing outside the station he'd known since he was a child.

At the head of the queue a German officer stood beside the freight clerk, observing the showing of papers and the collection of goods. The white silk scarf about his neck was smudged with grime along its creases. When George handed

82

his docket to the clerk the officer took it and glanced over its details. 'Ah, chickens,' he'd said in a delicately accented English as he passed the docket back to the clerk. 'My wife keeps chickens.'

A poster was pasted to the wall beside the desk. As the clerk worked through his files and papers George read the first few sentences.

Proclamation to the People of Britain

1. British territory occupied by German troops will be placed under military government.
2. Military commanders will issue decrees necessary for the protection of the troops and the maintenance of general law and order.
3. Troops will respect property and persons if the population behaves according to instructions.
4. British authorities may continue to function if they maintain a correct attitude.

The clerk was completing his paperwork. George scanned over the next directive, hoping to reach the end of the poster before he had to leave. But then number 6 stopped him in his tracks. He felt the blood drain from his face.

The officer gave George a curt smile and a short nod, indicating he could leave with his crate of chicks. As he carried the crate away from the station the two young guards watched him pass. George looked straight ahead, fixing his eyes on the brow of the hill over which he'd walk home. One of them strolled a few paces behind him then stopped. George heard the metallic snap of his steel-shod boots on the tarmac. When they stopped he thought maybe the soldier was raising his rifle, taking aim at the back of his head. A rush of fear rose through him. He felt vulnerable, exposed, as if an area the exact circumference of a bullet just above his neck had turned to liquid. He kept his eyes on the hill and carried on walking, the chicks bubbling away in the crate he held before him. Nothing happened, but still he didn't look back until he was out of sight and only then did he put the crate down and rest beside a signpost at the edge of the road, his hands quivering on his thighs. The signpost was new, the soil at its base freshly turned. The Germans had put it there, replacing the one removed by the Home Office five years earlier. The Germans seemed to have thought of everything, even bringing their own signposts. What else had they come prepared for? George thought again of that poster at the station, its sixth directive, so definite, so abrupt in its translation:

6. All civilians are warned that if they undertake active operations against the German forces, they will be condemned to death inexorably.

Shrapnel damage to left wheel arch of staff car.

George checked over the details of his latest observation then folded it three times into a chunky square of paper. Reaching under his bed he picked out one of the split tennis balls he kept there. Pressing each side of the ball he opened the slit as he would the mouth of a sheep he was dosing and slipped the folded rice paper inside. Then he put the ball in a canvas rucksack and put the sack under his bed, ready to take out that night, once his parents were asleep and he could move safely under the cover of darkness to the drop point at the barn.

This had become his regular rhythm. A week after Atkins's first visit four years ago he'd met the intelligence

84

officer again. As he'd suggested, George had kept an eye on the drop points and, sure enough, one evening there was a note from Atkins telling him to meet the next afternoon in the top ploughed field. It was another hot summer's day and once again George saw Atkins's fishing flies winking in the sun before he properly saw the man himself. As he stepped over the dry, crumbling ruts he couldn't help thinking that Atkins's 'cover' of a country fisherman didn't hold up too well out here in the middle of a ploughed field. But he knew why he'd chosen to meet here. No one could possibly over-hear them. The field was the farthest from the farmhouse and wasn't overlooked by any other buildings.

Standing there in the middle of the field Atkins tested George on the sheet of German insignia he'd given him on their first meeting. Holding it before him he alternated between asking George for the name of a unit attached to a certain insignia and asking him for the description of the colours of a particular unit. He watched him carefully all the time, his blue eyes keen over the edge of the illustrated sheet.

'Well done,' Atkins said when they'd finished. 'Only one wrong. The 6th Engineers have a black, not a red cross at the centre. Not to worry though, they're all engineers, and that's what matters.' Taking a match box from his waistcoat pocket he struck a match then held it to the corner of the insignia sheet. George watched as the paper curled in the heat, as the flame caught and climbed towards Atkins's hand like an animal reaching for the fingers of its feeder. The ashes fell to the ploughed earth and scattered over the young leaves of the potatoes growing at their feet.

'Shan't be needing that any more, shall we?' Atkins said, eyeing George again.

'No, Mr Atkins, I suppose not,' George had replied, relieved he'd passed this first test. As it turned out they did need another sheet of insignia. Over the years since that meeting in the ploughed field the war had moved on. Divisions had amalgamated, battalions were swallowed and whole new armies formed from volunteers in the occupied countries. So a couple of months ago George had found another note at the drop point from Atkins, this time accompanied with updated insignia details. That note was the last he'd heard from him. Ever since then there'd been silence. A hurried scribble, *G, Afraid you'll have to learn these on your own. Good luck! T. A.* and attached to it, the illustrated list of insignia, at least twice as long as the one he'd given George four years ago.

November 1st

Heavy rain through the night and into this morning. The river is very high, over the stepping stones. The stream flowing fast too. Washing a lot of earth with it.

Clear by this evening. A strong sunset. Maggie said it looked like the hills were on fire.

Finished the ditching today. I think this rain might have drowned it though.

Maggie said we'll start bringing the lambing ewes down tomorrow as it looks about to set in cold. She had some more news off her radio. London is still ours but they have a lot of the south. Maggie says they've even changed the time down there. German Summer Time. And they'll do the same if they come up here. I can't really see how.

They are close, Tom. The bells at Longtown were ringing without stopping for half an hour this evening. I could hear them clear. Maggie came straight over and then we went to stop in on Menna. Mary is up with Edith. Menna is very tired with her two.

I think we all know what the bells mean but Maggie won't have it. She still says they won't come up here. But it is frightening Tom. I am scared. Mary wants Bethan to go over to her cousin in Hay. I keep thinking of those stories we heard at the start. When the Germans went into Poland and Holland. I wish you were here.

Maggie's been into market twice now and says there's no word there. She didn't say anything, and neither would I, Tom. But I do wish I knew.

Just heard some planes. Heavy ones by the sound of it. Don't know if they are theirs or ours any more.

I hope you come back before it gets cold. I hate to think of you on the mountain in Winter. If that is where you are.

It was getting easier, this writing to Tom, but there was still so much she couldn't tell him. For some reason, after the first two weeks she grew to expect him back more than ever. As if two weeks was enough. As if there was a season for his missing, just as there was a season for everything else and it should be waning now, just as autumn was waning to winter. She began waking in the mornings feeling as stripped as the branches outside her window.

More than once she thought Tom had left signs for her. That he'd come back when she wasn't looking and left signs only she'd recognise. First it was a yearling ewe with foot rot in the yard in the morning. The dogs were lying down, still chained, watching it as it hobbled back and forth in front of the gate, bleating weakly. Sarah couldn't see how it would have got in. When she found it she went round the back of the house and looked up the hill, feeling her heart gulping in her chest like water from the hand pump. But he wasn't there, Tom wasn't there. Just this sheep in the yard with one foreleg swinging from the knee as it held its bad hoof off the cobbles.

Since then she'd seen some kind of a sign nearly every day. Tools she was sure she'd left out hung back in the lean-to; the coal-shed door closed when she thought she'd left it open; a couple more pleachers than she'd left the previous night, woven into a hedge she'd been fixing. Once it was a new tooth in the old haul rake, a fresh blond whittled peg plugging the gap she was sure she'd seen there just the day before. But then she was so tired. She couldn't always be certain and over the hours doubt would seep into her sense of revelation, until by the end of the day, as she climbed the stairs to bed, she was as empty as ever, giving herself to another night of bad good dreams or good bad dreams. Both left her feeling like those branches outside her window. Robbed, exposed, bare.

This evening, after a day of no signs at all, she'd gone looking for one of her own. Opening the dark wooden wardrobe in their bedroom she'd sat on the edge of the bed in her nightdress and pressed Tom's clothes to her face. There was nothing of him in his formal clothes, in his best suit or his pressed white shirts. Just the acid smell of mothballs. But in his working clothes he was still there, just. As faint as the indentations of his body in the mattress had been at the end of that first day. A stale sweat smell. Musty, worn, traces of animal.

Perhaps it was the smell of Tom that brought her bleeding the next morning as she sat shivering on the seat of the *ty bach* out the back of the house, watching the dawn light melt through the little window from black to blue to grey. She was disappointed. For a couple of months before Tom had gone she'd been slipping a day here or there in the calendar, hoping he wouldn't notice. And he hadn't, so when she was late this month she'd allowed herself a brief blush of hope. Maybe against all odds it had happened. Tom had always been firm on this. No children while there was a war on. No more mouths to feed until it's over. Sarah had never understood. They'd have enough food and she wasn't getting any younger. Twenty-seven next March. So she'd begun slipping the odd day here and there, convinced Tom would be pleased when she eventually fell pregnant. And now just when she realised why Tom had been so reluctant, she thought maybe, just maybe, she'd been able to keep some of him after all. But this morning had proved her wrong. She'd known as soon as she woke. The familiar long drag of pain below her stomach. And then on coming out here, the first drops of deep black blood. She'd been wishing for the impossible, she knew that now. She'd been working hard. She was worried, not sleeping well. Of course she might be late. It had been too much to hope for, especially with Tom gone when even the simplest hope, to have him back, seemed so forlorn. As she sat there, looking out at the lightening sky, Sarah even found herself placing these two hopes either side of a superstitious equation, with herself at the centre. Was this her punishment for trying to deceive Tom? Him and the others going like that? If it was, she wished she could turn back the clock now. To have Tom back, all of them back, that was the impossible she wished for now. That was all she wanted. The world back in place and the valley continuing as normal, whatever happened beyond it.

The still dawn she'd watched through that window turned into a crisp morning, brittle with brightness after the days of loose rain billowing like undone curtains across the valley. Every twig of every branch seemed redrawn, sharper. The edges of the hills were newly refined against the sky like old blades worked to a thinness on the granite sharpening wheel. When Sarah came out again later to untie the dogs she saw the valley wall opposite was run with several fresh scars. The waterlogged earth had given way overnight, slipping down the slope, leaving tapering brick-red marks in its wake. 'Like a giant cat's been clawing its way out of here.'

Her mother's voice again, echoing down the years. These landslips often happened after heavy rain. The valley was so steep it would always give in to itself in the end.

The sound of horseshoes scuffing on the track below Upper Blaen signalled Maggie's arrival. Seren and Fly pricked their ears, eyes fixed on the gate that led down onto the lane, and Sarah rubbed her gloved hands and stamped her feet against the cold. Together with Maggie they'd go up on to the hill and bring down the lambing ewes. Maggie would ride her cob mare and Sarah would try and work the dogs. If things went well they might be done by evening.

The women were through the wood, its canopy opened by the autumn leaf-fall, and making their way up onto the sheep tracks running through the shrunken bracken when they heard the hammering. It echoed off the narrow valley walls, each metallic hit answered by another knock, slightly duller, following close after. It was like the working of a massive buried clock that after years of silence had found its rhythm once more. Tick-*tock*. Tick-*tock*. Tick-*tock*. A pause, then the same again, regular and methodical ringing through the fragile November air.

Both women stopped. Maggie turned her mare into the slope and turned her good ear to the valley. 'It's comin' from The Court,' she said, 'or near there anyway.'

They listened in silence as the hammering beat on, paused again and started again.

'Reg?' Sarah asked, unable to suppress a breath of hope in his name.

'No.'

'But then who –'

'I dunno,' Maggie cut Sarah short. 'Constable Evans maybe? I saw him in market. Up from Pandy. Said he'd come by if he could, though I told him no need, of course.'

They listened again to the rhythm of the hammering. It was slight, a small hammer, metal. Not the wooden impact of a stake beetle or the heavy blows of a sledge hammer. On a different day with a wind up or damper air they might not have heard it at all.

'Maybe he heard The Court's empty. Brought up some board for the windows p'haps. That's probably it.'

Sarah could tell Maggie wasn't convinced by her own conclusion.

'Shouldn't we go and see? It might be Reg or one of the boys after all.'

Maggie looked down at Sarah. 'No,' she said simply. 'We've got a job to do, bach. It's already late to be bringing them down. Mary will go have a look, probably. Evans is one of her cousins after all, isn't he?'

With that Maggie shortened her reins and squeezed the mare on up the slope. Seren had trotted back down to them while they'd been listening to the hammering. Sarah gave her a light stroke, tracing a finger over her head between her ears, then followed on after Maggie up the hill.

'Hold on the tail,' Maggie called over her shoulder as the mare worked the incline. 'She won't kick, long as that dog keeps out the way.'

Maggie and Sarah worked on the uplands all morning. It was slow going. They had over a hundred ewes to bring down off the hill and parts of The Court's flock had wandered again. Maggie spent the first hour corralling these ewes from the broad expanses that opened out along the knuckles of the Black Hill. Sarah, meanwhile, set to trying to divide the flock with the dogs. Although the two bitches were instinctively aware of what they must do, they soon became confused by her attempts to guide them through the bunching flow of sheep. It was as if those invisible tethers by which Tom usually played them had become slack and unresponsive, incapable of carrying the pulses of communication needed to keep the dogs edging round the flock in the right directions.

Half way through the day they brought the first batch of ewes back down the hill to Upper Blaen. The day had failed to find its heat and their breath clouded thickly in the glassy air in front of them. Having enclosed the sheep in the lower meadows by the river, Maggie and Sarah made themselves lunch in the farmhouse, warming their hands at the range, the cold ebbing from their fingers in sharp stabs of tingling pain. Again Sarah suggested they go down and look in at The Court and again Maggie was dismissive of the idea. No time. Still half the lambing ewes to bring down at least. And no need. Mary would have been over.

Before they set out up the hill once more Sarah went upstairs. 'Now, don't you laugh,' she said as Maggie heard her tread coming down the staircase again.

'Good God, girl! What you thinking of?' Maggie said as Sarah entered the kitchen. She was wearing a pair of Tom's trousers puckered under a thick belt at her waist. One of his corduroy jackets hung loosely from her shoulders, its sleeves rolled thickly at her wrists.

'They still smell of him,' she explained to Maggie, who was staring at her as if she'd come down the stairs naked. 'The dogs'll pick it up, won't they? It might help.'

'Well, it might,' Maggie said, 'but looking like that you'll frighten the bloody sheep away too!' She hit the table with the flat of her hand and laughed. It was the first time Sarah had seen her smile for weeks.

By the end of the day they'd managed to round up all the lambing ewes and bring them down for flushing in the richer pastures by the river. After the coarse grazing of the hillside two weeks on this richer grass would improve their fertility. More ewes would take, and of those that did, there'd be more twins too. God knows though, Sarah thought, they had too many to deal with anyway. The splitting of The Court's flock had given all the farms in the valley more sheep than they could handle. If Tom had been here they'd probably have sold a third of these ewes by now. But he wasn't and they hadn't, so for now the farm and the sheep would have to cope as best they could. And so would they.

By the time Maggie left Upper Blaen the sun was firing up the sharp edge of the Hatterall again, setting its steep mottled sides a deep black. Sarah stood in the yard for a moment, watching the first stars appear in the blue-black sky above the ridge. Once again she was exhausted, the ache in her womb a nagging reminder of that morning's disappointment, which she still felt despite her more sensible self telling her she should be relieved. But beneath these surface sensations Sarah was also strangely contented. They had brought the sheep down. Over the afternoon the dogs had begun to listen to her, retuning themselves to her pitch and tone. The sheep had begun to flow. The job was done and the ewes would be ready for tupping. Tom would have been proud of her. Just for a moment all this lent her a sense of tired ease and she relished being alone in the yard, watching the stars dot to life against the sky like the first raindrops against a window at the start of a downpour. But even this ease was short lived. It scared her. She didn't want to feel any second of contentment while Tom was away. She was frightened that if she did, one day she'd become too used to this. She needed to miss him at every moment. If she didn't, then it would already be too late.

She went inside to rekindle the fire in the range and make

herself supper. These were often the hardest hours of the day. Preparing for bed alone. Eating alone. She'd begun reading her small selection of books again, finding some company in the familiar stories of Dickens, Hardy, Eliot and Scott. They were the books of her girlhood, given to her by Mrs Thomas, an enthusiastic teacher who'd thought she shouldn't have been leaving school when she did. She hadn't read them for years, hardly ever since she'd married. But tonight she was too tired even to read. She would eat, write her diary to Tom, clean up the kitchen and then go to bed, hoping as ever not to dream at all but to fall into a blank sleep instead. A sleep so deep and blind that it would, for a few hours at least, erase the dull ache of the missing body beside her.

Sarah was on her knees sweeping the ash from under the range when she heard footsteps outside followed by a sharp rap on the kitchen door. She looked up, still on her knees, to see it already opening.

'Hello?' she said.

The clear night outside was washed with moonlight. She could make out a figure silhouetted in the door frame. A man's figure.

'Tom?' she said quietly, leaning forward on the palms of her hands. The figure didn't move. 'Tom?' she said again louder, her frown unfolding to the tremors of a smile. The figure stepped forward into the kitchen and it was then, by the dim light of a single lantern, that Sarah saw the battered grey-green serge of Albrecht's uniform. She gasped and jumped back onto her heels, sending the rack of iron pokers and tongs beside the fireplace clattering over the flagstones.

'Please,' Albrecht said, slotting his pistol back into its holster and holding out his hand. 'Don't be alarmed, please.'

Sarah tipped herself further away until she felt the iron of the range's oven, still warm at her back. She held the brush she'd been sweeping with across her chest, its bristles over her heart.

'Please,' Albrecht said again, 'I didn't mean to surprise you.'

Sarah saw movement behind him. A darker shadow shifting in the night. There was someone else there, in the yard. Why were the dogs so quiet? She'd heard them barking but had been too tired to go out and silence them. She'd thought they were just excited from their day's work out on the hill.

'You are Sarah Lewis?' Albrecht said, looking down at a notepad.

She looked back into the soldier's face. The candlelight reflected off the lenses of his glasses. Without his eyes she couldn't read his expression. She nodded, unable to bring enough air into her clenched chest to do anything else.

'Good,' Albrecht said. The word dislodged a rattle in his throat and turning to one side he coughed heavily into his gloved hand. The cough was deep, hoarse. 'Excuse me,' he said, turning back to face her. He gestured to one of the chairs around the kitchen table. 'Please, sit down.'

His voice surprised her. He spoke an English Sarah had rarely heard. Clean, clear, precise, like the English of the estate owners around Abergavenny, but gentler, more careful. In this last request, however, she'd detected the slightest hint of an order. She didn't want to press that voice any further, so slowly she stood up and pulled out a chair from under the table. Still moving carefully, she sat in it. Tom's chair, she thought as she did, the chair her husband sat in every morning for breakfast. The chair from which she missed him every day, its blank seat always a reminder of that morning when she'd woken to the silences and spaces of his going. The thought of Tom brought the air back into her lungs.

'What do you want?' she asked, keeping her shaking hands on her lap.

'My name is Captain Wolfram,' the soldier said slowly. He held his peaked cloth cap in both hands before him, as an altar boy might carry a candle down the aisle of a church. 'I am in command of a patrol unit of the German army. I am here to inform you that myself and my men have established an observation post in your area.' He paused. 'I understand you were not aware this area is under German military control?'

Sarah shook her head. The hammering at The Court, it was them. German soldiers, here in the valley. After all Maggie had said. Maggie? She'd been going to check on The Court when she left this evening. Was she all right? Was she alive even?

'No,' she said quietly.

'Well it is,' Albrecht continued. 'I wanted to inform you of our particular presence personally and to reassure you that while we are allowed to complete our work here without obstruction then we will not disturb you, your belongings or your families.' He took a step nearer the table and, resting his hands on the back of a chair, leant towards Sarah. 'I do not anticipate we will be here for long,' he said in a more relaxed tone, a tiredness tingeing the edges of his voice. 'A week, perhaps two.'

Complete our work. What did he mean by that? Sarah's mind was racing, suddenly acute, trying to take in this sudden invasion. She looked over the German officer again. His uniform was worn, threadbare at the elbows. He wore a thick black belt about his tunic. The cross-hatched stock of his pistol protruded from a heavy leather holster on one side and a long knife hung to half way down his thigh on the other. No, not a knife, Sarah thought, a bayonet. Again she remembered the stories of the German invasions of Belgium and Holland.

Albrecht moved towards the dresser. 'Is your husband at home, Mrs Lewis?' he said, picking up their wedding photograph.

Sarah blinked rapidly, keeping her eyes fixed on the photograph as if it was her child he held so casually in one hand, not a picture in a cheap wooden frame. Suddenly she saw, felt, the taking of that picture again. A bright May day, standing on the steps of the chapel, her veil flicking into her face in the breeze. The path covered with a confetti of cherry blossom. Laying her hand on Tom's sleeve. Feeling the delicate tensing of his forearm under the heavy cloth of his suit.

'No,' she said, trying to stop her voice quavering. 'He's on the hill. We found a ewe with liver fluke. He's with her now.'

'Liver fluke,' Albrecht said quietly, weighing the term on his tongue. 'I see. Well, Mrs Lewis, if you could tell him of my visit I'd be most grateful.' He put the photograph back on the dresser and gave Sarah a tight smile. For the first time she saw his eyes beneath his glasses. He looked exhausted. Older than his voice. She saw too that his short black hair was flecked with grey, like when the river ran shallow over the stones, foaming white in the dark.

Albrecht gave a curt bow of his head. 'Good evening, Mrs Lewis,' he said. 'I am sorry for alarming you. I promise it was not intentional.' Stepping out the still-open door he turned back. 'I hope the sheep gets better,' he said, putting on his peaked cap. 'And that Mr Lewis is not away for too long.'

And then he was gone. He hadn't been in the room for more than two minutes. He hadn't even asked to search the rest of the house. Another hand closed the door. Sarah heard a few words of German, quick and impenetrable, and then the disjointed chorus of three sets of footsteps fading over the cobbles and down the track. The dogs gave a couple of barks and once again she heard the shuffle of their chains. Then there was nothing. Just the unending rustle and hush of the river below the house and the wind playing a hollow note in the chimney behind her.

He shouldn't have called after dark. He should have taken the old woman's word and come back in the morning. But he had to check, that's what Albrecht told himself as, flanked by Alex and Otto, he picked his way down the track from Upper Blaen. The long frozen puddles running between the peaks and ridges of mud crackled and split under their feet. Yes, he had to be sure. Not a single man in the valley. Because he hadn't believed any of their stories. They hadn't even kept to the same one. Farm sales, helping cousins, driving sheep to slaughter. They all seemed to have no idea. Such movement, such events simply weren't happening any more.

Otto and Alex walked either side of him, one slightly ahead, one just behind, swinging their sub-machine guns in slow arcs as they walked. Albrecht noticed how the moonlight caught the thin barrels, slipping up and down the polished metal as the two men swung them, left and right, right and left. Their anxiety was understandable. However important it had been to check all the buildings in the valley, it was still irregular to be out after dark in new territory. But then everything about this mission had been irregular from the very start. Ever since he'd taken that motorbike over to SS Southern Headquarters over a month ago. An SS order to a Wehrmacht officer. He should have known then that he was going into unknown territory, in every sense of the word.

The meeting with the SS colonel had lasted no more than five minutes but it had been enough for him to know this was no ordinary patrol. The colonel was evidently as unimpressed with the whole idea as Albrecht was confused.

'Read this,' he'd said, casting a cursory eye over Albrecht's dirty uniform and handing him a slip of paper. The colonel's own uniform was spotless; the leather straps polished to an ebony shine, his black tunic immaculate, the gold braids, intricate and bright. An Iron Cross hung solid at his breast. To have won that, Albrecht remembered thinking, he must have seen battle at some point. Once, early in the conflict, he must have known the fear, exhilaration, stench and dirt of this war. His uniform must have known sweat, blood, shit and soil. Once. But now it was unmarked, a peerless Nazi pattern of starch, insignia and personal tailoring, typical of the peacocking SS. Unmarked, Albrecht noticed with some satisfaction, but for two light galaxies of dandruff dusting each shoulder.

'Any questions?' the colonel had asked without looking up from his desk. 'The corporal outside has all the relevant maps and additional information.'

'Transport arrangements, sir?'

Only now, with just his eyes, without moving his head, did the colonel look up at him. 'You're to go to the transport pool and take what you need,' he said through a tight jaw. Perhaps he'd registered Albrecht's surprise, or perhaps he just needed to hear his own explanation on the air, to convince himself once more that this order must be obeyed. For whatever reason, he relaxed his expression, gave a short sigh and leant back in his chair before continuing. He spoke slowly, as if to a child.

'This has come from the top. Reichsführer SS Himmler. All of these special patrols have. The Führer himself is aware too. They both place great importance upon such missions. For the future of the Reich. In this case a suitably qualified officer could not be located within the SS. You, on the other hand, have all the necessary qualifications, as you can see. So to answer the question you were about to ask, that is why.'

Albrecht tried to imagine what bargaining had gone on between the Wehrmacht and the SS over this. Relations between the two organisations had been deteriorating ever since the end of the Russian campaign when the commanders of both had begun to detect the scent of victory. No doubt he was a chip bartered in a broader game. For the Wehrmacht to give him and his patrol up now, when the whole force of the invasion armies were being called upon, was quite something. For the SS to ask for a Wehrmacht officer to take on one of its own missions was unheard of. For that officer to then be given the pick of the transport pool was most remarkable of all. Many Wehrmacht companies were already dependent upon captured or requisitioned British and American vehicles among their units.

However unorthodox the order, at least he'd been right about not joining the offensive on London. Those first few days had been a real relief, for him and his men. To be taken away from the front, away from the fighting units. But since then their journey had been far from easy. Over a month of stop-start travelling, edging along behind the advancing front like a shoal of fish swimming in the wake of a whale. Several times they'd been drawn into the fighting, through necessity, as local commanders fended off enemy probes and counter-attacks. His men had accounted themselves well on these occasions. The reports about young Steiner had been accurate. They'd all kept their heads, fought well. Nothing too foolhardy or panicked. Sebald had been as active as he always was, bandaging and plugging, trying to hold the pieces of men together under fire. Otto remained as silent as ever.

These moments of fighting had helped pull the patrol together. Experiencing the intensity of battle among unknown divisions and companies crystallised their identity as a group apart from the general flow of events. They were like a wandering band of players, a strangely privileged gang of vagabonds, the SS slip in Albrecht's pocket always giving them licence and access. Suddenly they seemed to be moving through the war, not with it. Weaving through its veins and capillaries of supply lines and temporary locations rather than being pushed along at its vanguard, pressed against the enemy by the weight of it behind them.

They could never escape it completely though. Even when they were travelling deeper behind the front through the newly occupied territories, the violence still stalked them. Insurgents were becoming active across the country, often once the fighting units had moved on and been replaced by the softer occupation divisions. Albrecht had witnessed the unearthing of such a resistance group himself, in the countryside outside Oxford. The city itself had fallen quickly. 'The English would rather give up their women than lose their precious buildings,' Albrecht had heard one lieutenant remark. But outside the city sabotage activity had been increasing since its occupation. The railway dynamited; a high-ranking officer assassinated as he strolled on a village green. When they'd caught the men responsible they'd brought them to this same village green, an oak tree at its centre, the delicate shadow of a church's spire falling across the closely mown grass. Albrecht watched the prisoners marched out under guard, stepping a slug's pattern of footsteps through the shining dew. Five men. The oldest looked over sixty, the youngest less than twenty. They'd been

beaten. Two of them carried another. They wore khaki dungarees over their civilian clothes.

A Gestapo officer looked on as the captain gave a brief
account of these men's crimes. An interpreter shouted his
words to a small crowd, forced to watch, ringed by soldiers.
Then the captain took a step back and nodded to the sergeant at his side, who in turn nodded to the two soldiers
standing behind him. These soldiers walked forward to face
the bowed heads of the five men lined up under the tree.
Cocking their guns with one simultaneous slide and click,
they machine-gunned them with a tight left and right spray.
The spattering sound of the bullets rang off the Cotswold
stone of the surrounding cottages and the sturdy walls of the
church. As the soldiers lowered their weapons the echoes of
the execution faded on the air. The men, who had been
standing so still beneath the oak tree, jerked violently before
collapsing, like puppets whose strings had been randomly
yanked and then cut. A woman in the crowd fainted.
Another howled, clawing at her face with her nails.

Later that morning the captain who'd organised this execution took the Gestapo officer and Albrecht to inspect the
buried base of the resistance group. He'd led them through a
wood on a small hill. 'This rabbit hole?' he'd said as they
approached the trees, pointing towards a root-fringed hollow with his cane. 'An observation slot. See how good the
view is from here?' He turned and looked over the landscape, the ox-bow of the river, the railway embankments
slicing through the fields. 'Very clever,' he said. 'Very clever
indeed.'

Inside the wood a couple of guards had cleared the leaves
from a patch of ground. As they got nearer Albrecht saw the
thin grass was deeply scored with a neat square, as if a heavy
box had been set there for months. The captain nodded to

one of the guards who bent behind a tree as if to pick something up. To Albrecht's surprise the scored square slowly swung open, revealing the soft whirr of a dropping counterweight and the rungs of a ladder descending into a narrow brick-lined shaft. After a couple of seconds the whirring stopped, leaving the patch of turf suspended at an angle above the opening. The captain was obviously pleased with his little show. 'Please, gentlemen,' he said. 'After you. But be careful, that ladder is still slippery.'

There was barely room inside for the three men to move around but the captain was determined to give his guests a full tour of his discovery. 'The first, I am told?' he said raising his eyebrows in inquiry to the Gestapo officer. 'In England. No doubt there will be more, of course, but this is the first we've found. Yes the first.' He repeated this confirmation quietly, as if reminding himself of the honour his statement implied. Albrecht and the Gestapo officer followed him as he moved about the base pointing out various features. Chippings of coke in the paintwork to absorb moisture; a deep steel tray at the foot of the ladder to catch and contain the blast of a grenade dropped down the shaft; ammo store; wireless position; an angled escape tunnel (blocked by his men in the process of the capture); six thin bunks piled three high along each side of a narrow chamber off the main area. 'These,' the captain said, tapping a row of glass jars glowing faintly yellow in the lamplight, 'are filled with the insurgents' own urine. I believe they thought they could use it to confuse the dogs.' He flashed Albrecht a quick smile. 'It didn't work, of course.'

Of course. It was always of course with these party men. The captain, Albrecht could tell, had not always been a soldier. A merchant perhaps, a shopkeeper whose wife had left him. A cowed individual until membership of the Party straightened his back, put steel back in his nerves. A failed application to the SS, no doubt. He certainly relished his chance to impress a Gestapo officer. Whether he had or not was difficult to say. The Gestapo man remained silent throughout the tour of the bunker. Between his silence and the captain's verbosity Albrecht had felt suffocated, trapped. When they'd emerged back into the bright day filtered through the branches of the wood, he'd breathed deeply, anxious to fill his lungs with nature, with all that did not change. The damp musk of the mouldering leaves, the tang of the breeze already sharpening towards winter. The new air made him feel better and as they'd walked out of the wood he'd tried to draw the Gestapo officer on his thoughts. The man carried on looking ahead from under the low peak of his cap as they strode across the field, wearing his assumed authority like an invisible armour. 'Interesting,' he'd said at last. Albrecht could sense the captain behind them, trying to catch up to listen. 'Very well built. Better than anything we've seen before. But then of course the British have had a long time to prepare for this day.'

Albrecht nodded but said nothing more. 'This day.' He hated the way they spoke. Everything ordained, their quasi-biblical language, no trace of the months and years of failure, of the breaking of spirits and bodies. Just the inevitable march of time towards 'This day'. Of course, he'd repeated again and again to himself as they'd made their way back to the village. 'Of course, of course, of course.' The words wouldn't go away. They chased each other inside his skull, the one collapsing to the other, faster and faster. He couldn't rid himself of the phrase, the banal certainty of it chased him through his dreams. Of course, of course. He could not argue against it. He was part of it. The great 'of course' of National Socialism. He thought of the English translation, and again the semiotic flexibility of the language struck him as so suitable. Of course. On course. He was travelling along the Nazi course, its route, its path. There was no getting off, there were no side roads. Everything was planned and was falling into place and there was nothing he, Albrecht Wolfram, could do about it, other than join the flow. Of course, of course. Even two days later as he lay down to sleep in the comfort and quiet of Oxford itself, this insistent mantra wore away at his mind, eroding his consciousness until he finally gave way to a fitful slumber.

Oxford had been a welcome diversion from their irregular journeying. They'd spent three days in the city, enjoying the rest, the feel of fresh linen against newly washed skin. Albrecht's mind began to calm again. Freed from any specific duties he allowed the men to explore the city. He watched them walk away down Broad Street, this little band he'd extracted from the flow of the war. Otto and Gernot walked a few yards behind the others, their heads tipped back, drinking in the strange beauty of the buildings, the grinning grotesques and the pipe-swallowing gargoyles. As they turned the corner at the end of the street Albrecht saw Gernot stretch out an arm and point towards the skyline. He leant his other hand on Otto's shoulder. Albrecht thought he saw Otto smile as Gernot peeled away into the peculiar laugh of his, the laugh that had singled him out for this mission in the first place.

For Albrecht the city struck a more unsettling note. It was certainly a welcome return, to see his old haunts again, to find himself remembering the streets and shortcuts of the back alleys. But his memories were tinged with the echo of regret. A regret for lost time, for that year he'd spent here, out of the world which had been at that very moment racing so inevitably towards this; his return six years later, the heels of his jackboots clicking over the broken flagstones of silent college cloisters.

While the men roamed the parks and colleges of the city, Albrecht spent the three days roaming the stacks of the Bodleian Library running beneath its streets. Together with a surprisingly pliant English archivist he'd gathered a useful collection of books relevant to his mission. He wanted to learn as much as he could before he arrived, but he was also driven by a more general sense of pleasure at being among books again. It had been so long; the weight of words in his hand, the promises of opening pages. For years he'd been able to carry only a couple of volumes with him – a battered copy of Rilke's sonnets, von Eschenbach's *Parzival*. Now for three days he had the stocks of the world's greatest library spread out before him and like a desert wanderer stumbling upon an oasis, he drenched himself with the smells and textures of the printed page.

As always it did not last long. Advances in the west meant they could continue their mission and on the fourth morning they packed their belongings in the staff car and joined a convoy heading out of the city. Their lodgings had been more than comfortable. The rooms of a professor whose name had appeared among the thousands of others tightly printed in the Gestapo's 'Black Book'. The professor had been taken for questioning in his pyjamas on the morning of their arrival. The patrol moved in half an hour later and found his quarters just as he'd left them, food in the larder, fresh flowers on the table and a record slowing on a wind-up gramophone, the needle softly thudding in the final groove. When they left three days later Albrecht hadn't been able to resist and as Alex started the car he'd loaded the gramophone and a kit bag of recently introduced 33rpm records onto the back seat. Alex raised his eyebrows and said something Albrecht couldn't catch above the rumble of the passing traffic. 'Well,' he'd shouted in reply, 'we'll need something to keep us entertained up there!'

The roadside bomb had been a sudden and brutal reintroduction back into the war. They were just a few miles outside the city when it happened, the convoy snaking through the B roads between the Cotswold villages. The troop carrier in front of them had taken the force of the blast, its front wheels torn from the chassis, the driver's cab and the canopy set ablaze. Some shrapnel hit the left wing of their own car. Alex had to swerve violently to avoid the suddenly stilled truck and the men falling from its rear, cloaks of flame fluttering from their burning uniforms. Another piece of shrapnel hit Albrecht. Luckily the piece of metal ricocheted off his helmet, but the force of the impact still knocked him unconscious. He came to lying beside the road with the searing light of Sebald's pencil torch burning in his eyes, a thick plume of smoke rising into the sky behind him.

The unearthing of one resistance group was never enough. For the rest of their journey they encountered the aftermath of numerous incidents of sabotage and murder. Even last night, when they'd billeted with a young lieutenant down in Pandy, they'd been told about the killing of two young guards at the station. And not just killing either. Stabbed in the neck, then disembowelled, their livid purple and yellow entrails spread out on the forecourt beside them like macabre gifts for the afterlife beside bodies in a grave. The young lieutenant was still visibly shaken. He'd seen the murdered guards himself and he vowed to Albrecht he'd find the men responsible and kill them.

And now the patrol had arrived here; a remote and manless valley. They would have to be careful, although Albrecht knew they were probably in the safest place of all.

Resistance groups rarely operated near their own homes. There was a pattern to insurgency. This was something they'd all learnt over the last five years of the war. Regardless of nationality, creed, language, the same patterns always seemed to apply. As if this last act of defiance were such a deeply woven instinct that it crossed all borders. The tactics of winning wars differed from army to army, from general to general. The tactics of snapping at the heels of your invaders, however, were always the same. Albrecht saw no reason the British should be any different from the Dutch, the French, the Poles or the Belgians.

He should tell that young lieutenant in Pandy though. He may not have found an operational base like the one outside Oxford, but he'd stumbled upon the next best thing. The families. The homes. The standard SS and Gestapo tools of revenge and discovery. Again he'd seen it all across Europe. Hit the insurgents where it hurt them most. At their hearths and in their hearts.

But not yet. He wouldn't tell that pale, shaken lieutenant vowing revenge just yet. He'd do what he came here to do first. Find what he'd been sent to look for, work, for once, outside the Wehrmacht bureaucracy, without interruption. Then, once they were done, he'd let the lieutenant know. That way he wouldn't have to be here when it happened. When another soldier came through that kitchen door behind him and didn't holster his pistol or lower his machine gun. He thought of the men he'd seen marched out onto that village green outside Oxford. How they'd folded and fallen as if their skeletons had been whipped from out of them. Then he saw the same scene again, playing it over in his mind's eye with a new cast made of the women he'd met today. The worn, worried-looking one. The ignorant, confused young mother. The old stubborn one and now this last scared, feral young wife wearing her husband's clothes. He closed his eyes tightly for a few seconds and walked guided only by the crunching, splashing sounds of Alex's boots on the muddy track before him. He wouldn't imagine that again. He couldn't. Not everything was his fault or the consequence of his actions. He knew that, but he still had to learn it. After all this time this was still something he had to remind himself of, rather than something he just accepted, like the cough in his chest or the lice in the seams of his shirts. It would all happen anyway. Of course it would. Of course. It was always bound to happen as soon as their husbands left them. As soon as they turned their backs on these farms and walked into the war. It was them, their husbands, who had killed these women. Not him.

As they dropped down into the valley and onto the lane the trees on either side leant to meet each other, forming a fragile tunnel over their heads, the moon held in their latticework of bare branches and twigs. They walked on silently, Alex and Otto still swinging their guns left and right, right and left. Albrecht looked at Alex's broad back and for his sake tried to think like a soldier again. He mustn't be complacent. What else should they be careful of? The women? The women themselves? Would they be any trouble? No, he didn't think so. Not these women. Elsewhere he might have had cause for concern. In Russia, for example, they'd all learnt quickly enough to be as wary of the wives as the husbands. But these women? No, it wasn't the same here. This was a backward valley, a dead-end, isolated slice of life embedded in the clefts of the hills. Even the information he'd gathered in the last village indicated these hill women were considered a breed apart, outsiders.

'Well, they'uh a quiet lot, tha's foshaw. 'Ide behin' th'edge if they see yer, they do.'

Albrecht had found it difficult to understand the man he'd interviewed and not just because of his split and swollen lip. They spoke quickly in this part of the country, running their words together like shunting cattle trucks behind a braking train. He was unfamiliar with the accent too. It wasn't Welsh as such, but wasn't English either, the words slipping either side of the border just as their towns and villages did. No 'r's' in the speech at all from what he could gather, (he thought again of the telegram that had started all this, the faded R's ghosting the text) and a habit of asking questions as negative statements. 'You're not going up there, are you? Haven't got any chocolate, have you?' Still, by listening hard and filtering through the anomalies he'd got an idea of what he could expect in the valley. How many farms and who was in them. The Olchon was an outpost, even in the eyes of the village of Longtown, itself considered remote by the people of Pandy, which was in turn thought of as provincial in Abergavenny. And so on all the way back to London. A sliding scale of outlivers, outsiders. And now here they were at the end of it. There was no one else beyond here to call an outsider, no other settlement that even these farmers could look upon as being beyond the outskirts of usual living. There were just the hills, a great bald, pleated barricade of earth, rock, heather and bracken, rising up to the peat-pocked expanses of the plateaus before eventually descending again into another country altogether.

'Ahh!' Alex breathed in deeply, stamping his boots on the flagstones of The Court's covered porch. 'Roast pork! God! I haven't smelt roast pork for years!' He pushed open the door into the living room and stood in its frame, the lamplight casting his shadow behind him, an elongated shard of darkness connecting with the night. With his hands hanging at his sides he sucked in the warm air through his nose.

'You'd better believe it, farm boy!' Gernot shouted from the kitchen. 'Pork like you've never tasted! Private Ehrhardt 624687 at your service. The best field cook in this whole fucking army!'

'Field cook?' Sebald said from an armchair by the fire-place. 'I don't think so, private. This doesn't count as field cooking.'

Albrecht went and stood in front of the fire and began unbuttoning his tunic. Sebald looked up at him, his alert face more relaxed than Albrecht was used to seeing it. 'Well?'

Albrecht shook his head. 'Not a man in the valley. We'll post a watch through the night. I don't want to take any chances.'

Sebald nodded slowly and sighed. Leaning his head back he closed his eyes. 'And how about you? Smell that pork Ehrhardt's working on?'

Albrecht shook his head again. 'No. Nothing.'

'Ah well,' Alex said, coming back down the stairs and laying a hand on Albrecht's shoulder as he passed. 'We'll just have to enjoy it for you, don't you worry.'

The piece of shrapnel from the roadside bomb may have ricocheted off Albrecht's helmet but it had still left its mark. When Albrecht came round he'd seen Sebald's face peering down at him, he'd felt the damp ground at his back, the blades of grass at his neck and he'd heard the grind of traffic, the shouting of men's voices, even the crackling of the flames licking around the shell of the truck. But he hadn't been able to smell the smoke from the burning tyres or the singed tint of seared flesh. And when Sebald gave him a precious block of dark chocolate he may as well have been eating wood. However much he chewed on it, however much he turned it round his mouth, he couldn't discover the confectionery's bitter-sweet tang. The shrapnel had numbed his world.

Albrecht sat down heavily in the armchair opposite Sebald and looked about the room. It was well furnished. Better than anything else he'd seen in the valley today. A big fireplace, old heirloom books on the shelves, a well-equipped kitchen in which Gernot and Alex now argued over the cooking pots and even a well-tended vegetable garden out the back. Upstairs the bedrooms were generous and the beds soft. Albrecht had been told an old man lived here with his two sons. Well if that was true, then they'd kept the place as well as if they'd had a woman in the house. Although it had obviously been empty for a while it hadn't taken long for them to stoke the fire and breathe life back into the building. For the second time on their journey they'd arrived in a rare heaven. After the years of field living, sleeping in dugouts, on wooden plank beds, in fox holes, a place like this was a utopian dream. It made Albrecht feel clumsy, awkward, as if they were a pack of stray animals wandered into an empty palace. Their boots, their weapons, their talk, they all seemed too modern and harsh for this ancient farmhouse. Too fleeting. But like his men Albrecht was relishing the chance to enjoy the comfort The Court offered, to once again experience the touch of civilised living, despite his blunted senses which had left him feeling less human than ever. Now they'd come to the end of their travels he was also looking forward to beginning that other journey, to setting out on the real quest he'd come all this way to fulfil. Because the map was here, somewhere, that's what all the information indicated. Somewhere in this deep notch of a valley, hidden in its stones and trees and crevices. He thought of the folded maps in his kit bag upstairs, the intercepted communication, the code-breaker's version stapled behind it. Tomorrow he'd start looking, begin translating those maps into these hills and fields. Then, by the time he'd found it, all this might be over. Just a week perhaps, maybe two until the British finally accepted what they should have seen back in '41. After five years it would finally come to an end and all of them could stop being soldiers. They could leave the army, leave the war behind them and go back to their homes, or at least what was left of them.

As Albrecht settled back into Reg's armchair and listened to the logs shift and collapse over themselves in the fire, Sarah was closing the door of Upper Blaen and making her way out into the night. She wore a sack about her shoulders for extra warmth, its corners bunched in her fist below her throat. In her other hand she carried Tom's shotgun, its polished wooden stock slick against her fingers, a pair of cartridges nestled in the breech. As she walked and half-ran down the track she felt the wild skittering of her heart against her knuckles.

It had been so quick that at first she'd hardly been able to believe it had happened. Had he really been there? A German soldier standing there in her kitchen? She hadn't seen a man for over a month and his shape, his movements, his smell had all seemed so alien she wondered whether her tired mind was playing tricks on her. But then she'd gone to the dresser and picked up her wedding photograph, holding it to the candlelight. And yes, there, right across her own face was the imprint of the soldier's thumb; a thin autumnal web, a new veil to replace the one she'd thrown back to let Tom kiss her in the chapel. Desperately she'd rubbed at the glass with her shirt sleeve, smearing the thumbprint over Tom's suit, her dress. She rubbed it again until it had gone, all gone. She sat down, breathing fast. Her mind hadn't been playing tricks. He'd been here (what was his name? What did he say? She could only remember the first part, Wolf . . . Wolf . . .) and there were others too. A pack of wolves. In the valley, at The Court. They were here and they couldn't be rubbed away like a thumbprint over a photograph.

Coming to the end of the track Sarah turned right onto the lane. She would go to Maggie, check she was all right. Maggie would know what to do. Maggie would have an answer, a solution.

The sound of her nail-shod boots seemed impossibly loud. She wanted to be able to float over the ground, leave no mark, slip through the valley unheard, unseen. But as it was she felt she was being louder, more clumsy than ever. The stamp of her tread, the rustle of Tom's oversized shirt, the rasping of the sacking cloth. The familiar lane developed eyes and her blood pulsed in her ears.

But what if Maggie didn't know what to do? After all, she'd been wrong about the Germans, hadn't she? She'd said they wouldn't come this far, that they wouldn't come here. And yet here was exactly where they were. In her house, in her kitchen, in the valley. Maggie had been wrong.

Sarah strode on, wishing a cloud to cover the moon, to choke the lane with night. The ice puddles crackled under her feet, punctuating the rhythm of her thoughts. Maggie had been wrong. Wrong, wrong, wrong. The word recoiled back at her with every step she took, each repetition carving further into whatever substance had calcified within her these past months, paring away a hollow within her ribs. She wanted it all to be different. She wanted to turn back the clock to that night before the men left and she wanted Tom back more than ever. To counter that word, to fill the space creeping up through the whole of her body, leaving her heart suspended in its own beat, her head afloat from her neck. She wanted Tom back to reassert the world, to stroke her head like he did when the bomber crashed up on the bluff. To hold her and tell her, 'Shh, bach, shh now, it's all right. It's goin' to be fine. Just fine.'

NOVEMBER 1944–MARCH 1945

Hiraeth . . . a longing, but especially a longing for
something indefinable, perhaps unattainable . . .

Jan Morris, *Wales, The First Place*

November 3rd

There are six of them, Tom. Maggie went over to The Court this morning and saw them. She says as we shouldn't worry. That they're here for some piece of work and then they will go. But what work could they have here? Mary is frightened rigid. She hasn't let Bethan out of the house all day.

Maggie said it's true. All round here is occupied, everywhere. I took Bess up on the hill today to check on the flock. It's hard to believe it from up there. Nothing looked any different. No change in anything.

There was a wild herd up by the flushes. They had a couple of foals. One of the colts came close. He made me think of when you rode one last year, steering it with your hands over its eyes. That seems so long ago now, Tom, but it was just last summer. I do wish I knew you were safe. Did you know they were coming? Is that why you went? Maggie said it was to make us safer, and I can see how that might be now.

It's getting colder. There's a change in the clouds like new weather might be coming in. Maggie's meadow grass is getting short. She gave her cows the first of her hay today. She say's we'll tup soon enough. Next week most like. It was lucky William and Hywel got their rams over early this year.

The hazelnuts are ripening and the rooks up on the slope are louder than ever.

Sarah dug her fingers deep into the ewe's wool and gripped two handfuls, one just below the neck, the other over the rump. Pushing a knee into the animal's hindquarters she heaved it backwards and sidewards, tipping it off its feet towards her. The ewe shook its head and gave a thin bleat, trying to free itself from Sarah's grip. She felt her cramped fingers weakening, slipping through the waxy wool. Letting go with her left hand she caught the ewe at its neck. It bleated again and she felt the vibration of its throat across her fingers as with a final pull backwards she brought the animal to rest, up-ended between her legs. The ewe was panting, its small tongue poking out the side of its mouth, its slit nostrils damp and flaring with every breath. 'I know how you feel, girl,' Sarah said as she moved to make way for Maggie, already bustling in beside her. Sarah stood back, breathing heavily herself, and watched as Maggie took one of the animal's forelegs and got to work on its hooves with a rusty pair of shears. Its struggle lost, the ewe's head fell loosely to the side, coming to rest in the hollow of Maggie's apron stretched across her open knees. 'An' the next,' Maggie said simply as she lifted the other foreleg and began trimming the curling hoof, flexing the shears with short, twanging snaps of the blades.

They'd been doing this all morning. Working in a hurdle pen in Maggie's meadow below the farm, preparing the ewes for tupping. Maggie's ram was already in the next field, the tupping pad strapped to its chest. As it grazed, moving between the patches of richer grass, strands of the pad's blue dye brushed the tallest blades, tracing an elliptical trail through the meadow.

They didn't have to be doing this. They could have just let the ewes into the field. They would have been fine, Sarah was sure of it. But Maggie wanted to treat their feet first, check for foot-rot, cut back the hooves. William would have demanded this, she explained, so why shouldn't they do it just as if he were here? There were lots of reasons why they shouldn't but Sarah didn't mention any of them. She simply agreed and set to catching the ewes and turning them for Maggie, who'd hold them between her knees, snapping away with the shears or dousing their rot with a livid purple disinfectant, pumped from what looked like a beaten old genie lamp.

Sarah was getting down to the younger ewes now. They were stronger and faster and had, so far, managed to evade her. As she moved towards them they shoaled away from her. One reared onto the back of another, showing the whites of its eyes. Their breath steamed from their noses, misting above the confusion of wool, tails and small black faces. Crouching lower she approached the shifting current of bodies and made a lunge, catching one with both hands gripped in the wool over its rump. The ewe pulled on, taking Sarah with it. Her boots slipped in the churned mud and sheep shit. She found her footing again but the sheep still struggled and bucked under her hands. She tried to get a firmer grip but as she loosened her fingers the ewe pulled away harder, squirming like a trout hooked on the end of a line. 'You bugger!' Sarah said through her teeth as she tried to bring the animal closer to her body.

Then suddenly Maggie was with her, grabbing at the sheep's neck and forelegs.

'For God's sake, girl, jus' turn it!'

'Maggie your back . . .' Sarah began, worried Maggie would hurt herself. But it was too late. Maggie was already heaving at the struggling sheep and so Sarah pulled with her until it lay tipped back, its pink-teated stomach rising and falling between them.

'Hold 'er there,' Maggie said, grabbing a foreleg and angling the hoof's edge between the blades of the shears. She began cutting away furiously. Twice Sarah noticed she cut too close, nicking the skin and drawing blood. She seemed in a sudden tumult of grim energy. Looking up from the sheep Sarah saw why. There, just over the winter-thinned hedge at the end of the field, were the faces of two of the German soldiers, watching them from the lane. One of them wore a steel helmet with that curious step at the back, the other a soft peaked cap. Sarah recognised this second man as the officer who'd called at Upper Blaen a week before. She caught his eye for a second before Maggie spoke to her again, her voice strained.

'Sarah! Go get the next. An' make sure you catch 'er proper mind.'

Sarah understood what Maggie meant. Her arms were tired, hanging light as ribbons from her shoulders and her fingers were cold and stiff. But when she caught the next ewe she held it tightly, the wool coming through her fists like spurts of smoke between her knuckles. With one quick motion she swung it onto its rump. Maggie was already coming towards her, flexing the shears, the blades clean of rust along their edges where they'd slid against each other for years.

'Well done, bach,' Maggie said as she took the ewe from Sarah. 'An' again now.'

Sarah's back ached, her left ear, which had slipped from under her scarf, tingled in the cold wind. Again she grabbed a sheep and swung it over with a grunt of effort. As she did she let her eyes flick up to the hedge at the edge of the field.

They were gone. The two pale faces were no longer there and once again Sarah found herself wondering if she'd seen them at all. Everything looked so ordinary. There was nothing left in their wake. No mark or sign to point towards their presence. Just the valley itself, as always, shedding and greying towards winter.

This is how it had been for all of them over the past few days. Chance glancings, a rush of the heart beneath the ribs. The soldiers glimpsed like apparitions in familiar places. Cruel echoes of their own missing husbands. And then they were gone, passed on, and everything looked as it always did once more.

None of the women had spoken to the Germans since that first evening when Albrecht conducted his tour of the valley's farms. None of them except Maggie. Sarah had stayed at hers that night. She'd arrived out of the moonlit yard, Tom's shotgun held unbroken in her hands. She was shaken, pale, confused. Calming her had calmed Maggie herself and when she woke the next morning she'd known what she must do. Having seen Sarah back off to Upper Blaen she set out herself for The Court, her old bitch collie trotting along the lane beside her. As she approached the solid old farmhouse she became aware of the barrel of Gernot's rifle tracing her as she made her way up the lane. He held it at his shoulder, his head bent to its sights, one eye closed in aim. As she got nearer he called over his shoulder into the house and Alex appeared from the front door behind him, a submachine gun held at his waist, his finger shadowing the trigger.

Maggie stood in front of the two soldiers where she'd stood talking to Reg and the boys a thousand times before and asked to speak to Captain Wolfram. Alex looked down at her, frowning heavily and understanding nothing until he heard Albrecht's name, strangely flat in this old woman's mouth. He went back inside for a moment then appeared at the door again with Albrecht at his shoulder. He was in his shirt sleeves and braces, wiping the last flecks of shaving soap from his face with a towel.

'Please, Mrs Jones,' he said, pulling the towel over his hands. 'Come inside.'

Maggie hesitated, surprised again by his refined accent. She was unsure whether she should cross this old-new threshold of The Court's front porch but something in the way the two other soldiers parted for her, like a set of double doors opening to a secret password, seemed to leave her no choice. Telling the dog to 'cwtch ci', she followed Albrecht inside.

She did not sit down. Albrecht and she spoke standing on the flagstones in the front room instead, like two battlefield generals meeting at dawn to negotiate the day's engagement. The room smelt of solidified fat and old fire, cold ashes shifting under the grate in the breeze from the opened door.

Maggie made herself clear. They would not give the Germans anything. Food, supplies of any kind. The government had forbidden it and she wanted Captain Wolfram to know this now, to avoid any confusion. She would make sure that everyone in the valley stayed away from The Court while the soldiers were here. In return she wanted the Captain's assurance again that he and his men would leave them undisturbed and allow them to get on with their work of running the farms.

Albrecht nodded politely throughout Maggie's speech, shivering a last drop of foam still suspended behind the lobe of his left ear. When she'd finished he told her he agreed with everything she had said. He appreciated her coming and he understood her position. He and his men had plenty of supplies, both of their own and now from the larder and vegetable garden of The Court. 'I would, however, like to remind you, Mrs Jones,' he said with a tight smile, 'that whether your government forbids your co-operation or not is entirely irrelevant. This valley is, after all, like all of this area, under German military control.'

Maggie stiffened before him.

'But that is no matter,' he continued. 'You will not be disturbed. I assure you.' He paused, looking her straight in the eye. 'In any way.'

Albrecht gave Maggie a short bow. 'Now, if you'll excuse me we too must get on with our work.' He nodded to Alex who opened the front door and guided Maggie back out onto the lane that ran beside The Court. The old woman walked beside him, two of her strides to one of his, her head level with the scratched buttons on the chest of his tunic. When he stopped, Maggie carried on without a pause, consciously keeping her back straight, her head high. Only when she'd rounded the bend in the lane and was out of sight of Gernot's trailing rifle did she let her age fall in upon her once more, rounding her shoulders, shortening her stride and bringing her hand instinctively to the base of her spine to cradle the pain that never left there. As she walked back to her farm the old collie ran ahead of her, unaware anything had changed other than the arrival of a man scent back into the valley.

The German officer had said nothing about their husbands. She'd given him his chance. Because that's why she'd really gone to The Court. To invite it, to bring it to a head. Then she might have been able to negotiate. To explain. Or (and is this what she'd really wanted?) the captain would have told her, simply, that he knew exactly where their husbands were. That they'd been captured, weeks ago. That he'd seen them himself, that they were prisoners of war. Maybe even (and at this thought Maggie felt something fall away from behind her eyes, a loosening of her skull) that they were dead. Yes, even that. That is why she'd gone to The Court. To know.

But the captain had said nothing and, in the end, neither had she. The men had been as absent from their conversation as they were from the valley. But the captain knew. She was sure of it. He knew.

On Albrecht's part he was content with everything Maggie had said to him. This was how he wanted to keep things here. Simple and apart. After so many years and months of movement, after so many days of noise and fear and fighting, he wanted to give himself and his men a rest. So there was no need to impose his authority on these women. Especially with their husbands gone. To do so would just invite retaliation. No, better to have the lightest of touches upon this valley. Complete his work here and relish its silences, its pause in the world while he did. Let the women alone and let their husbands do their killing and being killed elsewhere.

It was never going to be easy for Albrecht to convince the rest of the patrol to share this approach. They were, after all, young men as well as soldiers and apart from some distant visits to a French brothel they'd all spent months beyond the orbit of women. So Albrecht wasn't entirely surprised when one evening a week after Maggie's morning visit he'd had to remind them all again that there would be no interfering with these farm women, in any way.

It was Steiner who'd forced the issue. Albrecht had taken to walking out early from The Court each morning. The recent years of army life might have been active but they had left him unfit. The lack of sleep, the bad food, the nervous smoking, the disruptive pattern of boredom punctuated with moments of intense fear. All of it had taken its toll. Ever since his promotion he'd rarely had to march anywhere. There was always a truck, an armoured vehicle or a staff car to ride in. Even in Russia, where they'd all become lean through long months in the field, he'd got little exercise beyond walking the perimeter defences.

Since they'd got to Britain he'd noticed his physical decline more. He'd put on weight but not in a good way and not in the right places. When he sat down there were soft ridges of fat where there hadn't been before. His chest was tight, gripped in a stubborn cough. His dark hair was shot with silver, his stomach was always unsettled and now, on top of everything, that piece of shrapnel had left a legacy of regular headaches. The war was taking his best years. He was thirty-three years old but he felt as if he'd aged much more. The body of a young man about the heart, lungs and skeleton of an old one.

Albrecht had started taking these early morning walks partly to ease himself into his mission in the Olchon, to get a sense of the area, to look over the valley's intimate places. But they were also for his old-young body. To make it work, to bring the fresh air pumping through it like a purifying draught through the opened windows of a long-abandoned house. Kill or cure, as the English would say. He'd leave by The Court's back door, leaning into the steep slope that rose directly behind the house. He always went alone, which Alex didn't approve of despite Albrecht's assurance there was nothing to worry about. He'd be careful and there was no need for concern. Things were different here from where they'd been before. Maggie's visit had convinced him of that.

The incline behind The Court was immediate and abrupt

and it wasn't long before his thighs were burning and his weak chest heaving. He often removed his scarf within the first five minutes of the climb, exposing his prickling neck to the November air. On the initial few walks he stopped regularly, suddenly stilling his body, the brushing and rustling of his clothes giving way to his own heavy breathing and the throbbing of his pulse; a crude, rhythmical beat to the unmoving view beneath him.

Just as the air purged his lungs so the views purged his sight. The valley was beautiful, there was no denying it. No tanks, no dugouts, no snouts of anti-aircraft guns protruding from behind sandbags. The few derelict buildings had fallen under age and weather, not bombs and bullets. It was nature in all its massive certainty, from the crowds of trees running along the valley floor to the barren challenge of its hilltops. He'd never seen anywhere like it before. He was a city man, born and bred in the city's landscape of streets, buildings on buildings and lone elms and sycamores levering up the pavement slabs with their roots. As a child there'd been outings to the countryside, true, and while at university he'd even taken to walking along the granite ridges and hills of Upper Lusatia with a group of friends. But he'd never seen somewhere quite like the Olchon before. Somewhere so still, so bluntly beautiful and yet possessed, within that same beauty, of such a simple, threatening bareness too.

He'd walk straight up until he was through the fields and on the sheep tracks that cut through the brown expanses of withered bracken. Then, long before he reached the top of the ridge, he'd turn and walk along the slope, the valley falling away to his right. He suspected it was a false horizon anyway, that there'd be more climbing before he'd be able to see the land on the other side of the ridge. Not that he wanted to see that land. That was where the war was, that was where they'd come from, and for now he'd rather just explore the valley itself and know nothing of what lay beyond.

On the day he saw Steiner Albrecht had followed the same route he'd walked on that first morning of Maggie's visit. Skirting along the west wall he passed above the old woman's farm and worked his way round to the steeper curve at the head of the valley, where the incline became cliff above him and the young river cut a deep crevice, arching from between clusters of rocks. Here, he climbed again, moving above the damp ground where the spring that became the river first surfaced through the thin soil. Using this spring as a pivot he walked down the slope and swung right again, crossing the river to bring himself back to rejoin his original path, the toe of his boot stepping over the heel of his previous footprints. He never went further around the head of the valley towards the east wall and the ridge of the Black Hill. Even then, on that first morning, he'd somehow sensed the unspoken border that would divide the valley while the patrol was there. The farm women would have the valley east of the Olchon, dark until late in the day, and they, the soldiers, would have the west of the valley, greying to night from the early afternoon onwards. Only Maggie's farm cut into this silent division of territory, but she kept to her fields and often worked with the others along the eastern wall. Upper Blaen, at the head of the valley, marked the apex of this invisible divide.

Sometimes, if the mood took him, or the view was of particular clarity, Albrecht would pause in his walking and sit on one of the rocks near the source of the Olchon. On the morning he saw Steiner it was the nature of the mist, lingering low in the valley, that made him stop and look out over the view. The edges of the stones nearest the stream were softened under mouldings of ice, air bubbles suspended like pearls under their transparent skins. The coarse grasses at the edge of the water were also iced, each individual blade encased in a thin tube, as brittle and fragile as the stems of champagne flutes. Albrecht carefully snapped one of these ice rods and drew it off the blade, leaving the pale grass exposed, quivering in the wind. Looking out over the valley clogged with mist, he blew through the delicate ice straw and felt his warm breath cooled against the palm of his hand.

The sun was just over the Black Hill, diffusing its light through the low mist and throwing shadows in unexpected places. Which was why, at first, Albrecht hadn't seen Steiner standing by a stone wall far down the slope below him. It was only when Steiner removed his radio pack that his movement, unfamiliar in the rhythm of the landscape, caught Albrecht's eye. The pink semaphore of his hands as he slipped the straps from his shoulders, then the lifting of those hands to his face. And then Steiner was still again, his uniform melding back into the greens, browns and burnished ambers of the early winter hillside.

It was the first time Albrecht had seen anyone on this walk. Had Steiner left The Court before him? He didn't think so. He must have taken the lane, the lower route through the valley, while Albrecht made his slower progress along the hillside. Why he was here, Albrecht didn't know. He thought of calling down to him but he didn't think Steiner would hear. He'd already learnt the valley threw visual illusions all the time, that perspective seemed to shrink and shift within its narrow parameters. Steiner was too far away for a voice to reach him. Albrecht watched his motionless back, squinting to sharpen his edges. He was waiting for him to move, to turn, so he could stand and wave to him. But Steiner remained as he was, standing by the broken stone wall, his hands held to his face and his elbows angular either side of his head. Albrecht recognised that stance. He'd seen it on hillsides all over Europe; officers and generals surveying a battlefield through the intimate distance of a pair of binoculars.

Taking the ice from his lips Albrecht twirled it once through his fingers then with a delicate pressure across his thumb, snapped the stem in two. He pushed himself off the stone and began to pick his way down the slope, the broken rod of ice melting in the warmth of his fist. As he neared Steiner he began to drift left, away from the course of the river ricocheting between the rocks. Steiner was armed. He'd spent the last month in constant conflict. Albrecht didn't want to startle him.

Reaching a buckled thorn tree he paused and watched Steiner again, one hand resting against its trunk. The young soldier still hadn't moved, transfixed by whatever filled the figure-of-eight view of his binoculars. Albrecht found himself mimicking this motionless; a hawk hovering above a hunting hawk until eventually Steiner broke their mirrored stillness, unfolding his right elbow and lowering one hand to his waist, as if looking for something in his pocket.

Albrecht walked on, sweeping his legs through the bracken hoping Steiner would hear his approach. But still he didn't move, the binoculars held to his eyes with his left hand, the right still searching on the other side of his body. Albrecht moved further down the slope again and it was only then, when he was on a level with Steiner, that he was able to follow the line of his gaze. There, further down the valley below the bracken line, one of the local women was moving through the low-lying heather and bilberry bushes, a wicker basket hung over the crook of her arm.

'Güten tag, Steiner.'

Steiner's whole body jolted as if shocked with a sudden voltage. Dropping the binoculars he spun towards Albrecht while reaching at the same time for his rifle, his right hand coming up to the stock of the gun, already half off his shoulder.

'Hey! Steady!' Albrecht stepped back, holding both his hands before him and for a frozen moment the two men faced each other like that; Albrecht with his hands out and his knees bent as if braced against a boulder, Steiner poised between flight and defence. Slowly Albrecht straightened up again, allowing himself a breathy half-laugh. 'I didn't come all this way to get a German bullet, private. Could have got that at home a long time ago.'

Steiner returned a weak-eyed smile, slipping his rifle back over his shoulder and making a half turn away from Albrecht as he adjusted himself. 'I'm sorry, sir,' he said. 'You caught me by surprise.'

Albrecht walked up beside the young soldier and looked down the valley.

'It's so quiet,' Steiner added, as if by way of further explanation.

'Yes it is, isn't it?' Albrecht said. 'Admiring the view?' He raised his eyebrows at the pair of binoculars hung round Steiner's neck. He was careful to keep his voice light. He still didn't know Steiner, not like he knew Alex or Sebald. He also had no idea why Steiner was here, out on the hill so early in the morning.

'Yes, sir.' Steiner said, his eyes playing over Albrecht's face trying to read his expression.

'Mind if I have a look?' Albrecht held out his hand, his palm still dewed with the melted ice. Steiner lifted the strap over his head and handed the binoculars to Albrecht.

Albrecht lifted his glasses onto his forehead and looked through the binoculars. They were Russian, the rubber about the eyepieces perished at the edges, cracked like the skin of drying lips. Turning the dial at their centre he brought the view below into focus, drawing the valley from an Impressionist myopia into flat precision. Making small movements that brought the landscape sweeping across the lenses he found the woman, still moving and bending among the bushes. He knew who she was before she lifted her face. The young wife he'd met at the last farm on their first night in the valley. He recognised her hair but he'd known it was her before that. When he was standing by the thorn tree, he'd known then. She was picking bilberries, methodically pulling them from the undergrowth and dropping them into the basket. She obviously had no idea she was being observed.

Albrecht watched her small hands deftly searching under the tight leaves and branches. She was wearing a large, shapeless coat, her hair tied back from her face. Putting the basket down, she stood up and arched the small of her back, working the muscles there with the knuckles of her fist. Even then, from this distance there was little apart from her long hair and the finer bones of her face to mark her out as a woman. The coat hid her shape and her skin was ruddy in the cold of the morning. He felt nothing and was, in some rational part of himself, relieved. But somewhere else, somewhere within him still untouched by the war, the questioning continued. Had that piece of shrapnel numbed him completely? Had it taken not just his taste and his smell but his desire too? He could see why Steiner would be watching her, and yet he felt empty. A lifeless but moving machine, possessed of enough residual knowledge to recognise what he once felt, even if he was no longer capable of sensing it any more.

He lowered the binoculars and turned to look at Steiner.

The young soldier looked back at him, the embodiment of everything he was not. His face had changed while Albrecht had been looking at Sarah. Albrecht recognised his new expression. Just like he'd recognised the stance of a man looking through binoculars, so he'd seen this look of Steiner's on the field many times before too. It was a different kind of searching. Steiner knew Albrecht no better than Albrecht knew him. He was waiting for permission, for licence, for the official nod to the unofficial operation. For the blind eye. How many times had a young soldier like Steiner looked in this way at a superior officer before? And how many times had that officer given the slightest of nods, or just turned away, as Albrecht did now. He breathed in deeply, looking out to the distant hills framed in the valley's broad mouth.

'Do you have any sisters, Steiner?' he asked.

The young soldier was wrong-footed. Albrecht couldn't see his face, but he knew his expectant expression had suddenly dropped.

'Yes, sir,' Steiner said.

Good, Albrecht thought, then this will be easier.

'I had two sisters before the war, sir,' Steiner continued. 'Now I have one, Hilda.'

Of course. That genetic subtraction all of them made these days. Families tapering to single figures, brothers and sisters diminished to the past tense. This would not make it easier.

'I'm sorry,' Albrecht said, still looking out over the view and wondering how it was you could live with a man for over a month and not know about the death of his sister.

'It was a British raid,' Steiner said, his voice clipped. 'Margaret was always last to the shelter. The sirens were faulty that night. My father looked for days afterwards. For anything. Some hair. A shoe. Just something. But there was nothing.'

So many stories like this. That's why he hadn't known. Because they were no longer unusual. So many ways for someone to leave, to be extinguished. Albrecht lowered his gaze to follow Sarah again, now just a pale patch without the binoculars' magnification. That would make it easier, he thought. From here, from this distance, it would be easy. And after all, why shouldn't he let Steiner have his revenge and his pleasure all at once? Give the young man his sympathies then walk on, stepping over his own prints, edging around the valley back to The Court. Walk on and let Steiner descend the slope behind him, waving casually to the uncertain, unnerved farm woman. Let him hold her face into those wet bushes, one of his hands spread against the back of her head. Let him lift that shapeless coat and the skirt beneath. Let him empty his grief, his anger and his sadness into her. Let him leave her, alive but with her life suddenly taken. Let him introduce her to the war with which all of them have had to become so intimate these past endless, dragging, unforgiving years.

Anywhere else and he might have let it be that way. Might have walked on and climbed higher up the slope as he went, so as not to hear her screams. He'd known it happen so many times before, why shouldn't it happen again?

Because he wouldn't let it. Not here, not now. Because this valley could be different. He'd already begun to feel the faintest of turnings within himself this past week. He knew it was the valley that had engaged this turning and he wanted it to continue, this slow rotation inside him like the tumblers of a lock edging into place. If it went on for long enough, until the end of the war, then who knows? It might just unlock him altogether. It might still not be too late and he could finish his war a victor in every way. Over his enemies and over himself.

'Why are you here, Steiner?' Albrecht looked away from him again, out over the deep valley before them.

'I had no choice, sir.'

'No, *here*. Now. On this hill.'

'That house is silent, sir,' Steiner said jerking a thumb at the radio pack lying on the ground behind them. 'The whole valley is. I was looking for a signal.'

'And did you find one?'

'Not yet, sir. But I think I will higher up. Up there.' He pointed to above the source of the Olchon at the head of the valley.

Albrecht followed the line of his finger up to the horizon behind them, its edge dark against the opaque sky.

'Well, let's see if you're right, shall we?' Albrecht said, handing the binoculars back to Steiner and starting to walk up the slope, pressing the heels of his palms into his thighs. Steiner didn't follow him but just turned and looked back down the valley instead, at the faint shape of Sarah moving between the bilberry bushes. Albrecht stopped his ascent and called down to him.

'She didn't drop any bombs, private. None of them did. They're farmers, that's all. Let them farm.'

Steiner looked up the slope at Albrecht. There was something unsettled in his eyes. Albrecht met his stare, one hand resting on the holster of his pistol. A crow cackled from a tree below. A pair of ravens spun, ragged in the wind. Eventually Steiner bent to the radio pack, slipped one of its straps over his shoulder and began climbing up the hill towards Albrecht.

'Come on,' Albrecht said when he was nearly with him. 'You never know. If we get through maybe they'll tell us its over. That we've won already.'

Steiner gave a resigned smile at the worn joke he'd heard

so many times before, a hopeless wish thrown at reluctant radio operators across Europe for the past four years. Albrecht walked on. He felt strange. He knew it was right, in what he remembered of the real world, to be walking away from the farm woman as they were now. And yet he felt wrong, as if he'd denied the war its natural course, disturbed the calibration of events. It reminded him of when, as a boy, he'd taken a still-breathing mouse from the mouth of a hunting cat. He'd intervened in nature, hiding the bruised and bitten rodent in the garden hedge. But he'd known it was only temporary. That he was only keeping at bay, just for a moment, what he knew all too well to be inevitable. The cat would find the mouse, the wolf will find the lamb and the war, like the river they walked beside now, would always rediscover its course, however much he wished to dam it with the insignificant pebbles of his own intentions.

November 11th

They're still here. Me and Maggie saw two of them today when we were doing her ewes. They were just looking at us and then they were gone. The officer and the tall one. Maggie was having none of it and set to with her shears harder than ever but it shakes me up every time, Tom. And what makes it worse is every time at first I think it's you or William or Hywel. Still, only a week or two is what they said. Then once they're gone maybe you can come back.

It's still clear. The mornings all start off with mist, but then it burns through until it's fine all day. The nights are cold though. Frost every one for the last week. But then I suppose you know all this, don't you? All the leaves have turned and every morning there's new spiders' webs in the grass.

Menna and Mary have got all their ewes down so they're tupping too now. The whole valley will be lambing at the same time. Mary's been hiding Bethan away ever since they came. I understand why she's done that but I think she's being too worried as usual. Apart from like today we see nothing of them.

I picked bilberries yesterday. I don't know why. Habit I suppose. It seemed wrong not to. Once I get a moment I'll try some jam with them. They won't make much but it'll be something.

Things have gone awful quiet, Tom. Reverend Davies was due last Sunday but hasn't been up since over a month now. Maybe he heard they're in The Court. Even so, you'd think he'd still come. None of us have had a chance to go into town. Maggie says the radio must have changed its waves or something because she's getting nothing, not even music.

I think the old cockerel will have to go. The young one is causing too much trouble. His spurs are long enough. I was waiting for you to come back but I suppose I'll have to do it. Best be rid of him before winter.

George pressed himself into the hedge until its thorns and twigs dug into the back of his head, clawed at his neck and scratched up around his eyes. He felt the sting of a nettle brush across the back of his knuckles. He should have worn gloves. Not because of the nettles but because if they swung those torches this way his hands would shine up like lanterns out of the dark. Edging the sleeves of his coat over his fingers, he held them there, tightly balled in his fists.

The patrols kept changing their routine. This was the third time he'd been caught out like this. So much for the Germans' infamous love of order. That was the one thing Atkins had said he could rely on. Once they'd established a pattern they'd stick to it. But they hadn't. Atkins had been wrong about so much. George was still here for a start. Still going out every night to check his drop points, to scribble observations on his dwindling supply of rice paper. In Atkins's world he should be dead by now. Or on a train or in a cattle truck shunting and rattling south. But he wasn't. He was still here. And he wasn't the only one. Those messages kept coming and his observations kept going, disappearing from the drop points as if the walls and gate posts were in collusion with him, swallowing his information, digesting it into the landscape, preparing the country for when it would throw off these invaders scurrying across its back.

The operational units had been at work as well, which is why he was having to press himself into the hedge like this now. Ever since those two guards at the station had been killed the young lieutenant at Pandy had made it his priority to find the men responsible. That's why the patrols kept changing, he was sure.

They'd done a round-up of men in the area the same day they found the guards with their guts spilt over the road. George himself had been pulled out into the farmyard at home. He'd thought that was the end then. Or at least the beginning of the end. The lieutenant barking questions he didn't understand into his face, the translator repeating them in a bored, irritable tone beside him. Why wasn't he in the army? Where had he been last Thursday? His mother scrabbling in the drawers of the dresser for that medical report from four years ago. 'Acute deafness in left ear.' That, at least, was something Atkins had got right.

George was sure if they weren't under orders to keep the farms going they'd have taken him there and then. As it was the lieutenant listened while the translator read the report, eyeballed George for a few long, frozen seconds then gave his sergeant the nod to clear the soldiers out of the yard. When they'd gone his mother sat against the trough and wept. His father had laid a hand on her back in a way George had never seen before, rubbing gently between her shoulder blades. When he'd looked up at his son it was in such a way as to make George think perhaps his father knew everything after all. Or perhaps he was asking himself the same questions the lieutenant had asked. Why wasn't he in the army? Why wasn't he in the Home Guard? Why wasn't he doing something at least?

Not everyone had been able to give the lieutenant as good a reason as George and fifteen other men from the area were taken away that day. They never came back. The lieutenant made sure everyone knew it would be the women and children next, the old men, the grandmothers. That next time it would happen here, in their homes and in their fields, not at the end of a journey in a truck.

Since then any news of operational units' activity came from far away. Attacks on the railway up towards Hereford, a munitions dump exploded outside Abergavenny. A new newspaper, the *Star*, distributed by the Germans to replace the papers that had stopped production in the weeks before their arrival, ran reports of these attacks. A vicious insurgency was determined to undermine the freeing of the British people. Funded by self-interested parties, these insurgents were attempting to destabilise the peaceful German occupation. Germany's war was not against the British people, but against Churchill's tyrannical democracy which had insisted on prolonging this conflict for five unnecessary years. The insurgency was the last, sputtering breath of this dying tyranny. The German army would, however, prevail. As they always did. Long live the Führer. Long live the Reich.

After the killing of the guards at the station the western edition of the *Star* had run just one other article about the area. The editors, whoever they were, had chosen to give this article more than the usual amount of space. INSURGENTS MURDER LOCAL POLICE CONSTABLE. George wished the headline was just another of the many lies the paper printed every week, but this time he knew it was true. Constable Evans had been shot through the window of his own house as he sat down to a cup of tea before bed. A single bullet, fired from long range. The *Star* said it was the work of the insurgents but no one believed that. Except George, for two reasons. Firstly, because Atkins had told him this would happen, that he shouldn't be alarmed when it did. That it would be necessary. Secondly, because the calibre and model of the rifle the *Star* said was used in the killing of Constable Evans was identical to that of the sniper's rifle George had, just the other night, taken from beneath his bed and buried deep in the manure heap piled in the corner of his father's farmyard.

George shifted his head slightly, trying to ease the pressure of a thorn pressing behind his ear. The soldiers were still milling around the idling truck in the middle of the lane. Its headlamps burnt into the hedge, casting a broken glow across the field beyond. The chassis shook gently over its engine and the exhaust fumes turned slowly in the cold air. There were six of them, though he couldn't be sure. He saw them only when they passed through or near the beams of the headlamps, or when they caught each other's faces with their torch beams. Ghosts, half-men appearing out of the darkness, hovering above invisible legs. Headless men, the buttons and webbing of their chests illuminated beneath faces and helmets eaten by the night. The cigarettes gave him more of an idea. Five of them now, their tips making slow loops in the air, glowing on and off, rising and falling like amber fireflies. George counted them down as they extinguished. Five, four, three, two. The last one burnt faintly all the way to the truck, hung suspended in the air outside its window, glowed brightly once more then went spinning to the ground, dying in a little explosion of sparks. Shortly afterwards the truck shuddered down its spine, a grating gear engaged and the vehicle began turning. Three of them were going, three were staying. If he timed it correctly he could use the noise and the cover of the truck to run along the hedge and slip over the gate further up the lane. He wouldn't be going any further tonight. Not this way at least.

He'd find another way. Because there was always another way, that's what Atkins had told him. 'Always another way, George,' he'd said, his hand on his shoulder. 'You've just got to keep your eyes open, that's all, lad. Keep your eyes open.'

His eyes wouldn't open. They seemed glued shut. With his own blood? No, not blood. It was a bandage. A tight bandage pressing down on his lids. But there was blood, yes. Dried. He could feel it, pulling on his skin.

Atkins moved his head. Everything spun inside him. White snow under his closed eyes.

His hands were tied. And his feet. Yes, he remembered now. Stupid. Stupid to be caught like that. He should have gone north with the rest. Regrouped. But someone had to stay, didn't they? Stay behind.

Who told? Who sent them to him? No one perhaps. But yes, always someone. Not their fault. What about him? What had he said? No, nothing. Nothing. Yet.

There'd been no time for the pill. They'd taken him by surprise. He tightened his hands so the base of his fingers touched. Yes, the ring was gone.

Stupid to be caught like that. Should have kept his eyes open.

What was that? A door opening. Closing. The click of a latch. Footsteps. They were coming for him again. He listened to their approach. A small room. They came close. He could hear their breathing, smell the fresh smoke on their clothes. Two of them. Why didn't they speak?

One set of footsteps now, moving behind him, then hands,

hands at the back of his head. Fingers at the back of his head. The bandage coming off, pulling at his eyelashes, peeling the blood from his skin – Oh Christ! Jesus Christ! Burning light. Burning, burning light. Hands at his face now, fingers pulling at his face, holding his head, thick fingers over his eyebrows, thumbs pulling at his lids, drawing them back, keeping his eyes open.

The snow came to the valley the same way the men had left it; suddenly, silently and overnight. When Sarah pulled back her curtains the next morning the day was still half dark, washed out in greys and blues. The only light shining into the room was from an undulating seam of white pressed against the lower panes of the window; a miniature range of bright hills, their contours bisected by the glass. She looked at it, her eyes still grainy with sleep, confused. There had been no warning, no sign this would happen. On going to bed she'd been able to see the stars but now the sky and the world beneath it were obscured. There was a wind too, wild about the house. She looked out at the branches of the trees. She could just see them, black behind the still-falling snow. Yesterday they'd been upright, motionless, but now they were all swept the same way like iron filings drawn to a magnet, bowing under the wind that pressed upon them.

The day was no lighter by the time Sarah was out in the yard, clumsy and heavy under layers of jackets and coats, a woollen scarf wrapped about her head, a sack over her shoulders. She fumbled with the dogs' chains, her fingers thick under gloves. Taking Tom's crook and a spade from the shed she began walking down to the lower field where she and Maggie had herded the lambing ewes just weeks before. She was walking against the wind. The snow caught in her eyelashes, melting her vision. With each step her leg sunk up to the knee. When she pulled her boots back out again she tinged her own footholes with red-brown mud, like the edging of blood around a punctured bandage. The world had turned white, the twigs of the hedges fleshed out with inches of snow balanced along their upper sides. With every step forwards she had to push herself against the crook, up and on, walking within her own sphere of mist, the rest of the valley extinguished. The dogs went before her, leaping through the snow like salmon against the current of a stream. Despite the wind Sarah was soon sweating under her heavy clothes. Her breath came hard and fast as she cursed Tom for leaving her like this, quietly at first but then louder, letting the wind snatch the damning of her husband from her mouth.

When she reached the field she knew immediately that at least a third of the flock was missing. Those that were left had bunched together at the far end where the snow was shallower. At the other end the wind had swept a massive drift over the height of the hedge. Fresh snow spun off its edge, sculpting a delicate curl like the blank page of an open book suspended in the breeze between turning and falling. That was where the other ewes would have been lying. Against the hedge, trying to find some shelter. And they were still there somewhere, trapped under the weight of drifted snow.

Sarah waded through the field and began poking her crook into the drift. She'd only ever known this happen once, and even then Tom had got to the ewes before they'd been completely covered. With William in the valley and Maggie's radio, they'd never been taken unawares by the weather. Sarah didn't know if she'd find the ewes alive or dead. Or even if she'd find them at all.

She called to the dogs, shouting above the confusion of wind and flurried air. 'Seren! Fly! Cumby now; cumby, girls!'

The dogs bounded up to her, their coats flecked with snow, their breath steaming. Sarah ran her crook along the drift, 'Cum'n girls, cum on now.' Fly was the first to climb onto the firmer snow at the base of the drift. She began trotting along its length, her nose low. Seren followed her and soon both dogs were pawing at the same patch, throwing the snow between their legs. Sarah joined them with the spade, digging until she saw a smudge of grey-white wool. Dropping the spade she dug with her hands instead, freeing the ewe's front legs, scooping the packed snow from off its back and heaving it into the field. It was alive. Stunned and dumb with cold, but alive.

In this way Sarah mined the ewes from the drift, the dogs scenting them out and her birthing them, their coats clogged with ice, into the morning's thickening blizzard. Each one was worse than the last and Sarah knew she'd soon uncover a body of wool no longer panting for breath. Her face burnt with exhaustion and tears. She hated Tom. And she hated the other men too. For leaving, for running away. Over the past two months the loss of their husbands had been changing within all the women and Sarah was no exception. The questions, the hurt and fear had been gradually overshadowing her concern. She'd felt it altering every day, felt the vacuum of Tom's missing curdle and calcify into something harder. This sudden blizzard had broken it open, but like an insect struggling from the case of its pupa, her grief had transformed, emerging bitter and injured into the cold light of day.

After half an hour of finding, digging and pulling the sheep from the snow, Sarah was too exhausted to be either surprised or scared when Albrecht and Alex emerged from the white-out behind her. The dogs signalled their arrival, standing on the drift, barking over her shoulder. Sarah turned in time to see them coming through the mist and snow, two ghosted bodies, their faces obscured with grey scarves. One of her knees was bent deep into the drift. Her left hand held the head of a ewe, gulping for breath. She remained like that until they were close to her. Albrecht bent to her ear, pulling the scarf from his mouth, flakes of snow melting against his glasses.

'Where are they?' he asked, raising his voice over the wind. 'How many more?'

Sarah waved her free hand along the drift. 'All along here. Follow the dogs.'

Albrecht turned to speak to Alex but he was already up beside the hedge, his legs covered to the hip, digging with a short-handled trench shovel. Seren barked beside him, her ears pricked and her thin ribs rising and falling under her wet coat.

It was Albrecht who found the first dead ewe. He was digging with his hands, excavating around the animal's back towards its head like an archaeologist uncovering a fossil. He knew before he saw its glassy eye that the sheep was dead. He'd seen enough death to recognise its pattern upon a body, human or not. Even so he pulled the animal free, bringing it sliding down the lower part of the drift, its stiff forelegs curled under its chest. Climbing out of the deeper snow he walked over to where Sarah was digging.

'This one,' he said, bending close to her ear again and thumbing towards the ewe's carcass. 'It's dead.'

Sarah looked up at him, frowning. The scarf had slipped from her head and her dark hair hung in wet strands across her face. For the first time Albrecht noticed her eyes; the flecks of gold in the green of each iris.

Alex shouted to Albrecht in German from further up the field. He too was dragging the lifeless body of a ewe out of the drift.

'And that one,' Albrecht said to Sarah. 'Also dead.'

Sarah returned to the hole she was digging. Albrecht waded into the drift and together they threw back the snow until Sarah felt the soft give of a sheep's muzzle. She cleared a space about the nostrils and removing one of her gloves held her bare palm before them. There was nothing.

Albrecht was still clearing the snow from the ewe's head but now Sarah stopped him. 'No, don't' she said, touching his arm. 'The crows'll only get the eyes.' With one sweep of her still-gloved hand she brought the freshly dug snow falling back over the hole, covering the velvet of the ewe's dead face.

'I'm sorry,' Albrecht said. Sarah didn't respond but just sat back for a moment, sinking into the drift. Feeling the hard-soft snow both support and embrace her, she suddenly understood how the sheep could have done this. How they could lie here and let themselves slowly drown. A gentle death. A warm, bright, gentle death. An easy death. All she'd have to do was lie there. Stay still and let this white world swallow her whole. Let the snow knit her shroud, flake by flake, until there was nothing left to mark her presence except the slightest of tremors across the drift's smooth surface as she allowed her last and longest breath to leave her.

'Mrs Lewis?' This time Albrecht shook Sarah's shoulder. The snow was still falling heavily and it had already settled thickly on her head and her arms. Slowly, Sarah looked up at him, as if rising through a dream.

'My sergeant says these two must be helped. They'll die if they stay here.'

Sarah turned to look at the two ewes lying either side of the big German soldier. They were alive but they'd given up. The others they'd freed had, after a moment of shock, made their way over to the rest of the flock at the far end of the field. But these two were still slumped on the ground. Their sides heaved with breathing but through no will of their own. They were already dead, but that didn't matter. She couldn't lose any more.

'Bring them t'the house,' Sarah said quietly, pushing herself out of the snow. Albrecht looked at her blankly, the flakes falling heavily between them. 'Those two,' she said again louder pointing to the sheep. 'Bring 'em up t'the house.' She turned away from him and walked along the destroyed drift, pitted with their searching. At the far end Tom's crook stuck out of the bank of snow like a question mark bereft of its question. Sarah grasped it as she passed, heavy-stepping on towards Upper Blaen, calling the dogs after her. She looked back just once to see Alex, one ewe already over his shoulder, lifting the other onto Albrecht's back. The German officer was bent over at the waist, one leg braced forward and his hands behind him. His uniform was soaked dark over his knees and clumps of snow clung around the cuffs of his sleeves. Stood like that he reminded Sarah of an illustration in one of her school books when she was a girl; Atlas crouched in anticipation, ready for the weight of the world to be set upon his shoulders.

By the time Albrecht and Alex reached Upper Blaen Sarah had already stoked the fire and fed it with fresh wood and coal.

'Put 'em there,' she said, pushing the table back to make room in front of the range. Alex laid one of the ewes on the flagstones as gently as if he were putting a child to bed, then took the other from off Albrecht's back and laid it beside it.

The two of them lay there, still numb and listless with cold. Alex said something in German to Albrecht.

'A cloth? A towel?' Albrecht said.

Sarah went into the porch and got an old flannel shirt Tom used for wrapping weak lambs in and gave it to Alex. Undoing his scarf and taking off his gloves, the big German sat down beside the sheep and began rubbing their necks and backs. A pool of water was already bleeding from under them as their frozen coats began to thaw.

'He's good with 'em,' Sarah said, not looking at Albrecht. 'Knows what he's doing.'

'Alex grew up on a farm,' Albrecht said. On entering the kitchen his glasses had misted and now he was cleaning them on a corner of his shirt.

Sarah sat down. Here they were again. In her house, in the kitchen. The enemy. The invading army. But it was different this time. As if the snow had shed them all of their history. She felt safe. For the first time in over a month, she felt safe.

'You're still here,' she said, looking up at Albrecht.

'I'm sorry?'

'You're still here,' she said again, looking at the red marks where his glasses had pressed over the bridge of his nose. 'In the valley. You said two weeks before.'

Albrecht glanced at Alex rubbing at the sheep with the old flannel shirt. He didn't understand English. 'Yes,' Albrecht said. 'A dispatch rider came. We're to stay for a little longer.'

'How much?'

Albrecht tried to smile but his face felt stiff and immobile with the cold. 'I'm afraid I can't tell you that, Mrs Lewis.'

Sarah looked back down at the sheep. 'I should heat 'em some water.' She got up, collected a tin bucket from behind the door and went out into the yard. When she came back in the bucket was half-filled with snow and her hair was shot with flakes. Albrecht was at the dresser, one hand holding the cover of the family Bible, the other turning its thin pages.

'Pump's frozen,' Sarah said walking past him and hanging the bucket on a hook above the range.

She sat down again and for a while none of them spoke. The only sounds were the falling of the coal in the grate, the hissing of the damp bucket above the fire, the wind at the window and Alex, murmuring to the sheep in German.

'It was Alex's idea we came to help,' Albrecht said eventually. 'When he saw the snow. He said you might need help.'

Sarah looked out the window at the obscured world. He knew then. They all knew. Of course they did. *You might need help.* He may as well have just said it straight out. Because your husband isn't here. Because your husband has gone. Sarah felt a trickle of fear run under her heart, like the returning voice of an old friend.

'My patrol have gone to the other farms too,' Albrecht continued. 'To help.'

Sarah thought how that must have been. The German soldiers wading over the fields. Knocking at the doors, peering through windows. What would the others have done? What had Maggie done? Were the Germans standing in their kitchens now? Somehow she thought not.

'D'they speak English too?' She asked.

'No,' Albrecht said, 'but I told them what to say. And I gave them notes.'

Sarah nodded slowly. Menna couldn't read.

One of the ewes shifted its legs, dragging a hoof over the stone.

'Where d'you learn yours?' Sarah said, looking back at Albrecht.

'I lived here. Before the war. I was a student in Oxford and then in London.'

Now it was Albrecht's turn to look away through the white window.

'You went to Oxford? The university?' Sarah said.

Albrecht turned back to her. 'Yes. For a year.' He was surprised by her question, by the knowledge it implied. He closed the Bible and leant against the dresser. 'Did you go to school, Mrs Lewis?'

'Only 'til fourteen,' Sarah said, glancing at a framed certificate on the wall. 'Then I had t'work.'

Albrecht went over to the certificate and looked it over. It was faded but had been as lovingly framed and hung as an old master. He read from its typed print:

Herefordshire County Council Education Committee

ON LEAVING SCHOOL

Dear *Sarah*

FOURTEEN YEARS OF AGE – You have now passed your fourteenth birthday. It may be your intention to leave School, or you may have resolved to continue your studies for a time. In either case, here is a message of friendly counsel and good cheer.

Great issues depend on this period in your life. Choices are being made now by which the course of your life for good or ill, for success or failure, is determined.

There followed a number of sections, each bearing a paragraph of advice. Albrecht cast his eye between them, the sound of the wind rising hollow in the chimney behind him.

THE GREAT CHOICE – The greatest of all choices is that between good and evil; whatever else you may be or do, strive to be good. Speak the truth always, whatever it cost you. Be courteous to everybody; to honour another is to honour yourself. Keep your temper. There is no harm in having a temper; the harm lies in losing it.

YOUR CHARACTER – Your most precious possession is a pure character. Guard it closely. It is easily lost; it is terribly hard to regain.

YOUR BODY – By fresh air, by cleanliness, by recreation, by regular habits, keep your body fit. Be temperate in all things. Beware of strong drink. Athletes in training abstain from alcohol, and surely it is our duty to be always at our fittest.

YOUR MIND – Good books are 'Kings' Treasures'. Read only the best. The best of all books is the Bible. Read it daily; get to know it thoroughly. The reading of a few verses every morning or evening is the best of all tonics for mind and soul.

NEVER BET OR GAMBLE – Gambling is an unhealthy striving to gain something without giving proper return for it. It is a great evil, destructive of character, disastrous in its consequences.

Albrecht didn't read any more. He didn't like this certificate. Its tone of 'friendly counsel' was tinged for him by the miles of printed rhetoric he'd seen fed to the children of the Reich. Moral directives. Orders that, given and followed enough times, would lead to the arrogance of that Gestapo officer in Oxford; to other fourteen-year-olds taking up guns and spitting at Jews. But that wasn't the only reason this certificate left a bad taste in his mouth. Standing there, in that farmhouse kitchen in another country, he couldn't shake the sense that somehow its vacuous advice was intended for him too, both advising and admonishing him at once.

'Some good advice,' he said turning away from the certificate and leaning against the edge of the dresser again. Sarah stood and fetched a wooden spoon to stir the melting snow in the bucket. Albrecht looked back at the certificate.

'May I ask you about these names, Mrs Lewis?'

Sarah looked up at him, her eyes like the first night he'd seen her, fierce and fearful in her husband's clothes.

'Richards and Thomas,' Albrecht continued tapping at the two signed signatures in the bottom right hand corner. 'These family names are also Christian names. Richard and Thomas?'

Sarah went back to stirring the snow, nodding in reply.

'And yours too? Lewis? This can be a man's Christian name?'

Sarah nodded again, her throat had gone dry. Why was he asking about their names? What did he want to know? What had she done, letting them come in the house? The snow was deep outside. Too deep for anyone to get here quickly. Even if they heard her cries at all.

'I think it is common here. This type of family name?'

Sarah sat back down at the table, her eyes still on the bucket of heating snow. Alex began turning one of the sheep, shifting it onto its other side.

'I was wondering why that is,' Albrecht said more quietly, half to himself. The woman seemed to have stopped talking. He went over to look out of the window again, trying not to look too comfortable, too used to walking around a stranger's house. But he'd done this so many times he couldn't hide his familiarity with authority. He'd walked in too many strangers' houses for the ease he'd so difficultly acquired to shed that simply.

'It's from the Welsh,' Sarah said suddenly, still keeping her eyes on the bucket. 'When everyone spoke Welsh a son was given the first name of his father. They passed it on so as they got to have long names,' she glanced towards the Bible on the dresser. 'My mother's grandfather still signed himself Hywel ap Thomas ap Dafydd. Son of Thomas, son of David.' She looked up at Albrecht. 'When the English came they made it easier for them to understand. That's why.'

She remembered her mother telling her just this story one day when they were walking down through the fields from delivering milk and eggs to old Mrs Roberts up the valley.

Albrecht nodded. Her sudden talking had startled him. 'Yes, of course,' he said. 'Thank you.' He'd only ever read of Welsh in his studies. 'My family name too, is a first name,' he continued. 'Wolfram. Wolfram von Eschenbach was a medieval poet. From Bavaria. I think at some point my family took the name from him.'

Sarah stared back at the bucket, trembling slightly on its hook, the heating snow tapping against its sides. She didn't want to know about his name. She didn't want to know anything about him.

Alex had stopped working on the sheep and was looking up at Albrecht. He'd heard him tell Sarah his name, as clear in the flow of incomprehensible English as a stone within a stream. Why was the captain talking so much to this woman? Why was he telling her his name again?

Albrecht returned Alex's stare. 'Alex is from Bavaria,' he said before continuing in German to his sergeant. Alex laughed. His voice was deep, welling from some far place inside him. 'But Alex is not a poet,' Albrecht said in English, shaking his head and smiling. Then suddenly, without warning, he saw Alex in Russia again, locked in a struggling embrace with a Red Army soldier. Alex losing his rifle, the

Russian lifting his knife. Alex biting at the man's throat, tearing out his windpipe with his teeth. The man falling at his feet, bubbles of blood popping under his chin, spreading through his greying stubble like ink through blotting paper.

Albrecht's smile left him and he looked out the window to try and ease the rush of panic this vision always brought. Alex went back to tending the sheep, still smiling at Albrecht's joke.

Sarah fetched a shallow bowl and, taking the bucket off its hook with a teacloth wrapped about her hand, poured some of the heated water into it before laying it before the two ewes. Then she walked out of the kitchen into the yard without saying anything or looking at Albrecht.

When she came back inside she tipped a handful of calf nuts into the water. Alex nodded in approval and smiled at her. She ignored him and sat back at the table.

'This will make it hard for you,' Albrecht said, studying the thick folds of snow over the shed's slate roof.

Sarah felt another shudder of fear. There, again, he knew. *This will make it hard for you.* Because you're on your own. You all are. Because there isn't a man in the valley to help you. That's what he meant.

She traced the whorls of wood in the surface of the table, her mind racing, searching for a way to lead his talk away from her own situation. *Fingerprints of those gone before.* She let the wood's smooth whirlpools lead her.

'I knew a poet once,' she said quietly. 'When I was a girl.'

Albrecht turned to face Sarah, frowning. 'A poet?'

'Yes. You said your family took their name from a poet. I knew a poet. He lived up at the monastery above our farm. He'd been a soldier before but he was a poet when I knew him. And a painter.'

Albrecht looked at her blankly. What was she talking

about? How did she know a poet out here? Why was she telling him this? Perhaps the snow, the exhaustion, had got to her. Or maybe that light in her eye he'd thought the glimmer of intelligence was, after all, no more than the glint of rural insanity.

'Really?' Albrecht said strolling over to the dresser again. He stood with his back to her, studying the certificate once more but not reading it. He could hear the sound of the sheep lapping at the mix of water and nuts behind him. Leaning against the dresser his hand knocked something over and he found himself picking up Sarah's wedding photo again. There she was on her wedding day. With her husband. Thick shouldered, a farmer in any language. She was smiling, her dark hair pinned up under her veil to expose her neck, fine and slender in the light. She looked like a different woman and he wished he'd known her then. He hated her for changing. He looked up from the sepia image and caught her eye.

'When did they leave?' he said flatly.

Sarah made a sound as if she'd been punched in the stomach, a long empty gasp. Her eyes welled and her mouth worked like a fish gulping the air for water.

Albrecht felt ashamed. And he felt satisfied. 'Your husband and the others,' he continued, his voice colder than before. 'When did they leave you?'

Sarah looked at the floor. She felt sick. Her head spun. One of the sheep made a weak groaning bleat and she snatched at the sound like a drowning swimmer grabbing for a lifeline. Dropping to her knees she took its head in her hands, found her own reflection in the brown convex pool of its eye.

'You can go now,' she said, not looking up from the sheep's face. Her voice grated in her throat.

She pushed the bowl nearer to the ewe's muzzle and waited. Waited for him to ask her again, for him to order his sergeant out of the room, for his hand to grab her from behind. But instead he just spoke quickly in German to Alex, who got up off the floor and began putting on his gloves as they exchanged a few more words.

'Alex says the sheep in the field will need feeding. They can't eat the grass.'

She didn't answer him. Silence. Silence was all she would give him now. Keeping her head bowed to the ewe she listened to their footsteps over the flagstones then felt the cold blast as they opened the door onto the porch and then the front door. She didn't lift her head or turn round. He was still there, she could feel him. She could feel his eyes. The silence of his presence pressed at her back, pulled the air taut around her for what felt like minutes.

'Why do they do it?' he said at last from the open doorway, his voice half taken by the wind. 'Why do they let themselves be covered like that?'

Sarah stroked the ewe between its ears, felt the animal's skin warming under her touch.

'Because they give up easy,' she said quietly, not lifting her eyes from the ewe below her. 'They let go too easy.'

The cold wind blew at her back. In the corner of her eye snow swirled in across the stone floor. The flames of the fire beside her guttered and flagged. Then the door closed. The turning snow settled, the wind died and the flames burnt taller once more. She waited for a minute until she could no longer hear them, then got up off her knees. Her wedding photograph was lying on the table, face down. She picked it up and placed it back on the dresser, then slid the Bible back onto its shelf. She should never have left it out. Taking a broom from the corner of the room she began sweeping the snow back towards the door. One of the ewes, scraping a hoof over the flagstones, shifted its weight and stood up.

That evening the clouds cleared and Sarah was able to stand at the back of Upper Blaen and look down the simplified valley, illuminated under moonlight. The snow-thickened ground had risen within feet of the trees' lower branches. The trees themselves wore a foliage of frost and half a foot of white on every limb. Every hedge and every fence was covered, their presence reduced to long undulations like the banks and ridges of Tom's body carved into the horsehair mattress by the weight of his sleeping.

For two months now the women had lived alone. It had been a gradual shedding of company. First, at the outbreak of war the sons and farmhands had left, drawn from the valley by the faraway conflict. Then, years later, their husbands had followed, swallowed overnight by the hills. Now, with the advance of the German army, what few visitors to the valley there ever had been had stopped coming. Reverend Davies, the Baptist minister who held their fortnightly services at The Court, the doctor, the district nurse, the blacksmith. Even the Ministry men with their clipboards and pamphlets. Finally, Maggie's radio, their one intermittent contact with the outside world, had been defeated. Maggie still switched it on, but only to hear it tune hopelessly through static, listening to nothing but the white noise of its silence.

No road had ever run through the Olchon and now it was as if no road had ever run into it either. Absorbed in their work, in thoughts of their husbands, the women had become amputated from the world beyond. It was as if it had forgotten they ever existed. And now the snow had perfected their isolation. If the silence, the absence of their situation, could have been made corporeal, it would have looked like this. A thick shroud over the fields, the farms, the river. A great white dust sheet laid over the entire contents of a locked and abandoned house.

And yet they were not alone, as Maggie proved in more ways than one when she came knocking at Upper Blaen later that evening. Sarah had been expecting her. She knew she'd come in the end, Maggie always did. She also knew that she should have gone down to see Maggie first. That she shouldn't have let the older woman struggle up through the snow to Upper Blaen. And she would have gone too, if she hadn't had to take hay to the sheep, smash the ice in the troughs, settle the two ewes in the shed, dig a hole over the submerged hen house and lean over it to listen for the warm, buried clucking of the hens as she tipped in their feed. Even then Sarah would have gone to see Maggie but only if she hadn't spent so much time sitting in the kitchen watching the snow fall and fall and fall, wondering whether to curse or bless its coming. Only if she hadn't sat for an hour beside the fire staring at her wedding photograph, aching her brain trying to remember what Tom felt like, smelt like, sounded like. Trying to remember what it was to love him as him, and not as her missing husband. Trying to remember what it was to love him at all. Because her anger had not subsided with the cold in her fingers. She still didn't understand. How a man could leave his wife to all this; to the war, to those soldiers, to herself for so long.

And then the sharp pangs of guilt and worry. Perhaps Tom had no power over his missing. What if he was lying months dead in the hills or, worse she somehow thought, languishing in a German camp somewhere on the continent? She just didn't know. And it was killing her. All she did know was this. The falling snow. The glowing and cracking coals. The wind, funnelling down the chute of the valley. The simple smells, sounds, lives and deaths of her animals. And, of course, Maggie and the others, all enduring their own versions of this left-behind limbo. Each so unique and yet so much the same.

When Maggie came through the door her face was red with effort and cold. She sat by the range, unwrapping herself and stamping her boots, dislodging threads of snow from their treads.

'Well, better this than a green one, bach,' she said, massaging her hands back to life. 'Tha's all I can say. Better than a green one.'

A green winter. Sarah's mother had always had the same fear. A winter without snow. It was bad luck. The old people would die. Maggie was the oldest in the valley.

Sarah looked out at the Hatterall Ridge, a dark curve between the stars and the snow-plump fields. 'No, Maggie,' she said. 'I think you'll be safe with this one.'

Maggie looked up at her and Sarah saw the uncertainty moving under the old woman's features, like a submerged brook running under fragile ground. The soldiers had come to her too. Or at least one of them had.

'I didn't know what to do when he held out that note,' Maggie said, warming her hands on a mug and studying the still-swirling tea within. '"Medic," he kept sayin'. "Medic." Well, I thought he wanted one, not that he was one. But then I read the note, see. "OK," I says, "well, follow me then, Medic."' Maggie looked up from the mug, 'An' he was good as gold after that.'

Between them Maggie and Sebald had freed her lambing ewes from an upper field and brought them down to the meadows beside the farmhouse. Then Sebald had cleared the snow from her front door and path and carried bushels of hay to the sheep. Maggie spoke no German and Sebald no English, but Maggie recognised the language of hard work and was quietly grateful for his assistance.

'And what about Menna and Mary?' Sarah asked.

'Oh, they're fine,' Maggie said. 'Another couple of the Germans went to them as well. Only thing is they must have seen Bethan I s'pose.'

'And have you seen them then?' Sarah knew there was no way Maggie could have battled her way over to the other side of the valley through this much snow, but she needed to believe that somehow she had.

'No,' Maggie said, looking back down into her tea. 'No, I haven't seen them myself but I know they're all right. The captain told me.'

'He came to see you?' Sarah had known he would. That he wouldn't leave them alone any more.

'Yes.'

'An' you believe him do you, Maggie? That they're safe?'

Maggie met Sarah's stare. 'Yes,' she said, 'I do, Sarah. Why would he lie to me?'

Ever since that first morning meeting Maggie had felt instinctively that she and Albrecht understood each other; that there was an echo in their positions, their situations, that was slight but still significant.

Sarah knelt to the fire and stoked the hot coals, releasing a breath of sparks from their breaking hearts. 'He knows,' she said, looking into the flames. 'He knows, Maggie. About Tom. And the others.'

She couldn't look the old woman in the face but she heard Maggie sigh behind her.

'Yes, bach,' Maggie said, 'I know he does. He told me too.'

Sarah sat back down opposite her. The night outside was

still and quiet after the hours of endless wind. The temperature was dropping. Sarah was sure she could hear the ice forming over the house, crystal by crystal. 'So what do we do now?' she asked.

Maggie took a gulp of her tea and stared into the broken coals and glowing embers.

'Oh nothing for now, bach,' she said. 'Not while it's like this.' She carried on staring into the fire, a glaze forming over her eyes. 'Nothing 'til the snow's cleared. 'Til then I reckon we'll need them as much we can.'

That night Sarah couldn't sleep, her mind restless between the memories of two men no longer with her; Tom, her missing husband, and the poet she'd once known as a girl. Sarah hadn't thought of the poet for years. Every now and then after he and his colleagues had left the old monastery they'd been mentioned in whispered tones by her mother and father. Soon, however, they were not and the poet became no more than a faint summer memory, surfacing just once again in the month she'd left school when she was fourteen years old. Mrs Thomas, her teacher, had also known about the poet. She'd never met him, although she'd met the others living up at the old monastery, the artist and his daughters. When she discovered Sarah had seen the poet, and even spoken to him, she'd sat her down and questioned her about the time they'd spent together. Sarah had answered her as best she could. It seemed the poet, a man called David Jones, was also a famous artist and this was why Mrs Thomas was so interested. He'd recently had an exhibition of his paintings in London. Mrs Thomas showed Sarah a newspaper cutting, a review of this exhibition. Because of this review, this exhibition, the questions were very important to Mrs Thomas. She wanted to know everything Sarah knew about the poet.

It was as if, just briefly, Sarah was the teacher and she was the pupil. Mrs Thomas had promised to show Sarah a book with some of the poet's work in it, but when she'd left Llanthony shortly after Sarah had finished school she took her talk of the poet with her, so as Sarah grew older she'd left him and his stories behind her. But now, with the wild scattering of her mind, with the German captain's questions, with his mention of a poet of his own and most strange of all, with her memory of those diagrams from 'The Countryman's Diary', she had thought of him again. And now she couldn't not think of him.

A rumpled man perched on a rock in front of an easel, shrunken within a heavy greatcoat lashed at his waist with a thick leather belt. This was how she'd first seen him. She was nine years old and her mother had trusted her with delivering the butter and milk herself. The people at the old monastery had been making their own milk and butter, but now they'd stopped.

'Thought that wouldn' last long,' her mother had said to her father when he'd come in and told her. 'They're only playing at farmin' up there.'

She was speaking from the kitchen and Sarah's father, safely out of sight in the living room, rolled his eyes in response, making Sarah giggle in the chair where she sat playing with the kitten. Ever since her brothers had left he'd been more like this. Gentler where once he'd been hard. More fun where once he'd been serious. It was as if the wound opened by his sons' leaving had shown him where he'd been wrong inside, and now he was trying to fix himself, however late he'd left it.

'I'm not goin' up there twice a week mind!' Her mother's voice had risen above the sound of her clattering at the sink. 'However much you pays me!'

'Well, you won' 'ave to,' her father had answered, winking at Sarah. 'The littlun cun take it up to 'em. Can't you,
bach?'

This was before the stories of what went on in the
monastery filtered out into the valley, after which her parents forbade her ever to go near the place again. But in those
early weeks of summer, before those stories had leaked
beyond the monastery's thick walls, Sarah relished this
twice-a-week chore. She felt as if she'd crossed an invisible
boundary and passed over into a new, adult world. The som-
bre sense of responsibility, the excursions beyond her familiar orbit, the robust, imposing building of the old monastery
growing before her as she walked up the hill.

Usually one of the daughters would take the milk and butter at the front door. Once a week, on every second trip,
they'd give her some coins in return which she carefully
tipped into her coat pocket. She never saw any of the men.
Just once or twice she heard a man's voice from within or
from above; snatches of conversation through an open window between the sawing and hammering of carpentry or the
lighter taps of a chisel against wood. So it came as a surprise
to her when, one day after three weeks of this routine, she'd
crested the hill on the way home and seen the poet perched
on his rock in front of his easel. He was facing away from
her looking up at Y Twmpa, the steep flanked hill rising at
the end of the valley. Sarah crept closer, trying to see what he
was painting, but all she could make out was a wash of faint
colours, vaguely echoing the shape of the landscape in front
of him. Suddenly he turned round. He looked straight at her
with no hint of surprise, his tufted blond-brown hair lifted
off his forehead in the light wind. He was small. A boyish
face. Dark eyes with heavy lids behind a pair of round-
framed spectacles. Then he'd turned away again and

returned to his easel in the way the wild ponies on the hill would fix her for a moment, then drop their heads to graze again. But the turn away had also seemed like an offer; to come closer, to watch him work. Which is what Sarah did.

She sat just behind his right shoulder, her knees to her chin and her arms round her knees, locked in place with a hand gripped at each wrist. He was silent. She couldn't even hear him breathe. There was just the brush across the paper; an irregular, slow breathing of weak colour. Sarah watched the painting evolve. It was a watercolour and if she leant forward she could just see the faint pencil lines already marking out the landscape in front of them both. As he filled these spaces with colour, with washes of his brush, she saw that the painting wasn't, after all, this landscape before them. And yet it also was. It was as if the scene had been put through a fairground mirror; distorted, crooked, its features enlarged, the curves of the trees made fluid. The poet continued, sometimes pausing for long minutes, doing nothing but looking. Sarah did the same, following his eyes up to the hill, then dropping them to the easel again as he filled a patch of sky pink, then grey then blue.

He never spoke. After weeks of hearing the men's voices she'd finally met one of them, only for him to be silent. Even without his voice, though, she could tell he was different from any man she'd met before; from her father, her older brothers or her uncle. His eye was quick within a still body. When he lifted his hand to paint, his arm moved as though through water. He smelt different too. Not of animals and earth but of sawdust and paint. Of books and a long, quiet pain. In that way, she thought now, lying in her dark bedroom so many years later, he'd been like an animal. A wounded animal that couldn't speak of its sickness, of how or where it hurt, but could still, somehow, wear the knowledge of that pain. Unspoken, unheard, but so definitely there.

He'd said nothing to her that first time and eventually after a few minutes, thinking of her mother's scolding, Sarah had got up and carried on walking down the hill, the loose coins chinking in her coat pocket with every step down the slope. The next week she walked home the same way and he was there again, so again Sarah sat down and watched him work. This time, made brave by the repetition of the situation, she'd spoken to him.

'S'cuse me, sir,' she'd said. 'Wha' yer doin'?'

He paused in his looking. 'Writing a poem,' he said, splaying his brush into a pale green tablet and lifting it to the easel. 'I've started writing a poem.' He turned to look at her. His face was serious with just the hint of a smile at the corner of his mouth. 'I think it's going to be a long poem, although right now, it's rather short.' He went back to the painting. 'And actually it might not be a poem at all.' Sarah laughed nervously. She didn't understand him. He wasn't writing a poem. He was painting. His voice, too, had caught her off guard. It was high, slightly tremulous, the vowels flattened under the weight of London. She tucked her chin back behind her knees and decided not to say anything else.

'Do you speak Welsh?' he asked her, not looking away from his painting.

'No sir. Me mam does. A bit.'

'Oh,' he said. 'That's good.'

He went back to his long looking. A pair of flies were buzzing around his head, but he seemed not to notice them. Sarah began to get bored. She thought of leaving, but there was nothing but chores for her back at the farm. She thought of her brothers. How now they'd left there were more chores than ever for her to do. How her father was always tired.

'It's too much, cariad,' she'd heard her mother telling him when he came in late and slumped in the chair by the fire. 'Too much for jus' you now.'

'Would you like to hear a story?' The poet's strange voice brought her back sharply.

'Wha' kinda story?' Sarah said. Her brothers had told her a ghost story once, about 'Hanging Judge Jeffreys' down at Pandy. They'd been drinking at the Skirrid Inn. The landlord had shown them the rope marks in the beams where Jeffreys had strung up the Monmouth rebels. When they got back, beer on their breath, they'd sat on her bed and told her how the ghosts of those unfortunate rebels still roamed the inn, their necks hideously elongated, broken and bruised. She hadn't been able to sleep for a week.

'A story about that hill,' he said, pointing his brush at Y Twmpa. 'About all these hills.' He swept the brush wider as if the real hills were his canvas now. He turned to look at her again. 'A story about your ancestors.'

And that was when the poet began to tell Sarah his stories, recasting the land and hills she'd known all her life as the backdrop for his Celtic myths, for tales of saints and soldiers, of kings and bards. His stories worked upon the valleys around them like his paintings. He spoke of places she knew or that she'd heard of before, St Peter's Well, The Abbey, The Cat's Back, St David's Cell, but the lens of his stories made them all new again. Some of the stories she'd even heard before, but never like this, never growing from the very hills of her birthplace. Stories of King Arthur, Lancelot and Percival. About Welsh princes, Irish princesses and English armies. The stories were not always about the Black Mountains though. Sometimes he'd tell her stories from his own life too, about growing up in London, or about his time in France during the war. But while his stories of the

173

hills were often full of war, of Llewellyn ap Gruffydd, Owain Glyn Dŵr and the barbarous armies of Edward I, his French stories were not war stories. They were stories about the villages he'd lived in, about the French dogs and the French children. About the flowers and birds of the French countryside and, just once, a story about Christmas in the trenches. About how up and down the line one Christmas Eve the soldiers had hung wreathes on their 303s and climbed out into no-man's-land to play football and share cigarettes. How for a day, the sky was quiet again. It was after that story Sarah asked him if he'd ever been shot. She'd heard her father talk with a strange admiration about men he knew who'd been shot. He'd farmed throughout the war and seemed almost envious of their scars. The poet didn't say anything in reply but just drew up his loose-fitting trousers to expose a bullet wound puckered above his left knee. His legs were thin and white, the veins ice blue and shallow beneath the skin. The wound was in the shape of a melted star. After a few seconds he lowered his trouser leg and went back to his painting and Sarah felt sorry for asking.

It wasn't always easy for her to find the poet. As long as it wasn't raining he was nearly always outside, painting, even when the weather got colder. But he kept changing where he painted. Sometimes it was on the slope just below the old monastery. At other times she'd find him down between the two streams, trying to capture their movement, their white water and ferny banks. But she always tried to find him after her delivery, in the hope of another story, or just to spend an hour watching his brush uncover a strange, supple version of the land around them.

Then suddenly the poet wasn't there. Somehow Sarah had always known that one day he wouldn't be; that he was as much a product of the season as the tall hay fields or the swallows tying knots in the air. As inconstant and brief as the spring blossom or the long, blood-streaked summer evenings. Her mother had prepared her for his going. 'They won' last long, mark my words,' Sarah had overheard her say to her father. 'It's a holiday for them, tha' place. Another winter'll see 'em off, you watch now. Back to their towns soon enough.'

Sarah first told her mother about the poet when she was helping her with the washing, feeding a pile of wet clothes into the wringer while her mother worked the handle. She told her about his stories, about his paintings. She didn't tell her about his wound. Her mother had frowned down at her, shaken her head and gone back to turning the handle. 'Stories never put food on the table, bach,' she'd said as the flattened clothes emerged from between the rollers. 'Work, tha's what feeds yer. Now, put in tha' shirt there, will you?'

Her father had been more positive. 'No harm in it, is there?' he'd said to his wife when she'd voiced her concern about their daughter spending so much time in a field with a blow-in poet and painter. 'Do 'er some good more like. Get out a bit, hear about the world. He was in the war you know?' Seeing Sarah standing in the door frame, watching them, he'd moved closer to her mother and added in a lower voice, 'She misses her brothers, see.'

But then the other stories about the people at the monastery started to come out. Stories Sarah only ever really understood or heard properly years later when she was an adult. Stories about the poet's friend, Eric Gill, the artist who first brought them all here, arriving as a group in a pony and cart in the middle of a downpour four years ago. About his ways. The stories began in whispered knots of women outside the chapel and spread like gorse fires throughout the valley. Sarah's mother came home one

175

Sunday and held Sarah against her chest so hard and for so long that Sarah had to push back against her arms to catch a proper breath. Then her mother had asked her questions, a strained look on her face. 'No, Mam,' Sarah had replied to the same enquiry asked several different ways but never asked straight. 'He jus' told me stories an' did 'is paintin'. Tha's all.' For weeks after that her father kept himself low and quiet about the house, treading carefully around his wife for fear of spilling her boiling anger. 'Catholics,' Sarah had heard her mother say over tea with a visiting friend weeks later. 'What can you expect?'

So Sarah never got a chance to go back to see if the poet ever returned to his rock in the field. Her mother forbade her to ever go near that end of the valley again, and over the years since, apart from Mrs Thomas' brief flush of interest, she'd forgotten the poet and his stories. Until now. Until the captain's mention of his namesake and its resonance against those diagrams from 'The Countryman's Diary' that had so haunted her these past months. Those sketches and plans of subterranean bunkers, submerged under the earth and peat of the hills. They made her think of the poet and his stories again. One story in particular, about a sleeping lord and his army. There was a king, that's what the poet had told Sarah one afternoon as he painted by the streams. A Welsh king and his army beaten into the hills by Edward I. Beaten, but not killed and not captured, even though no one ever saw him or his army again. That, the poet had explained, was because they'd never come back from those hills. Thousands of men swallowed within the muscles of earth that formed Wales' natural defences against her invaders. And they were still there. At this point the poet had paused in his painting, placed his brush into a cloudy jar of water and leant closer to Sarah's listening face. His voice dropped, so quiet she could barely hear him over the running of the streams. Yes, he'd whispered, still there. In the hills, deep inside them, buried under the peat, heather, gorse, rowan, bog-cotton, stone and soil. Asleep. Not dead, asleep. An entire army and their king, sleeping in the hills, ready to wake and defend the country in its hour of need. The sleeping lord and his sleeping army is what the poet had called them and as he'd described them, Sarah saw them; a glimmering seam of armour, chain mail and swords, just as she'd seen in her history books at school. A rare ore of sleeping men, embedded in the hearts of the hills, waiting.

Had he known then somehow? Had he known that years later, when that little girl was a woman, her husband and all the other husbands in her valley would disappear into those same hills? That they would go underground, deep underground? If that's where they were. She could hardly remember the pictures in that pamphlet now. Had she really ever seen 'The Countryman's Diary' at all? Why did Maggie have to burn it? So quickly. She'd been numb then, so soon after learning. Why couldn't Maggie have waited?

Sarah turned over in the bed which still felt too wide for just her body. She was being stupid. All these hours alone. It was a story. A story for a little girl. She was a woman now, she couldn't believe such things. But she wanted to. Wanted to believe so badly. That Tom and the others would be coming back. *To defend the country in its hour of need.* But wasn't that hour already here? German soldiers in her kitchen asking questions, turning the pages of her family Bible, holding her wedding photograph. She *was* Tom's country and she was in need. But he hadn't woken. Tom hadn't come to her. He was still out there, dumb and unseen, absorbed into the hills' unending green. And deeper still now, under the snow too. He was sinking deeper from her every day.

She had to remember him. Properly, with all her senses. When she'd held that photograph by the fire this evening, she'd felt nothing. It was just paper in glass, light on paper. She couldn't even conjure the memory of its taking any more. Her memory was the photograph, she saw that now. And that wasn't enough. Not if she was going to hold on to him, to stop him sinking further away from her through the centuries of soil and earth. She must conjure him, not memories of him. Conjure him, Tom, here, into their bedroom. Like Edith trying to conjure her son back from the dead. But Sarah didn't need any boards with letters on, any upturned glasses. She had him already, inside her. She just had to draw him up to her again. Draw him up through the layers of her forgetting like stubborn ground water drawn up into a well.

The first time she saw him. Surely she could conjure that again? The moment she first saw her future husband. As a girl playing on her own in the fields she'd often thought about that man. The man who would be the father of her children, a little boy playing somewhere in another field at exactly the same time, oblivious of their impending meeting. Or maybe he was a young man already working on a farm. For a few months of her schooling he'd even been an earnest young student bent over his books in a town with spires and old stone buildings. And then after all that wondering years later she'd finally seen him. It was at a dance in the village hall in Longtown. One of those dances organised by the community to make the young of the valleys, who spent their lives divided by the long fingers of the Black Mountains, mix and meet. The kind of dance at which countless other women in the area had met their own future husbands.

She hadn't wanted to go. Her father was keen she should, though. He and her mother were getting older now. 'Can't have you stuck wi' us old'uns every night, bach,' he'd told her. He'd got his friend's daughter Branwen to call for her, to make sure they went.

There was a band. A live band with one of them playing a fiddle and another on a trumpet. The men drank beer, cider and wheat wine. Some of the women did too. It was the end of September, the hard part of the year over with until winter. The air in the hall was thick and musty with released energy, with anticipation.

Branwen got talking to one of the men they'd not seen before, a thin dark-haired builder with a thick moustache. It was he who introduced Sarah to Tom, to stop her hanging around Branwen like a mute chaperone. Tom had been drinking cider. She could smell it off him, sweet and rich. She'd spent all day bottling pears, all day with her fingers in their soft yellow bodies. When they'd danced, after an hour or so of talking, their smells mingled, apple and pear. 'Together we make an orchard,' she'd laughed into his ear. Tom hadn't understood her but he'd still smiled at her and after that first dance he'd carried on smiling all night. It was more than he'd ever smiled since but by the time he'd called on Sarah a couple of times over the following weeks that didn't matter any more. By then she'd come to like his serious silence. It was solid, like him; a strong, secure quiet, still as a sudden pool in a shallow running river.

It was a winter courtship. For the next few months after the dance Tom would ride over the Hatterall once a week on a Sunday to meet Sarah and walk with her. They always walked, even when the weather got cold. Through the lanes, down to the ruined abbey and sometimes up onto the bare hilltops where birds started away from under their feet and a herd of wild ponies witnessed their first kiss. Tom knew every plant and bird they saw and sometimes his conversation consisted of no more than a list of names accompanied by short nods of his head in the direction of whatever he was naming. Sarah told him he was like Adam walking through the garden of Eden, naming the animals for the first time. He'd looked down at her and she'd seen that again he hadn't understood her, but she'd also seen again that it didn't matter. Her arm through his, sharing the hillside in evening light, resting her head against his shoulder as they walked. These were what mattered to her then.

One Sunday after their walk Tom came in for tea. Her mother made too much of everything, bread and butter, *bara brith*, piled slabs of cheese. Tom and her father talked about farming and that was when he told her parents about Upper Blaen, his late uncle's farm over in the Olchon he'd be taking on come spring. After tea her father took Tom out to show him his prize ram. That must have been when Tom asked her father for Sarah's hand because the next Sunday, as they were standing by the river watching the snow melt in its eddies and foam, as she warmed her fingers under his jacket, he'd asked her to marry him.

After the wedding they'd come straight to Upper Blaen, and then, that night, they'd come here to this bed. Sarah had no older sister to speak with and her mother had long since retreated too far behind her sayings and phrases to ever talk straight about anything. Still, Sarah thought she knew what to expect. She'd lived on a farm all her life and even Branwen, whom she'd seen some more of since the dance, had at times talked of their future wedding nights.

Now, years after that first night together, after five years of marriage and two months of Tom's missing, she tried to remember completely. Everything. The sound of him washing in the basin as she lay waiting; the scent of the skin on his shoulders; his hands touching her clumsily where they'd never touched her before; his hair brushing coarse against her cheek. The way he'd moved above her, the weight of him. The way he'd groaned as if in pain and the way he'd suddenly shivered the length of his body, the muscles of his back quivering like a horse's flank under the touch of summer flies. The way he'd shrunk away from her afterwards, like sand through an hourglass.

Sarah hadn't shivered like Tom that night and she didn't for many nights afterwards until early one morning, when Tom was out on the hill, she'd discovered she could move herself in a way that Tom never had. Lying there on her own that morning, with the grey wash of the dawn seeping through the curtains, she'd made herself lighter. It had felt as if she was turning a cord within her, tighter and tighter, until eventually it broke inside her, releasing her thighs to clasp about her fingers as she fell from the height of her rising. As she'd fallen Sarah's blood had switched within her, flicking the wrong way down her arteries and veins before subsiding back, diminished with its return but still charged with the resonance of that sudden momentum. A slow burn dissipating across her pelvis and hips like the concentric ripples of a sinking stone, spreading and fading over the surface of a lake.

Sarah gasps. Lying alone once again, in her dark bedroom, she lets out a short, rasping gasp. The dogs in the yard below bark, their sounds muffled through the snow at the window. She'd wanted to conjure Tom. She'd wanted to salvage him from the depths of his missing with all her senses. And she had. He'd been here again, with her in their bed, looking down at her. But then as she'd lain beneath him his face had begun to change until it was no longer his she saw above her, but that of the captain's. The German captain's face, looking down at her, the snow melting in his hair as he removed his glasses to reveal those two red impressions, imprinted like shallow brandings either side of the bridge of his nose.

The coming of the snow made a choice for the whole valley that Albrecht had already made for himself and his men. They would not leave. They could not go anywhere. The Olchon was choked with snow, frozen closed. Even the distant view, had they been able to climb the hills, had gone, obscured behind low cloud and mist. It was as if his silent prayer had been answered and for once the weight of his own decision taken from his shoulders. It had even been Alex who'd suggested going out to help the farm women. So all he'd had to do was respond, respond to circumstance just as any good Wehrmacht officer should. That was why he'd gone to see the old woman afterwards. To ensure some kind of a working balance, an equilibrium in their shared and now forced isolation, for however long it might last.

The visits to the other farms by his men had gone well and he'd wanted to capitalise on this moment. Boredom; that, as ever, was the greatest danger. The patrol must not be allowed to get bored. So far they had all, he knew, relished this caesura in their war. None of them were in a hurry to return to the front. But soon they would get restless, ask questions of him. Especially the younger ones, Gernot, Otto and Steiner. So they must have more involvement, more work. This is why Albrecht made the choices he did.

He'd allocated them to each farm carefully, making quick

calculations of their characters. Sebald he'd sent to Maggie because he was closest to her age. He was also a medic and so had acquired the trustful, patient face of someone who'd listened to countless chronicles of pain. If the old woman could be won over by someone other than Albrecht himself, that might be enough.

The silent Otto he'd sent up to the simple woman on the top of the hill. The young soldier still carried a fragility about him and Albrecht felt that the woman, whom he'd been told had lost her only son early in the war, would recognise that fragility. He'd seen it before, a kinship of damage, a shared recognition of fractured souls. Although he suspected the woman couldn't read he still gave Otto a note explaining his presence. Even if she could read, Albrecht felt the boy's silence would communicate more to her than words ever would.

Alex he'd taken with him to Sarah's, while Gernot and Steiner he'd sent over to the other side of the valley to the middle-aged woman and the young mother. That had been a mistake. Their journey would be the hardest, through the deepest snow. They were the fittest in the patrol and that was partly why he'd sent them. He hadn't been too worried when he'd watched them leave. The middle-aged woman would present no attraction to them and he thought that neither of them, despite Steiner's actions on the hillside, had reached a point where a mother with young children would be in danger. They were, thank God, both relatively new to the war and so had some idea of moral dignity beyond any militaristic code. And these were British women. Had they been Slavs or Russians he might have thought again. Had he known the two soldiers would return excitedly reporting the existence of another woman in the valley, a young girl, he would certainly have thought again and probably would not have sent them at all. She was the daughter of the middle-aged woman. Somehow her mother had kept her hidden from them for these past two months. When they told Albrecht this he felt a rush of panic. What else had they kept hidden? They hadn't really been looking since that first night, but still, what else were these women keeping to themselves?

Despite their excitement at discovering Bethan, Gernot and Steiner assured Albrecht they'd carried out his orders in the manner he'd asked; with respect and humility. As genuine offers of assistance and not the actions of an occupying force. But still it was evident from their report of the girl, how Gernot had described her in the air with his hands and how Steiner spoke of her mother's worry, that their discovery complicated matters. What was more important to Albrecht right now, however, was the effect of this enterprise on all of them. They had all returned invigorated by the work they'd undertaken and by the contact they'd made. Even Otto's excursion to the top of the hill had been a success.

When Otto hadn't returned by the late afternoon Albrecht had started to worry. Perhaps the simple woman was insane too. Perhaps she'd wreaked her vengeance on the war upon Otto, recognising not, after all, his fragility but just the colour and nationality of his uniform. But when Sebald and Alex went to investigate they discovered Otto safe at the woman's table, eating a thick soup, a newly made fire crackling in the hearth beside him. Far from seeing her son's killer in the young German the woman had, it seemed, simply seen another son, a boy of her own boy's age appearing out of the snow and wind like a gift from some capricious god, who, having taken her warmth and security with one hand, had given her Otto with the other.

All of this together with his own experience at Sarah's

farm had sent Albrecht to Maggie, to meet once more like the leaders of two stand-off armies. This time, however, rather than negotiating the rules of engagement, he came offering a truce, a recipe for mutual survival through this sudden winter and, in a longer view, through what was left of this war.

At first Maggie had remained at her door, leaning against the frame with her arms folded while Albrecht spoke to her from the yard, the snow falling thickly over him, settling on his cap and shoulders. She'd even stayed there after he told her about the patrol's visits to the other women. 'Kind of you,' was all she'd said with a curt, tight-lipped nod of her head. There were steps up to her door. She was looking down at him. Albrecht, meanwhile, had shrunken against the wind and the cold, his hands clenched under his armpits. She was in the dominant position, in every way. Somehow he had to break through to her. With his men, if this was going to work at all, it had to look as natural as possible, a consequence of the vagaries of war. His own will and guiding hand must not be seen, not yet at least. But with Maggie honesty would be the only way forward, however much of a gamble his sudden openness might prove to be. He remembered Sarah's school certificate hanging on the wall at Upper Blaen; *Gambling is an unhealthy striving to gain something without giving proper return for it. It is a great evil, destructive of character, disastrous in its consequences.*

'I know where your husbands have gone, Mrs Jones,' he'd said simply, looking up at her through the falling snow from beneath the peak of his cap. 'And why they have gone.'

Maggie's expression didn't change. She'd just continued looking down at him, a face of stone. 'But I promise you,' he'd continued, trying the slightest of smiles, 'that I have no interest in drawing this information to the attention of my superiors or to any Reich authorities. We both know what they will do here if I did.' He coughed into his hand, a rattling, mucous cough, as if his confession had loosened the infection in his lungs. Maggie still didn't move. 'I understand that might sound like a threat,' Albrecht continued, 'but it isn't. I can assure you I want to see them here as little as you do. You see, Mrs Jones, none of us, myself or my men, are in any hurry to rejoin this war. Regardless of this,' he freed a gloved hand and opened his fist at the snow, 'it is no longer in our interest. So you and I, Mrs Jones, we are, in a way, in the same position.' He stamped his boots to try and warm his feet. 'Neither of us wants to see the Gestapo in this valley, but what is the point of surviving them if we do not survive this winter? That is why I have come to see you.'

Maggie looked over his head at the valley, so changed overnight. She knew in her bones this was set in; that this was no brief spell of cold. That they were in this now, this winter, this altered world, for a long time. Still looking over his head she'd eventually swung one shoulder back as if she herself were hinged to the door frame. 'You'd better come in then, hadn' you?' she'd said, walking on before him into the dark hallway. 'Stamp your boots on the step mind,' she called over her shoulder. 'I don't want you bringin' that snow in look.'

Inside the farmhouse, sitting at the same table where the women had first seen 'The Countryman's Diary' two months earlier, Albrecht told Maggie what he had not yet told his own patrol. That in his opinion, although this war appeared to be nearly over and although major operations might soon come to an end, the low-level guerrilla fighting, here and in Europe, would continue for some time. That the Nazis needed war, dissent of some kind, as a plant needs light and water. That the Reich would always need them in the army, as part of an occupying force somewhere. That despite this, for some reason, his commanding officers appeared to have forgotten him and his patrol. That he was pleased to be forgotten. That while the fighting in England continued he wanted to stay in this valley with his men, for as long as they could be of help and not a hindrance to Maggie and the others.

Other than his opinion on the guerrilla fighting, about which Alex and Sebald agreed, Albrecht had said none of this to his own men. As far as they and the rest of the patrol were concerned the mythical dispatch rider he'd mentioned in Sarah's kitchen that morning was a reality. Albrecht told them he'd met the motorcyclist at the mouth of the valley while he was out on one of his walks and that was when he'd taken the order sheet. The orders were clear, if surprising. Although their primary mission was already complete they were to remain in the area as a temporary observational outpost. They were to await further instructions.

Every word was a lie. There had been no dispatch rider. There had been no contact of any kind since they'd arrived in the valley. Studying his maps on the big kitchen table at The Court Albrecht suspected he knew why. Their position lay on the border of two command sectors. The commanders of each sector would be all too quick to shift responsibility for a nomadic patrol onto the other's shoulders. The army supply lines were stretched, they were fighting a desperate, defending nation. Winter had come upon them like a second attacking front. Any concerns they might have had about a patrol in their sector would have been drowned out in the noise and confusion of war. Albrecht and his men had inadvertently slipped off the stage of battle.

But what of the other map? The one he'd been sent here to look for? If the SS thought it important enough to form this patrol, to break with protocol and commandeer a Wehrmacht officer, then surely it was important enough for them to chase him up? But they hadn't. For a month now there had been nothing but silence despite Albrecht's regular listening. Because he had, after all, been awaiting further instructions. That much at least was true. But that was all he'd been doing. Waiting and listening, nothing more.

The morning he and Steiner climbed to the head of the valley they had, as they'd suspected, found a radio signal. Together they'd sat on two bilberry hummocks either side of the radio and listened as fragments of the world beyond came to them out of the cold mountain air. Snatches of orders, information, captains reporting to colonels reporting to generals. As Steiner tuned through the frequencies they'd heard the war again. Gunfire, mortar explosions, even once the moans of an injured man faint in the background. When he'd switched frequencies they'd heard music too. Classical, big band, swing and even some jazz. 'Negro music,' Steiner had said with distaste, holding one earpiece to the side of his head and frowning.

They also heard the news. Faintly, from far away in English on the BBC and then stronger and louder in German on what Albrecht presumed was the new services propaganda station. The two voices gave very different pictures of what was happening in the heart of England. They both agreed on one point, however. London was still standing, as Albrecht knew she would be. She was surrounded, her supply lines cut off, but she was still British. But now there was a second offensive on Birmingham too, a double-pronged attack on England's two major cities. According to the German station, its news declared in declamatory style, the Japanese were also making further advances in the Pacific. Meanwhile lost territory in North Africa and the Western

Desert was being reclaimed by bolstered Italian and German forces. The Allied armies were scattered and stretched. The Axis alliance was on the verge of victory. But still the war was grinding on.

After the silence of the valley, its deep solitude of centuries, the radio was a sudden and awful reminder of where they'd come from and, for Albrecht, of what they must avoid. It also reminded him of exactly who they were: two invading soldiers living in a stolen house watching over a group of frightened farm women. And that is why they'd just listened that morning. Albrecht did not order Steiner to transmit anything. At that point there had been nothing to report beyond the missing men anyway, but even if there had, Albrecht would have ordered silence instead. It was then, after tuning into the world beyond, as they'd descended back into the isolation of the valley that Albrecht began lying to his own men, before he'd even spoken to any of them.

To Maggie in her kitchen, however, he was more honest than he had been for years. Help, that is both what he was offering and asking of her. At first she'd stuck to her original position. She couldn't supply them with anything. None of them could. That would be collaboration. But gradually Albrecht had explained that collaboration was not what he was asking for. His men would simply work for her and the others. To help them through the winter with the jobs that Maggie knew all too well they would never cope with on their own. All he asked was that the patrol be allowed to take back The Court's original flock, so they might have some extra meat and so the women's own flocks would be more manageable. Alex could help Maggie with the cows and her horses. 'Horses,' he'd explained, 'are in Alex's blood.' Sebald, meanwhile, could offer his medical expertise while the others could offer their energy, their bodies. He was laying himself and his men at her disposal. To get them all through this difficult time while they waited for the world to right itself again, to find its balance.

At some point in that visit, as Albrecht talked to her across her own table, Maggie had glimpsed the man behind the uniform. She'd also seen a man who knew what was happening in the world beyond the valley. Finally, as he'd explained the complexity and seriousness of the situation, quoting from directives in his invasion handbook and showing her a poster he'd been issued with in Oxford, she'd recognised the man who might just keep them all alive. For this reason the next day, after another early morning snowfall, Albrecht, Alex and Gernot were allowed to begin driving what elements of The Court's original flock they could still find back to The Court's lower fields, where Sebald was already smashing the ice in the troughs and filling the mangers with Reg's stored hay.

Sarah didn't understand how Maggie could have given in so easily. With the men just two months gone. With the war still being fought, with her own sons in the army. She said as much when all four women met that same day in Mary's front room. Maggie sat in the armchair by the fire, her skin damp from both the snow and the exertion of her walk to Mary's. It had been difficult for her to cross the valley. The usual paths were no more than vague depressions in the thickening carpet of white. And under the snow was ice. In all her years in the valley it was the worst she'd seen. 'Well, least it's not a greenun,' she'd panted to Sarah again over her shoulder as they'd made their way up through the trees on the other side of the river. But there was no way she wouldn't have come. The soldiers had begun clearing the paths and driving the sheep across early that morning. It was important to Maggie they all agreed on what was happening. Which they didn't.

'It's treason, Maggie, that's what it is,' Mary said, speaking with the authority of a mother whose long distant son had served in army Intelligence. 'An' it's a sin too. I pray for you, I really do, Maggie.'

'I know why you done this,' Sarah said, eager to avoid Mary's preaching. 'But there's no need for it. We don't need their help. We've been gettin' on just fine, haven't we?'

'Maybe you have, bach,' Maggie replied, 'but I haven't. I'm done in an' we all will be soon enough with this upon us.' She looked at the window, at the ice formed on both sides of its pane. 'An' anyway, if we hadn't taken Reg's flock in the first place, then those sheep would be theirs as it is.'

'You know that's not the point,' Sarah said. '*Nothing which would be of the slightest help to the enemy.*' She raised her eyebrows towards Mary's 'Stand Fast' leaflet tucked into the edge of the mirror above the fire.

'What will Constable Evans say?' Menna said quietly. Maggie shot her a look before addressing Sarah again.

'You want to tell me about advice in leaflets, bach? Then how's this for some advice?' She reached into the pocket of her cardigan and pulled out the rolled poster Albrecht had given her. Taking her glasses from the other pocket she flattened the piece of paper over her lap, lowered her head and read in a slow, careful voice.

'"If the population initiates active operations *after* the completed conquest of a locality, or in places *behind* the fighting front, the inhabitants involved in the fighting will be regarded as armed insurgents. When taking hostages, those persons should if possible be selected in whom the *active* enemy elements have an interest."'

Maggie looked up at the faces of the three women.

'He knows about William an' the others, see,' she said. 'He isn't stupid. So those *persons* are us isn't it? Now, if they wants to stay here an' carry on with a bit of farming 'stead of going off an' wagging their tongues to their superiors, I reckon that's fine by me. And if they want to help us through this,' she waved a hand at the frozen window, 'that's fine too. Because if they don't, I reckon it's the Germans'll be coming for us, never mind no Constable Evans. And not ones like this lot either.'

Sarah looked into the fire. Maggie was jumping ahead again, as if she knew what their husbands were doing, where they were. 'But William an' the rest,' she said, still staring into the flames, 'we don't know what they're doing. I mean, that book, we don't . . .'

'We don't know nothing, bach,' Maggie interrupted, her face set hard again, 'we don't know nothing about anything. But he does, see. He does. They got a radio, haven't they?' Her face softened, sagging under her age and the weight of the moment. 'So he knows. He knows what's going on out there, and believe me, bach, you don't want to hear the half of it.'

Over the rest of that winter, the longest and harshest any of them had ever known, the women's lives in the valley resembled one of the landscape watercolours Sarah used to watch the poet paint down by the two streams of the old monastery. They were the same as they'd always been and yet were also entirely different; recognisable as their lives, but dramatically altered at the edges. Their days existed of well-worn routines of feeding, fixing, cutting, making, all turning around many of the same concerns and chores they always had. And yet each day was also another unreal awakening into a world they didn't know.

Over the weeks following Albrecht's visit to Maggie the patrol managed to gather the rest of The Court's flock from the other farms, although many were lost up on the higher reaches of the hills. With this source of fresh meat along with the provisions they'd found in the house and their own dwindling supplies, they remained self-sufficient within the valley. Now and then they assisted the women, trying to keep certain pathways and tracks clear, drying and cutting wood when stocks became low. Alex regularly helped Maggie with the feeding and handling of her cob mare and foal and sometimes with the early milking of her cows, the only source of milk in the valley. In return she'd let him take back a jug of fresh milk which he'd have boiling on the range in The Court as the others began to wake. Gernot took on the cooking responsibilities while, under Alex's guidance, Steiner helped manage the flock. Sebald began to take an interest in the vegetable garden, carefully clearing the blanket of snow and tipping hot water over the frozen soil to uproot the parsnips and carrots, hard as steel. Otto helped Edith move down to Maggie's, clearing a path from The Gaer and then carrying her battered leather case behind her as she slowly picked her way down the hill muffled against the cold with one of Roderick's old jumpers wrapped about her head.

The women, meanwhile, all found their own ways of coping with the isolation, fear and missing their husbands. Mary increasingly found solace in the Bible, reading and re-reading the Book of Job. She took it upon herself to fill the vacuum left by the absence of Reverend Davies, reading to the others in a voice not her own when they came to her front room on a Sunday; 'Naked came I out of my mother's womb, and naked shall I return hither: the Lord gave, and the Lord hath taken away; blessed be the Lord.' She focused her worries where she could see them, on Bethan, rather than upon Hywel or her sons, both of whom she'd had no word of since the invasion.

Bethan herself kept up a sullen doggedness, spending most of her time helping Menna with her two children. She missed her father badly and mistook her mother's distractions as a lack of love for her husband. She was painfully aware of her youth, precious and wasting inside her, and felt increasingly suffocated by the other women, by the whining and crying of Menna's two children. Before the winter she'd found some rare moments of solitude riding her pony through the sheep tracks up on the hills. The snow had put a stop to that and now, on the rare occasions when she could sneak away from her mother and Menna, she crossed the valley instead, walking beside the hedges to hide her tracks, and climbed the facing slope, skirting around to higher ground above The Court. From here, crouching behind a thorn tree, she'd spy on the Germans. When she saw one of them, either through The Court's large back windows or when they came outside, she'd try out curses under her breath; 'Fritz bastard, Nazi scum, fucking fascists,' and once even the old-fashioned 'dirty Hun' she'd heard her father mutter when listening to reports of the bombing of Swansea on Maggie's radio. None of her curses was charged with real venom and by the third or fourth time she'd crouched behind the thorn tree they had faded to a half-silent instinctive chant, dislocated from any meaning and increasingly obscured by her growing fascination with these men, some of them young, as young as her perhaps, who washed, talked, pissed and yawned below her. One of them, particularly, had begun to draw her attention beyond mere curiosity or interest. There was something about his laugh, so natural, so open, that it seemed to belong to another time, long before this war. Bethan felt herself lighten every time she heard it and she often waited until she'd caught a glimpse of Gernot before making her way back to the other side of the valley.

Maggie worked on, faithful to the two standards of her new existence: to continue as they always had and to keep the other women in the valley alive, both physically and mentally. She missed William more each day and saw him in every nook and corner of the farm they'd shared for over thirty years. She saw him in the loose slates he'd never fixed, in the snow collected like piled white books on the iron cleats of the silent tractor, in the space on the dresser where his pipe and folded pocket knife once lay, waiting for his return from the fields at the end of the day. She saw him most of all though in the young colt, not yet a year old, they'd foaled together at the end of last summer.

Maggie never spoke of the depth of her grief to any of the others and she only ever spoke to William when she was alone with the mare and her foal in the cramped stable in the corner of the yard. Standing in the warmth of this stable, icicles hanging from the guttering above the half-door, she'd stroke the foal's new mane as his mother pulled and chewed from the rack of fresh hay.

'Comin' up lovely, isn't he, Will?' she'd say under her breath as she ran her hand over the swirls of hair above the colt's shoulders. 'Going to be a beaut mun. A good colt for us, Will. Imagine that, eh? Running a yearlin' like this come the summer.'

And it was only then, when she thought of the days and seasons to come that she would have to endure without her husband, that Maggie cried. Silently and to herself while the mare tore at the hay and the colt nuzzled her pocket for a treat of oats, she shed private tears. For all the years they'd lived together, for the sons they'd raised, for the son they'd lost and the way their shared lives had been extinguished overnight, so suddenly and certainly by a faraway war that had only now, at the very end, come calling at their door.

Sarah did not cry to herself like Maggie because, unlike the older woman, Sarah still believed. She believed that even if what 'The Countryman's Diary' suggested was true, the men were still coming back, one day. This is why, of all the women, Sarah resisted the assistance of the patrol the most. Since the morning of the first snowfall she'd been especially wary of Albrecht and wanted no more contact with him and his men than was absolutely necessary. Once they'd helped her clear a path down to her lower fields she'd had little need of any further help anyway. But even if she had, she'd rather have coped on her own despite the harshness of the winter, which became so cold she often couldn't go into the parts of Upper Blaen unreached by the warmth of the fire without layering herself with her and Tom's coats. Every morning she woke with a headache brought on by the bitter nights and she spent two whole afternoons filling the gaps in the larder wall with mud, scraped up from down by the stream below. It was too late for most of the vegetables stored there. The potatoes had blackened in the frost and when she sliced an onion its layers were seamed with crystals of ice. She sunk into routine, hibernating the parts of herself unnecessary for the day-to-day survival of her mind and body. She worked hard, fixing, mending and feeding as best she could the chickens, the pig, the sheep. Every day she threw Bess larger armfuls of hay than she should, determined to reverse the shedding of the pony's flesh that had left her ribs showing sharper each morning through her ragged coat. In this way Sarah kept up a solid resistance to the siege of snow and ice that pressed upon her as if to drown her, as it had already a third of her flock. In between her chores she wrote to Tom in the back of their accounts book, held their wedding photograph trying to remember, and in her evenings alone, when she felt she could spare the oil and wicks for the lamp, she read, either from the Bible or from the few books that Mrs Thomas had given her when she left school: *The Mill on the Floss*, *Jane Eyre*, *Great Expectations*, *The Mayor of Casterbridge*.

Although she vaguely remembered the brush strokes of these stories she read them as if for the first time. The night after she read of Henchard selling his wife in *The Mayor of Casterbridge* she dreamt that Tom was selling her at market. A crowd of German soldiers were raising their hands and nodding in response to the auctioneer's rhythmical chant. She'd woken in a cold sweat to find the tether at her neck was just the sheet wrapped about her throat, but that the anger she'd dreamt was real, still burning in her chest and flushing over her cheeks.

It was a bleak Christmas. In the absence of Reverend Davies, on Christmas morning the women met at Maggie's, where Mary read to them from the Gospels of Matthew and Luke, giving special emphasis to the angel's visit to the shepherds and glancing at Maggie when she read, 'Then was Jesus led up of the Spirit into the wilderness to be tempted by the devil.' They sang carols around the fire and Maggie uncorked the stone flagons of last year's cider that William kept under the pig-killing bench in their larder. Edith didn't speak much, Christmas always being when her talking turned more to Roderick than those who were with her, but she sang the loudest, asking for 'the Bread of Heaven' so strong and sure that it made Mary shake her head and Bethan laugh out loud. Mary had brought some wheat wine and for the first year, despite her giggling at Edith, she let Bethan take a glass. Maggie gave them all a small wrapped parcel of cheese she'd made that week, and for Menna's two children some of her own boys' soft toys that she'd kept all these years.

Sarah found herself often looking out of Maggie's front window, just as she had on that first morning after the men's going. Again, she half-expected to see the Germans coming into the yard, but this time in the way the poet's Germans had come over the trenches into no-man's-land on Christmas day 1914; offering presents, cigarettes and company rather than occupation and fear. But they never came. The week before, Gernot and Steiner had called at all their houses to give them wreaths they'd made from holly, evergreen leaves and long strands of ivy. Only Maggie and Menna had hung them on their doors but now Sarah wished she had too. Somehow she'd thought she'd see them on this morning, and somehow, it being Christmas, that it would have been all right when she did. But they stayed away and for Christmas Day the valley remained another kind of no-man's-land, vacated of their husbands and filled with nothing but the ghosts of their memories haunting the lanes, fields and beds they'd once shared with their wives.

The winter clung on, stubborn and freezing into the new year. For all of them, the women and the patrol, the silence it brought was the worst. Not the silence of the valley itself, of the stilled brook, of an empty field under heavy snow, but the silence of beyond the valley, the silence of the rest of the world.

By this stage of the war Albrecht, Alex and Sebald had no one left to write to, but for the younger three soldiers this was not the case. For Otto it was his mother in Hamburg, for Steiner and Gernot their parents, school friends and sweethearts back home. No army postal service could have reached them in the valley, even if they'd known they were there, and it was futile trying to free the staff car or the motorbike to ride into any of the surrounding towns. So they lived on, deprived of the distant voices that had, at irregular intervals, kept them connected with their homes.

For the women too there had been no mail since a week or so after the invasion. Mary had family over the hill down in Hay-on-Wye, Menna a sister and cousins in the mining valleys, and all of them except Sarah had brothers, sons, uncles in the war. But there was no word from any of them and every morning they woke to nothing more than the snow's blank page, written across with a filigree of bird prints, a daily reminder of the letters that remained unwritten and unsent from the world beyond.

Apart from the occasional red glow in the night sky from the steel works over in the mining valleys (working for whom, the British government or the Germans, they didn't know) the patrol's radio remained the valley's only connection with the rest of the country. Despite the difficulty of climbing through the snow Albrecht and Steiner kept up regular walks to higher ground, searching for a signal and the news transmissions which would tell them how the war was turning without them.

In this way Albrecht witnessed the gradual ending of the war; the violence, the disruption of the conflict that had shaped their lives for the last five years translated into a montage of reports, speeches and announcements, all played out against the silence and stillness of the winter mountains. When the German announcer read out the impossibly large figures of sunk merchant ships Albrecht was studying a striking red moss he'd uncovered with the toe of his boot. When the fainter voice of the BBC condemned the cowardly onslaught of V1 and V2 rockets upon London, he was holding a kestrel's frozen feather in the palm of his hand, staring intently into its intricate frosted structure. When, two weeks later, the German service described how Nelson's Column had been sliced in two and tipped onto the loading platforms of a transport lorry to be taken as a trophy back to Berlin, Albrecht was watching the intimate torture of an insect, impaled by a shrike on the thorns of a nearby bush. And when he listened, two weeks later again, to the description of the Führer's surprise visit to London, he had, once more, been slipping fragile sheaths of ice from the blades of coarse grass at his feet. He let the ice melt in his hand as he listened to the announcer describe how Hitler had stood on Parliament Hill promising 'to bring peace at last to this nation, misguided for so long by the corrupt democracy that once sat in those shattered buildings beneath us'.

And yet the ever fainter voice of the BBC still broadcast, hinting that perhaps the optimism of the German reports was not entirely true, that the whole country was not yet under the Nazi's iron heel. The BBC did admit, however, that Churchill had, along with many of his Cabinet, followed King George and sailed for Canada. Despite assurances that he would die in his bunker at Neasden, armed with just a pistol and his motto, 'You can always take one with you', the Prime Minister had left these shores 'to better continue the fight against the evil of fascism', until that day when he would return 'to rout the invaders from our land'.

Through it all, over those fragmented weeks of listening to the fall of London, Albrecht became acutely aware of the multitude of hinges in events that had brought about this unfolding present. Of how easily, given the alternative tipping of countless moments of chance, he could have found himself sitting on another hillside, somewhere else, listening to a parallel description of the fall of Berlin. Had Stalin not boarded his train and abandoned Moscow; had the British arctic convoys been successful in supplying what was left of the confused Russian defence; had America answered Churchill's call sooner; had the Führer himself not overseen the resurrection of the Luftwaffe.

And even after all of these factors had played into the war's script, still it could have been so different. What if the Allies' attempted invasion of mainland Europe had not been delayed by bad weather? If their giant floating harbours had not listed and sunk? If their floating Shermans had made it to shore and broken the beachheads, destroying the bunkers in which he and the others had crouched. What then? Would they have rolled back the relentless Nazi advance?

One piece of information repeated within his mind more than any other. Something he'd been told by one of the few contacts he still had in Wehrmacht Intelligence. That maybe all this, a German victory, the end of the war, was down to one man. Not a general or a chief-of-staff, but a long-term sleeper agent who'd discovered the Allies' elaborate deception plans; a massive fake army of inflatable tanks, cardboard bombers and plywood landing craft stationed at Dover facing Calais. A dummy invasion force, complete with rows of speakers broadcasting the sound of a mobilising army across the narrowest point of the channel. It had almost worked. The elite Case 3 Panzer divisions had been ordered to remain in Calais. Thousands of crack SS and Wehrmacht troops poured into the area to await the false invasion. But then one man, who had for the past ten years gone about his business as a bank clerk in Brighton, discovered indisputable proof of the charade and broadcast the truth to Berlin just moments before the British picked up his signal and broke down the door of his bedsit.

The rest was already history. The Case 3 divisions and the

infantry reinforcements were released from their positions in Calais and were waiting in Normandy on that overcast morning when a choppy, truculent sea offered up so many men to the slaughter. The thought that one man might have made this possible and everything that had happened since, even his own situation, huddled under a ledge on a barren winter hillside, a pair of headphones clamped to his ears, both numbed and excited Albrecht to the core.

The excursions to higher ground were not just an opportunity for Albrecht to furnish himself with as much information as possible. They were also a chance for him to try and get closer to Steiner, to tune into the younger soldier's emotional frequency just as he tuned into the voices of the airwaves. Steiner was the only direct witness of Albrecht's reluctance to make contact with any of the surrounding command units. He was also the one member of the patrol whom Albrecht anticipated would be most resistant to his plans. Steiner was more serious than Gernot and less damaged than Otto. Unlike Sebald and Alex he'd seen relatively little fighting. The death of his sister in a British air raid, meanwhile, still burned within him and he had not, as yet, been in the war for long enough to have his enthusiasm for the causes of National Socialism blunted. Out of all of them Steiner had the least to lose from re-joining the war, and it was this that worried Albrecht. As such, Albrecht was aware he needed a more intimate bond with the boy, so as to better prepare the ground for when the subsiding winter meant he'd have to reveal his intentions to the rest of the patrol. So when they weren't listening to the radio Albrecht encouraged Steiner to talk instead. At first he was hesitant, unused to such informality with a commanding officer. But he soon opened up, telling Albrecht more about his family in Hamburg. Both his parents were teachers, his father of maths, his mother of French. He showed Albrecht photographs of them, drawing them, curled and weatherbeaten from his wallet. One was of the whole family in a garden. Steiner was there, his young man's face just traceable under the last years of his boyhood puppy fat. His sisters flanked him, Hilda with dark hair and Margaret with blonde. His mother stood behind them, a hand on each of her daughters' shoulders. All three children wore the uniform of the Hitler Youth.

As the radio reports became more optimistic, as London fell to both the winter and the German advance, Steiner began to speak more of his plans for after the war. He wanted to go to university and study sound engineering. And then he wanted to work in film. That was the future of sound, he told Albrecht, blowing into his gloved hands to warm his fingers, film sound. After the war he would travel the world with a film unit, sending their newsreels and films, all with detailed, intricate soundtracks, back to Germany from the far reaches of the Empire of the Third Reich.

In return, although Albrecht said nothing of his future, he did share glimpses of his past. He told Steiner about his time at university studying medieval history and literature; how he had come to Oxford before the war to study for a doctorate and even about the subject of his thesis, the thirteenth-century Ebstorf World Map, destroyed just last year in an air raid. His mention of the air raid was purposeful, leading Steiner on to speak again of his killed sister. Albrecht listened and then shared his own stories of loss, telling Steiner how in one night both his parents and his fiancée, Ebbe, had been killed in the same raid over Dresden just months before the renewed Luftwaffe fought back the British bombers.

Albrecht had lost his only photograph of Ebbe somewhere on the Russian Front so he described her to Steiner instead, recalling her delicate bones, 'like the hollow bones of a bird', her sallow skin, her jet-black hair cut short in the modern style. Closing his eyes he even described the curious half-twist of her smiling lip that had so caught his attention in the lecture hall at the beginning of his first year. Her name, he told Steiner, came from Old German. It meant the returning of the tide. And that is what he'd written to her in his last letter. That like her name, one day he would return to her. That after ebbing away on the retreating current of the war for so long, he would return, rushing back to her like the sudden tides of the flat Friesian coast they'd once run away from, holding hands on a summer's day before the war. But he had not. He had not returned and she had died without him, burnt alive by a British incendiary bomb.

Having Steiner close at hand also meant Albrecht was able to dampen the boy's enthusiasm in response to the increasingly triumphal German broadcasts. By retuning the radio to the faint transmission of the BBC he could counter the German claims with the British reports, well known among German soldiers to have a history of being closer to the truth. Albrecht still remembered when it was pointed out to him, early in the war, that the Nazi's massive tallies of sunk Allied shipping actually outstripped all the ships ever built in the world. Nodding his head grimly throughout the BBC reports, he'd translate for Steiner, carefully undermining the previous German transmission, allowing them some degree of credibility but always leaving the picture several shades bleaker than at first painted. Again he was thankful no one else in the patrol spoke English.

'That's it!' Steiner had exclaimed when they heard the report of Hitler's visit to Parliament Hill in London. 'It's over. We've won. The war's over.'

'No,' Albrecht had said, placing a hand on his shoulder. 'Not quite. They haven't said that yet. There's been no surrender. London has fallen, that's good, but it isn't over yet.' Steiner had looked at him, failing to understand his pessimism. He knew that older soldiers like Albrecht had been waiting for this day for years. 'Soon though,' Albrecht had continued, giving Steiner's shoulder a tap. 'Soon, for sure.'

What Albrecht said was true. There had been no official British surrender. There was still fighting in the Far East and new unrest in Russia. America was, in theory, still in the war, although now impossibly stretched on all fronts and under siege from a growing band of reinvigorated isolationists at home. The Führer's visit to London was strange too. Why no description of Wehrmacht divisions marching up the Mall? Hitler addressing the world from outside Number 10 Downing Street? Could it be that only certain areas of the city could be guaranteed as safe? That the lightning visit was, in fact, a desperate measure in an ongoing war of propaganda? But Steiner was also right. The war would, officially at least, soon be over and what would Albrecht do then?

In the end both the thawing of the winter and Sebald's intuition of Albrecht's intentions forced his hand. Towards the middle of February they woke to the sound of dripping water. The temperature had risen above zero for the first time in months and the icicles outside their windows were melting. It was like waking from a long dream. For the past three months all of them had settled into the winter and The Court. Alex had thrived, the contact with animals and with Maggie reviving a part of him long numbed by the war. Gernot, meanwhile had proved ever more resourceful and inventive in the kitchen. Both he and Steiner had asked Albrecht for some English instruction which Albrecht had given them. Their interest was, no doubt, fuelled by their chaste glimpses of Bethan, which always provoked a bout of friendly rivalry and banter between the two younger soldiers. Albrecht was more than happy to encourage their distant admiration of the farm girl, especially in Gernot, in whom he'd recognised a growing infatuation with Bethan beyond a young man's bravado. Otto had begun to speak again.

Sebald, meanwhile, had visibly softened. The years of patching bits of men's flesh together under fire had taken their toll and he'd arrived in the valley as tightly wound as a spring coil. But over that winter, something loosened inside him. A keen amateur artist before the war, he began making sketches of the views around them and even of the other members in the patrol. It was as he was sketching Albrecht while he read beside the fire on the evening before the beginning of the thaw that Sebald first gave an indication that he might approve of Albrecht's as yet unspoken plans.

'Did I ever tell you about Hermann?' Sebald said distractedly, not looking up from his sketch book.

Albrecht paused in his reading. They were the only ones in the room. Gernot was whistling in the kitchen, Otto was on sentry duty and Alex and Steiner were upstairs. 'Hermann?' he said. 'No, I don't think you did.'

'A doctor I knew at the start of the war. Well, I only met him a few times really, taking men back to a château we were using as a holding hospital.' He paused, frowning over a patch of shading. 'But I got on with him. Look back down, will you?' Albrecht did what he said, looking back down at the book, an English biography of the poet Walter Savage Landor, the stamp of the Bodleian Library faint inside its cover.

'We used to share a quick smoke while our boys were transferred. I'd give him the low-down on them, which ones would be going home.' He stopped sketching and looked up from his pad. 'I should have known then, I suppose. Every time I said that, "Seven tickets home in this lot, Hermann," that kind of thing, he'd look, well, terrible. Sick.'

'Should have known what?' Albrecht asked, looking up at Sebald.

Sebald went back to his sketching. 'He was being asked to kill them.'

'Who?'

'Those boys with the home ticket wounds. Hermann had been ordered to kill them. Bad for morale, apparently, seeing young men with no legs on Potsdamer. Hardly the Party's ideal of Blitzkrieg, is it?'

'I don't understand; how do you know this?'

'It was all in his note,' Sebald said, licking his thumb to smudge the background of his sketch. 'He cut his own throat.'

'Hermann?'

'Yes. He was a good soldier, you see. Followed orders. But he was a good doctor too. Injecting young men with lethal doses of morphine, well, he couldn't do that. So he killed himself instead.'

'Cut his throat, you say?'

'Yes. I never understood that either.'

'Were other doctors ordered to kill wounded men?'

'Oh yes. But not many of them did. And not for long. The order was recalled. If only Hermann had waited. But he didn't.'

Albrecht tried to catch Sebald's eye, but he was still sketching. He didn't know why he was telling him this.

'You think he was wrong?' Albrecht eventually asked.

Sebald glanced up from his pad. 'Hermann? No, he was right, of course he was. But there were other ways around that order. You know how it is. There always are.' He went back to his sketch again but carried on speaking. 'His duty was to his patients. They were worse off without him. He should have thought of them over himself.'

'But he was thinking of them, wasn't he?'

Sebald looked directly at Albrecht, but into his eyes, not merely at his face as he had done for his drawing. 'No,' he said. 'He saved himself. He wasn't saving them. Just himself.'

The next day the thaw gathered pace. The valley was both shrinking and expanding about them, the river swollen and the lanes flowing with water. It was a clear day, the sun burning warm in a blue sky. Albrecht knew he could wait no longer. That evening, bolstered by what he thought to be Sebald's implicit approval, he gathered the whole patrol in The Court's front room and told them.

In the end it was easier than he'd expected. He'd failed to appreciate how over the last three months the men under his command had come to trust him in a way he would never understand. He had also misjudged the effect upon all of them of time away from the war. No gunfire for months. No dugout sleeping, no crouching over your haunches emptying your bowels under mortar fire. And most importantly, no fear. No expectant death. Life had returned to them, the prospect of a continuing life after the war, and it was Albrecht who'd led them to this perspective. It was like a drug and having tasted this hope, this expansion of the self through the years ahead, none of them was willing to give it up. None of them, except Steiner, whose voice was the first to break the silence in the room following Albrecht's announcement. Made more confident by their conversations on the hillside, the young soldier spoke to Albrecht with a surprising directness.

'But wouldn't that make us absent without leave, sir? That's a court martial offence.' The other men all turned to look at Steiner, flickers of tension passing at their temples. Albrecht could sense their unspoken willingness to go along with his plans, but Steiner's question was enough to plant a seed of uncertainty. An anxiety that they were disobeying a higher authority that would, one day, have its vengeance upon them. Albrecht tried to ease these worries, casting his and now what he hoped to be their shared intentions in the most innocent of lights.

'I am not,' he told them as they sat round The Court's large table, 'talking about disobeying orders of any kind. As you all know we have completed our mission here, and completed it well. No doubt at some point because of this Western Headquarters will come looking for us soon enough. But until then all I am proposing is that we do not draw unnecessary attention to our presence here.'

He paused to cough into his hand, as if to demonstrate the strain and duress through which all of them had already put their bodies.

'We have fought well in this war, all of us.' He looked at Steiner, trying to tell him with his eyes as well as his words that he need not feel any guilt. 'But now the war has changed. It is ending. A German victory is certain. Because of this I should tell you I feel my duty, too, has changed.' He glanced at Sebald but the medic was looking down at the table, arms folded. Had he misjudged their conversation the previous night? Even if he had it was too late now. 'My duty is to you now,' Albrecht continued. 'Not towards victory. We will still be vigilant, of course, but we will not be reckless. I truly believe it is in Germany's greater interest that all of you return home to your families, your hopes, unharmed and alive.' He looked at Steiner again and was met by the frowning young soldier's face, intent upon his every word. 'They say London has fallen, but there are other cities. These people have their backs against the wall. I think we all know it will take longer than they say. I also know that every one of you, if you had to, would still fight, and fight well, if it was asked of you. But as yet, no one has asked you and until they do I see no reason why any of you should risk everything now, when we are so close and you have already given so much.'

He paused, allowing his last words to hang in the air.

'If any man does want to rejoin the regiment,' he concluded, sitting back in his chair, 'that is, of course, his right and he would have my blessing. All I would ask is that he do so at no risk to the other members of this patrol.'

Albrecht had no idea how this could be done but he felt it had to be said. That he had to leave a door apparently open, even if they all knew what he asked was impossible. The offer was unnecessary anyway. At the end of his speech Steiner had looked towards Gernot. The two of them had become close over the last months. Steiner valued this friendship, and admired Gernot's lighter ease with the world. He looked up to him in many ways, and that was why, when Gernot gave the slightest of indications to Steiner that he agreed with his Captain, Albrecht knew it would be all right. Gernot's deepening interest in Bethan meant any concerns he might have about Albrecht's intentions were eclipsed by more powerful desires. He would not leave the valley now unless he had to. And if Gernot stayed, so would Steiner.

One by one, with the slightest of nods, each man agreed to what Albrecht had proposed. There was just one condition, voiced by Gernot.

'What about our letters, sir?' Their letters. The letters they had written over the long nights of the winter. Of course they would want them posted, so their families and loved ones might know they were safe, that they had survived the invasion and would be coming home soon.

Albrecht nodded, smiling at Gernot. 'Don't worry about them,' he said. 'I'll send them myself.'

And that was why two mornings later, when the snow had reduced to uneven patches on the valley's slopes and ragged strips skirting the fields, Albrecht kick-started the motorbike and rode down the lane towards the railway station at Pandy. It made sense for him to be the one to take the letters. As an officer he was less likely to be stopped or questioned, he was the only fluent English speaker and because the patrol's silence was his initiative, it somehow seemed apt that as a concession to this, he be the bearer of their voices to the outside world.

Albrecht was willing to accept the responsibility but only because he had no intention of delivering the letters. To him, it was madness. What was more important? These men's families being informed of their safety or that safety being ensured by their silence? He still went through the routine of censoring the letters, omitting any mention of their position or whereabouts, but purely for the sake of the younger soldiers for whom, he realised, it was vital they believe their words were going home even if they weren't.

At first he'd intended to ride the motorbike just far enough for its engine to no longer be heard at The Court, until he was out of sight and sound of the patrol. But the sensation of its speed, of movement after so many days of stillness, caught him unawares. It was another bright day, sudden on the senses. His taste and smell, although still blunted, were both improving and he could just make out the steeliness of the air as it rushed past him. Snowdrops were budding in the banks of the hedgerows and the steep sides of the valley were baring their nerves, the brooks and streams swollen white with the thawing snow and ice. All of it got the better of Albrecht and he rode further than he'd planned, beyond the mouth of the valley and on down the narrow lane towards Llanvoy.

Albrecht had already stopped the bike and was about to dismount when he saw a young man cycling up the lane towards him. A brief wave of panic overtook him. This was the first person outside the patrol and the farm women he'd seen in over three months. There was no one else around, not even a house or farm in sight. A story from his days in Holland at the start of the war came back to him, about a cyclist in the Dutch resistance whose quickness of drawing and firing his pistol from the saddle was so feared that soldiers took cover and cocked their rifles whenever a lone man on a bicycle approached. But then Albrecht remembered where he was, who he was meant to be. He resisted the urge to twist the throttle and ride away and stayed put, the motorbike's engine thrumming under him as the young man leant over his handlebars to tackle the gradient of the slope.

'Stop, please.' The order felt strange, unfamiliar on Albrecht's tongue.

The man was almost level with him and clearly hadn't been intending to even pause as he passed him. Now he pulled up, panting from the effort of the hill behind.

'Your papers?'

The young man took off a glove and pulled a booklet from the inside pocket of his jacket. He was in his early twenties, if that. A sullen look to him, blond hair, clean shaven, small and thin.

'Where are you going?' Albrecht asked, inspecting the pages of the booklet.

'Up the Olchon,' the man replied. 'Got some letters t'deliver.'

'You are a postman?' Albrecht said, looking at his jacket, the dirt under his nails, his rough cord trousers and worker's boots.

'No.' He looked at Albrecht for the first time. 'Post Office has a backlog from the winter. Said I'd help out.'

'Let me see them,' Albrecht said, passing back the booklet and holding out his hand.

The man drew out a thin bundle of letters from another pocket and gave them to Albrecht. Albrecht untied the string and leafed through the envelopes, reading the addresses. *Hywel and Mary Griffiths. William and Margaret Jones. Tom and Sarah Lewis.*

Taking a pen from his own pocket he wrote across the front of each envelope, as clearly as he could. *Deceased. Return to Sender.* He handed them back to the young man who read what Albrecht had written then looked back up at him, his sullen expression slipping.

'There is no one left in that valley,' Albrecht said simply. 'Tell the postmaster he needn't send any more letters there.'

The man looked at Albrecht, straight in the face, a muscle twitching at his jaw. For a second it seemed as if he might speak, but he didn't. Slipping the letters back into his jacket, he put on his glove and slowly, still looking at Albrecht, turned his bicycle to free-wheel back down the lane. Albrecht watched as the young man's back shrunk down the hill and around the corner of the lane. His heart was beating hard. It was the right thing to have done. By killing the women he had saved them. By inscribing death across their names he had given them life. This is what he told himself as he dismounted the motorbike, crouched by the side of the lane and put a match to the corner of his own men's letters, turning

214

the bundle slowly in the air until he felt the heat of the flames against his hand. He dropped the sheaves of paper, still burning, into the long grass. A light wind rose up the lane. Albrecht stood and watched as it lifted the ashes of his men's words, printing them across the unthawed patches of snow.

George cycled back down the lanes, his mind spinning as fast as the wheels of his bicycle. *Deceased. Return to Sender.* It was true then. What old Bob Kelly had told him was true. The railwayman had been working up the line when he'd seen a body carried through. The dead man wore dull khaki dungarees over a thick woollen jumper. An insurgent, he'd been told by one of the guards, caught the night before laying charges on the line. Although Bob hadn't seen the man's face, he'd sworn it was William Jones of the Olchon. This was why George had offered to help out with the backlog post when the thaw set in. Although he'd never knowingly met William Jones he'd told the postmaster he had to visit him, so he could take the letters for the Olchon, seeing as he was going there anyway. But he hadn't even had to enter the valley to discover that what Bob had said was true. The German officer had made that clear enough. William's family, and all the other families in the Olchon it seemed, had paid the price for his, and probably others', involvement with the Auxiliary Units.

George couldn't remember recording any recent troop movements in this direction and the lanes had been impassable for months. The soldiers must have come into the valley over the Black Hill instead, a pack of them descending on horseback, just as they had elsewhere throughout the winter.

What was most shocking to George was not what the German officer had written across those letters, but his own lack of surprise. He'd heard enough similar stories over the last three months to half expect this, to cycle into a deserted valley. The Germans had been true to their word. Ten civilians executed for every German soldier killed. That was what it said on the posters signed by Feldmarschall Walter von Brauchitsch, the newly appointed Reichsprotektor of Occupied Britain. The 'insurgency', as the Germans called it, hadn't faltered in the face of this threat and had left a trail of massacred villages in its wake. Von Brauchitsch had ordered the confiscation of all private wirelesses, so it was hard for George to tell for certain, but from the muted reports in the *Star* and other Nazi-backed newspapers he thought the insurgency was still causing the Germans trouble. Although most of the Americans had been shipped back to defend their homeland against the Japanese he knew that many British regular fighting units had melted into the civilian population and were also taking part in guerrilla activities. Ever since the BBC had moved to Worcestershire the railway up to Hereford had sustained regular attacks.

But the tide was turning. Again, the new press couldn't be trusted but George had heard for himself the inauguration speech of R. A. Butler, the German appointed Prime Minister of the new British government in Harrogate. The Germans played it from loudspeakers strapped on the roofs of trucks and printed the full speech in the *Star*. Butler, an Under-Secretary at the Foreign Office during the war, assured the British people that he came to power reluctantly, but as a patriot, thinking only of their welfare. 'Common sense,' he told them, 'and not bravado must govern our actions in negotiating with the German authorities.' Shored up by the credibility of support from Lloyd George, the country's victorious leader in the last war, Butler's administration had already won a muttering allegiance, especially in areas of the country he'd saved from direct Nazi rule.

There were also rumours of a return by the Duke of Windsor. In the wake of the King and Queen's sailing for Canada accompanied by Lord Halifax and other members of the Free British government, there was a vacuum left in the country which many thought would be filled by Edward VIII. The *Star* had been busy for the past few weeks recasting his pre-war abdication as an act of deposition, thus preparing the way for his return, no doubt under the same patriotic banner as Butler. To heal a wounded nation. To bridge the differences between Britain and Germany and build towards a united Europe, standing strong against the capitalist Americans in the West and the Bolsheviks in the East.

Most worrying for George, however, were the widely reported actions of Sir Will Spenser, the Regional Commissioner for Civil Defence for the Eastern Region. Spenser had been the first British official to openly turn against the Auxiliary Units, promising to 'arrest any members operating in the Eastern Region'. George knew this was an attempt to stem the tide of vicious German reprisals but how long would it be before Spenser's sentiment took over the rest of the nation? Before a desire for peace, for safety, for some kind of future, outweighed the desire for independence from the Nazis?

George had already seen this kind of slippage closer to home. It appalled him more than the actions of the official collaborators, who could perhaps have been forgiven for acting with genuine patriotic ideals. This easy slide towards a kind of normality, however, was unforgivable in his eyes. In the towns the shops were trading again and all the banks back in business. People were returning to what could be described as their normal lives. The long winter had tightened the focus of their concerns from a national to a personal level. The Germans had capitalised upon this, fulfilling their role as providers of food and warmth with one hand, while deporting men of military age, resettling thousands of Jewish families and killing women and children in acts of reprisal with the other.

And yet relations between the local population and their occupiers had been steadily improving. His own sister served German soldiers when helping at the village shop in Pandy. Hotel owners laid out their dishes in front of Wehrmacht officers and lieutenants. In return the occupying soldiers were, on the whole, polite and even considerate. After the brutality of the first wave of fighting troops, followed by the fanaticism of the young Arbeits Dienst detachments brought in to work on the railway and destroyed bridges, the older and calmer occupation troops were a relief. There were already toddlers in the area whose earliest memories would be of sitting on the knee of an avuncular German sergeant as he bounced them up and down while telling their mother about his own little boy or girl at home in Stuttgart, Berlin or Munich.

For George it felt like the most personal of betrayals. Four years ago Atkins's approach across that field, the flies on his hat winking in the sun, had initiated George into the war. In the space of half an hour he was involved, one of its millions of intimates. Atkins's prophecies had not come true that summer of 1940, but when they did last autumn, George tasted once more the potency of his secret duty. But then he survived. Atkins's fourteen days passed and turned into fourteen weeks. Atkins himself disappeared, the flow of messages dried up and after a brief period of activity, the war moved on, leaving George behind to his usual existence of daily farm work and long evenings reading the newspaper after his father had finished flicking through its pages. He should have been pleased but he wasn't. Once inside, he now felt outside again. With only the Nazi press to rely upon he had to make do with a diet of rumour and hearsay. The sieges of cities happened far away from him. Even the activities of operational Auxiliary Units only ever reached him as echoes from Hereford, the mining valleys or even further afield in Worcester and Salisbury. The drop points were always empty and he had long given up leaving his own observations to rot in the damp holes of walls and fence posts.

As he freewheeled down the hill towards his father's farm he knew he was cycling back to nothing more than the drudgery of his work and a family who saw him as an ineffectual coward, 'too clever by half', who'd jinxed his way out of the army and even his Home Guard duties. This same family now sold eggs and milk to the soldiers of an occupying force that were, elsewhere, enacting their revenge upon the nation they blamed for prolonging the war.

He wanted never to stop cycling. To let the bike go whizzing past the entrance to his father's yard and cycle on madly through the village, through Abergavenny and on and on, never having to stop again; never having to come to rest in a country and a life he no longer recognised.

March 4th

We've been getting low on meat these past weeks so Mary killed her sow yesterday. How is it they always know? It took three of us to pull her to the bench. She screamed all the way, and as we lashed her down too. Mary stuck her. I couldn't watch after that. I've never been good with pigs, you know that. They sound too human. Mary did it all just as if she's always been doing it. Maggie took the gouting blood then we put her up on a ladder for the scalding. Mary says as she'll do the butchering tomorrow.

Maybe it was seeing the sow strung up, but I had a nightmare again last night. Same as before, about Jeffreys and the rebels down at the Skirrid. Only this time, when he came to hang them the rebels was you and William and Hywel instead. I was six when my brothers told me that story but it's been coming back all the time, Tom. All the time.

The river is back down again and its warmer too. I saw a raven with nesting twigs this morning and a couple of hares, fighting in the meadow.

Maybe now the snow's gone they'll go too. I heard their motorbike the other day, so perhaps they're getting ready to leave. I hope so. Then maybe you can come back.

Sarah laid the book and the pen on the table and went to stir the *cawl* simmering on the range. They hadn't been able to kill the sow on their own, she was too strong. It was Alex who had got her onto the bench. And Alex who had strung her up afterwards. But Sarah couldn't write that to Tom. She had no way of telling him without it sounding wrong. So she left it out instead, as if it had never happened.

Sarah's eyes were immediately drawn to the thick square leather case Albrecht carried in his right hand. It was a blustery spring day. His fringe blew about his face as Seren strained on her chain and barked behind him.

'Good morning, Mrs Lewis,' Albrecht said simply with a smile. 'May I come in?'

Since the thawing of the winter the women had seen more of the German soldiers. Once Maggie's explanation of their mutual dependence had sunk in, some of them had even relaxed enough to call upon the patrol for help with heavy work. Mary had begun to let Bethan walk over to The Firs to look after Menna's children on her own. Only Sarah still kept her distance. But they could not be avoided entirely. She often saw Alex ushering Maggie's four cows up the lane early in the morning and several times now she'd been sitting at Maggie's table when Albrecht called to give her an update of the situation in the world beyond. She didn't like the way the two of them talked. Like confidants almost, with an air of assumed greater knowledge. Whenever Albrecht mentioned the insurgency he did so as if it had no personal bearing upon the women of the valley. The men, their husbands, missing from their lives, remained missing from the conversation too. And yet it was also around this time the women began confiding to each other that they had seen the departure of their husbands coming. Small signs. The way they spoke, the way they didn't. The way they touched them, the way they didn't. Sarah meanwhile kept up a vigilant watch for small signs of her own. Unspoken messages from Tom like the new tooth in the hay rake or the ewe she'd found in the yard that day. But there were none and she wondered again if she'd imagined these signs in the first place. That Tom had, after all, just gone and left nothing other than a fading scent on his clothes and the ghost of his impression in their mattress.

She couldn't take her eyes off the case. It was a rigid box covered in dark leather, battered and scratched with use. Her mind raced to wild possibilities as to what it might contain. This was the first time the captain had called on her since he'd carried those ewes back from the field with his sergeant at the start of the winter.

She looked up at his face. He seemed lighter, younger than he'd appeared on that day.

'Cwtch ci!' she shouted at Seren over his shoulder. The bitch sank back on her haunches, the links of her chain playing a brief scale on the cobbles of the yard.

She looked back at Albrecht. 'I s'pose so,' she said and stepped back from the door to let him in.

Albrecht walked through into the kitchen. He still wore his uniform, threadbare at the elbows and knees. The collar of his shirt was broken and frayed. Over the winter some of the other members of the patrol had begun mixing their uniforms with clothing they'd found in The Court. At first Albrecht was worried about this, thinking it would offend the women's memories of their husbands. But Maggie had put his mind at rest. 'Jus' clothes, aren't they?' she'd said. 'Jus' clothes. An' your boys need to keep warm, fair enough.' Then she'd snorted a strange half-laugh. 'I saw them the other day mind,' she said, shaking her head.

'Looked like a bloody bunch of refugees they did. Right old mish-mash of stuff they had on.'

Albrecht had laughed with her, relieved and relaxed by her response. 'Well, maybe that's just what we are, Mrs Jones,' he'd said, 'all of us here. Refugees.'

Her look had cut him dead. 'Oh no, Captain Wolfram,' she'd said, all humour pared from her tone. 'This is our home. This is where we live. We're not refugees from anything, an' don't you forget that.'

Albrecht placed the leather case on the kitchen table. 'I hope you don't mind,' he said, flicking two steel latches and lifting the lid. 'But I wanted to bring you this.'

Sarah looked down at the gramophone on the table. 'Why?'

'Because it is your birthday today.'

It was true. It was her birthday, however much she'd tried to forget it. She hadn't mentioned it to any of the other women and she'd tried not to even mention it to herself. There was, she felt, nothing to celebrate. Twenty-seven years old. Childless. Abandoned in a world gone sour. Just the afternoon before she'd ridden Bess up on the hill and watched a pair of crows circle and dance about each other in the air. When they'd landed they'd rubbed shoulders and Sarah had felt again, as if for the first time, the pain of her solitude. Even the carrion crows who ate the eyes of her dead ewes had companionship while she, as ever, had just the blood-pulse of the wind in her ears and the heat of Bess's neck to keep her company. Not for the first time, she'd wanted Tom dead. Not because of what he'd done, but instead of what he'd done. In death he would have given her an answer. She would have known where he was. As it was, she just had nothing. Even the women whose husbands had gone to war, they'd always had something: letters, days of leave.

She'd once seen a crowd of these women down at the station in Pandy. They were wearing their best dresses, their cheeks rouged and their lips bright red, waiting for a train to take them into Newport. There, they would wait on the platform for the fast train carrying troops from the training fields of west Wales up to London and the ports of the south coast. The train didn't stop at Newport, just gave a couple of blasts on its whistle and steamed on through. But these women always went to watch it pass, dressed as if for a dance. Just for the chance of seeing the faces of their husbands, their lovers, as the long line of carriages clattered and rushed past them trailing its heavy plume of steam. It was often a hopeless journey but the women still went, just for that chance, that glimpse. But Sarah didn't even have that. There was nowhere she could go in the hope of seeing Tom. No reports she could read with her heart in her mouth. And no letters she could wait for. Just an empty vigilance for some sign, some hidden message and her long rides up on the hills, forever facing up to their blank answer.

Sarah sat down at the kitchen table. 'Who told you that? That it was my birthday?'

'No one' Albrecht said, slipping a black vinyl disc from a sleeve on the inside of the gramophone's lid. 'I read it in your Bible' he said more quietly, aware that mention of that day would unsettle her, when right now he wanted nothing more than to make her glad he was there.

He busied himself at the gramophone, taking the small crank from out of its clip in the box and fitting it to the square bolt at the back. He began winding, slowly at first, then quicker, talking to Sarah as he did.

'You have no music here,' he said with his back to her. 'I thought you might like some.'

Sarah didn't reply. Her head was bent to the table as

she traced the knots and whorls in the wood with her finger. She felt awkward in his presence, remembering the last time he'd stood in this kitchen; the veil of his thumbprint across her bride's face. Albrecht was determined, however. In the past two weeks spring had come to the valley and with it his senses had returned. It was as if he'd never experienced a change of seasons before. Bare stone walls revealed purple crocuses along their jagged tops, the birdsong multiplied, the melodies of song thrushes and blackbirds shot through with the sudden drilling of a woodpecker. He felt lighter than he had ever done, possessed of a quick, fragile potential. The turning within himself he'd first detected on those early walks through the valley was complete. He'd unlocked, and in doing so had woken another part of himself too. As if waking from a deep sleep into a clearer light of reality, he'd found himself thinking of Sarah every day.

For the past months he and his patrol had regularly listened to the Oxford professor's gramophone and records. The music had stilled them. At times it had lifted them too. Now Albrecht wanted Sarah to experience this. More importantly, he wanted to share the experience with her. Not for the music, but for the sharing, for the creation of a common ground between them. A common ground that was not a consequence of war, but was in spite of it.

Albrecht lifted the polished steel arm and lowered the heavy stylus to the revolving record. The needle met the groove with a sudden crackle and hiss.

'Bach,' he said simply as he stepped back from the table and leant against the window sill, folding his arms in anticipation. 'The Cello suites. No.4.'

He lowered his head and at the same time, as if his movement had created it, a bow drew itself deeply across a single bass string before melting to a higher note that fell back towards the first. At the end of that descent, the bow drew across the bass string again, ricocheting the notes higher once more to repeat the movement, the same as the first, but different too. Each time the bow pulled across that bass string, brief and sonorous, a scattering of breadcrumbs on the table near Sarah's hand vibrated over the wood.

Sarah's kitchen had not heard music for months. Before all this happened she used to sing to herself as she worked in here, cleaning the grate or peeling potatoes. Each chore was lightened and quickened by song, a hymn hummed or sung just under her breath. But since Tom's leaving she hadn't sung to herself again. With this record, with the sound of this single cello emanating from a battered leather case, everything in the room, the table, the dresser, the range, the horseshoe over the door, seemed in contact with a new element. The trees she could see through the window over Albrecht's shoulder now moved not with the buffeting wind as before, but under the command of the rise, fall and procession of the music.

The pattern of the music changed, the stab of a sudden high note rising through a smooth flow of the other phrases. The surprise of it picked at Sarah's heart and she found herself suddenly looking up at Albrecht. She was met with the top of his bowed head over his folded arms. Standing there like that he looked like a body prepared for the coffin.

The bow was moving quickly over the strings now, building rapid ascents before falling back to the familiar foundation of that single bass note. Sarah remained motionless at the table but inside her mind was racing after those notes. It had been so quiet. So silent. And now this. So much sound, so intricate and yet so simple. The weight of the winter months seemed to collapse about her, undermined by this music like the blocks of snow along the banks of the Olchon, weakened and loosened by the river's renewed energy.

The first movement came to an end with a return to the original phrasing, closing not with the single bass string that Sarah unconsciously anticipated, but with a smoother, longer note, drawn out to a sudden silence. The stylus hissed and popped in the record's grooves, riding the slight waves of its surface like a boat anchored out at sea. The wind outside seemed amplified and a blackbird's song rang through the yard, as if all the sound about them had been washed clean in the cello's music.

'The Allemande,' Albrecht said barely audibly, his head still bowed. Sarah didn't understand, but again he appeared to conjure the music, as with these words it began once more, lighter, faster, with contralto vibrations at its heart.

Again Sarah and Albrecht remained motionless as the battered gramophone filled the room with its music; Sarah seated at her table, pockmarked and scored by generations of hungry farmers, and Albrecht standing at the window, the coldness of the wind penetrating the panes at his back, his eyes closed and his inward vision travelling back to distant concerts with Ebbe before the war.

At the end of the second movement he spoke again, even quieter than before, 'The Courante.'

Again they listened, and Sarah too found herself transported, not to a faraway past but to her present. In all the months of silence she hadn't been able to think, to once make sense of things, to see clearly. Now, with her kitchen filled with more sound than it had ever heard, she found a silence in which to think, a cavern of reflection carved from the notes piling and crowding about her.

The end of the Courante caught her unawares, a series of

foreshortened ascents that slipped back, once more, to that bass string, trembling the breadcrumbs beside her fingers.

Albrecht, however, had been ready. She turned her head to see him standing over the gramophone, his hands poised either side of the revolving record as if he would pounce and catch the final dying note before it slipped into silence. He did not, and waited instead until its faintest resonance had passed before raising the stylus from the disc with one finger, as he might the chin of a crying girl. Swinging the arm to one side he flipped the record, wound the crank and lowered the needle again, all in what looked like one swift movement.

'The Sarabande,' he said, not looking at her as he took up his position by the window again. There was something in the way he said this, a promise in his tone, that made Sarah strain to catch the first note from the record's initial grooves of empty static.

When it came she understood. Languid, slow, pregnant with sorrow, the strings seemed to belong to another instrument altogether. A regretful but wise and saddened cousin of the cello that had played the first three movements. Sarah found her own head dropping now and her eyes closing. It was beautiful but she could not bear it. The music seemed to know. About her hours on the hillside, the wind like the sound of her own blood in her ears, the long nights lying awake in her abandoned bed. It was as if the notes of her heart over these past three months had been dictated directly to the hand that drew this bow over these strings to describe, so perfectly, the complex yet simple geometry of her damaged soul.

The movement closed, not as the others had with definite strokes across a string, but with the lightest of touches, almost accidental, the contact so slight that the final note

229

barely breathed from the string before extinguishing, leaving a resonance of more substance than the note itself.

The gramophone hissed. The wind shivered the panes of the window. 'The Intermezzo,' Albrecht said in a whisper, 'a bourrée.'

The suite played itself out as it had begun, with a strong pass across a deep bass note that left its imprint on the air as physical and real as if a pebble had dented the atmosphere of the farmhouse kitchen. The needle ran to the end of the final groove and stayed there, riding the revolving thud of the record's silence, the pulse of nothing playing into the room. Albrecht didn't move. If he did he felt he would spill whatever it was he held so delicately within him.

The record turned, its regular heartbeat the only sound now other than the playful, intermittent wind outside. He stared at the stone flags at his feet, feeling the resonance of the music settle within him. Eventually he could bear it no longer. Slowly, he raised his head.

Sarah was looking directly at him. Her eyes were glazed with tears, the skin about them blushed with unspent crying. He allowed himself the slightest of tender smiles.

'What are you doing here?' she said. Her voice was clean and hard as bone, pared of all depth by her anger. Her eyes remained locked on his. 'You've won this war. Why don't you just leave now? Leave us alone.'

It was no good, Albrecht saw that now. He was not, as he had hoped, the sum of his parts, of the parts of himself he'd rediscovered in this valley. He was, after all, no more than the sum of this uniform, of this war. He had no power to shape his future. He could not extract himself, escape from what he had done and what he had been part of, through no will of his own, over these past five years.

'I know what you think,' Sarah continued in the same cold

tone. 'Just because we live out here, because we spend our days with animals, that's all we are.' She let her eyes flick towards the gramophone before staring back at him. 'Think I've never heard music before? Well I have, like you'll never know too. From people, not from a record either.'

She stopped. The Sarabande still played within her. The fragility of its sadness had turned her chest to shivered glass and her head into a cloud of gathered tears. She glanced at her row of novels on the top shelf of the dresser then returned her eyes to him again as she continued, more quietly than before. 'I read, you know. I read books. So don' come here with your music. I know what you've done. We all heard the wireless. In Belgium an' Holland. Them Jews weren't just taken to new homes were they? So don't come here and cover yourself with this music. Because I see you,' she said, her words no more than a whisper. 'I see you.'

She was tearing it down. Everything he'd wanted to create; a rare sharing. He'd selected the suite specifically with her in mind. He had brought it to her, brought her music and himself to this cold, lonely, silent house. And now she was destroying it. Albrecht felt the pressure of a childish frustration gather in his chest at the loss of the moment, at this injustice done to him and his character.

'Do you really think they'll come back if we go?' he said quietly, trying to suppress the anger in his voice. 'Do you really think they're alive at all any more?'

Sarah's eyes didn't falter. 'Yes,' she said. 'Yes I think Tom's alive. I know he is.'

Tom. She used her husband's name like a needle to pierce him. Albrecht broke from her stare, his eyes falling upon the plates, leaflets and books on the dresser. They came to rest on Sarah's wedding photograph. He let out a sigh. 'I hope for your sake you're right, Mrs Lewis,' was all he said.

The single heartbeat of the record was slowing as if the pulse of the house was weakening. Albrecht crossed to the gramophone, lifted the stylus and swung the arm back into its clip. Placing one hand on the record he stopped its turning then stood there, his head bowed, as the silence seeped back into the room.

'You think they're dead, don't you?' Sarah said quietly, her voice her own again.

Albrecht closed the gramophone then leant against it, both his hands on its lid, his head hung low between his shoulders, his eyes closed.

'Maybe not,' he said. 'They know this area well, I imagine,' he paused, clearing his throat. 'And from what I've seen men like your husbands have been well prepared.' He thought of the bunker he'd visited outside Oxford, the rows of glowing jars filled with urine, the stacks of supplies under the bunks. 'And God knows,' he continued with an empty laugh of a sigh, 'this war might be full of terrors, but it's full of miracles too.'

'Like here?' Sarah said.

'Yes,' Albrecht replied, his eyes still closed, nodding his head. 'Like here.'

They remained like that for several seconds before Albrecht straightened up and turned round. 'I should leave. I am sorry if I've upset you, Mrs Lewis.' He fastened the latches on the box and slid it off the table. He was walking to the door when Sarah stopped him with her question.

'Why d'you come here? In the first place I mean. Why here? Was it t'look for them?'

Albrecht turned to face her, a faint smile playing on his lips. 'Oh no, Mrs Lewis. We came here to look for something much more interesting I'm afraid.'

'And did you find it?'

'Yes,' Albrecht said, his eyebrows raised as if surprised by his own answer. 'Yes, we did find it.'

Sarah frowned and shifted in her seat. 'So what was it?' she asked. 'Or can't you tell me that either?'

Albrecht rested a shoulder against the door frame, the gramophone box still held in one hand. He looked down at his feet for a moment. When he looked back up at Sarah his face had changed. There was, once again, some of that light-ness Sarah had seen when she'd first answered the door.

'Something my superiors wanted,' he said. 'Something they wanted very much indeed.'

He appeared on the verge of laughing at some secret joke. Sarah was both irritated and intrigued. 'Here? They wanted something from here?'

'Yes,' Albrecht replied, nodding his head deliberately. 'Yes they did.' His smile slipped for a second before returning with a new energy. 'Will you let me show you?'

Again he looked like the younger man who'd come calling for her on a blustery spring morning. 'It's not far, and I think perhaps it might prove a better present for you than this,' he said, lifting up the battered leather case. Lowering the gramophone again he watched as the nick of a frown-line appeared between Sarah's eyebrows. Remaining at the open door, he stood there, motionless, waiting for her answer.

It was sacking cloth. Sarah could see that now, its folds and pleats longer and smoother than the jagged stone walls around them. As Albrecht moved towards it the torch beam lit up its coarse surface. Sacking cloth. Just like she'd put about her shoulders all through the winter.

Albrecht took hold of the corner and pulled. The cloth slid off whatever it covered and fell to the floor with a slow slump, like thawing snow breaking from a cornice. There was another sheet underneath, tarpaulin this time, like the tarpaulin Reg used to cover his hay ricks. Albrecht pulled at this and it too fell away. At first Sarah could see nothing but the glare of the reflected torchlight. She squinted away from it, the beam sudden on her eyes after the darkness of the cavity they stood in. But then Albrecht shone the torch at the wall instead and when Sarah looked back she saw the pale wood of the packing crate raised on a pallet, and then the darker wood of the frame within. Inside this frame again she could make out a lighter surface that almost filled it, shaped like the gable end of a house and stained with darker patches. She moved closer and saw this surface was covered in illustrations and blocks of written text.

'What is it?' she asked.

Albrecht's voice came from behind her, out of the darkness. 'The world,' he said. 'Or at least an idea of it.'

Sarah had not come here easily. Although she'd eventually agreed to let Albrecht show her why his patrol had come to the valley she'd grown nervous once they'd left Upper Blaen. She didn't trust him and as they'd walked up towards the head of the valley, then around its western wall above Maggie's farm and The Court, she'd stopped several times, shaking her head, telling him she wouldn't go any further. But in the end something had brought her here. Something in his tone, in his look had convinced her she needed to see this. To make sense of things, to explain what had happened to her life over these past four months. So by the time they reached the Red Darren, a sandstone cliff jutting from the head of a scree slope high up the valley's wall, Sarah was ready to follow Albrecht as he collected a torch from behind a boulder and stepped inside a tall, narrow crevice in the rocks.

Although the stone of the Red Darren was most often split horizontally, making it look from a distance as if it had been built from massive rough-hewn bricks, several vertical rifts like this appeared irregularly along its half-mile length. Sarah had never been inside one of these rifts and she was surprised how quickly the only light was that of Albrecht's torch illuminating the damp, angular walls. She gripped the hazel walking stick she'd taken from her porch, the V at its head worn smooth as glass by the pressure of Tom's thumb over the years, and hoped the dogs, which she'd left waiting at the mouth of the crevice, would still come to her if they heard her calling.

When Albrecht had stopped in front of her and shone his torch at the back wall her heart had begun racing once more. There was nothing there. He had lured her into this cliff and now there was nothing there. She gripped the walking stick with both hands and leant her weight towards the entrance, ready to run back towards the light at any moment. But then Albrecht had moved closer up to the rock before stepping sideways and disappearing into a larger cavity. Sarah followed him, coming out into a man-made hollow with wooden struts and a brattice running along its sides. The struts were split and splintered, as if they'd been hammered into place in a hurry. Sarah looked around her, remembering how Tom had once told her how soft this stone could be before it was exposed to the air. 'Like butter it is,' he'd said on one of their early walks together as he'd slipped his hand into a crack in the cliff and pulled out a clump of crumbling rock. Albrecht shone his torch about the hollow, following Sarah's gaze with its beam until she finally saw the sacking cloth which had fallen away to reveal this frame and the world inside.

*

'It would have had more colour when it was first made.' Albrecht came up beside Sarah and ran his fingers along one of the long brown channels penetrating the lighter parchment like roots through soil. 'These rivers were blue,' he said. 'Bright blue.' He moved his hand down to a larger patch of brown. 'And the seas were green.' His hand went to the top right-hand corner of the frame. 'Except for the Persian Gulf and the Red Sea. These were red. You can still see traces of the original colour.'

Sarah nodded slightly in reply.

'The lettering of the continents and the compass points were in gold leaf,' Albrecht continued. 'And of course the whole parchment would have been white. Bright white. It must have been beautiful.'

Albrecht seemed to be no longer talking to Sarah but to himself. He stood close to the glass of the frame, moving his fingers over its surface as he studied details of the map.

'How old is it?' Sarah's voice was hoarse, lowered in deference to what she didn't understand.

'Medieval,' Albrecht said. 'Late thirteenth century most probably.' He crouched down and pointed at an island in the bottom left hand corner. 'See here?' he said. 'These castles were built by Edward the First in the north of Wales. In . . .' he paused, bringing the torch closer to this corner of the map, 'Conway? Is this how you say it?'

'Yes,' Sarah said, kneeling beside him.

'And here, in Car . . . Car . . .?'

'Caernarfon.'

'Yes, Caernarfon. Well, this one was begun in 1283, so the map must have been made after that date.'

Sarah thought of the poet's stories. How he'd creased his face in disgust when he'd told his tales of Edward I's occupation of Wales. How the English king had killed the bards to

236

silence their voices of dissent. She bent closer to where Albrecht had pointed on the map.

'Why is England an' Wales down there? That's not right is it?'

'I did say it was only an idea of the world,' Albrecht replied. 'And an early one too. But this, around Europe is actually where the map is most accurate. The whole thing is tilted you see, so east is up here,' he shone the torch to the top of the map, illuminating the circle of paradise beneath its apex. 'And west is down here. But this is as much a mythical and religious map as a geographical one. Look,' Albrecht shone the torch at a faded illustration of two men hacking away at the limbs of a body. 'These are the Essodenes of northern Asia. They were said to eat their parents rather than bury them. And here, beside them, you see that? That is the golden fleece.' His voice had taken on an unfamiliar charge, a tone of impassioned instruction.

They both studied the illustrations in silence for a moment, kneeling in the powdery earth on the floor of the hollow. Then Sarah stood up, as if suddenly remembering where she was and with whom.

'What's it doing here? Why's it here?'

Albrecht stood up beside her and leant back against one of the wooden struts. 'It is being hidden.'

'From you?'

He raised his eyebrows, 'I suppose so, yes. Or at least from the SS.'

The SS. Even Sarah, living out the war in her relative isolation, had heard enough about the SS for those two letters to quicken her pulse again.

'What do they want it for?' she said.

Albrecht shone his torch over the Mappa Mundi as if he'd discover the answer to her question somewhere in its inscriptions, cities and sea monsters. 'To be honest,' he said, 'I don't really know. But they do want it. Himmler. You know who he is?'

Sarah thought for a moment. 'The small one? With the spectacles?'

Albrecht laughed. 'Yes, him. The small one with the spectacles. Well it's he who wants this map so much.'

How much else should he tell her? It all seemed too fantastical now, after his months in this valley. Would she even believe him? If he told her the famously frugal Himmler had, according to intelligence reports, spent $3.7 million building a castle at Wewelsburg. That inside this castle there was an Arthurian round table at which the 'knights' of the SS sat, a silver disc with their names inscribed on the back of each pigskin covered chair. That alongside Himmler's museums of weapons and Masonic regalia the castle was packed with treasures like this Mappa Mundi, looted from occupied territories across the globe. It was of no coincidence, Albrecht thought, that Himmler had chosen Wewelsburg as the site for his castle. The town had, after all, been named after Wewel von Buren, an infamous robber-knight.

But as for Sarah's question; what did he want the Hereford map for? He still couldn't answer her because he didn't know himself. He could only guess that the map played some part in the ritualistic jigsaw of the occult and the ancient that Himmler had constructed as the background for his racial ideology. That somewhere within the legends and Roman topography of its mythic world the small man with spectacles had located yet another justification for the destruction he and the Nazis had unleashed upon the real one.

In the end he gave her just the simplest facts. 'The Nazis are more cultured than you might think, Mrs Lewis. It could be argued that Adolf Hitler is currently the world's greatest collector of art.' English may have been Albrecht's second language but he was fluent enough for Sarah to catch the note of sarcasm in his tone. 'All over this country,' he continued, 'art treasures like this map were hidden from the bombing. This was very wise of your government.' He thought of the Ebstorf World Map which he'd lovingly studied for two whole years. A contemporary of this Hereford map, it had been destroyed in a second by a British bomb. 'The entire collection of your National Gallery for example is, as we speak, stored inside a mountain in North Wales.' He shone the torch to the bottom of the map, illuminating the crude illustrations of Conway and Caernarfon castles once more. 'But now these treasures are hiding from the Reich itself, and not just their bombs any more.'

'From you.'

'Yes,' Albrecht admitted with a resigned nod of his head. 'From me.'

'An' they sent you because of your studies?'

'I suppose so. And because I was here, nearby. And because of my English.'

'So how d'you know it was here? In the valley?'

Albrecht moved closer to the map again, which now seemed to glow dully in the dark, possessed of its own light. 'At the start of the war the map was evacuated from Hereford Cathedral and stored in the wine cellar of Hampton Court outside London. This was when the finial was removed.' He passed his hand across the top of the dark wood frame. 'Later in the war, probably during the Blitz, it was evacuated again, this time to a coal mine in Bradford-on-Avon near Bath. Then, shortly after the German counter-attack reached British shores, it was moved again and brought here. I can only assume its original keeper at the cathedral came for it, as a mother might come for her child, and brought it home. Or as near to home as was safe, which was here, Mrs Lewis, in your valley.'

He held her stare for a moment then placed his finger directly at the centre of the parchment upon what looked like a round cog. 'This,' he said, 'is Jerusalem. Right in the middle of the map.'

Sarah came and stood beside him. 'Thus says the Lord,' she said quietly. 'This is Jerusalem; I have set her in the centre of the nations, with countries round her.'

Albrecht smiled to himself, remembering Sarah's school certificate; *The best of all books is the Bible.*

'The book of Ezekiel,' she said.

'Exactly.'

Again they stood in silence, letting their eyes wander over the map's most intricate details.

'How d'you know all this?' Sarah eventually said.

'My studies,' Albrecht replied, not taking his eyes off the map. 'In Dresden and Oxford.'

'No,' Sarah said shaking her head. 'I meant about where the map's been. How it was here.'

Albrecht kept moving his fingers over the glass of the frame, leaving slight imprints where he pressed over a certain inscription or illustration. 'They have their methods,' was all he said, a darker expression briefly clouding his face before turning back to his explanations of the map. 'You see this heavy scoring? Especially over Paris? Why do you think that is? Some say it was a sign of anti-French feeling in these parts in the later fourteenth century.' He bent down and, removing his glasses, leant his face closer to the cross-hatch of long, straight marks over the multiple-towered illustration of Paris. 'I'm not sure though,' he said almost under his breath. 'In the early nineteenth century some glass lanterns were leant against the map when it was out of its case. I think these are from those lanterns perhaps.'

'What are these?' Sarah's voice came from above him. She was peering at something at the edge of the frame, dimly lit in the faint spillage of light from his torch. He straightened up and shone the beam where she was looking. 'This,' she said laying her finger beside an O encased in a roundel outside the main boundary of the map. 'An' this one too.' She bent to touch the glass over an R in a similar position lower down. Both letters still bore traces of their original gold leaf. The flakes caught the torchlight and shimmered against the sepia parchment like fool's gold in base rock.

'Everything within this boundary,' Albrecht said, running his fingers around the outer circle of the map. 'Is God's creation. This is the world. These letters,' he said, pointing to the two letters and another pair that faced them in the same positions on the opposite side of the map, 'spell MORS. They represent death, which dwells outside God's realm.'

Again they were silent but in a different way than before. It was a deeper silence, the silence of waking, as if that one word had made them remember everything again. Everything which they had, for the briefest of moments, been allowed to forget.

'You do understand why I wanted to show you this, don't you, Mrs Lewis?'

Sarah couldn't see his face but his voice had changed again, returned to the voice she'd always known.

'This map is why I came here, into your valley. And it is why I am still here too. This map,' he turned towards it once more. 'It deserves more than a castle in Wewelsburg. It deserves light, not darkness.'

Sarah shifted her feet in the dry earth. She felt afraid again but this time she didn't know why. 'I should get back,' she said at last.

'Yes,' Albrecht said. 'Of course.'

He lifted the sacking cloth and tarpaulin from the floor and pulled them across the packing crate, obscuring the world within. Then, taking the lead but shining the torch behind him so Sarah might see her footing, he led her out of the cavity into the natural crevice, and then out of the Red Darren altogether onto the hillside and its steep slopes of scree. Outside, Seren and Fly were on their feet, stretching their backs. The blustery day had pushed what few clouds there'd been over the Black Hill and as Sarah emerged from the crevice she had to squint in the brightness left in their wake. She looked down the valley, and for the second time in her life saw everything held within its steep walls cast in an unfamiliar light.

It was a week after Albrecht had shown Sarah the map when Atkins, half-blind and missing all the fingernails on his right hand, came stumbling down the valley's west wall towards The Court. Stopping at an outcrop of rock he crouched behind it and peered down at the moss-covered slates of the farmhouse below him. His vision rose and fell with his heavy breath. There was a milky cloud always drifting across his left eye, the watermark of a blow from one of those unseen hands that had, for months now, assaulted him every day.

Atkins was exhausted but still energised by the ebbing adrenalin of his escape. By the sheer luck of it. The bullet in the back had never come, however much he'd expected it as he'd scrambled down the railway embankment and rushed headlong into the trees at the edge of the siding. He'd lain in the drainage ditch for the rest of the day, motionless but for his shivering, the water making his joints ache with cold.

A tool shed in a cottage garden on the edge of the village had supplied him with the file with which he'd spent most of the night, running the chain of his cuffs across it as slowly as he could for fear of the noise it made. The cuffs themselves he'd had less luck with. He'd never been much good at picking locks and so he still wore them on each wrist, a few links of chain hanging from each one, still tarnished with the blood of the guard from the train.

Just before dawn he'd set out for the valleys. There were Auxiliary Units out there, or so he hoped. He didn't know for certain. The Special Duties Section had always been his only responsibility, but he thought it was likely that somewhere in those remote hills there'd be a bunker and men who could help him. Or at least, if not a unit, then this, a local farmhouse so isolated even the Germans had left it alone. And inside, people like this young boy coming out to feed the chickens. People who could also help him. Who could feed him, hide him, until he made contact with the units.

Atkins watched the boy scatter the mash inside the chicken pen then stand still in the midst of the stabbing of the birds' beaks at his feet. Slowly, the boy crouched lower until he was almost at their level. Then, just as slowly, he reached out an arm to stroke the oil-spill feathers of one of the cockerels. The bird let him do this, tame to human hands, and only gave the lightest of resistance when he picked it up and carried it out of sight around the corner of the house.

The boy didn't come back and Atkins had to wait for over an hour before he saw another person. This time it was an older man, dressed in a similar way to the boy, in a farmer's way, clothes that Atkins had come to know and trust. An old tweed jacket, a flannel waistcoat beneath and heavy cord trousers pulled tight at the waist with a thick leather belt. The boy's father perhaps. Atkins watched the man pull a fork from where it was stuck in the ground and begin working over the soil of a vegetable patch. He felt a wave of tiredness wash over him. These were the people he was fighting for, for whom he'd endured these months of pain. Men of the earth, men who knew their landscape as intimately as they might a lover. This man, he would understand.

Standing from behind the rock Atkins began walking down the slope, the chain of each cuff held in his palms so as not to alarm the farmer. He felt as if he was walking towards the gates of Eden. A rare sanctuary just when he thought the game had been up. The man continued with his work, absorbed in his digging. Atkins walked on, the dew from the longer blades of grass soaking the bottoms of his trousers. He filled his lungs with the fresh mountain air, with freedom, with life. When he was near enough he paused in his descent, took a deeper breath and called down to the man below him.

'Hello there! Good morning!'

Sebald looked up from his digging to see a tall man standing on the slope above him, raising one hand in the air. He was speaking English. Any soldiering instinct still silting some-where within him failed to show itself. Dropping the fork, he ran back inside The Court, clattering through the back door into the kitchen and on into the front room where Alex and Albrecht were eating their breakfast.

'A man,' Sebald said to them, the air gulping in his throat. 'An Englishman. Outside on the hill.'

Atkins knew he'd made a terrible mistake the moment he saw Alex's boots. Surprised by the farmer's reaction, he'd walked a little further down the slope hoping to put him at his ease and so was closer to the house when Alex came round the corner. Even through the cloudy patch of his left eye he saw immediately that the man's boots were not those of a farmer's but regular Wehrmacht issue. It was all Atkins needed to know and he was already turning to run when Alex swung a machine gun from behind his back and aimed it up the hill.

Atkins felt a sudden burn of energy flooding through him

as he half-ran, half-fell up the slope, grasping at roots, branches, rocks, anything that would propel him up and away from that gun behind him. As he ran he once more waited for the crack, for the momentary bumble-bee whine of the bullet as it sped towards his back. But it never came. Just the scramble of loose stones and soil falling away behind him and the panting breath of another man, drawing closer and closer. Suddenly the breath became touch as he felt a grab at his trailing ankle that brought him smashing into the ground and sliding backwards. Then another hand on his other leg. He kicked out, made contact, then felt his ankle gripped again as he was dragged down the slope. Then more hands on his back, pinning his arms, on his head, pushing his face into the sweet smell of the young bracken, its fronds still curled like the fists of a foetus in the womb.

Albrecht paced back and forth before the range in the front room of The Court, the heel of his boots scuffing over the flagstones. Atkins sat in a chair with Alex standing behind him pressing the muzzle of his gun into his neck. A bruise was deepening under the sergeant's eye where Atkins's boot had caught him. Albrecht kept his hands in his pockets because they were shaking. With rage, with fear, with sadness.

He hated this Englishman sitting before him, his head bowed, his hair matted and stinking. Not because he was English. Not because of those defiant, hard blue eyes. Not even because he was his enemy, but simply because he had come here from there. He had brought the war back into the valley and so had also brought with him the choices Albrecht so hated and the parts of himself he so wanted to forget.

Albrecht stopped pacing and looked down at Atkins. The

man was obviously British Intelligence, otherwise he'd no longer be alive. He bore the marks of the Gestapo all over him; those denuded, bloodied fingers. He must have something they wanted, otherwise they would have shot him by now. He must have held out, somehow. That was why he was still alive and still here. So it was no use questioning him further. If he'd stuck out the Gestapo's interrogation then anything Albrecht might try would be child's play in comparison.

He went and sat at the table, his head in his hands. The dark wood of its surface was stained with even darker pools, worn smooth in little hollows where generations of men had placed their elbows. The table was a map of all the humanity who had lived in this house. Of all those who had nurtured food from these bare hills and sat here to eat the fruits of their labours. Men who had given to the soil, but only to take. This was the equation here, he saw that now. This was the pattern by which these farm women lived. The cycle of husbandry and farming was a simple one. Give life and take life, so there may be life once more.

Albrecht sighed, feeling the weight of his own head in his palm. 'Take him away,' he said to Alex without looking up from the table. 'Get rid of him. Quietly.'

APRIL–JUNE 1945

And I have asked to be
Where no storms come,
Where the green swell is in the haven's dumb,
And out of the swing of the sea
      Gerard Manley Hopkins, 'Heaven-Haven'

Albrecht watched as Sarah dressed the orphan lamb in the flayed skin of another. Just moments before he'd observed her with equal fascination as she'd run the blade of her knife about the dead lamb's neck, hooves and rump then peeled the skin from its body, drawing it over its head like a jumper.

'You'd best bury that one,' she'd said to him as she turned the skin back the right way round, her small hands as bloodied as a butcher's. Albrecht took the raw body, mottled with globules of fat, wearing its head like a mask, and dug a shallow grave down beside the river. When he returned Sarah was still preparing the orphan lamb, slipping its legs through those of the skin jacket. She pulled the new coat tight over its back, making sure it covered the tail where the ewe would smell to recognise her own offspring. Brushing a strand of hair from her eye and tipping back on her haunches, she inspected her work. The skin still hung loose about the lamb's midriff.

'I'll need some string,' she said. 'Hold it for a second, will you?'

Albrecht knelt beside her. There was a pale pink smear of blood across her temple where she'd smoothed back her hair. He wanted to lick his finger, press it to her temple and rub the mark away, but he just took the lamb instead, holding it with both his hands, his fingers touching under its belly. He could feel its skin beneath the adopted coat, supple over the bone, its ribs, thin as twigs and the rapid tremor of its heart beneath its ribs again. A cloud passed from over the sun and a quick tide of light slid down the valley, over the farmhouse, the two waterfalls on either side and then across the lower field where Sarah was walking away from him towards her coat, hooked over the gate post like the body of a hanging man. Without that coat he could make out her shape more clearly. She wore a cardigan over a blouse tied at her waist, which was narrower than he'd expected. From this distance it looked as if his hands would encompass it completely, as easily as they did the body of this lamb.

The tide of light reached him, bringing with it a warmth that had seemed impossible all through that long winter. Such light was a rare gift in this valley, he'd come to appreciate this now. A cloud passing, or the sun rising over the Black Hill could transfigure the landscape in seconds; from a dark notch of earth and broken stone into a gilded wound, as if the mountains had been scratched and revealed to be pure gold beneath.

The lamb moved under his hands, lithe and fragile, just hours old, its dark eyes still filling with light. If there had ever been any rhetoric of National Socialism that struck a faint note in him, Albrecht thought, then perhaps it had been this. The idealism of the simple, rural life, a celebration of the German peasantry and their values. He'd lived his life in cities and towns but this lamb, its delicate heart, the borrowed skin, the sudden sun, the waterfalls that never stopped; all of it countered the years of war behind him and made him feel whole again. It also made him feel younger, a child once more; ignorant but learning, edging his way towards a knowledge that seemed more elemental, more connected than anything he'd ever studied in the libraries of Dresden or Oxford.

Sarah returned with a ball of string from which she cut a length to tie the skinned coat about the lamb's stomach.

'What if this doesn't work?' Albrecht asked.

'Use the dogs, I s'pose,' Sarah said, pulling the skin tight over the lamb's rump.

As ever, her speech was sparse, but Albrecht had come to understand that for every word spoken there were another ten shadowing it, unsaid within her. The words she did speak were like stones dropped into a well to determine its depth. Few, but resonant beyond their own sound.

Checking the tightness of the string Sarah took the lamb from Albrecht and let it into the pen where the surrogate ewe was already grazing. Together, they leant on the top rail of the hurdle fence and watched.

Ever since Albrecht had shown Sarah the map a month ago she'd engaged with him and the rest of the patrol more in the manner of the other women in the valley. Still infrequently, still guarded, but in a pragmatic spirit of circumstance; as fellow subjects of events and not as occupier and occupied. She'd even allowed him to visit her with the gramophone again, and play her some of Bach's other cello suites.

Sarah had agreed not to mention the map to the other women. At first, when she'd said this to Albrecht as they walked back from the Red Darren that day, she thought she'd still have to tell Maggie. But then she'd found she hadn't wanted to. Maggie's air of privileged knowledge whenever she spoke with Albrecht, her taking matters into her own hands, had irritated Sarah. She felt she had no reason to share the existence of the map with her, that somehow

Maggie didn't deserve such confidence. So she'd kept her promise to Albrecht and over the weeks it had worked upon her. There was nothing she could do about it. The shared knowledge of the map created something of an understanding between them. She felt this most when they were with others. Nothing was said, but the experience was there, shadowing them. The flakes of gold leaf, the faded towers of the cities, the once blue veins of the rivers. Albrecht's silent witness confirmed her own. It made her feel, for the first time in months, in control of something.

As Sarah watched the ewe and lamb, the crease between her eyebrows deepened. The winter had taken a heavy toll on the flock and she couldn't afford to lose any more. A week after the first thaw she'd ridden up on the mountain with Maggie to see the damage. Nearly all the sheep they hadn't got down at the start of the winter had died. Some had been so hungry they'd eaten the wool off the backs of others. They'd even found a huddle of mountain ponies frozen together, still standing in a circle, their backs to the wind. 'It's their nature as kills 'em,' Maggie had said as they'd ridden past. 'Won't ever take shelter, see? Just huddle in like this an' wait.' The few sheep still alive stood motionless, their ragged coats hanging like wet rugs over their backs. Murders of crows floated above them, biding their time until one of them would finally drop to its knees and lie down.

Once lambing started they'd lost even more. At first hardly any of the ewes took their lambs. They just wandered off, the afterbirth still trailing behind them. The grass was black and poached and they didn't have the energy to suckle the bleating bundles of legs and bones struggling on the ground behind them. But gradually their strength and instinct had returned and they began to feed their offspring.

Last week had seen several strong lambs born. It was still sometimes too much for the ewes though, which is why this one was an orphan. Just moments after Sarah had pulled it free of its mother the ewe had laid down her head and died.

'The dogs?' Albrecht said. 'How do they help?'

'We put the dogs in with them,' Sarah said, not taking her eyes off the lamb in the pen. 'The lamb's got t'feed first, without the ewe scenting it. Then we put the dogs in.'

The lamb tottered towards the ewe, moving awkwardly under the weight of its new skin. It let out a reedy bleat, lifting the ewe's head from her grazing.

'And what do they do? The dogs I mean?'

Sarah turned to look at Albrecht, the ghost of a smile across her lips. He'd been more like this recently. Like a boy, understanding nothing but wanting to know everything.

'The dogs,' she said, turning back to examine the ewe and lamb again. 'They're a threat. Ewe's instinct is t'take the lamb, protect it.'

'And that's enough?'

'Should be. Once it's fed a bit.'

Albrecht nodded then watched in silence with Sarah. There was that same equation again. The give and the take, protection in exchange for fear, a dead lamb skinned so this one may live. If this was always the pattern then perhaps it would apply to them too. Wasn't the war like those dogs? Its teeth bared outside these steep hills? But then who were the orphans? The women, abandoned, or him and his men? It didn't matter. What did was that instinct. The instinct of a ewe to protect one of its kind, the instinct that would force them, against the weight of all the years of war, to recognise their shared humanity.

But with Sarah there was another instinct too, he knew

that now. Over the past weeks they'd spoken about the men again, about Tom and the others. Early one morning, when he and Alex had come over before dawn to help with the lambing, Sarah had asked him what else he knew. They'd spoken openly, more openly than they ever had before, as if those hours prior to daylight were not yet the day itself, and so neutral territory. He'd told her about the bunker outside Oxford, describing in detail its construction and supplies, hoping this would make her feel better about her husband's possible situation. She'd nodded as he spoke, as if he were confirming what she'd already seen for herself. He didn't mention the men who'd occupied that bunker he stood in, the men he'd seen marched out onto that village green, and she hadn't asked.

He wanted to tell her she was holding on to nothing. That her husband and the others were probably dead before the patrol even entered the valley. Badly designed air vents, faulty explosives, a mis-set timer, tracker dogs, the Gestapo, the SS, informers, that unending winter; any of these could have killed them by now. But he remained silent and hoped instead events beyond the valley would do his talking for him.

The old woman's wireless was, once again, picking up news broadcasts. The original home frequencies had been reactivated by the new administration. It was clear, however, that although the announcer's voice was unerringly English, this was no longer the pre-invasion BBC. As such, the messenger was as eloquent an illustration of how the world had moved on as the message itself.

In America, Roosevelt had lost the November elections to an increasingly isolationist Republican Party. The new President Dewey had, like millions of Americans in the face of the Allies' failures and losses in Europe, reverted to his

1940 views. Roosevelt, he told the American people, had led the United States into a war that was not hers to fight; a European war of imperialism in which not one American boy should have died. Following Japan's act of aggression America would still secure her rights and safety in the Pacific and along her Pacific coast, but with words as well as weapons; with diplomacy not deaths. More bloodshed was not the way forward. In keeping with this approach negotiations with Berlin would begin immediately. Any active American units still fighting in Europe would be ordered to withdraw. Roosevelt's sabre-rattling and the refusal of his War Department to warn the commanders of Pearl Harbor, despite their ability to read the Japanese diplomatic codes, had led to the Japanese attack that had in turn led America into war. Now it was time for Dewey to lead her into peace.

Closer to home Butler's government in Harrogate had begun the first steps towards rebuilding a shattered Britain. The first British prisoners of war were released from German camps, having signed agreements of non-aggression towards their new rulers. New semi-military home organisations had been established to 'put Britain back on her feet'. Air Chief Marshal Sir Arthur Harris of Bomber Command had been taken to Berlin to stand trial for war crimes against the German Reich.

The country, however, although occupied and no longer officially at war, was still far from settled. The wireless also carried reports of the ongoing 'insurgency' in the north and west and even broadcast a blustering speech made by an ailing Churchill in Canada. Albrecht couldn't tell if these reports were true or whether they were German propaganda, the necessary friction required by the administration to justify their actions. In the end, he realised this didn't matter either. Fact or fiction, these reports were still enough.

Enough for the women to want to keep their missing husbands a secret and for him and his men to want to remain out of those teeth of the war.

The lamb reached the ewe and began butting its head in the crook of her hind leg. The ewe, in response, bent to smell the lamb's back. She lingered over the skin, scenting the dried remains of her own amniotic fluid. The lamb, shaky on its legs, kept up its jutting motion under her stomach. The ewe sniffed once more about its tail, then lifted her head and walked away to graze again.

Sarah let out a heavy sigh. 'She's rejected it,' she said, shaking her head. 'Even with the bloody skin on, she didn't take it.'

The lamb, bleating thinly and shaking its tail followed the ewe, but when it reached her she walked away again, oblivious to its cries as if she were alone in the pen.

April 12th

*Mary sent Bethan away today. Over to Hay to her cousins.
She doesn't even know if they are still there. She gave Bethan
a note and a packed lunch and that was it. I saw them walk
past on the old track this morning then later Mary walked
back on her own. Mary swears Bethan won't say anything.
Maggie was set against it but Mary was having nothing of
that. She was sure Bethan shouldn't stay here any longer.*

*Two more this morning. One black, one white. Good
strong ones, up on their legs straight away. Still some weak
ones coming through though. The crows find them before I
do. They even took the tongue of one. It was still alive.*

*Maggie had a pair of twins joined at the head and back.
That shook her up bad. She broke one up to get the other
one out but it was no good. She lost them both and the ewe
too. She says she's never known it before.*

*I come out yesterday and saw The Gaer bright as any-
thing. Edith has done her whitewash new. Can you believe
that? After all these years.*

*Still no one come into the valley. I don't know why they
don't. They must see our smoke. But they still stay away.
Maggie says its best that way for now. Until we know for
sure what's going to happen.*

*I don't know if you can see the hawthorn where you are,
Tom, but it's come out full here again. Even some pink down
by the river. Bluebells coming through early in the wood too.
There's a woodpecker in there somewhere. I haven't seen
him yet but I hear him every day.*

*I put that orphan in with the dogs but she still didn't take
it so he's here now with me, wrapped in your shirt by the fire.
I never thought I'd be doing this without you, Tom.*

I hope you are safe.

   Sarah

Sarah found the writing easier now, the words running
smoother to the pen, but her letters still weren't complete.
They still didn't translate the days she lived. Like the poet's
watercolours they were representations but untruthful. She
didn't tell Tom everything; no longer because she couldn't,
but because she didn't want to.

Just as their husbands were absent from the valley, so the
German patrol had become absent from her letters in the
back of the accounts book. They were there, but unseen,
shadowing every event. It was Otto who had whitewashed
The Gaer in preparation for Edith's return. It was Sebald
who had broken up Maggie's conjoined lambs. It was
Albrecht who'd found the weak newborn with its tongue
torn out at the root by the crows. It was Bethan's responses
to the attentions of Gernot which had persuaded Mary her
daughter should leave the valley, and it was as much
Albrecht as Maggie who'd been so concerned by her leaving.

Sarah had tried writing her days as they were, but it was
no use. Her pen hung over the page and the words blocked
in her mind. If Tom were here she could explain it all. How
it was just the way of things. How there was nothing to

worry about. How without the help of the patrol they'd all have sunk under the weight of the winter.

But Tom was not here so instead she told him about her days as if the Germans didn't exist. It left her feeling unfaithful, to him and to herself, but she'd rather this than not write to him at all. Rather some words than none. Because anything was better than silence. She understood that now. Anything was better than the silence of the mute hills, the creaking quiet of her bed, the still hours before dawn. Any contact, any words written to him and him alone, even if they were hollow and echoed with the silence of all the words unwritten behind them.

They had kissed only once. No more than a brushing of lips, as light as swallow's wings nicking the water's surface when they dipped to drink. Even as he leant in towards her, she'd already been pulling away from him, shaking her head. But she must have paused, just for a second, because their lips did meet. And when they did it had felt so right, more right than anything he'd done since he left home a year ago. But now Bethan was gone. Her mother had sent her away. For what? A brushing of lips, a moment of shared breath, nothing more.

Gernot had first seen Bethan watching them over the winter. The thick snow on the hillside behind The Court seemed to absorb some of the light during the day and release it again through the evening and night. At least, this was how it had appeared when he'd looked out of his bedroom window at dusk that evening. The snow, faintly luminescent, showed up the darker outlines above it. The posts of a fence, the wind-withered thorn trees and there, behind one of them, the shape of a young girl crouching at its trunk looking down at them. Gernot had not yet lit the lamp in his room so he was able to stand there, at a little distance from the window, and watch Bethan as she watched them. He didn't move until she did and even then, when he went downstairs to prepare the patrol's dinner, he didn't tell any of the others of what he'd seen. How the hillside had briefly birthed a dark-haired girl, a wood spirit who was watching over them.

The next time he saw her he was ready. Sitting on the edge of his bed he rested his elbows on the bedside table and lifted the binoculars up to his eyes. The magnification of their lenses shut out whatever light the snow emitted, so although they brought Bethan closer to him, they also hid her further in the gathering night. The fading light became grainy and her face no more than an oval of shading, her features merely suggested by pools of black and grey, all framed in the deepening darkness of her hair. Even then though, he could see her lips moving. Not all the time, just intermittently. A dark crease in her face mouthing silent words. He wanted to know what she was saying. He wanted to understand. And even then, through the opaque shreds of the dying daylight, he wanted to kiss those moving, then still, then moving lips.

He never caught her there again. When working in the vegetable garden or out the back of the kitchen, or even in the further away fields, he'd look up at the slope, find the thorn tree and search for her shape behind it. Although he never saw her that didn't stop him planning what he'd do if he did. How he would walk up the slope towards her, how he would speak the few words of English Albrecht had taught him. How he would take her in his arms and kiss her. Lying in his bed at night he recreated her shadowed face behind his closed lids, shedding light over it to illuminate her skin, her eyes and those two moving lips.

A couple of times over the first weeks of the thaw Gernot had seen Bethan in the distance, riding out on her pony on the other side of the valley, but he'd had to wait until the first full weeks of spring before he saw her properly again. He'd worked at the women's farms several times over the winter, and at her mother's farm more than once, but Bethan had never been there. Then one day Albrecht ordered him and Alex to help Mary plough and plant a small field of potatoes down beside the river.

Alex worked the single-blade plough, his big arms floating it above the turning soil. Gernot and Mary followed in his wake, pushing the seed potatoes into the freshly exposed earth. There had never been much ploughing in the valley so Mary's old cart horse was unfamiliar with the harness and the movement, with the weight of the yoke at his shoulders. This was why Bethan was with them. To walk at the horse's head, one hand hooked in the rope halter as she talked softly into his ear or encouraging him on with short clicks of her tongue against her teeth.

Gernot watched her, eclipsed and then revealed over Alex's shoulder as the plough rode its own furrow like the needle of the gramophone in the grooves of the records they'd listened to over the winter. Once again he saw her lips moving and again he could not hear what she was saying. As they repeated their gradual procession, up the field, turning, then back, he put words to her moving mouth. He imagined she was talking to him. First in English and then in German, but always words just for him, whispered into the crook of his neck.

On each turn their eyes met. It was a silent connection, a wordless thread spun through the clamour of each turn; the cart horse sucking his big hooves from the wet earth at the field's edge, Alex ushering him on, the chains and hinges of the plough clattering and creaking. And yet for Gernot each glance drowned out the noise around him and seemed possessed of such a resonance that he couldn't believe either Alex or her mother hadn't heard them.

For the next two days, whenever he could, Gernot

watched the slope behind The Court from his bedroom window. He was convinced those brief moments on the turn of each furrow had been enough. On the evening of the second day his belief was rewarded when he saw Bethan appear through the new bracken and crouch behind the trunk of the thorn tree. Leaving himself no time to question, he walked out of the room, down the narrow stone stairs and out of the farmhouse, his head light above his body and the skin across his temples throbbing with his pulse.

The lowering sun had not quite set behind the Hatterall ridge, the last sliver of its disc flaring from over the silhouetted horizon. Gernot walked into a kaleidoscope of transparent orange and yellow spheres and hexagrams, long streams of light playing through the branches of the trees. He knew where the thorn tree stood, however, and he made his way steadily up the hill in its direction, painfully aware that the light blinding him would illuminate his face for Bethan as he walked towards her.

When he reached the thorn tree, she was still there. He'd somehow thought she would not be. That like a deer spotted in the woods, or a fox paused in a garden, he would arrive to find nothing more than the imprint of her feet and a branch still quivering from where she'd passed.

She did not seem afraid when she looked up at him. As she did, Gernot clearly saw the last ebbing of the girl still within her, and it made him aware of the shadow of the boy still in him, the boy who had been submerged so rapidly with his entry into the army.

'Hello,' he said, the English word thick on his tongue. 'I am Gernot.'

She smiled, 'I know.'

Gernot sat down beside her. So far this was all as he had forecast, as he had planned a hundred times before in his mind. But now he seemed unable to follow the script he'd written for himself. He tried to picture it, reaching out an arm about her shoulder, drawing her close, then both of them slowly tipping back against the bracken behind them. But it was no good, so instead he just sat beside her and looked out over the valley as she did.

Opposite them, on the other side of the valley, the setting sun had cast a broad band of amber along the ridge and upper slopes of the Black Hill. The sky behind the hill was lit an impossible blue. Together, they watched this strip of evening light tighten, a seam of burnished earth compressed between the land and sky, deepening in colour as it narrowed until just the hill's long spine shone bronze and everything below it was night.

'It is beautiful,' Gernot said, struggling with the last word.

She turned to look at him. This time she did not smile.

'You are beautiful,' he said, still looking out at the darkening valley.

She kept looking at him, so when he turned to her she was there, her face near his. And that was when he'd leant in and kissed her. That was when he'd felt her breath on his mouth, when he'd brushed her lips with his.

But then she was pulling away from him, frowning, shaking her dropped head. 'No,' she said, the word no more than a breath on her lips.

And then she left. Suddenly, she stood up and left. Gernot turned in time to see the herringbone pattern of her coat disappearing into the bracken out of which she'd emerged just minutes before. He heard her brushing through the stiff stems and leaves. And then she was gone. It was as if in kissing her he had banished her. As if she had been just a reflection and the lightest touch of their mouths had shattered the mirror between them.

Sitting there, alone on the hillside, Gernot thought he'd see Bethan again the next day. That they would look out over the valley once more tomorrow. But she hadn't come back and now he'd learnt that her mother had sent her away. For how long he didn't know. Why had she done this? Was it really because he'd kissed her? How could her mother have known? What trace of him had Bethan carried with her back to that dark farmhouse on the other side of the valley?

Whatever it was he wished he could retrieve it, take that kiss back, if it meant she would return to him. Now, with her gone, he'd rather live with the promise of those moving lips than with the knowledge of their brief taste. But he would wait, that is what he would do. He had waited before, through the longest of winters, just to see her, and he could wait again. He'd entered this war expecting to die, expecting each day to be his last. But he'd been wrong. The war had led him not to death, but to her, and to life. So he would wait for her and then, when she returned, when she came back to him from over the hills, his waiting would be done and they would leave. Leave this valley, the patrol, the other women, and walk out into a new world together, as young and unknown as their love.

May 16th

Maggie's radio says as it's over, Tom. Here at least. Butler is working with the Germans. Its over. So why don't you come back? I know you're still there. I feel it. But its been so long, Tom. I'm twenty-seven. I'll never be twenty-seven again. It's not just you that's been gone these months, Tom. It's me too.

I wish we'd said more when you were here.

We'll have to dip soon, and shear. And then there's the hay. I see the meadows growing and I remember last year. You working with Reg and the boys. How hot it was. Will it ever be like that again, Tom?

I don't think Mary should have sent Bethan away. It's going bad with her being so alone. But then it's bad for all of us.

The radio says its over but there's still trouble with insurgents. That's what they call them, Tom. They say as no one wants them any more. That it's time to move on.

The elder's flowered, and the laburnum. I found a nest dropped out of the hedge yesterday. There were three eggs still in it. Two sparrow and one cuckoo.

Albrecht and Sarah were walking back from the Red Darren, picking their way through the dark landslides of broken scree and sandstone. Sarah had wanted to see the map again. Although surprised by her request, Albrecht had been pleased too, so he agreed to meet her early in the morning at the mouth of the crevice. Inside he shone his torch over the dappled canvas for her once more, illuminating and translating the handwritten texts and illustrations. He showed her the mapmaker's impression of the Magi's journey, an almost comical series of sepia loops and diversions across Asia and the Middle East. In return Sarah had mentioned the poet again. She said the traced wanderings of the Magi reminded her of an afternoon she'd spent with him as he recounted the story of Percival and his own wandering journey in search of the grail.

Now, back in the morning light, silence had settled upon them once more as they walked down the slope, dislodging fragments of rock from under the larger slabs they used as stepping stones. Albrecht stopped to prise out one of these fragments from the broken sole of his boot. 'There is a book I have been reading,' he said, his voice sudden and unfamiliar on the air. 'About another poet who lived here.'

Sarah stopped and turned to look back at him.

'Well, not here in this valley,' he continued. 'But over there. Where you lived as a girl. Landor. This is his name.'

'Squire Landor?' Sarah said, raising a hand to shield her eyes from the low sun. 'My father used t'tell me stories about him. My grandfather rented a farm off his estate. Wanted t'plant the whole valley with cedars he did. An' he tried bringing in a Spanish flock.' She half smiled and shook her head. 'From what my father said the valley gave him a hard time of it.'

Albrecht smiled back at her, nodding. 'Yes, it seems they did.'

'I didn't know he was a poet though,' Sarah said, frowning.

'I think he was many things, from what I can tell.'

They walked on in silence, testing their footing before trusting their weight to each piece of broken rock. The valley below them was waking. The bleats of lambs pestering their mothers for milk filtered up from the fields below.

'His house is still there you know.' Sarah said, pausing again between two slabs of sandstone, one of them rocking slightly under her foot. 'Landor's. Just ruins, but I could show you if you wanted.'

Albrecht looked her in the eye for a moment. He wanted her to smile again. The few times he'd seen her do so were like the gift of light to this valley. The slightest lifting of the corners of her mouth transformed her features, making her face at all other times seem like a mask. But if anything Sarah looked scared now, timid in the wake of her offer to show him Landor's house. Even so, as he looked at her for that brief moment Albrecht could not believe he'd once felt numb to her. Roughly attired though she was he knew that given the same cut of clothes, lipstick, hairstyles as women he'd known in Dresden, London and Oxford, her broad face, green and gold eyes, delicate lips, would eclipse them all. Maybe even Ebbe, whose memory he still considered more seductive than most women he'd met in the flesh.

He drew his eyes away from her face and looked over her shoulder towards the mouth of the valley. From here, in the clear morning, the country was laid out before them. He could even make out the clusters of hamlets and villages in the distance. It all looked so close and yet so impossibly far away. But it was there, that couldn't be denied, waiting like a long-postponed tide on the verge of breaching the coast once more.

He looked back at Sarah but it was she who spoke next. 'If we went early no one would see us,' she said. 'It'd be safe.'

Albrecht felt the muscles across his brow ease. She understood. This was a choice beyond just his own. 'Yes,' he said at last. 'Yes, I'm sure it would. Thank you.'

Bethan's leaving the valley had caught Albrecht off guard. At first he couldn't understand why her mother would commit such a self-harming act. He knew she was concerned by Bethan's attraction to Gernot, but she'd already lost all contact with both her sons and her husband, and now she was depriving herself of her daughter too. And at what cost? She knew as well as the others the consequences of their being linked to the insurgency in any way. His concern, however, was not just for Mary. Bethan's leaving had endangered them all.

Since the onset of spring the valley had found a strange harmony, more settled than Albrecht could ever have hoped. Alex spent much of his time rediscovering the farming of his boyhood, and therefore himself. He worked with Maggie's cows and horses, helped her halter train the colt, built fences and when needed handled the plough. Otto had also stumbled upon his own kind of peace, finding an understanding in Edith's ragged world, confused at its edges but possessed, for him, of a clarity at its centre. The others, meanwhile, even Steiner, had come to accept the valley as a refuge in which to bide their time and wait for what would happen once the dust of the war had settled. For Sebald, it was perhaps, even more than this. 'As good a place to end up as any,' is what he'd once said to Albrecht when they'd paused in a walk to take in the full view of the valley's length. 'And better by far than most.'

The women too, appeared to be more accepting of the situation. At times Albrecht even thought he detected a genuine gratitude for their presence. When Maggie looked to the tasks waiting in the months ahead, for example; to the shearing, dipping and hay making, the old woman seemed relieved to think they would not be facing these alone.

At first Albrecht had been careful to limit the contact as much as he could, but now the dependence between the women and the patrol had developed its own rhythm and metre. He was no more the conductor of events, but merely an observer of what he'd created. Slowly, despite the language barriers, he felt the patrol were becoming less German in the women's eyes and more just men. Men who'd been washed up on their doorsteps, carrying with them their own losses, just as the women did the loss of their husbands.

This shadow of their missing husbands was, of course, always there, and made darker by the intermittent wireless reports of the ongoing insurgency. But even this was now woven into the everyday fabric; an unseen and mostly unspoken weight of absence which together with the war worked as a counter-balance to their lives in the valley. Reminders of why all of them were still here, sharing this slice of isolated land between the thumb and forefinger of the Black Mountains Hand.

When Albrecht noticed the change in Gernot's behaviour after Bethan had left, he knew why Mary had sent her daughter away, but it did little to ease his concern. The balance they'd achieved in the valley was just that; a calibration that kept their fragile vessel upright but which might be tipped at any moment. In leaving the valley Bethan had punctured the hull of this vessel. She'd left behind a hole in the shape of herself through which Albrecht feared they would be contaminated. Just like the sandstone out of which the valley was made, they would all, once exposed to the realities of the outside world, be forced to calcify and harden.

Bethan's leaving, however, still worried Albrecht far less than her return. When he'd asked Maggie about this the old woman had been unclear as to when the girl might come back. His only hope was that when she did she would bring with her nothing more harmful than confirmation of the news reports that kept them here. The reports that still spoke of the war in the present tense. That hinted at a Russian resurgence behind the Urals threatening to break out into the west. The reports that suggested the war was not dead, just dormant, and it could still kill them all, given half the chance.

Albrecht was perhaps most affected by the ease with which Bethan had left. A packed lunch, a walk to the valley's head, a thousand yards across the plateau and she'd been gone. That was all it had taken for her to leave their world. Still six miles or so from her destination of Hay-on-Wye, but gone. The simplicity of it stirred something within him. A desire, despite all his better judgement, to see outside the valley walls himself. Not to leave them, but to see, just for a moment, the outside world close to his face and not from the distance of a view. But this desire, this sudden need in him triggered by Bethan's leaving, was not the only reason he accepted Sarah's offer to show him the ruins of Landor's house. It was the first time she'd ever given him anything, any possibility beyond the present. As a consequence it was also the first time since he'd taken her the gramophone and played her the cello suite that Albrecht could allow himself some hope.

'There, see that track? Where it goes in the dingle? That's where it is.'

Albrecht followed the line of Sarah's pointing finger. He could see nothing but a clump of trees, thick with new foliage. But the position would have been right. According to the biography he'd read Landor had been at pains to build up the slope, away from the ruins of the priory beneath.

Sarah dropped her arm. They were sitting on a stile at the edge of a small wood. It was the first time they'd stopped since they started out from the Olchon just before dawn. The plateau of the Hatterall had been broader than Albrecht expected, thick with bilberry bushes and purple heather. Twice they'd disturbed skylarks from their nests and stood and watched as the startled birds ascended above them, disappearing up the threads of their songs.

Over the past five years Albrecht had travelled through countries, over seas and into countless sectors of unknown territory, and yet this short walk over the Hatterall, no more than an hour, had felt the most adventurous of all his expeditions. This sensation was accentuated when they descended the other side of the ridge and the Llanthony valley began to open out before them. After his months in the Olchon, after all the days waking to its familiar shape and character, this suddenly different view invigorated him. The interlocking spurs of the high-backed hills gave the valley a folded appearance, while the broad glacial floor was patched with rich alluvial fields. Compared to the deep notch of the Olchon it was more open, more gentle and, with the ruins of the priory settled within it, more resonant with the mark of human hands. Albrecht felt like a Victorian explorer stumbling upon a hidden discovery. He knew, however, he was discovering nothing more than the depth of his own retreat these past months. The extent to which, apart from that brief motorbike ride out of the valley, he'd shrunk his world to a scale he could know and control.

The ruins of the priory were impressive. A great wrecked ship of a building run aground on the valley floor. A morning mist hung low about its walls. Many of its arches and long windows were still intact, framing the hills opposite and lending the ruins a beguiling impression of both order and chaos, of studied construction and natural decay. Its ragged towers and fallen walls emerging from the mist reminded him of another priory he'd seen in France. That too, had been a ruin when he saw it, but its remains had risen out of grey smoke, not mist. The priory had been used as a dressing station and in its crypt they'd found more than a hundred wounded men. Only the low grind of their moaning indicated some of them were still alive. In the chancel Albrecht had found a statue of the Virgin fallen from her pedestal, her head resting on a pillow of shattered stone and dust. The paint on her face was chipped below her eye in the shape of a tear. Albrecht was not a religious man, but at that moment he'd been willing to believe that someone, somewhere, was crying for what they had done.

'My father said Landor wanted that track t'be a road right

over to Longtown.' Sarah was still looking in the direction of Landor's house. 'But he never got it further than that field.' Albrecht traced the track away from the trees to where it faded and petered out into a grassed depression, then nothing.

The walk over the ridge seemed to have energised Sarah too. There was a new animation about her that lit her features. Every time Albrecht looked across at her it took some effort to make himself look away again. She had, he supposed, been away from the valley of her birth for a long time. While they sat on the stile she told him what she knew about its history.

'That's the Honddu,' she said, pointing towards the river meandering between the spurs of the hills, shining metallic in the first light of the morning. 'Means "black water".' Sarah lowered her hand. Albrecht felt her shift her weight on the stile beside him. She scratched her calf with the toe of one her scuffed boots. She seemed nervous.

'They say St David came here. Down there, where the chapel is, see? That's where he had his cell. He came here late on, when he was old,' she added before pausing again. Albrecht thought of the orphan lamb, awkward in its unfamiliar skin.

'William de Lacy built the chapel. He was a Norman knight. Came into the valley on a hunting trip an' never left. The priory came later. Didn't last long though. Locals wouldn't leave the monks alone so they left in the end.'

Albrecht began to feel uncomfortable too. She'd never spoken to him like this before. She'd never offered so much of herself. Was she trying to tell him something? This valley and its history was, after all, a graveyard of failures, littered with the remnants of men foolish enough to think its geography sufficient to extract themselves from the world.

What Albrecht didn't know was that ever since their walk back from the Red Darren yesterday Sarah had been mining her memories for everything she'd ever been told about the valley by her father, Mrs Thomas and the poet. It wasn't that she wanted to impress Albrecht. It was more important than that. He'd shown her the map, he'd explained its secrets to her, and now she wanted to be able to guide him in return. She wanted to be his equal, to show him that although she had none of his studying, she could still navigate the history of this living map below them.

'The old monastery, where David Jones lived with Eric Gill and the others? That's further up. You can't see it from here.' Sarah was careful to use their names. To call them as she always thought of them, as simply 'the artist' and 'the poet', seemed childish now. And she did not want to appear a child to him. This was her valley and she wanted to reveal it with all the authority and love with which he'd translated the map.

Albrecht nodded in response to Sarah's observations, interjecting now and then with, 'I see, yes,' or just a murmur of understanding. She said nothing he didn't already know. The books he'd obtained in Oxford had already told him everything she mentioned, and more. In a history of the valley he'd read the original extracts from Giraldus Cambrensis, who'd first referred to the tradition of St David's Cell. The biography of Landor he'd been reading at The Court had described how William de Lacy, sick of the trivialities of the royal court and seduced by the valley's isolated beauty, had resolved to restore the squat chapel below them and take up a life of contemplation and prayer. And from a recently published walking guide to the Welsh Marches he'd learnt how the monks had been harried from their cloisters by the lawless peasants whose ancestors had, no doubt, earned the valley its other name of the Vale of Ewyas, from the old Welsh word *gwyas*, meaning 'a place of battle'.

The sun was rising. The people in the valley below would soon be stirring. 'And that is where Landor built his villa?' Albrecht said, pointing once more to the trees at the end of the overgrown track. He looked down at the cows moving in and out of the ruined priory.

'It's all right,' Sarah said, getting off the stile. 'They're beef, not dairy. We'll be good for a bit yet.' Turning away from him she began walking across the open field.

Albrecht was suddenly panicked. Years of battle had left him with a natural wariness of such open pieces of land, even though it was now just the eyes of strangers he feared, not bullets or mortars. But those eyes could still be lethal. They could still take it all away. And that's why the panic fluttered in his chest. Because he did not want to lose her now. Not after so long, not when he could sense them becoming closer by the day. He slid off the stile and followed her, looking anxiously down at the ruins and the farm beside them, ready to retreat back into the woods at the first sign of life.

Over the long winter nights of reading his biography by the fire in The Court, Albrecht had grown fond of the eccentric and rebellious Walter Savage Landor. He somehow thought he understood what fuelled the eclectic gentleman poet who'd bought an estate in this valley with the vision of creating a feudal Utopia; the energetic dendrophiliac who'd planned to plant ten thousand Lebanon cedars on the bare Welsh hills. The ruins of his house were, therefore, a disappointment to Albrecht, and a sorry monument to the man and his ill-fated dreams. A few free-standing piles of fern-topped stones and four broken-topped walls of brown-red sandstone round a square of bare earth was all that remained of the villa Landor never saw finished. The ground within the walls was shot with nettles and cut up by the hooves of sheltering cattle. The unfinished cellar beneath these walls was dank and thick with the smell of sheep droppings. The only roof was provided by the trees; saplings when the foundations were laid. These at least, Albrecht thought, would have pleased Landor.

Sarah watched Albrecht as he moved slowly about the ruin, running his hand over the flaking sandstone just as he had across the surface of the map. He still wore a pair of grey-green uniform trousers, Wehrmacht-issue boots and an army water bottle on his belt. But from the waist up he was dressed in clothes from The Court; a heavy tweed jacket over a shirt and dark blue jumper. Sarah wondered who the jumper and jacket belonged to. Reg or one of the boys? She thought of Reg's son Malcolm, dragging his heavy foot over the hill. Leaning back against one of the ruined walls she let herself slide down its rough surface until she was crouching at its base. How had it come to this? Alone with a German, half-soldier, half-farmer, in the ruins of a house in which she'd played as a child. She'd probably seen those clothes before, when she'd talked with Reg and the boys or watched them at their work just months ago. Maybe that was the very shirt Reg had been wearing last summer when she'd come across the stubbled field with a flagon of cider. When he'd paused in pitching his forkfuls of freshly cut hay onto the wagon to drink thirstily from that flagon, spilling some of it down his front, before handing it back to her with a playful wink and a hoarse, 'Thank you, bach.' Perhaps if she got close enough to Albrecht she'd still smell that spilt cider. Still smell another man's summer on the clothes he wore now.

279

She looked up at him. The low sun caught the frame of his spectacles. He didn't look like a soldier any more, but more like the scholar he said he once was, running his fingers over the remains of this ruined house. His hands looked pale against the dark stone, long-fingered, delicate almost. She was too far away to see the veins branching over the knuckles, but she already knew how blue they were under his pale skin, like mapped rivers under ice.

Tom's hands were rougher, broader. Other parts of Tom, his smell, his face even, were fading from her, but not his hands. She remembered them. He'd worked with them all his life. Each finger bore the scar of a slipped knife or a barbed-wire nick. Each knuckle held some of the cold and heat of the many seasons he'd worked outside in all weathers. They were heavy, thick hands. When Sarah touched them she used to think he'd only feel her if she dug her nails right in or pressed with all her weight into his palm.

She looked again at Albrecht's hands. They were hands for turning pages, holding books, for passing slowly over the surface of ancient maps. They were not the hands of a soldier. She couldn't imagine them holding a gun, a grenade, pulling a trigger. But she knew they must have. She'd seen it for herself that night he came into her house. That night she'd thought he was Tom, back at last, only to see Albrecht standing there, one of his pale hands holding a pistol.

Sarah got up and walked over to where Albrecht was leaning against a corner of the ruin. He was looking down towards the priory as if he wanted to remember its every keystone and fallen arch. She stood behind him, at his shoulder.

'Have you killed people?' she said quietly, speaking as if they were in a crowded room and she wanted no one else to hear them.

Albrecht didn't move, just let out a brief, almost imperceptible sigh, like an escaped fragment of something larger collapsing within him. His gaze shifted from the priory to a buzzard catching its balance on the morning air in the field below them. 'Yes,' he said at last.

'How many?'

'I don't know.' He watched the buzzard drop then turn a slow glide over the field.

'You wouldn't think it,' Sarah said. 'You'd think t'see it. But you don't.'

'No,' Albrecht said, 'you don't.'

He pushed himself off the wall and walked along the track that ran away from the ruins, trying to get a better view of the priory below. Sarah followed a few feet behind him until he stopped and sat on a hummock of moss under a tree. Looking down at the ground he tore a few blades of grass from between his feet before looking back up at her standing beside him. 'What will you do?' he said. 'When this is over?'

'Nothing. Stay here, with Tom.'

Albrecht smiled and nodded his head as if he'd been stupid to ask such an obvious question. 'Of course,' he said, 'of course you will.' He ripped another handful of grass from between his legs. Sarah came and sat beside him.

'You are a remarkable woman, Sarah.'

The sound of her name in his mouth caught her unawares. She looked up at him but he was staring back down at the priory again. In all the months they'd known each other they'd never used each other's names. She had always been Mrs Lewis and he, whenever she spoke of him to Maggie or the others, was 'the Captain'. In calling her Sarah it was as if some game they'd been playing was suddenly over. Except she'd never been playing at anything.

'You really believe they'll come back, don't you?'

There was no challenge in his voice, just a quiet admiration. Nothing for her to resist or to provoke her anger.

'Yes,' she said. 'I do.'

She was lying, but only partly. She didn't know about the other men but she did know about Tom. And she did believe he would come back, or at least that he was still here, that he wasn't dead. She wouldn't believe that he could die and she wouldn't know, somehow. A shift in the air about her, a tint upon the light of the day. Somehow, she'd know.

'What about you?' she asked Albrecht. 'Will you go home?'

Albrecht followed the buzzard as it made another slow spiralling descent before coming to rest in the upper branches of a tree at the edge of the field. The bird stretched its wings once then folded them, disappearing to a dark bud, invisible to the passing eye.

'I have no home to go back to,' he said. 'I was a student before the war. Always on the move. My parents' house is no longer there. It was destroyed in an air raid. The same one that killed my fiancée.'

He'd never mentioned Ebbe to Sarah before. She had never wanted to know anything but the barest of facts about his past. 'I'm sorry,' she said.

He leant back against the tree. 'I was in Russia when they died. I didn't know until over a month later. For over a month I wrote to all of them, but they were already dead, and I never knew.'

She wanted to reach out and touch him then but she couldn't. He was wearing those clothes. To touch them on him would be a betrayal of everything she was holding on to. 'Germany though,' she said eventually. 'That's your home, isn't it? You'll be going back there when it's over, won't you?'

Albrecht rested his head against the trunk of the tree, closed his eyes and tilted his face towards the sun rising over the Hatterall ridge behind them. 'When I was stationed in Holland,' he said, speaking with his eyes still closed, 'I used to go to a park every Sunday to listen to a band that played there. They were very good. I got to know the band leader. One day I saw a Party official also watching the band. He was holding a clipboard, making marks on it with his pencil. When they were packing up I asked the band leader what the official had been doing. He looked at me as if I was mad not to know. "Checking we're playing within the regulations," he said. "No sideways swaying of the saxophone. No muted trumpet. No ostentatious trills or double-stopping." What he meant was nothing that might resemble "Negro music", as he called it.' Albrecht thought of the distaste on Steiner's face when they'd tuned through snatches of jazz on the radio. 'I am German,' he said, turning his face away from the sun and looking back down at the abandoned priory. 'But Germany is not my home any more.'

For some minutes they sat there, beneath the tree, saying nothing. A blackbird sang from one of the ruined walls beside them. A crow cawed, brash and harsh, as it fought in the tree above with a pair of magpies. It was going to be a warm day. Sarah could feel it, the potential heat heavy in the air. She was in the valley of her childhood, where she'd grown up. She knew the contours of the land about them intimately. And yet she was also in a place unfamiliar to her, somewhere off the edges of any map she'd ever known.

Eventually it was Sarah who spoke again.

'That night,' she said, speaking slowly as if it was an effort to draw up the words. 'The night they left. All of us woke late the next morning. We've never spoken about it, but we did. Slept right through. Never heard a thing. All of us. I've tried speaking to Maggie. Ask her why she thinks that was. But I can't. She knows why though, an' so do I. I even went looking for the bottle. But I can't ask her. It'd be too much, I reckon.'

Albrecht shifted his back up the trunk and turned to look at Sarah. 'Your husbands did the right thing,' he said. 'It is what men all over Europe have done. It is what I would have done.'

'That's maybe,' Sarah said, sighing through a weak smile. 'But that don't make it any easier. I'd rather they were wrong an' here than right an' not.'

Albrecht turned back to face the valley, then looked over again at the ruined walls of the house Landor had only ever dreamt of living in. 'You know, he was a very fine writer of letters, Landor,' he said, still looking at the ruins. 'There's a line in one of them that has stayed with me ever since I read it: "More people are good because they are happy than happy because they are good." This is what he says. And he is right.' He glanced back at Sarah. She met his eye then looked away. 'It is very hard to be good now,' he continued. 'But after all this, when we are able to be happy again, then I think maybe we will be good to each other again too. In ways that do not have to be so painful.'

He kept his eyes on her face, willing her to turn back and look at him. But she did not. She just looked down at the grass, nodding her head, as might a child who wasn't really listening to the words being spoken to them.

'This is what I hope, anyway,' Albrecht added more quietly as he unclipped the water bottle from his belt. Unscrewing the cap he offered it to Sarah. She shook her head without looking at him. He tipped the bottle to his own lips and drank briefly, before finding himself swallowing at nothing but air. He upended the bottle and a few drops of water landed in his palm.

'Here,' Sarah said suddenly, holding out her hand. 'There's a standpipe in the yard of the farm.'

Without thinking Albrecht passed her the bottle. As he did he saw her eyes were glassy with tears and the frown line cut deep in the middle of her brow. She stood up, brushing loose bits of moss from the back of her blue dress, and it was only then that he realised what she'd meant. 'No, Sarah, you can't –' he began, but it was too late. She was already walking away from him over the fields towards the priory and the farm.

Albrecht watched her shrink away from him down the shallow slope through the yellow scatterings of buttercups. It seemed to take her hours, not minutes, to cross the field and the one beyond. For a moment he saw the whole scene from the perspective of that buzzard, high in its tree. Him, sat beside the ruins of Landor's house, and her, walking through the acres of green and gold towards the arches of the priory, with nothing more than the lengthening thread of her footprints in the dew to connect them. By the time she slipped round the corner of the farm she was no more than a dot of blue against the priory's grey stone. Albrecht was suddenly convinced that was it. That she wouldn't come back. That like Bethan's easy departure, Sarah had simply walked away from him, knowing he wouldn't follow her. He sat under the tree, his mind reeling. Should he go after her? Should he try to bring her back? Had she really just left him like that, after everything they'd said? After several minutes of straining his eyes at the ruins of the priory Albrecht could bear it no longer, and he was about to risk going after her when he saw the blue of her dress again appearing round the corner of the farm as she began to re-trace that thread of footprints over the fields back towards him. He felt a wave of relief, the sudden gratitude of a reprieve. Closing his eyes he tilted his head back against the tree once more, thanking the God he didn't believe in.

As Sarah got closer he saw she was holding something other than just the water bottle. It was a piece of paper, a yellow piece of paper which she folded twice then placed in her pocket before reaching him. When she did her face was flushed from her quick walk up the slope and her eyes were clear of tears again. 'Come on,' she said, 'it's getting late. We'd best be going now.'

'Maggie, you can't. It's madness.'

'Don't be silly girl. Nothin' mad about it,' Maggie said from over the rim of her mug. 'An' we've got to do something, anyway. Mary's right. It's gone on long enough. The show's as good a place as any to see how thing's are lying.'

Sarah was sitting at Maggie's kitchen table again, just the two of them. Maggie had a bad cold and had brewed herself a pot of elderflower and honey. The bright morning cast the window frame's shadow across the table's surface, a dark cross separating four squares of light gradually slipping over the scarred and pitted wood. One of the squares caught the corner of a yellow piece of paper lying between them, its heavy type buckled at the creases where Sarah had folded it into her pocket the day before.

By Permission of the Office of the Reich Sub-Area
Commandant for the Western Region

Saturday 9 June
Llanthony Agricultural Show and Country Fair
Ploughing Match, Sports, Horse and Stock Showing

'But why him, Maggie? You'd find someone at the show, wouldn't you?'

Maggie frowned at Sarah as she took another sip from the

steaming mug as if to admonish her for asking such a stupid question. 'You've seen him with the colt,' she said, placing the mug back on the table. 'He's good with him. The horse likes him, knows him. You know it was him not me as first haltered him don't you? Even Will never did that.'

Sarah knew Maggie was right about this at least. She'd watched Alex handle the colt, seen the relationship he'd developed with the young horse which had grown into a strong yearling, too much for Maggie now, thick at the neck, big-boned, alert and quick. Alex, however, had found a manner with him. The colt's head only came to his shoulder but he was still as slow and gentle about the young horse as he would have been around a frail old woman.

The amount of milk produced by Maggie's cows had been declining for weeks now. When Alex came over to help her he'd had more time to stay on and work with the colt. At first the horse was skittish, familiar for so long with only the smells of the mare and Maggie. But each day Alex moved a little closer, talking to him all the time, until one morning the colt let him run his hand the length of his neck. By the time he came to halter him there'd been hardly any struggle. Maggie had looked on nervously from over the stable's half-door as the colt tossed his head a couple of times and began quick-stepping his hind legs sideways. As soon as the halter was on, however, he'd settled, allowing Alex to stroke his mane and talk once more, low and soft, into his ear.

Maggie never understood what Alex was saying to the colt, and Alex didn't understand Maggie either when she talked away to him as they worked. But this hadn't stopped them communicating. With the colt between them they didn't need a common language. Everything was movement and rhythm, sound not words, a shared instinct for how the young horse would react, how he'd shift his weight, moments before he did. The first time Alex ran him in the meadow, his hooves flashing out high, his thick neck curved tight, was also the first time since her husband left that Maggie had felt, for the briefest of moments, a lightness inside her.

'I still don't understand why you'd want t'go now,' Sarah said, turning the poster round to look at it again. She wished she'd never brought it back from the priory, wished she'd never gone down there at all. It had certainly been a mistake to show it to Maggie.

'Don't you, bach?' Maggie gave Sarah a long look. Again she saw how she'd fallen so much earlier than the younger woman. She stood up and moved over to the dresser. Standing on the tips of her toes, she picked out a long card from behind the plates on the top shelf.

'You know what Will could be like,' she said, her back to Sarah as she looked over the card. 'Never so pleased with himself as when he'd run a good yearling.' She shook her head, 'Daft bugger,' then turned back to Sarah. 'He'd have wanted to run this colt at Llanthony, I know he would. So that's why. Because we should be carrying on as usual where we can, doing what we'd be doing as if this never happened.' She paused, looked out the window then back down at the card in her hand. 'Because it's what Will would have wanted. That's why, bach.'

Through all of Maggie and William's years together the yearling cobs had been the only part of their daily lives they'd really shared. The other chores and tasks on the farm had remained the territory of one or the other of them since their first day of marriage. Making the bread, butter, cream, keeping the chickens, feeding the pig and the fire; these were Maggie's responsibilities. Milking the cows, looking after the flock, the vegetables and the farm; these were William's.

Breeding cobs from a succession of working mares had been their only mutual interest and the only activity to which they'd devoted time that wasn't directly related to keeping the farm going. Once they'd had some good results with a yearling in the local shows the young horses would be sold on at a tidy profit, often much to William's delight and Maggie's regret.

This latest colt, Glyndwr Llwyd, was never meant to be. They'd agreed they were getting too old for breeding, that they'd had a good run at it and now, what with the turn in the war, it was best to rest on their laurels. But then one day William came home from market with the stud card Maggie held in her hand now. As she sat back down at the table she glanced at the door, remembering how he'd stood there that afternoon, one hand on the door frame, the other pulling the card from his waistcoat pocket.

'He'll only be here a couple of days,' was all he'd said as he'd placed the card on the table as carefully as if it were made of bone china and might break at any minute.

Maggie was baking bread. She'd dusted off her hands on her apron, sat down where she was sitting now and turned the card round to face her.

Season 1943
THE FAMOUS WELSH COB STALLION
CARDI LLWYD, 1665
Holder Of Premium for Brecon and Radnor.

Fee, £3. Tenant Farmers, £1 10s. Groom, 5s
Breeders: PARRY BROS., Llwynfynwent,
Llangwyryfon, Cards.

CARDI LLWYD is a beautiful Dark Dapple Dun Colour Cob, 12 years old, 15 hands high. He is one of the grand old Welsh type, now almost extinct; short to the ground; proper height and any amount of bone and substance; with such a look out; perfect temper, manners, and any amount of courage; and one of the finest goers in the country.

People who may not have the Stud Book at their command will be interested to know that investigation of this Pedigree reveals the possession of four strains of CYMRO LLWYD, probably the best of the many good horses that have contributed to the maintenance and improvement of the Welsh Cob.

Sire – Ceitho Welsh Flyer, 1080, W.S.B.
g. Sire – Caribaldi Comet II, 711, W.S.B.
g.g. Sire – Caribaldi Comet.
Dam – Gwyryfon Nancy, 8935, W.S.B., by Welsh Model, 620.
g. Dam – Gwyryfon Betty, 7141, by Trecefel King, by Grand Express.
g.g. Dam – Polly, by Satisfaction, by Welsh Jack.
g.g.g. Dam – Eiddwen Bess, by Eiddwen Express, by Express (Cotrell).
g.g.g.g. Dam – Fly, by Welsh Jack, by Cymro Llwyd.

Concerning the remarkable pedigree behind CARDI LLWYD, one could write much, but for the time being I must confine myself to the general comment that it would be difficult to find a better combination of type, speed and action, handed down by individuals of outstanding merit.

All Mares are absolutely at owner's risk but the utmost care will be taken.
All Mares tried by this Horse will be Charged for.

'I thought we'd said no more, Will?' Maggie had said, still reading the card and trying to put an edge to her voice.

'Well, yes,' he'd replied, coming round behind her, placing his hands on her shoulders and giving them a squeeze. 'We did, didn't we? But Cardi Llwyd? It's not every day you get quality like that in the area.'

'You've been drinking.' He only ever squeezed her shoulders like that when he had.

'Just a couple with Watkins.' He moved round to sit beside her. 'It was him as showed me the card. The stallion's standing at his place, see?'

'I bet he is,' was all Maggie said under her breath.

'So, what d'you think? She's in season isn't she?'

'Three pound,' Maggie said looking up at him. 'That's a lot, Will.'

And that was when he'd let his mouth grow into a slow smile, deepening the crow's feet at his eyes. As soon as Maggie had looked up he'd known. Just a year later Glyndwr Llwyd, a fine looking bay dappled colt, unsteady on his big-kneed legs, was suckling from the mare, and William was gone.

'He won't let it,' Sarah said, sitting back from looking over the poster again. 'He won't let him go.' She didn't have to say Albrecht's name for Maggie to know who she was talking about. 'You saw how he was about Bethan.'

Maggie kept looking out the window as if trying to make out a vague figure in the distance. Eventually she went over to the Rayburn and poured some more hot water over the elderflower in the bottom of her mug. 'Oh he will,' she said as she sipped at the hot drink, both her hands around it. 'He'll have to.'

June 8th

Maggie takes her yearling to the show tomorrow. She's set on it. I was going to go with her but now she says it will be better if I stay. I'm not so sure but she's set on that too now. You know what she can be like. She says it's time. That we need to see how everything is going outside the valley.

She's right, Tom. We can't go on like this for long. The lambs will have to go to market soon, if there is a market. Her cows need serving if we're to have any milk. We have hardly any coal if it turns cold again. And then there is the dipping and shearing and hay coming up. It will be too much.

I think it has been too much for Mary already. And maybe Menna. Mary's reading the Bible all the time, to Menna and her two little ones when not to herself. Edith is fine. Maggie says it's like they're crossing over those two, Mary and Edith.

I am still scared though, Tom. About Maggie going to the show tomorrow. Only thing makes me feel better is she might come back with news of you. I hope she does. It has been too long, Tom, and it's all over now anyway.

I put the first lambs on the hill this morning. The gorse out the back is in full flower. Every time I go round there I smell it. Like coconut.

Stay safe, Tom. I hope soon I'll be able to read these to you when we are together, instead of writing them when we are apart.

Sarah

She placed the cap back on the pen, closed the accounts book and put them both in the drawer of the dresser. The bottle of ink from which she filled the pen's cartridge was already in there. Picking it out she tilted it to measure how much was left. It was almost empty, the deep blue liquid drained from the bottle just as she'd drained herself from these letters to Tom. It didn't matter. The pages at the back of the accounts book had filled out over the months until now she was just a couple away from meeting the columns and figures of her previous life. She knew soon there would be no more room for the letters. Either inside the book or inside her.

When Alex arrived at Maggie's farm on the morning of the show the sky above the Hatterall ridge which had, just a few hours before, still borne the last indigo streaks of dawn, was already ripening into an early summer blue. Maggie was already in the yard, washing the colt. The cobbles about the horse's legs were polished dark by the water running off his flanks and flecked white between them where the soapy rivulets trickled down to the drain along the fence. Glyndwr's coat shone like a chestnut freshly split from its shell. Maggie worked over him with a towel, rubbing it in big circular movements over the slabs of muscle across his shoulders and rump. The horse lifted his head as Alex approached, pulling his tether tight before lowering his muzzle again to the calf nuts lying in the German's outstretched palm.

'Don't give him those now, mun. You'll only excite him,' Maggie said.

Alex smiled back at her, not understanding yet also understanding at the same time. A swallow darted from under the eaves of the stable. Alex followed its flight as it banked and carved above them, the blades of its wings, the cut throat of its chest, quick against the morning sky.

'Here,' Maggie said throwing him a pair of red bandages. 'I've chalked his socks. Put these on him to keep them clean. We'll be off soon enough now.'

Maggie had been right again. Albrecht had, eventually, agreed to Alex accompanying her to the show in Llanthony. At first he was firmly resistant to the idea, reminding Maggie again of the consequences if their husbands, and therefore themselves, were linked to the insurgency in any way. But then Maggie had given him some facts and consequences of her own. The practicalities of keeping the farms going made it clear they could not continue with their isolation for much longer. At some point the seal on their estrangement from the world would have to be broken. Menna was already threatening to follow Bethan out of the Olchon and take her children back to the mining valleys. They were low on coal, and oil for the lamps. They would soon have no milk and therefore no cheese and butter. The lambs were to be slaughtered, the wool sold. In time someone was bound to come into the valley. Much better, surely, they choose when and how they make their contact with the world beyond? And anyway, Maggie told him, she'd be going to the show whatever he said. Unless of course the captain wanted to stop her by force.

In the end it was the poster that convinced him more than anything else. He recognised where it came in the arc of occupation. He'd seen similar posters during his time in Holland back in '41. After months of nailing proclamations and orders to doorways and fence posts beginning with the word *Forbidden* and ending *On Pain of Death*, the administration would finally issue one like this. *By Permission of the Reich Sub-Commandant for the Western Region*; the benevolent new rulers allowing local traditions and customs to continue. It was a subtle sign of strength, one of the finer points of Nazi technique. Gather together, it said, continue as you did before all this. We have nothing to fear and neither do you. There is no need for concern. Nothing, you see, has really changed. At the show itself there would still be soldiers, but in the background. Small groups of young men in grey-green serge hovering at the edges of the marquees and stock rings. A friendly faced guard standing alongside the local woman taking the entry fees at the gate. Later, maybe some of these young men would remove their jackets and heavy boots and, trousers rolled to their knees, take part in the sports. They would laugh, make eyes at the young girls and everything about them would say, 'We are the same as you. It is nearly over now, this war. Let us be friends while we are thrown together.' Elsewhere on the showground there would be stalls, even out here in the country; new women's and mothers' groups with slogans about 'putting Britain back on its feet'. Information desks about the opportunities of work in a new United Europe. Albrecht saw all of this in the yellow poster, quartered by creases where Sarah had folded it into her pocket. He recognised how it advertised much more than just the show. How it advertised victory too, a seal on the disruption of the war years. It was a sign that the world had moved on. 'Why resist,' it said, 'that which is already here? That which has only altered things for the better and brought you peace.'

Albrecht had known for some time that what Maggie said was true. Ever since the first days of the thaw. However much he may have wished it otherwise, he recognised they could not continue like this. He hoped it would last through the summer, through the diversions of shearing and hay making, when the help of him and his men would be vital for the women. And maybe it still would. Maybe those letters he'd returned would be enough. But if the old woman was determined to go now, then so be it. She would not be stopped and perhaps she was right; perhaps the time was already upon them. It was impossible to tell from intermittent radio reports alone. He could only be sure by testing the waters of the real world outside this valley, however much that might put them at risk. The world of hunger, boredom, resentments, fear, greed and need. And that, in the end, was why he'd allowed Alex to appear at Maggie's yard that morning. To run her colt, the colt Alex himself had come to love, but also to act as a barometer for Albrecht and the rest of the patrol. To take the measure of the pressures in that real world beyond the valley, and gauge whether they could risk entering the erratic flow of its currents once more.

There were conditions. Maggie must enter her class, compete and then leave. There was no need for Alex to appear until the showing itself. Indeed, until the colts were run, Maggie could handle the horse on her own. Alex must not speak to anyone. There was little danger of any of the units at the show recognising him, but the consequences of a German soldier dressed in a farmer's clothes arriving with a local woman were obvious. It would be a disaster, for both Maggie and Alex. They would be seen as a collaborator and a deserter. For the duration of their time out of the valley, therefore, Alex would be 'Arthur', a mute cousin of William's returned from the army to help on the farm. The residue of shell shock was the reason for his silence. When Albrecht heard himself outlining this scenario he couldn't help but feel ridiculous. Would anyone really believe such a story? Maggie seemed to think they would. She understood the consequences of Alex being found out and there was a forthrightness in her manner that eventually convinced Albrecht too. Even so, it was with a level of anxiety he hadn't experienced in months that Albrecht watched the two of them leave Maggie's farm that morning. They were no more than two specks against the hillside, and not much clearer through Steiner's binoculars. But still Albrecht had watched them from the slope high above The Court, following their distant progress as closely as if they were a battalion of soldiers marching off to battle.

Sarah, still confused and shocked by Maggie's decision, had also watched the pair leave, leaning against the sill of the narrow window on the landing outside her bedroom. Maggie was riding the mare while Alex followed behind, leading the colt. The red bandages around the horse's hocks flashed on and off as they picked their way through the patches of scree and waist-high bracken. From this distance Alex could easily have been one of Maggie's missing sons. He wore one of William's caps, a rough herringbone jacket, waistcoat and trousers and a white shirt that, although spotless and stiff when she'd taken it from the wardrobe, Maggie had newly starched for the event. His boots were still his battered Wehrmacht-issue ones but he carried another pair in a bag slung over his shoulder. They were laceless ankle boots that Reg had hardly ever worn, removing their wooden trees for no more than a handful of weddings and funerals. They were smart and light and although half a size too small, perfect for running the colt at the show.

By the time Sarah came out of Upper Blaen to feed the hens Maggie and Alex were almost at the top of the ridge. She watched them rise, vague and indistinct against the greens and browns of the slope. When she bent to the hen house then looked up again she lost them. She scanned the hillside for movement but only caught them again when they crested the ridge. For a moment they were silhouetted there against the pale sky, their heads at the same height despite Maggie being on horseback, before walking on and disappearing over the horizon.

The cool morning warmed into a beautiful day, almost cloudless but for a few high puffs of loose vapour. There hadn't been much wind these past months and the apple blossom on the trees down by the river was already turning into the buds of new fruit. Sarah rode Bess up onto the hill to check the flock. It was smaller now, after the winter, even with the addition of the new lambs. Those that had survived, however, were growing big and strong on the spring grass on which they and the ewes grazed hungrily. Higher up on the top the wire grass swept blond over the plateau, patched with dark shallow peat pits, wisps of cotton grass and swathes of bilberry bushes hummocking into the distance. Riding back down the slope Sarah saw again the beauty of the Olchon as she had that first time when Tom had driven her into the valley on his father's pony and trap one spring evening seven years ago. Throughout the rest of the day, however, her mind was not in the Olchon valley but in Llanthony, where, in the fields beside the priory, she knew Maggie and Alex were meeting the world again. She was restless and couldn't settle to anything. Just after lunch Gernot arrived at her door with an eel he'd caught in the river. He seemed relaxed, light with life, despite his missing Bethan, and blissfully unaware of what might have been happening at that very moment, just over the ridge; of what terrible news Maggie might have been hearing as they stood there at her door in the midday sun. Sarah thanked Gernot and watched him leave, ruffling Fly's head as he passed through the yard and on down the track. Taking the eel inside, she sprinkled it with salt then began carefully peeling back, inch by inch, the slick dark skin, exposing the white flesh beneath.

Albrecht sometimes called in the early afternoon but when he still hadn't arrived by two o'clock Sarah went over to

Mary's instead and then on to The Firs, where she took Tudor and Emma off Menna's hands while their mother washed their clothes and prepared their supper. By five o'clock she was walking back along the valley's eastern wall, glancing up as often as she could at the opposite slope. She'd done the calculations. Maggie would have had to register Glyndwr for the class no later than eleven. The yearlings were usually early, say around one o'clock at the latest. The route back up from Llanthony was steep. So give them two hours in all from the start of the class, maybe three if it had been a large entry. That meant they should be coming back over into the valley around five, around now. Sarah looked up at the Hatterall, hoping to see their silhouettes again on its ridge. But there was nothing. Maybe they'd won the class? In which case there was no doubt Maggie would have stayed for the parade and the final judging. William had only ever won the champion of champions at a local show once. If she had then it would be nearer seven, eight even, before they'd be back in the Olchon.

In the end it was around six o'clock, as Sarah was coming round from the coal store at the back of the house, that she saw them, the colt's bandages flashing red again in the lowering light. They were far down the slope, almost at Maggie's farm. Sarah couldn't wait. Leaving the coal bucket in the porch she grabbed her coat off the back of the door and started down the track, her heart suspended within her ribs as delicately as the pocket of air between the bars of a spirit level. Fly and Seren, surprised by Sarah's sudden leaving, rose from where they'd been lying in the open shed, shook the loose straw from their bodies and trotted down the track after her.

By the time Sarah reached Maggie's farm Alex had already

left. Sarah couldn't find Maggie either. Perhaps she'd gone with him to The Court for some reason? But then she heard Maggie's voice, muffled and low, coming from within the stable in the corner of the yard.

'Stupid bugger. How d'you manage that?'

'Maggie?' Sarah said as she approached the stable. 'That you?'

Looking over the half door she could just make her out in the darkness, crouching on the floor beside the colt's off-hind leg.

'Got right worked up he did,' Maggie said, a wad of cloth between her teeth. 'Caught himself on the way down. Even with the bloody bandages on an' all.' She took the cloth from between her teeth, dipped it in a bowl of warm water at her side and gently ran a corner of it down the length of the cut on Glyndwr's hock.

Sarah stood at the door, waiting for Maggie to offer something else, but she just kept on dabbing at the cut, muttering the odd word under her breath, more to herself than to Sarah.

'Well?' Sarah said eventually. 'What happened, Maggie? At the show?'

Maggie looked at her from where she crouched, swilled the cloth in the bowl of water then stood up, wringing it dry over the bed of straw. Glyndwr tore a mouthful of hay from a rack on the wall and chewed on it rhythmically. Maggie walked up to the door so Sarah could see her face. She was smiling.

'Oh he ran well, bach,' she said, running her hand down Glyndwr's neck. 'Really well. He's a beautiful mover. The boy did him proud.' She leant against the top of the half door, still looking at Glyndwr. 'Watkins had a lovely colt in, mind, another one thrown by Cardi Llwyd. Least he was beat by his own brother, I s'pose.' She turned back to Sarah. 'An' a couple of others. Fourth in the end. Just out of the colours. Never mind, eh?' She patted the horse's neck a couple of times.

Sarah could feel her heart beating against the wood of the stable door. Couldn't Maggie feel it too? The steady hammer of it passing through her ribs and skin into the thin, knotted planks. 'That's good,' she said quietly nodding her head. 'But what about everything else? Who d'you see?' Her breath was tight in her throat. She paused and gave the colt a rub on his nose. He bucked his head under her touch. 'What was it *like*?' she said, pulling her hand away from Glyndwr's searching mouth.

Maggie let out a heavy sigh then looked down at the piece of cloth as she folded it into tighter and tighter squares. 'Oh,' she said. 'Not much different really. Some soldiers there, of course, but apart from that it was like as always, more or less.' She smiled again, still looking down at her hands. 'Think most folk thought we'd copped it over the winter.'

'Were they surprised then?' Sarah said. 'T'see you I mean?'

Maggie looked back up at her then beyond to the darkening ridge. The sky above it was deepening again, slowly bruising towards dusk. It was still light but she could just make out the first stars. 'It's been a hard time of it, bach, that's for sure,' she said. 'Think people have had their own worries without botherin' about us.'

Sarah couldn't hold back any longer. 'But what about Tom and William, Maggie? Did you hear anything?'

Maggie looked back at Sarah, at the deep crease of the frown between her eyebrows. 'No, bach,' she said, shaking her head. 'No, I didn't.' She sighed heavily again. 'I told them Will couldn't run the colt himself because he was over here working. Getting back after the winter. None of them so much as bat an eyelid.'

Sarah's pulse throbbed in her head and she tasted the bitter tang of bile at the back of her throat.

'I did see Helen Roberts though,' Maggie continued, as if they'd just been passing the time with general gossip. 'From over Hay? Said she'd seen Bethan in town. She's doing fine, helping her aunt with the shop, she is.' Maggie paused but Sarah had turned away from her, her back against the door. Where was she going? Maggie wondered. Where would the girl go once the hope was gone?

'I asked Helen t'tell Bethan to come back over for a bit if she could,' Maggie continued. 'Said it'd do her mother some good t'see her.'

Sarah knew what Maggie meant by this. She'd seen it herself when she'd called that afternoon. Mary was a boat loosening from its moorings. She needed Bethan there. They all needed her there. To anchor her mother, to stop her drifting away from them completely.

Maggie reached out and laid a hand on Sarah's shoulder. 'Look, lets talk about this in the morning, is it?' She felt Sarah flinch under her touch. 'I'm done in, girl. Let me get this fixed an' I'll come up tomorrow. We can talk it over proper then.'

Sarah turned round to look at Maggie. She didn't know her any more. There was something missing, as if she'd left a part of herself over the ridge in Llanthony. Maybe she was loosening like Mary. Maybe she'd already gone.

'It's best, bach,' Maggie said, forcing a smile. 'Get some rest yourself now.'

Sarah left Maggie's yard feeling as if the last threads of hope had been winnowed from within her. Calling the two dogs after her she turned back up the lane towards Upper

Blaen. All about her the trees were electric with the birds' evensong, marking the passing of another day. As the incline of the lane rose up the valley she saw the moon through the lower branches, rising over the Black Hill. It was a full moon, just like the one that had shone over the men's departure; a clean disc of pitted white, bright with the light of their own dying day.

Back in her yard Maggie fetched a bottle of disinfectant from the shed then returned to the stable and the colt. Tipping the open bottle to the corner of the folded cloth, she began cleaning the cut again, telling Glyndwr to 'shhh now, shhh,' and stroking his flank above her with her free hand. The cut was deep with fragments of stone in it; the horse must have caught himself on one of the many slabs of sandstone that littered the valley walls. She worked the cloth firmly into the cut, edging it under the loose skin at the sides. Glyndwr flinched, lifting his hoof off the ground every time she touched the wound, but Maggie wanted to make sure. She didn't want any proud flesh. A badly healed scar on a yearling as good as this would be such a shame. William would never forgive her.

When she'd finished treating the wound she began unwinding the bandages from his other legs. As she knelt to undo the knot of the bandage tied around one of his forelegs he nuzzled the top of her head, nibbling at her hair with his lips. 'Get off with you,' Maggie said, gently pushing him away with one hand while still fumbling with the knot with her other. She couldn't seem to get it undone. It was pulled as tight as an unripe berry, her fingers felt clumsy and thick and the knot itself kept blurring and distorting in her vision, however many times she blinked away the tears from her eyes.

Maggie had lied, but it wasn't what she'd said to Sarah that made her cry as she crouched beside the colt in the stable. It was everything she hadn't.

How the women in the secretary's tent had looked at her when she'd walked in; as if they were looking at a ghost.

How pale they went.

How, although the show looked like every other she'd been to, it was totally different.

How people's faces were strained at the edges, taut across their brows and temples.

How there were so many she didn't know, and so many she did who weren't there.

How one of those women from the tent, Edna Kelly, had followed her out and called her name after her.

How Maggie had turned to see that expression still ghosting Edna's face and how Edna's eyes had welled as she stood there, one hand held to her chest, the other on Maggie's shoulder.

How Edna had asked tentatively after William and how Maggie had lied to her too, saying he was on the farm, working.

And then how she'd had to stand there in front of Edna, the show turning about them, the announcer's clipped voice rising through the Tannoy, as she told Maggie how relieved she was; how there were so many rumours now you never knew what to believe; how she knew she'd been right; how she'd said to her husband, 'William Jones would never be caught up in all that, not him.' How she'd never believed it when they'd said it was him brought off the railway line. How (leaning closer now) those lot had it coming anyway; she didn't understand why they couldn't let it rest. How she'd never liked a mess and say what you like, at least the Jerries have put a stop to some of that.

How after Edna had gone back to the secretary's tent, giving her a squeeze of the arm as she left, Maggie'd had to walk away through the show, with Edna's words and all they'd implied swirling through her head.

How she'd seen groups of soldiers at the edges of the rings and hanging around the stalls selling cakes and small jars of sweets.

How she'd felt again the fear and anger of that first night when Albrecht came knocking at her door with his pistol in his hand.

How Glyndwr was the best in his class by far, with the most perfect confirmation, carriage and paces.

How Alex had slipped into the ring from nowhere, big and quiet and gentle.

How William would have been so proud to see the colt run like that, all power and muscle, a barely contained wildness simmering under the sheen of a deep bay coat, a flowing mane and four flashing, white-socked hooves.

How somehow the judges had known about Alex and that was why, when Maggie took the colt back from him, they'd left her circling long after they'd called the others in.

How she'd led Glyndwr around that ring, his head tossing, his hooves stamping, three more times before they'd eventually told her to take her place at the end of the line.

How when they finally left the ring, the crowd had parted about them without a word.

How she'd felt their anger, tense on the air.

How they were wrong.

How what she'd done was not, as they thought, an act of collaboration, but an act of love; her last for the husband of forty years who'd so suddenly left her life, silently and without warning as she'd slept one night last September.

June 9th

Maggie came back with no news. What does that mean, Tom? It could mean nothing I know. But it doesn't. To me it means everything. Am I writing to a ghost, Tom? Are you never coming back? After all this time. I don't know what to do.

George lay on his stomach at the edge of the coppice, the morning sun filtering through the leaves above him, warming his back and neck in patches that shifted with the breeze. The rifle case lay beside him. It still smelt of the manure heap, years-old animal shit impacted in the grooves around the two steel latches. He looked through the telescopic sight at the farmhouse below, moving the unsteady cross hairs slowly over its roof, across the yard and back again. He hoped this was the right farm. Watkins had already had a skinful by the time he'd got to him yesterday, celebrating his wins in two different classes. Then George had had to buy him another beer to keep him talking, so when Watkins finally told him where to find Maggie Jones's place he'd barely been able to understand him. This farm below, though, it looked like the right one. It was certainly in the right part of the valley and there were no others near it. He just had to wait, that was all.

The show had come as a welcome distraction for George. Over the past months his life had, within the confines of the occupation, reverted almost entirely to its pre-war familiarity of farm work and boredom. He was no longer an active member of the Auxiliary Units Special Duties Section. He was just his father's son again, a local farm boy, twenty-one years old but looking seventeen. To make it worse he was also increasingly the butt of the odd angry aside or bitter joke. After all, what had he ever done? Wriggled his way out of conscription then never even joined the Home Guard. No girl would look at him. He'd done nothing in the face of the war other than work on the farm, that's what they thought. Nothing. And yet George knew he would have given everything. He'd followed Atkins's orders to the letter. For months after the German troops arrived he'd regularly visited the agreed fallback position of an old barn on a hill two miles from his home. This, Atkins had decided, would be where he and the others would meet should the network of messages be disrupted. George never knew who these others were. He didn't need to and it was safer not to, that had been Atkins's line. And he still didn't. Despite his frequent visits he'd never found anyone or anything at the barn, other than bats in its eaves and, once, a sick ewe sheltering from the rain.

In the meantime he'd had to live and work under the eyes of the occupation troops while also witnessing a general slide towards mass collaboration. It seemed impossible for people not to. They had to eat, after all, and they had to earn money. The Germans, meanwhile, controlled the food supplies, handed out the ration tickets and were the only ones with cash to spend. George had seen them walking through the streets of Abergavenny, cruising the local shops jingling the loose change in their pockets. He'd watched the shop-keepers attend to them, eager-eyed and keen. He'd even seen his own sister laugh as she served a group of young recruits, joking with them over their bad English. 'They're no different from you,' she'd said when he'd told her she shouldn't behave like that. 'If we'd won our boys' (she didn't say him, he noticed) 'would be over there doin' the same. They're harmless, George, these ones. Just children really.'

But the Germans were not harmless, everyone knew that. London was a shell of a city. Gutted, starved, shattered, more of a ruin than a capital. St Paul's, the Palace of Westminster, the Royal Albert Hall, Westminster Cathedral, even Buckingham Palace. None of London's landmarks had escaped the bombing and shelling of that long winter siege. Its population had halved, scattered or killed. Elsewhere tens of thousands of men of fighting age had already been deported. The German propaganda machine and William Joyce's BBC were calling these deportations Britain's contribution to 'the rebuilding of a new United Europe', but everyone knew it wasn't as simple as that. And everyone knew about the Jews as well. Many escaped to Canada in those first chaotic weeks after the invasion but now, under the veil of order, administration and bureaucracy the Nazis were paring the nation of any remaining Jewish families, assigning them for 'resettlement' in the occupied Eastern territories.

Closer to home there had been waves of reprisals in response to the insurgency. George had heard of entire villages outside Hereford that now lay empty. Neat rows of pock-mark bullet holes in the walls of village halls and churches were the only reminders of what had happened there. No, the Germans were not harmless.

There was, however, also hope. Not within the official channels of proclamations, speeches and wireless reports, but in the unofficial currents of rumour, in quiet asides in country pubs before closing time; there you could hear the occasional whispers of an alternative future. These might be nothing more than reports of anti-fascist graffiti in the towns, painted over before most saw it, or old songs overheard in the street given new, anti-occupation lyrics. Nothing more than seeds of discontent. But even these,

George had to believe, could be enough. Alternative news also filtered in from abroad. American volunteers, many of them Jewish, were flocking over the border into Canada. The Canadian and Free British governments were mobilising an army of liberation. There were plans for an assault along Britain's western coastline, and even talk of commando landings already here in Scotland and Cumbria. Everyone knew, meanwhile, that the German occupation forces were being weakened by the month. The Russian breakout from behind the Urals was draining the Wehrmacht in Britain of its most experienced and best regiments. Faced with a choice, it was thought Hitler would rather let Britain go than allow the communists to edge any closer from the east. George had even listened to the opinions of some who thought America could be convinced to re-enter the war in Europe. They were still fighting with Japan, but if a Canadian and Free British assault could gain a foothold, then a shift in public opinion could well force the US administration's hand.

Such threads of hope were fragile, however, and the ache for peace, the desire for anything other than war, was growing stronger. The British administration in Harrogate had given its support to regional commissioners who were now actively assisting the Germans in locating and destroying any remaining insurgency cells. The Herefordshire Gestapo office had, George knew, been receiving a steady trickle of anonymous tip-offs about suspected insurgent activity. And hadn't he, George Bowen, already reneged on his duties? Not those given him by Atkins, to whom he felt he'd been nothing but faithful, but the duties he'd accepted from the other man who'd visited him that summer four years ago. The other man from British Intelligence who had brought him the rifle he held against his shoulder now, lying at the edge of a coppice, the morning sun warming his back and his neck.

The man had never told George his name, never even gave himself a sobriquet like 'Tommy Atkins', so George had always thought of him simply as 'the man'; dark hair, short, stocky, with stern, serious features and a neat moustache. He'd first approached George in 1940, two weeks after Atkins had strolled across that field, the fishing flies on his hat winking in the sun. George was driving the new Ministry-issue tractor down the lane, taking a pile of hurdles and pallets from the top field to the yard. The man had been leaning against a gate post so George had only seen him when he stepped out from the hedge and flagged him down.

The next time they met was in the wood beside the same old barn Atkins had chosen as the fallback position for their communications cell. It was in that wood that the man had told George what he wanted him to do.

'Seems like you're a sought-after lad,' he'd said, referring to Atkins's previous visits. 'Not surprised really. Wheels within wheels at the moment, and all of them in motion. We're bound to land on the same chap now and then.'

It was best for George, for everyone, the man explained, if he didn't tell Atkins anything about this. Nothing at all. 'This' was a long, narrow wooden case lying on a tree stump between them with an adapted Enfield Mark IV sniper rifle and telescopic sight inside it. 'Designed up at Coleshill,' the man said as he'd lifted it out and fitted the thick, dark silencer.

Had George ever fired a gun before? Shotguns? Good. The man spoke with the same directness as Atkins, but never broke it with a smile like Atkins did. Everything he said seemed carved from the air. Precise and exact. He'd brought a bag of apples on which he'd asked George to practise, balancing them on fallen trunks and the lower branches of the trees.

'One thousand, two thousand, three thousand, four thousand and . . .' The rifle had bruised George's shoulder that first time. It was, however, as the man had promised, almost totally silent. Just a sharp rush of air and then an apple bursting in the distance when he hit, or white sparks of wood spinning off a branch when he missed.

'I know this is a heavy duty,' the man had said to George as he'd dismantled the rifle and packed it away in the case. 'But I'm convinced you can handle it. It's vital, after all, that the local population understand. Collaboration is simply not an option.' He'd paused slightly, clicking the lid of the case shut and looked up at George. 'It will not, in any circumstances, be tolerated.'

George never saw the man again but what he'd said in the wood that day had stayed with him ever since. He'd practised with the rifle regularly, just as the man had told him to, aiming at the pencil dot on his bedroom wall and counting in his head up to the squeeze of the trigger. But then when the invasion finally came, four years later than when Atkins and the man had told him it would, they'd been occupied and it had got too dangerous. After he'd seen his mother sitting on the trough in the yard, weeping, his father's hand on her shoulder, he'd hidden the rifle under the manure heap and the man's words under his fear. By the time he'd gained the courage to confront them again, he didn't know where to begin. There was collaboration of a kind everywhere. Should he shoot his own sister? His father for selling the Germans food? The policeman who'd replaced Constable Evans, who went on his rounds accompanied by a pair of Wehrmacht privates? The man's words, however, never left him and because of them George knew he was 'perishing in the common ruin' rather than accepting his duty. He had abandoned the position that had been his to hold. But it was not too late. If the rumours, however fragile, of a Canadian and Free British assault were true, if the occupation might be overthrown, then he could still contribute. He could still play his part, however small. And that's why, after what he'd seen at the show in Llanthony yesterday, he'd woken before dawn this morning and dug out the rifle from the manure heap. And why he'd then cycled to the edge of the Olchon before walking up to here, a coppice high on the valley's eastern wall overlooking Maggie's farm on the opposite slopes below him.

A brief flash of sun from the farmhouse focused George's attention. Shutting one eye he peered through the sight again. Nothing. A window was open on the upper floor of the house, catching the sun as it swung in the breeze, but nothing else. His eyes were grainy with tiredness. The birds sang in the trees above him. A jay landed on a nearby branch, stripes of electric blue streaking each wing. It looked at him for a moment, then flew on again. The twigs and undergrowth below him dug into his stomach and forearms. He wished he'd had something to eat before he left.

Half an hour later George finally saw someone moving in the yard of the farm. No more than a shifting of shadows, but somebody was certainly down there. He looked through the sights once more and traced Maggie through them as she led the yearling colt out of the yard and through the small orchard of apple and pear trees. It was certainly her, and the horse, which still had one of its hind legs bandaged, was definitely the same yearling he'd seen run at the show ground yesterday.

George had watched Maggie and Alex descend the Hatterall ridge from where he'd been sitting on one of the priory's ruined walls overlooking the show. It was the year-ling's red bandages that had first caught his eye, as clear as autumn hawthorn berries against the green and beige of the summer hillside. Had it not been for his encounter with Albrecht when he'd tried to deliver those letters to the Olchon several months earlier, George would have thought little more of it. But those returned letters with those words written across their addresses had been hard to forget; as had the offhand way the officer had told George, 'There is no one left in that valley.' And yet now here was a woman and man bringing a horse over the Hatterall, the angle of their arrival suggesting they could have come from nowhere else but the Olchon.

George watched them make their way down through the lower fields, over the stream and then past him towards the show ground. They stopped before they reached the outer tents and the woman dismounted, handing the reins of her mare to the man then leaving him with the horses while she walked on towards the secretary's tent. By then, however, it had been just the man George was watching. He was certain he'd seen him before. He couldn't think where exactly, but there was definitely something about him that snagged in his memory. The way he carried his head, his height, the promi-nent jaw, the impassive expression of his angular face, even his nervous blinking. George dropped off the wall and moved a little closer, walking up the slope behind him so as not to draw attention to himself. Had he seen him at the sta-tion perhaps? Or at the market in Abergavenny or the sheep sale in Longtown? Then he remembered. The staff car with markings he didn't recognise back last November, shrapnel damage denting its left wheel arch. He'd seen it driving through Pandy, two or three weeks after the first troops arrived. This man had been the driver of that car. His hair was longer now and he wore a farmer's jacket and cap instead of a soldier's tunic and helmet, but George was sure of it. This was the same man. He moved nearer again, trying to see his face as he stood between the two horses, looking over the showground. A steady stream of people were coming through the main entrance, others were milling about the newly erected stalls and tents, but up here beside the priory, there was no one else around.

Suddenly the Tannoy system crackled into life, 'Testing, testing. Good morning everyone. One, two, three . . .' The yearling colt reared its head and spun away from the man, pulling the lead rope out of his grip. Grabbing at the trailing rope he'd pulled it tight, bringing the young horse back to him while still holding the reins of the mare. 'Shhh,' he'd said, bringing the same hand up to the yearling's withers and stroking him under the mane. 'Sshhh, *halt schon ruhig, halt schon ruhig.*'

George didn't have to tell many people what he'd heard for the word to spread. Although he'd yet to discover any organised civilian resistance in the area, he still knew which men and women harboured nothing but resentment for the German occupation. There were some who had become more ambivalent, who secretly welcomed what the Germans had brought: a promise of peace and a chance to get back to their pre-war lives. But even among these people there were levels of tolerance. And then there were those few at the other end of the scale who took it upon themselves to openly challenge the occupiers, within the bounds of safety, whenever they could. The chief judge in the cob ring was one of these men. A well-heeled farmer originally from up near Penderyn, he'd taken the cases of his workers and their families to the local commandant's office and fought hard for their rights on several occasions. And there were others too, in the crowd, at the edges, to whom just a nod and a whisper had been all that was needed, so that an hour later, at the end of the yearling cob class, George was able to watch with fascination as Maggie Jones led her colt out of the ring in last place and almost total silence.

Shifting himself a little higher up the ridge he lay against, George lowered his head to the eyepiece of the sight. His whole body felt transparent with lightness, the pulse of his blood heavy in his veins. The circular view of the sight wavered and trembled, eclipsed by thin crescents of darkness at either side, as he watched Maggie reach the end of the orchard and undo the latch of the gate to lead the colt through into the long grassed meadow. There were tall thistles at the field's edge, between which a charm of goldfinches flitted and sparked. As the colt came into the meadow he whinnied to the mare grazing in the field beyond. Maggie slipped off his head collar then watched as he trotted away to nose with his mother over the hedge. Excited by the sudden space of the field after his night in the stable, the colt cantered down and up the slope, eventually coming to a stop near Maggie, where, after sniffing at the grass, he dropped to the ground to roll, shifting himself from one side to the other with grunts and snorts through his nostrils. When he stood again he began to graze, letting Maggie walk up and stroke his neck and flanks as he did.

George could see Maggie's lips moving. She was talking to the horse as she brushed her hand over his mane. He tried to control his breathing which had become rapid and shallow. The trigger felt cold as his finger touched it, making the cross hairs shiver over Maggie and the yearling. 'Simply not an option. Will not in any circumstances be tolerated.' He heard the man's voice in his ear again, steady and sure. Then he thought of the empty villages outside Hereford (one thou-

318

sand), of his mother, weeping on the trough (two thousand), of the young lieutenant barking questions into his face (three thousand), of loose change jangling in the pockets of soldiers (four thousand), of his sister, laughing.

Maggie was looking up at the Hatterall ridge trying to see where the flock were grazing when she heard the bullet's whine followed immediately by the soft thud of its impact. When she turned round Glyndwr was still standing, a dark pearl of blood welling in his right ear. But then he began to fall, slowly at first, tilting up the slope, his legs buckling until he collapsed to the ground with the sound of a woolsack, full to straining, thrown from the back of a wagon. Only then, when he lay at her feet, did Maggie see the horse's left eye, exploded into a purple and red pulp, like an over-ripe damson undone by the beaks of hungry birds.

Albrecht was shaving from a bowl of warm water that Steiner had brought him when Maggie arrived at The Court. He stood opposite her in the front room just as he had on that first morning she'd called, wiping the soap from his face with a towel, his shirt sleeves rolled to his elbows. Maggie, however, looked like a different woman from the one who'd challenged him so defiantly in that same room seven months before. Her skin was ashen, her eyes unfocused and her speech hesitant. 'She's in shock,' Sebald said, guiding her into a chair with his hands on her shoulders. 'Alex, get me a blanket.'

Albrecht hadn't been able to sleep all night. Ever since Alex came back yesterday and told him what happened at the show, his mind had been racing, playing out the configurations, trying to second guess what would happen next. He'd placed the men on double guard duty then retired to his room early, so he could think. While he'd expected a reaction, a consequence of some kind, he was still shocked by what Maggie told him, at the swiftness of the retribution. He sat opposite her, his head bowed, trying to gauge what this meant and how much time he might have. Had their husbands done this? Had they been watching them all along, waiting? No, he didn't think so. They would never operate in the area of their own homes. But then, why shouldn't they? Perhaps they thought they had nothing to lose now and there were, after all, no rules. Had he really forgotten that so quickly? No rules and no boundaries, he knew that.

He looked back up at Maggie. Her face was haggard and loose, the light in her eyes dulling even as he watched them with his own. He brought his hand up to her cheek and held it there, cupping her face in his palm. 'Look,' he said quietly to Sebald, 'at what it does.' He knew this face too well, had seen it too many times before. In Holland, Belgium, Russia. Its features knew no borders, no nationality. He'd created this face in others, and even worn its mask himself, in a bunker on the outskirts of Moscow, a letter dated months earlier falling from his hand. It was not the face of war but the face war left in its wake. The numb, ghosted expression that set upon the features at the moment of a spirit's leaving.

Albrecht lowered his hand. 'Put on your uniform,' he said to Sebald, still speaking quietly, as if Maggie were asleep and he might wake her with his speech. 'Then take Mrs Jones to Mrs Lewis and stay there with them.' He stood up and walked over to a desk in the corner of the room. Tearing a piece of paper from a notepad he wrote over it quickly, then folded it once. 'Give this to Mrs Lewis,' he said as he passed the paper to Sebald. Then he walked over to Alex, who was standing silent at the side of the room. 'I'm sorry,' he said in a whisper, placing a hand on his shoulder. Then, almost as quietly, as he walked up the stairs, 'Battledress, double time.'

At the top of the house Albrecht opened a window and scanned the valley with Steiner's pair of binoculars as the clatter of the men assembling rose up through the rooms below him. Slowly pulling the fields and trees through the circular view he eventually found the colt. The horse was, just as Maggie had said it would be, lying in the meadow beside her farm, the grass around its head stained dark with blood. A black ruff of crows fluttered about its neck, busy with their beaks, their wings clamouring above them.

When Albrecht came back down into the front room the rest of the patrol were waiting for him. As he ducked his head under the low beam at the bottom of the stairs Alex brought them to attention with a scuffing of heels and a rattling of weapons and webbing. As Albrecht looked over them, at their threadbare uniforms, their helmets spotted with rust, their rifles and machine guns cumbersome in their arms, his heart sank in his ribs and a faint nausea rose in his stomach. One bullet. That was all it had needed for this to happen, for the men he had come to know so well to slip behind the uniforms of the soldiers he no longer did. The uniforms were necessary though, and not just to prevent any incoming troops mistaking them for British insurgents. No, Albrecht needed them too. He was grateful for them. They would make it so much easier for him to hold his resolve and stay true to the promises he'd made to himself yesterday.

While Alex and Maggie were at the show Albrecht had spent much of the day in the hollow up at the Red Darren, sitting before the map once more. The darkness of that cavity in the cliff, the map itself and its resonance of centuries had calmed him. Illuminating it with his torch he'd stared into its half-imagined countries and illustrations, searching once more for the answers to the questions within him, and it was then, as he'd studied the map in its makeshift chamber, that he'd decided. He would not go back, whatever happened, even if there were a way of doing so safely. He would not return to the life he'd endured for the five years before fate and this map drew him to this valley. He would continue with his escape, reach again for the life he'd discovered to be his. But he would not do so alone. That was the other decision he

322

made, sitting before the map in the dark. There would be no point in reaching for his life, in fighting for his life, if he left the woman he wanted to share it with behind him. So he would take Sarah with him. After the seven months he'd spent with her, he couldn't imagine it being any other way. But not yet. First there were the other women to be protected and these men standing before him, the men he'd chosen as they rested on that lawn outside a burnt-out cottage on the coast. He'd chosen them, he had decided their fate, and so he must stay with them until the very last moment, until it was time, at last, to leave them. Gathering himself, he walked towards the four soldiers standing to attention in their faded uniforms, placed his steel helmet on the table and began issuing his orders.

The first thing Gernot saw when he came to was the crows. A pair of them, hopping between the low bilberry bushes, close enough for him to make out the layered feathers on their chests and the points of light reflected in the beads of their eyes. He turned his head and the crow nearest him flapped away, cawing brashly at his movement. There were high clouds above him scudding across a deep blue sky. The low sun threw a light across the hills the colour of honey. He couldn't tell if it was early morning or the beginning of evening. Suddenly he felt a shock of pain pulse up his leg and through his back, then another stabbing at his hip. And then he remembered. A bird disturbed, a grouse skimming away from the hooves of Bethan's pony like a flying fish from the prow of a boat. The pony shying at the grouse and bolting from under him. His vision suddenly all sky, all ground, all sky as he lost his seat and fell from the pony's back. And then nothing. Just the sound of the pony's hooves resonating through the dry earth of the mountain, slowing, fading away from him, and then silence.

Where was Bethan's pony now? He tried to shift onto his side and raise himself on an elbow. The pain pulsed through him again and the ground swelled beneath him. He fell back, groaning, sweat pricking at his temples, the taste of bile rising at the back of his throat. Another shot of pain ran through his leg, like a voltage deep in the bone, making him cry out and drop his head back to the ground. He lay there, breathing as heavily as if he'd just sprinted up the slope behind him.

His forehead throbbed inside his helmet, which felt heavy and awkward after so many months without wearing it. Unbuckling the strap at his chin he let it fall away behind him, allowing a welcome breeze to brush across his brow. His rifle was still on his back, digging into his spine. With a movement that made him grimace, he edged its strap over his head until he could lie flat on the ground again.

It had felt strange for Gernot to be wearing his uniform again, to be clipping ammunition cartridges to his belt and strapping on his webbing. Even stranger to have the captain issuing orders, telling them to leave The Court and make their way across the valley in combat formation, swinging their rifles over the same fields he had, just yesterday, strolled across to go fishing down by the river. At The Firs they'd picked up Menna and her children. The captain had explained to her what had happened to Maggie's yearling. She'd looked over them with shocked eyes as he did so, the men who'd been helping on her farm now standing before her as German soldiers again. Once she'd understood what was happening they'd escorted her to Mary's, where the captain had ordered Gernot to stay and guard the house and the women while he, Alex and Steiner performed a sweep of the valley opposite Maggie's farm. As the three others left Mary's house Steiner had looked back at Gernot, his face pale under the rim of his helmet. Gernot had waved to him from the door, as if to say, 'It's all right, this is all right,' although he knew in his heart it wasn't.

The crows had come closer again, made bold by his stillness. He raised his head to look at his broken leg and they hopped backwards, flapping their wings. There was no blood, no bone protruding and yet still the slightest movement brought a wave of pain and nausea washing over him. His hip felt dislocated. He raised himself higher on both his elbows and looked about him. The scene swam before his eyes, but there, across the hummocks of the bilberry bushes and heather, he could make out Bethan's pony. It was grazing, the reins loose about its head. He thought about trying to crawl over towards it but even the slightest attempt to turn his leg made him cry out in pain. He fell back to the ground again, cursing the captain, Mary and his own stupid impulse.

The rest of the patrol had been gone for no more than ten minutes when Mary had come into the front room. Gernot was sitting at the window, his rifle at the ready across his chest. Without looking at him she'd walked to the front door and opened it. 'Get out,' she'd said.

Since Bethan had left the valley Gernot had stopped asking Albrecht for English lessons, but he'd understood Mary clearly enough. He didn't know what to do. He wore the uniform of a soldier but he no longer felt like one. Should he order Mary into the back of the house, lock all of them – her, Menna and the children – in a room and stand guard at the door? That's what he would have done before. But now, after the months they'd spent here working alongside these women, tasting civilian life again, that would seem ridiculous.

'Get out,' Mary had said again, looking him in the eye, her fingers still hooked on the latch of the door. 'What d'you think you're protecting us from, anyway? It's you as should be worried, boy. Not us.'

Gernot had felt himself blush. He stood up but Mary didn't move, just held the door open, looking at him as if he were a child. Through the open door he saw the top of the valley, the sweep of its curve, the bareness of its slopes over which this woman had sent Bethan away. His embarrassment turned to anger. It wasn't meant to happen like this. He was waiting for Bethan to return, to fulfil the promise of that kiss. Until then nothing should be changing. This is what they'd agreed, this is what the captain had promised. They'd seen too much of war, known too much of its stench and pain. They were all waiting for it to be over, but now the captain had ordered them into their uniforms and told them to carry their weapons again. Why? Because they were being threatened; because everything they'd hoped for was threatened. Well, if it was, and he had to be a soldier again, he wasn't going to stay here guarding women and children. He wanted to defend what he cared for: his chance to be here when Bethan came back, the chance for them to sit in the bracken once more, watching the evening light compress and darken over the hills.

Gernot walked up to Mary, holding her stare, and stood before her. He could feel the fear emanating off her, the fear of him, of everything. He'd recognised it because he'd felt it too. His knuckles were white on the stock and body of his rifle. 'Get out,' she'd said again, her voice smaller and cracked. Breaking her stare, Gernot looked out at the bare hills, turned back to meet Mary's eyes once more, then walked out into the valley. He heard Mary close the door behind him, but he didn't look back. His mind was suddenly clear. He would track down whoever shot the horse, and he would kill him. And then they could go back to living in the valley as before. They could take off their uniforms and he could go back to waiting, to watching out of his bedroom window for Bethan to appear at the thorn tree above him.

After leaving Mary Gernot had gone straight to the paddock at the back of the house where Bethan's pony was grazing. He'd watched her ride it up on to the hill before the winter, and again after the thaw, so he knew where she kept the saddlery in the lean-to in the yard. He'd never ridden much himself, but several times over the past few months he'd been out to check the flock with Alex, riding one of the two old cart horses kept at The Court. The captain had sent Otto to The Gaer, from where he was observing the mouth of the valley. The rest of the patrol were sweeping the woods and fields lower down. If there was anyone still there they'd be driven up onto the hills. So that is where he would go, up on to the plateaus that surrounded the valley.

Swinging his rifle across his back he'd caught Bethan's pony by its forelock and begun leading it down towards the yard, keeping an eye on the side door of the farmhouse in case Mary should try and stop him.

Bethan had been walking since mid-morning. At first, when Helen Roberts had called at her aunt's house just before curfew last night, she hadn't believed what she'd said. But Helen was adamant. Margaret Jones in Llanthony, clear as day, and her mother wanting her back, soon as possible. Once Bethan was convinced Helen was telling the truth she hadn't needed any more persuading. She'd left Hay-on-Wye this morning, carrying just the same bag over her shoulder with which she'd set out from the Olchon six weeks before.

Bethan recognised her pony long before she could see her properly. She'd ridden her since she was a girl and would have been able to identify her outline against the sky even if she'd been standing with a herd. It was only when she got much closer, however, that she saw Gernot, lying on his back in the distance. She went to the pony first, picked up the reins and led her over to where Gernot lay. Letting her go to graze, she went and knelt beside him.

At first, when Gernot opened his eyes and saw Bethan looking down at him, he thought he was delirious. But then he felt the touch of her fingers at the back of his neck as she lifted his head.

'Here,' she said, holding a bottle beneath his chin. 'Drink this.'

Gernot opened his mouth and let her tip the bottle to his

lips, which were dry and parched. He drank thirstily until she pulled the bottle away. 'Thank you,' he said, his voice hoarse in his throat.

Bethan stood up and looked about her. She'd been away for less than two months but it felt like a lifetime. During her stay in Hay-on-Wye she'd witnessed another occupation to the one she'd experienced in the valley. Before she'd left for the town her mother had made her swear on the family Bible to remain silent about the missing men. But that oath had been unnecessary. She knew now, all too well, after what she'd seen and heard in Hay, about what happened to families found to have links with the insurgency.

Her second cousin, Eve, whom Bethan had known only vaguely before the war as a childhood playmate at family gatherings, had become her guide through the realities of life under occupation. They'd shared a bed at the top of the house above her aunt's grocery shop. Every night, before they went to sleep, Eve would tell Bethan another story about what the Nazis had done in the town, and in other towns and villages too. It was only recently, however, when she could no longer hide the swelling of her stomach from her roommate, that Eve had told Bethan her own story. Finding Bethan's hand in the dark, she'd guided it onto her distended belly. She was, Eve told her, carrying the child of a German soldier. She had no way of knowing which one because there had been two of them. At this point Eve's voice had wavered and broken. Bethan had stroked her hair and said it was all right, she didn't have to tell her if she didn't want to. But Eve said she did want to, very much, and so she'd continued.

It was early on, a few weeks before Christmas. There had been more sabotage attacks and all the men, including her father, had been rounded up in the town hall. That's what they'd said, anyway. Eve didn't believe them. She thought it was planned, that the commanders wanted to give their troops a Christmas present. Because she hadn't been the only one that night.

The two soldiers were drunk. She and her mother were closing the shop, but the soldiers wouldn't leave. Her mother understood a little German and she'd leant over the counter, straining to make out what the two of them were saying. 'They say,' she'd said slowly to Bethan, 'what they want isn't on the shelves. That they want . . . something from behind the counter.' It was only when she heard herself translate their words that her mother went suddenly pale, and that was when the dark-haired one flipped up the counter flap and led Eve out the back of the shop and up the stairs. She'd tried struggling but he held the barrel of his rifle jabbed into her hip. The fair one had stayed behind, watching over her mother, then later, when the dark-haired one had finished, they'd swapped. It was a small building above the shop, a cheap conversion with thin walls and floors. Her mother would have been able to hear but she'd never said anything to Eve since except, that same night when she'd come and stood at the door to her bedroom. 'Don't tell your father,' her mother had said quietly, the streetlamp outside Eve's window casting a sodium glow across her face. 'It would kill him if you did.'

Even now Eve's mother refused to acknowledge her daughter's swelling bump. Eve said she was planning to go away, to Hereford. She'd heard they had places there where you could have your child, then leave it. That, she said, is what she planned to do.

Everything Eve told her made Bethan disgusted with herself. She felt like a child who'd only just woken to the adult world. The curses that had softened with her visits to the thorn tree above The Court hardened again, and every time she passed a group of soldiers in the street she muttered at them under her breath, energised with real venom once more.

During her time in the town Bethan had also become disgusted with the other women in the valley; women older than herself who should have known better. Just the other day they'd heard that David Lewis, Tom's brother, had been confirmed killed in action during the counter-attack. And there was his sister-in-law, Sarah Lewis, allowing that German captain to visit her every day, taking walks with him beside the river, even letting him play her music records while her husband was missing and his brother had died fighting the fascists. She hated the world she'd discovered outside the valley but she still wanted her mother to leave the Olchon and come back with her to Hay. Better by far to live in the truth and know it, however bad it might be, than hide yourself away behind ignorance and habit.

Bethan put the bottle of water back in her bag, slung the bag over her shoulder and walked away from Gernot towards where the pony was grazing. When she reached her the pony nuzzled at her pockets, hoping for a treat of some oats or calf nuts. The reins were tied at her neck to stop them falling to the ground. Bethan undid them, then swung them over the pony's head to lead her back to where Gernot lay among the bilberry bushes, his right leg angled awkwardly from his hip.

Gernot had closed his eyes again, the last of the evening light playing under his lids in bursts of orange fragments, just as it had across his vision that day he'd climbed the hill to find Bethan waiting for him beside the thorn tree. When he opened them again it was in time to see the pony's legs passing his head. One of her hind hooves caught the back of the opposite foreleg with every step, punctuating the steady rhythm of her walk with the faintest of metronome ticks. He turned his head slightly and the pony's legs swiped their shadows across his face as the tick, tick of her overreach passed by his ear, then faded away as Bethan led her back onto the track that dropped down towards the valley's head. As she led the pony on down the slope away from Gernot a pair of crows circled above her, cawing and tumbling in the last amber light of the day.

Sarah was sitting alone in Maggie's kitchen with William's shotgun loaded on the table before her. Maggie lay asleep upstairs, her pale cheeks sunken, breathing thinly through her open mouth. It seemed as if she'd aged years since last night when Sarah had watched her treat the colt's cut in the stable. As soon as she'd seen her like this, looking small and fragile in the sidecar of the motorbike, she'd handed the note Albrecht had written back to Sebald and, closing the door of Upper Blaen behind her, told him to take them both to Maggie's farm. Eventually Sebald had understood her and with Sarah mounting the motorbike behind him, he'd driven them back down the rough track, Seren and Fly straining on their chains, barking behind them.

It had been much harder, once they'd settled Maggie in her bed, to persuade Sebald to leave them completely. But Sarah had pleaded with him; he couldn't stay, not now, not after what had happened. Something in her expression, a note of desperation in her voice must have finally connected with him. '*Ja, ja,*' he'd said, nodding his head and picking up his rifle from beside the door. '*Ich verstehe.*' Sarah stood in the hallway with her back to the door and listened as the motorbike engine gunned into life then faded out of the yard and on down the lane.

Since then Sarah had been alone with just her confused

thoughts for company. She'd checked on Maggie regularly, given her water when she could, but the woman she knew was no longer there. For the rest of the day she'd sat downstairs in the kitchen and waited, for what, she didn't know.

Sarah felt she was to blame. Someone had shot the colt. Someone from outside the valley and because of what had happened at the show. But Maggie would not have known about the show if Sarah hadn't brought that poster back from the priory and shown her. She hadn't even needed to go down to the priory; they could have filled the water bottle in the streams. But she'd had to get away from Albrecht, that was why she'd gone. For her own sake, she'd had to get away from him then, and she'd had to see the chapel and the priory too. Not just see them either, but touch them, smell them. That chapel was where she'd married Tom and she'd hoped, she supposed, that the place would still hold a resonance of that day. That somehow, standing within its bare walls, looking up again at the high, simple windows, she would have been able to gather the echoes of how she'd felt then; Tom's forearm contracting under her touch, the smell of starch on his collar and the wind picking at her veil. But she'd found no memory and heard no echo other than her own footfalls over the worn gravestones laid in the flagstone floor. All she'd brought back with her was that poster, taken from the chapel's notice board, which had led to this; Maggie lying upstairs, no more than a husk of herself and her, sitting in the kitchen as the day darkened at its window, not knowing whether to be terrified or joyful at her husband's possible return.

As Sarah lit one of Maggie's oil lamps she heard Maggie's two dogs moving outside, their chains dragging on the cobbles of the yard. They began barking, the younger bitch's thin yelps over the older bitch's less regular, deeper growls.

She replaced the glass chimney over the wick and the flame grew inside, its illumination expanding and growing within the lamp. Standing there, motionless with the lamp in her hands, she listened hard. She could hear faint footsteps getting louder, quick footsteps, then the front gate opening and closing. Someone was coming into the yard. The dogs settled as the footsteps approached. Sarah put the lamp on the table then reached for the shotgun and went out to stand at the back of the hallway, pointing the gun at the closed front door. The hallway was dark. Whoever opened the door wouldn't see her straight away. She would have a second, maybe more, to decide.

At first, when Albrecht stepped into the hall Sarah didn't recognise him. She'd grown used to seeing him almost every day, but not like this. For the past few months he'd been wearing clothes from The Court like the rest of the patrol. Now, however, he stood before her wearing the same full uniform as he'd worn that night when she'd first mistaken his footsteps for the tread of her husband. The bulky leather holster of his pistol hung at his hip and his tunic was undone, as were the upper buttons of his shirt beneath. His hands were stained with earth and soil.

'Sarah?' he said, peering into the dark. She lowered the shotgun and stepped forward so he could see her. 'Sarah,' he said again coming quickly towards her and taking hold of her shoulders. 'We must leave.'

Albrecht had never once questioned his decision to guard the women in the wake of the colt's shooting. If their situation was known, then surely they were in danger as much from the British insurgents as from the Gestapo and the German army. So when he got back to Mary's house he hadn't expected her to tell him coldly that she'd asked Gernot to leave, or when he returned to The Court that he'd find Sarah had asked the same of Sebald. 'They don't want us near them,' Sebald had explained to him. 'Surely you can understand that? If their husbands are coming back, we're the last people they want protecting them.'

Sarah went back into the kitchen and Albrecht followed her. She sat down, putting the shotgun on the table while he went to the window and looked out anxiously at the gathering night. He turned back to her and leant against its sill. 'It's Steiner,' he said with a sigh. He looked exhausted, a vein at his temple pulsed under his skin as he spoke and his hands were trembling. 'He's taken the radio. He's contacting the local command unit.'

Sarah sat very still, taking in what this meant. 'What will he tell them?' she said eventually, drawing the lamp closer to her across the table.

Albrecht ran his fingers through his hair, leaving a streak of mud across his forehead. 'I don't know,' he said, sighing heavily again and shaking his head. 'Report insurgent activity? Give them our position? Ask for reinforcements?' Suddenly he laughed, brief and shallow. 'Report an officer unfit for duty perhaps?'

He looked back out of the window, searching for points of torchlight, listening for the crunch of boots on the lane. This was his fault, he should have seen it coming. When Gernot hadn't returned Steiner had got anxious. He'd wanted to go out and look for his friend. But Albrecht didn't let him go. He hadn't wanted to let the young soldier out of his sight. He'd wanted to follow the plan he'd made the night before. Well, now Steiner had made the choice for him. He didn't blame him. Everything was fraying and unravelling and all of them must look to save themselves now, however they could. Steiner had been clever. This would go well for him at the court martial; reporting the discovery of an insurgency cell. And couldn't Albrecht have stopped him if he'd really wanted to? Couldn't he have drawn his pistol and aimed it at Steiner's back as he'd scrambled up the slope behind The Court? Or couldn't he even have caught up with him? Steiner was, after all, carrying the heavy radio pack. But he hadn't. He'd just followed him instead, and when Steiner did eventually pause to look down the slope, Albrecht had stopped too and looked back up at him. For a moment they'd remained like that, a mirror image of their positions on that day when Albrecht had first persuaded Steiner to walk with him to the top of the hill. They didn't say anything and they didn't have to. In those few seconds both men saw and knew each other more clearly than ever before. And that was why when Steiner turned and carried on up the hill Albrecht didn't follow him again, but just watched him shrink away out of sight instead before continuing himself, running not up, but along the slope towards the head of the valley and Maggie's farm.

'Was it them?' Sarah said, trying not to become panicked by Albrecht's behaviour.

Albrecht looked at her, frowning as if he hadn't heard her. 'What?'

'Was it Tom?' she said more clearly. 'Was it Tom an' the others who killed Maggie's yearling?'

'No,' Albrecht said emphatically, shaking his head again. 'No, it couldn't have been. Not here.'

'How d'you know?'

He didn't know, but that didn't matter any more. Leaving the valley, that was all that mattered now. He came and sat down at the table beside her. 'Sarah,' he said, speaking more slowly, the muscle tensing at the hinge of his jaw. 'Do you understand what I said just now? Steiner has radioed out. They will send soldiers, a whole company perhaps. The Gestapo will come with them. If we stay here, they will kill us.' He paused, lowering his head so she couldn't avoid his eyes. 'We will die.'

Sarah looked into Albrecht's face as he stared back at her intently. There were spots of dried mud on his glasses. His eyes behind their lenses were bloodshot, making the pale blue of his irises darker than she knew they were. His face was taut and drawn. He was frightened, she saw that now. More frightened, perhaps, than she was herself.

'You know I can't leave,' she said at last.

Albrecht looked down at the table. When he looked back up at her it was with an expression of such incredulity it seemed to border upon contempt. 'You would really rather stay here and die than leave and live?' he said, annunciating each word slowly and clearly. 'What for? For who are you making this sacrifice? For your husband who left you?'

Sarah looked away from him, a sudden anger rising in her chest like the flame that had risen in the oil lamp. He'd never spoken to her like this before and she hated him for it; hated him because she knew he was right. There was nothing left for her here. Maggie was gone. They'd all held on for as long as they could, survived however they could, but the men had not come back. And now it was too late. Even if they did return, she knew it was too late.

Albrecht reached across the table and took her hand. 'The world is changing,' he said more gently. 'Nothing will be the same again. But it will get better. This will stop one day. And when it does, you can live as you wish again, maybe even come back here to the valley. But for now, if you stay, you will have no future. You will not be able to return. If you stay here you will have no life to live.'

Sarah withdrew her hand from under his. 'Where'd we go?' she said, still looking away from him and speaking so quietly that Albrecht could barely hear her.

'West, to the coast,' he said without hesitation. 'And then to Ireland. And then, if we can, maybe to America.'

Her head was light and throbbing and the room seemed unsteady about her. If what he said was true, then she had no choice. In the space of one day and night everything had changed completely. She had waited, for months she had waited, but now it was the end. It was over.

'All right,' she said quietly, frowning into the table and nodding her head. 'I'll go.'

Albrecht smiled at her and took her hand again. 'It is the right thing to do,' he said urgently, squeezing her fingers in his. 'We will be safe, don't worry.' He stood up, still holding her hand, scraping the chair behind him over the flagstones. 'But we must go immediately.'

'What about the others?' Sarah said, still sitting at the table.

'I've sent them notes. To warn them.'

'An' the map? What about the map?'

Albrecht let her fingers slip from his grip and went over to the window again. She saw his reflection in its pane as he looked out over the darkening view. 'The map,' he said still looking out at the hills and nodding. 'Yes, they will get the map. But there is nothing we can do about that.' He turned back and came towards her, offering her his hand again. 'We must go, now,' he said. Sarah looked at his outstretched hand, at the pale blue veins crossing at his wrist. Eventually she lifted her own and took it, feeling his scholar's fingers close about her palm as he led her out of the kitchen into the hallway.

They were almost at the front door when Albrecht stopped suddenly, cursing under his breath. 'My uniform,' he said, looking down at his open tunic. 'I need some clothes.' Letting go of Sarah's hand he strode towards the stairs at the back of the hallway, the heels of his boots clicking over the flagstones.

'No,' Sarah said from behind him. He stopped, half way up the stairway. 'William's won't do. He's too small.' Albrecht turned to look at her and for a moment they stood there like that; Albrecht paused on the stairs, one hand on the banister, and Sarah standing in the hallway framed in the dim rectangle of light cast through the open kitchen door. 'I'll bring you some,' she said at last, holding his gaze. 'Some of Tom's.'

Albrecht came down the stairs and walked back along the hallway towards her. He couldn't travel beyond the valley in his uniform but he didn't have the time to go back to Upper Blaen with Sarah either. It was, however, him and not Sarah the patrol would come looking for.

'It's all right,' Sarah said quietly, laying a hand on his arm as he reached her. 'I'll be quick, an' I need to get some things anyway.'

Albrecht held her by the shoulders once again. 'Thank you, Sarah,' he said. 'I know this isn't easy.' He didn't want to let her out of his sight. He was scared he would lose her now, just when they were so close. But she seemed calm, as if in making her decision she'd settled herself or, he dared to let himself think, as if her decision had already been made long before he reached her tonight.

'Where shall I meet you?' he said.

Sarah looked down at the floor for a moment, biting her lip, before looking back up at him. 'Landor's ruin,' she said. 'In the cellar. Wait for me there.'

Albrecht smoothed a strand of loose hair away from her face. 'Be quick. Bring a lantern but don't use it tonight.'

'Don't worry, I'll be fine,' she said, looking up into his face and seeing again the fear running under his features. He wore an expression of intense searching, as if he were looking for her on a distant hillside and not standing so close she could see her reflection in his glasses, her own face ghosted over his eyes. Sarah looked up at this reflection and tried to recognise the woman looking down at her, tried to see herself clearly, but she couldn't. As Albrecht bent his head towards her she watched herself slide away and evaporate up the lenses of his glasses, disappearing completely as his forehead touched hers. He closed his eyes and breathed in deeply. 'Be careful,' he said to her. 'Please be careful.'

'Go,' she whispered, drawing her head away from his. 'You must go now.'

Sarah stayed standing in the hallway for several minutes after Albrecht left. She listened to Maggie's dogs bark again as he passed, and then to his footsteps fading out of the yard and down the lane. Eventually she roused herself and went to the foot of the stairs. She wanted to say goodbye to Maggie, but then she thought better of it. She must do nothing that might shake her resolve. Better to leave quickly, as if she were coming back tomorrow. So turning away from the stairs she walked down the dim hallway and opened the front door, closing it carefully behind her, as if she might wake whichever god had stopped watching over her.

Sarah moved through the rooms of Upper Blaen quickly and efficiently by the light of a single oil lamp. As she went from room to room she placed a few items in an old canvas bag she used to carry into market; the accounts book, her pen, her wedding photograph, a box of matches. She tried not to linger anywhere for too long in the fear that a familiar object or a certain corner of the house would snag on her memory and unpick her decision. But Albrecht had been right. She was calm, strangely settled and focused. She had, after all the months of waiting, reached an end. After so much not knowing, she was waiting no longer. All her life she'd been left. By her brothers when they'd argued with her father; by the poet in the summer of her ninth year; by Mrs Thomas her teacher; by her elderly parents; and lastly by Tom, suddenly and with no warning one night last September. She didn't want to be left any longer, so she was going, she was leaving the valley, Upper Blaen, all of it behind her.

As she closed the front door Fly and Seren emerged from their shelter in the yard. She tried to ignore them but as she walked down the track they barked after her, their thin chains rattling over the cobbles, just as they had the morning they'd woken her to the cold impression of Tom's absent body.

She was almost at the bottom of the track when she turned round and walked back up to the house. Going around into the larder she unhooked two sides of bacon from the ceiling, then took them into the shed in the yard. Coming back out she placed a piece of bacon in front of each dog. 'Good girls,' she said as they sniffed at the meat and began to eat, pinning the slices to the ground with their paws.

As Sarah crossed the valley she saw the windows of The Court were lit, as were several of the windows at Mary's. The birds had stopped singing and the valley was silent. The sun had gone down but the sky was not yet dark and threads of light, deep mauves and indigos, still streaked across the deepening grey. The curves of the lane were traced out before her by banks of cowslip on either side, thick in the hedgerows and glowing dimly white in the gathering dark.

The full moon of the previous night was partly obscured

by cloud so Sarah found it hard work climbing the slope on the other side of the valley without a torch or a lantern to guide her. The bracken was thick and every time she lost the path her legs got caught up in the tangle of its stems. Eventually she rose high enough above Maggie's farm to begin walking along the western wall towards the valley's mouth. As she passed above The Court she paused and looked down at the thin rectangles of light cast from its windows across the orchard and vegetable garden. She could just make out some voices from inside, but nothing else. Then she saw Alex, standing at the front of the house, looking up towards the valley's head, motionless in the faint moonlight as if it had cast him into stone.

It took Sarah another half hour of scrambling over the scree to reach the cleft in the Red Darren. Even in the deepening night she could make it out as she approached; a dark slit tapering up the face of the cliff looming silver-grey above her. She paused at the entrance to catch her breath and take off her coat. She was sweating from the climb, strands of loose hair sticking to her forehead and cheeks. Reaching behind the boulder she found Albrecht's torch then walked into the shadow of the crevice. Once she was deep enough inside, she turned the torch on. As before it looked as if the split in the rock ended before her in a sheer wall of moss-streaked stone but on reaching this stone she saw again the wooden struts and brattice leading deeper into the man-made cavity, scooped from the soft sandstone of the hill. Edging herself through the narrow gap, she came out into the hollow, the torch beam lighting up the jagged damp walls before landing upon the smoother folds and pleats of the sacking cloth and tarpaulin.

Putting the canvas bag down at her feet Sarah pulled the cloths from off the packing crate to reveal the map within its

344

frame inside. She didn't want to risk damaging the torch so she kicked at the earth at her feet until she dislodged some fragments of rock. Bending down, she picked one up and felt its weight in her palm, turning it in her hand until its sharpest edge protruded from the bottom of her fist. Holding the torch in one hand and the stone in the other, she stood and stepped up to the map. Standing so close to it again she couldn't help casting her eye over its details once more, passing her own reflection over its strange creatures and towered cities. Whichever part of its half-imagined world she looked at she misted with her own breath, obscuring the cartographer's ink, the gold leaf, under brief patches of clouded glass. She didn't look too long, however, worried that, as with the rooms of Upper Blaen, she might be weakened by memories no longer of any use to her in her altered world. Lifting the stone to the top right-hand corner of the case, she brought it down with all her strength against the glass.

The first time she hit the glass the stone left no more than a granular smudge and a long fracture, running south-west across the map as far as the Red Sea. The second time, however, the glass splintered, tiny shards showering down between the map and its frame. The third time it shattered completely, with more shards falling at her feet and then larger pieces peeling away like the slabs of ice she'd pulled from the frozen troughs over the winter.

Sarah stood back from the crate. The map was entirely exposed and for the first time she could shine the torch over its surface without the reflected light obscuring her vision. It was beautiful, the most beautiful thing she had ever seen. Kneeling to her bag she took out the box of matches.

The first match she struck guttered and extinguished in the breeze that came channelling through the narrow rift in the rock behind her. She moved closer to the parchment, so close she could smell its scent of musty hay and the tang of ammonia used to preserve what colours it still held. She lit a second match, this time cupping the flame in her palm as she lifted it carefully to the bottom right-hand corner of the map.

The centuries-old parchment took with the sound of autumn leaves burning on a bonfire. It curled and blackened before the flames, the faint blue dye of the rivers bleeding from their imagined banks before disappearing completely. As the fire reached the brown seas its flames flickered green, as if the heat had released the spirit of their original colour. The gold leaf of the compass points burnt brightest, cracking and peeling away like shavings of pure light.

The heat was sudden and strong and Sarah had to shift herself quickly backwards, the constellations of broken glass crunching under her boots as the flames tore up the rest of the map, washing over the score-marked Paris, the cog of Jerusalem and on up towards the circle of paradise at its eastern head. By now the cavity was filling with billows of thick grey smoke and Sarah was worried the light of the flames might somehow be seen in the valley below. Picking up her bag, she made her way out of the man-made hollow and on through the natural split in the rock, the sound of the world burning and splitting behind her.

As she came out into the cool night air Sarah saw the headlights of two cars and a truck tracing the ribbon of the lane up towards the mouth of the valley. She watched them shudder over the rougher parts of the track then slow and swing around the tight corners, sweeping their beams through the hedges and over the fields. As the truck ground its gears up an incline its headlights shone into the sky; two soft pillars of light briefly rising and falling in the otherwise motionless night.

346

Sarah didn't want to see them drive any further, so shouldering her bag she turned her back on the valley and began climbing up towards the ink-black horizon of the Hatterall ridge. The slope on this side of the Red Darren was steep and covered with shale and scree that gave under her feet. Each step she took sent a running sigh of stones down into the valley below. As she rose higher the fragments became larger, unsteady stepping stones, tipping and swaying under her weight. She stopped and looked back just once to see the three sets of headlights part as the truck and one of the cars took the lower lane towards The Court and the other drove higher towards The Firs and Mary's farm. She turned back to the hillside and carried on climbing, using her hands as well now, grasping at fistfuls of rock, her face so close to the slope she could smell the rivulets of water trickling beneath her and the young ferns and mosses fed by their flow.

As she rose higher towards the horizon of the ridge Sarah saw a sudden point of light up the valley. It was, she realised, one of The Gaer's windows shining out onto the blackness of the upland slopes. She climbed on, her own breath hard and fast in her ear. As she climbed she thought of Edith, barefoot on the mountain top looking for her son; her startled face above that board and upturned glass. She paused, her chest heaving, then bent to the slope once again, thinking now of the ponies she and Maggie had found frozen together on the plateau, and then, as she finally crested the ridge and the night wind came at her, throwing her hair around her face, about another of the poet's stories. It was one of the earliest ones he'd told her, about the Iron Age people who'd first lived in these hills; how they'd built their forts on these promontories and how they'd only ever walked between them along the ridges and high places. Where they could see clearly, where they knew they were safe.

Sarah stood on the top of the Hatterall ridge and looked back towards the valley, but she could no longer see it. There was nothing but the night below her and the stars and clouds above. Adjusting the strap of her bag and tightening her coat about her waist she walked on, north-west along the ridge, along the border of two countries, the wind flinging itself around her. She hadn't brought any food or water and the summer nights at this height were still cold. She knew she didn't have much time, a couple of days perhaps, but she also knew this was no longer important. It was the looking that mattered. The belief and the looking. These were all that were left now and that was why she walked on along the ridge, blind into the night, clutching her bag tightly to her chest with the accounts book of her letters inside, the last of its pages still unwritten.

Private Jonathan Stevens of the newly formed SS Albion division stepped over the bodies of the two dogs they'd found last night then cautiously pushed open the front door of the farmhouse with the barrel of his rifle. It was the morning after the raid and most of the company had already left the valley. Just a small unit had stayed behind to go back through the houses looking for intelligence or any documents that might be used as evidence at the court martial. He stood in the doorway, scanning his rifle across the room before moving through the kitchen to look over the range and the sink. Standing at the dresser he slung his rifle over his shoulder and began to take down the books off the top shelf, fanning their pages over the table then throwing them aside. He came to the Bible last. It was heavy with a partly broken spine so he laid it on the surface of the dresser instead. Opening the front cover he saw the list of names and dates on the inside page, the copperplate fading back through the centuries to the late 1700s. He was about to move on into the other rooms of the house when the final entry stopped him. He checked the date on his watch, 11 June, then looked back at the final name and the numbers written beside it. The last date was written in a darker ink, fresher than any of the others.

Sarah Lewis, 15th March 1918 – 10th June 1945

Afterword

This novel is a work of fiction set in an alternative recent history. The seeds of the fictional past I've imagined, however, are sown in what many feared to be, at one point in time during the summer of 1940, an all too possible future.

I first heard about the plans for a British resistance organisation one summer when I was working for a builder in the Llanthony valley. We were taking the stone tiles off a barn, loading them onto a trailer behind a tractor, driving them through the valley then fitting them to the roof of a new conversion. It was hot, repetitive work, but over those weeks, between the lifting, loading and unloading, our conversations had the space and time to range and wander freely. One day Charles, the builder, told me how during the war some farmers in the area had been given caches of arms which they'd hidden in underground bunkers in the hills. Should the order have come, these farmers were to leave their homes and wives and take to the Black Mountains to resist the occupying German army. It was a seductive tale and from all the stories told over those summer weeks, it was this one that lived with me as others fell away over the following years.

I was reminded of Charles's story on the morning of September 11 2001 when I heard a radio interview on the *Today* programme. Papers had recently come to light detailing the real plans that had lain behind his tale of farmers as a resistance force in waiting. The presenter, Sue MacGregor, was interviewing George Vater. As a young man farming near Abergavenny during the war George had been recruited into the Auxiliary Units Special Duties Section, a network of farmers, vicars and other local people trained and prepared to run messages and spy on an occupying German force. At the end of the interview Sue MacGregor said, 'So you have no doubt, had there been an invasion, you would have repelled the lot of them?' 'No,' George replied, releasing laughter from the studio. After a slight pause he continued, speaking clearly and steadily, his words cutting through, then silencing the laughter. 'I'm very sorry to say, no. We were told that perhaps we would work for fourteen days, and that was our full lifetime I presume.'

I knew George Vater. His family farmed near my parents' house in Llanddewi Rhydderch. They also ran the local school mini-bus service. For seven years I was picked up at the bottom of our lane by one of George's sons or daughters, and sometimes even by his wife or George himself. For the last four of those seven years George's grandson sat on the bus beside me. As a lifelong supporter of Pontypool rugby club, George had recruited me for their colts side when I was seventeen.

George's reply at the end of that radio interview haunted me for many years after I heard it. Eventually, together with the story Charles had told me, the idea of a British resistance organisation and what they'd been expected to do in the event of a German invasion got the better of me. Taking the opportunity of a weekend visit home, I called George and arranged to meet him the following morning at his family farm in Llanddewi.

Sitting in his living room, surrounded by cuttings, maps

Inaugural meeting of the Monmouthshire Auxiliary Units Association,
December 1945

and photographs, George told me that morning how, in the
summer of 1940, he'd been approached by a man calling
himself 'Tommy Atkins'. He explained how Atkins had
given him a sheet of German insignia to learn and told me
what would have been expected of him as a member of
Atkins's Special Duties Section. George also told me where I
could still find the locations of several Auxiliary Unit 'operational bunkers' in the surrounding area, and he showed me
a photograph (above) of the inaugural meeting of the
Monmouthshire Auxiliary Units Association, taken after the
war in December 1945.

George and the men in this photograph never had to put
their training into practice as part of a British resistance
force, nor did they have to test whether their forecasted life
expectancy of two weeks was accurate. My conversation
with George did, however, enable me to imagine a world in

353

which the plans for such an organisation had to be realised. I'd hoped that one day George would be able to read the novel I wrote partly inspired by his experiences, but unfortunately I'm writing this on the morning of George's funeral. I can, however, still thank George. Not just for being so generous with his memories, but also for being willing, along with the thousands of others like him, to risk everything in what would have been the darkest days in the struggle against fascism.

There were, of course, many other influences upon this novel, and among them are some more seeds of fact that may be of interest. The Mappa Mundi really was removed from Hereford Cathedral and, after a stint in the cellars of Hampton Court, kept in a coal mine in Bradford-on-Avon for the duration of the war. The poet and artist David Jones, meanwhile, did live in Eric Gill's artistic community at Capel-Y-Fin between the years of 1924 and 1927. Similarly, both von Brauchitsch's 'Proclamation to the People of Britain' and the 'Guide on How Troops are to Behave in England' are taken from a series of real Most Secret draft orders and decrees issued to senior Wehrmacht officers in September 1940.

While these notes of fact, and others, have been woven into this novel, apart from Upper Blaen and The Court, the positions, names and number of houses in the Olchon valley, along with the characters living in them, have all been imagined. To borrow from Lawrence Durrell's note upon the city in *The Alexandria Quartet*, only the valley is real.

29 June 2006

Acknowledgements

I am very grateful to the staff and administrators of the following institutions: The Museum of the British Resistance Organisation; The Usk Rural Life Museum; Duxford Radio Society; The London Library and the British Library.

Many books informed this novel but David Lampe's *The Last Ditch* and John Warwicker's *With Britain in Mortal Danger: Britain's Secret Army* were both particularly invaluable sources of information on the background, training and operational details of the Auxiliary Units. *Of Wet and Wildness* by Odie Robey and *The Farming Year* by J. A. Scott Watson provided crucial insights into 1940s rural life.

I am also indebted to the many individuals who helped with my research, including: Nancy Selwood, William Gwyn, Ruth Parry of the Longtown Historical Society and her mother Mrs Lewis, George Vater, Edward Main and Juliet Gardiner.

For their support and guidance I'd like to thank Lee, Angus and everyone else at Faber, Zoë and Susannah at Rogers, Coleridge & White, Trevor Horwood for his accurate eye, Luke Epplin, Eric Chinski, Dilwyn, Lisa for her unfailing encouragement and advice and of course my ever resourceful parents.

ff

Faber and Faber is one of the great independent publishing houses. We were established in 1929 by Geoffrey Faber with T. S. Eliot as one of our first editors. We are proud to publish award-winning fiction and non-fiction, as well as an unrivalled list of poets and playwrights. Among our list of writers we have five Booker Prize winners and twelve Nobel Laureates, and we continue to seek out the most exciting and innovative writers at work today.

Find out more about our authors and books
faber.co.uk

Read our blog for insight and opinion on books and the arts
thethoughtfox.co.uk

Follow news and conversation
twitter.com/faberbooks

Watch readings and interviews
youtube.com/faberandfaber

Connect with other readers
facebook.com/faberandfaber

Explore our archive
flickr.com/faberandfaber